TAIWAN

Also by Christopher Wood

TERRIBLE HARD, SAYS ALICE
FIRE MOUNTAIN
DEAD CENTRE

TAIWAN

CHRISTOPHER WOOD

THE VIKING PRESS NEW YORK

With many thanks to Leslie Boxer

LIBRARY OF CONGRESS CATALOGING IN PUBLICATION DATA
Wood, Christopher, 1935–
  Taiwan.
  I. Title.
PR6073.0576T3   1982   823'.914   81-69975
ISBN 0-670-69067-8   AACR2

Printed in the United States of America

CHAPTER ONE

The death of the snakes was horrible. Half a dozen of them were already dangling from loops of cord, a medusa coil of splay-mouthed, entrail-bulging, blood-spattered, twisting shapes, slowly writhing and buckling, their movements losing momentum according to the order in which they had been butchered.

As Lee Fong Yu looked on, a curved steel skewer was inserted through the roof opening of a wire mesh cage and a brown viper hooked beneath the middle of its body and drawn from the churning mass of snakes. There were three cages of vipers, one on top of the other, and a crate beneath the reeking table that contained cobras. The viper plopped on to the table and the Snake Man swiftly pinned it down behind the head with his skewer. Lifting it between finger and thumb, he squeezed hard until the tight mouth sprang open and the sharp fangs in the upper jaw stabbed air. On the other side of the table from the crates was a wooden tray containing sixteen grubby tumblers still splashed with water from the bucket in which they had been rinsed.

The Snake Man swept up a tumbler and quickly forced the viper's fangs over its lip, squeezing again until an obscene blob of creamy venom was ejaculated to cling precariously to the inside of the rim. The glass was returned to the table and the viper's head inserted through one of the many prepared loops of cord dangling from a wooden pole. The loop was pulled tight and the snake's mouth opened wider and wider as its neck contracted where the cord was cutting into it. The Snake Man was pulling the viper by the tail and for a moment it seemed, as he reached for the blood-stained scissors, that the snake was a hank of coarse hair that was being drawn from its sister coils so that it could be trimmed.

Then the pointed blade of the scissors entered the flesh about three inches from the tail and within painful seconds the creature's public ordeal was over and it could be left to dangle with its fellows until it died. Its death would never be a

5

lonely one and by the end of the evening it would be difficult to find it beneath the weight of twitching corpses.

With a professional flourish the Snake Man dashed a tot of transparent spirit into the tumbler and swirled it aloft until the liquid became cloudy and streaked with crimson. He reminded his audience that its consumption would cure impotence and rheumatism and improve the circulation of the blood. This time there were no takers. The Snake Man waited for a few moments and then placed the tumbler on the counter behind him. There were twenty-four identical tumblers on it containing mixtures of snake blood and venom. The Snake Man picked up his skewer and reached for another adder.

Lee Fong Yu wondered why he was so absorbed in watching every item of this spectacle. He had seen it so many times in the narrow, teeming alleys behind the Lungshan Temple of downtown Taipei that it had ceased to make any impression on him. It was like the pattern on a familiar plate. But tonight had been different. He had watched and he had been absorbed. The plight of the snake had affected him. Not with pity but with a strange kind of identification. With a start of fear he realised that he had the same doom-laden sense of foreboding as one of the adders in the crates. His time was running out.

The Snake Man had pulled the string tight and was reaching for the scissors. Lee Fong Yu turned away almost hurriedly and pushed into the crowd. He had taken two steps when a sharp pain in his side made him cry out. It was not so much the pain itself as the unexpectedness of it in relation to what he had just been thinking — or perhaps, the expectedness. He started back instinctively and something hard pressed against his kidneys.

'Lee Fong Yu.'

He heard his name being spoken and his heart jumped. The prick in his thigh came again but this time he was expecting it. He looked down and saw the glint of silver in the man's hand. He could feel blood trickling down his leg. The muzzle of a gun pressed against his back.

'Take a glass. We will sit down.'

The man with the knife was Chinese and spoke Mandarin. Lee Fong Yu did not argue. He turned towards the Snake Man and raised his hand. The muzzle of the pistol pressed more firmly into his back. There was no possibility of fleeing into the crowd without

6

taking a bullet with him. The Snake Man gestured towards an assistant, who handed Lee Fong Yu a glass from one of the trays. Lee Fong Yu took it and walked past the layers of snakes into the sitting area behind the counter. Here there was a disorder of tables and benches, some with empty glasses on them. A fan turned slowly and in the background a grandmother and a woman suckling a baby were watching a wrestling match on a large colour television set.

Lee Fong Yu sat down at a table and the two men positioned themselves opposite him. They had hard expressionless faces and tight mouths. He thought he had seen the one with the gun before. He wore a jacket and now spoke for the first time.

'You know why we are here. You know what you have done.'

There was an explosion of noise from the television set. Lee Fong Yu did not judge it the right moment to say anything. The man with the knife turned his head quickly towards the noise. The other did not move his eyes from Lee Fong Yu. He was the leader, the senior *nanchi*, or hit man. Both his hands were beneath the table. Lee Fong Yu looked at the position of his arms and tried to work out where his gun was pointed. Almost certainly at the stomach. The bullet would not penetrate the table but rip into his entrails. Lee Fong Yu thought of the snake and felt a cold fear that formed itself like a solid object at the back of his throat. He tried to swallow.

'You have betrayed your brothers and you know the reward.'

Lee Fong Yu nodded. He was looking down at his glass in a gesture that he hoped would be taken for penitence. The venom had separated and was floating like a blood-stained cloud at the bottom of the tumbler. 'I regret what I have done.'

'Regret is useless.'

Another customer came into the sitting area carrying a glass. Once again, the man with the knife was distracted, but his superior did not take his eyes from his prey. Lee Fong Yu cursed silently. If only the man with the wandering eyes was carrying the gun.

The newcomer sat down three tables away. He had a drinker's heavy face and an unsteady hand. He raised the tumbler to his lips slowly and drained it in one gulp. His gaze strayed towards the television set. The wrestling had finished and a girl wearing a scarlet chi-pao was singing in a high-pitched voice.

7

'In recognition of the services you have provided in the past, the Leader has graciously decided to be lenient.' Lee Fong Yu's hopes rose momentarily. 'He is granting you an honourable death.'

Lee Fong Yu inclined his head and pressed his hand against his forehead. From beneath it he squinted sideways. Something had caught his eye when the new customer came in. Near a collapsing rattan partition was a foul-smelling bucket. Lee Fong Yu could not see inside it but he guessed that it contained the chopped-up remains of some of the larger snakes that would be used to feed domestic animals or perhaps make a stew. What gripped his attention was the thick, heavy handle of the hatchet that protruded from it. It was black with engrained fat and reptile fluids and the base of the hilt was bisected by a dimly visible silver line. This line was wide and it hinted that the blade of the invisible hatchet was solid and heavy. Lee Fong Yu cowered behind his hand as he calculated how many steps would be needed to reach it.

'You will swallow this.'

Lee Fong Yu moved his hand and studied the table before him. The gunman slid a hand into the pocket of his jacket and placed a small sandalwood box beside the tumbler. It was cylindrical and decorated with paintings of tiny, brightly coloured flowers. These had been varnished and in places the varnish had chipped off, carrying the illustration with it and leaving only sections of pitted wood. There was something so incongruous about the faded prettiness of the box that in itself it inspired mistrust and fear.

Deferentially, Lee Fong Yu leaned forward and drew the lid from the box. It parted with a soft exclamation of escaping air and a small oval pill was revealed, dark blue and gleaming like a precious stone. Lee Fong Yu stared at it, feeling as if the polished surface had the power to rob his limbs of movement merely by its texture. As a hangman knows a noose, he knew what lay before him. A cyanide tablet. The Leader's gesture of munificence. Lee Fong Yu raised his head and looked towards the two men. The man with the knife wore an expression that bore the faintest resemblance to a smile, an anticipatory smile. It was a facial contortion probably only performed at moments like this, when taking another human being's life. The man with the gun nodded

8

briskly as if to emphasize that there was nothing else to be said. No expression passed across his face. With his eyes on Lee Fong Yu he emptied the box into the palm of his hand and let the pill drop into the tumbler. Almost instantly it fell apart and the contents of the glass turned dark green. The man pressed down the lid on the empty box and there was a gentle hiss.

Three paces. That was what it would take to reach the hatchet. In the outer shop the Snake Man was talking to his audience. Across the room the baby changed breasts. The girl on the television was still singing, accompanied by four other girls who spun parasols. The man with the gun pushed the glass towards Lee Fong Yu. He closed his hand round it, feeling a chill that perhaps did not exist. The man with the knife leaned forward expectantly.

Lee Fong Yu started to raise his glass. What was the exact position of the gun? He bunched his toes against the cap of his shoe and edged his leg forward. The tumbler trembled before his lips. The knifeman's eyes were gloating. The gunman's forearm flexed downwards. Lee Fong Yu's foot left the floor. He began to tilt the glass. The vile liquid filled his mouth and he half closed his eyes, feeling the tension build up inside him like an electric charge.

Summoning all his strength he lashed out with his foot and spat the poison into the knifeman's face. His toe crashed against the hand holding the gun and drove it upwards. There was a thud, a cry, and a charge of pain exploded in his foot. He hurled the glass and threw himself backwards pushing away from the table with his left hand. The chair tilted and he was twisting in mid-air to land, sprawling, beside it and launch himself at the hatchet. Three paces and his hand closed round the haft. He glimpsed a mishmash of entrails and spun round expecting to meet a bullet. The man with the knife was on his feet, his weapon in his hand. His companion was beneath the table. Lee Fong Yu screamed and charged towards them. The man with the knife panicked. He hurled his knife and the hilt jarred against Lee Fong Yu's chest.

Lee Fong Yu was not interested in him. The other man, gun in hand, was scrambling from beneath the table. His head came into view and Lee Fong Yu sank the hatchet into the side of it between hair and eye, shattering a cheek bone and unleashing a stinging whiplash of blood that spattered the wall twelve feet away. The hatchet bit deep enough to be held and then broke free as the other man threw himself on Lee Fong Yu's arm and was dragged across

9

the table. He clung like a man drowning in his own panic. Lee Fong Yu struggled to wrench free the hatchet. He had dragged himself this far from the brink of death. He was not going to slip back now.

A table collapsed and a chair disintegrated. Women were screaming in the background. Locked together like ill-matched partners in a dance marathon the two men crashed through the flimsy furniture. Faces looked up to intervene and then fell back as they saw the bloody axe that was locked between them. The counter shuddered under the force of the two bodies and a tray of tumblers spilled half its contents. In their cage the cobras stirred, swaying backwards and forwards with the movement of the combatants. Lee Fong Yu let the man expend his energy by clinging to the hatchet, and forced him back, step by grudging step, until the evil mass of the snake crates glinted behind his shoulders. The man's eyes were an inch from his own, sweat glistened at his temples. Lee Fong Yu pulled him off balance and then tripped him backwards so that his body became a battering ram smashing against the crates. The top one was knocked askew and there was a sharp hiss that matched the intake of breath from the onlookers. The snakes reared up and the unbalanced crate toppled over and fell into the street. The lid burst open and a brown mass of adders slithered across the cobble-stones. Like a wave receding, the crowd shrank back, climbing over each other in their rush to escape.

Lee Fong Yu had the man pinned down with the back of his head pressing against the second crate so that it forced apart the thin metal bars. The snakes reared and hissed, striking indiscriminately. The man's mouth and eyes were wide with pain and terror. He twisted sideways and Lee Fong Yu pressed down harder so that flesh bulged through the parted bars. A snake struck and found the man's cheek, seeming to hang from it for the fraction of a second. He screamed and Lee Fong Yu wrestled the hatchet away and struck downwards. There was more blood, but the man launched himself forward with crimson spurting from the half-severed fingers that had parried the blow. He threw himself at Lee Fong Yu's throat and the two men blundered against a side awning which collapsed under their weight. For a second the man was enveloped and Lee Fong Yu lashed out repeatedly until a dark stain spread through the canvas and the man's body sank with it to

10

the floor like a toppled tree, only his twitching legs protruding.

Half blinded by blood, Lee Fong Yu kicked over the table with the remaining snakes on it and ran down the street. Half a dozen steps and he dropped the hatchet and darted into a side alley. People loomed up and he glimpsed their startled faces as he sped past. Behind him there were shouts but they soon died away. The crowd thickened as he came to an intersection and he tore off his jacket, rubbed his face on the lining and burrowed into the heaving mass of people.

Donald Neville Ryman heard the police-car sirens as he left his office in the Ai Kuo West road. It was not an unusual sound in Taipei and he paid little attention to it. He also had other things on his mind. He avoided the motor scooters parked along the pavement and moved to the curb. The rush-hour traffic was in full spate, feeding the pall of smog that hung over the city and making his eyes smart. There was a time when Ryman would not have permitted himself a cynical smile if told that the East possessed a mystical scent. Now he would have stated that the scent was composed of a few types of Chinese cooking, exhaust fumes, untreated sewage, squashed bed bugs, stale linen, sweat, damp and decay. A decay as much mental as physical but possessed of an odour that permeated every surface he touched including, he felt with increasing frequency, his own flesh. It was a melancholy observation but one from which there was no escaping. He yearned for more abrasive climes, an autumn England with mornings as crisp as bites from apples that would purge his nostrils of the all-pervading, gagging, too-sweet scent of putrefying syrup.

A Chinese family went past on a motorbike. There were five of them. Mother behind father on the pillion and three children wedged between father and the handlebars. The smallest in front, they fell back like parts of an interlocking toy. Ryman raised his hand and a taxi stopped almost immediately. A battered yellow Datsun which separated quickly and dangerously from the mass of hooting vehicles that scraped the sides of the road.

Ryman told the driver where he wanted to go and squeezed into the car. He was a big man, nearly six feet four, but beginning to spread round the waist as he approached his fiftieth birthday. He had once played a lot of squash, but now it was tennis and that only occasionally. The taxi jolted forward before he was properly

11

settled and he fell back cursing. In Taipei a cab meter only ticked up according to the mileage covered. Time spent in traffic jams was money lost. And Taipei was one large traffic jam. Ryman balanced his briefcase on his lap and then found a more comfortable position for it as he wriggled behind the driver. He was following his own maxim: 'Let the driver punch the hole through the windscreen; then follow him if absolutely necessary.' As if to prove the wisdom of this advice, the driver stood on his brakes and the passenger seat beside him snapped forward briskly to clout the glove compartment.

'Stupid bastard!' Ryman was addressing the world in general. He drew his head back from the driver's shoulder and twisted to squint out of the window. The cause of the near accident, a locally made Yue Looney saloon, looking like a pregnant Peugeot, accelerated away into the traffic, horn blazing. Taiwan drivers never stopped sounding their horns. Even on an open stretch of road devoid of traffic they would toot peremptorily from time to time as if wishing to make sure that the apparatus was still working. It was the most obvious manifestation of a national neurosis, a continual slap in the face on the way from the airport to all those new arrivals who had been raised on the myth of Chinese calm and inscrutability.

Ryman sat back in his seat and stared at the garish litter of Chinese calligraphy and neon signs that crowded the sides of the buildings. The streets were like fast-flowing rivers that had deposited colourful debris along the banks. Food stalls and shops were still open, but other vendors were wheeling in the displays and slamming down the steel blinds. Soon they would look like a row of garages tucked beneath the arcades with only the ubiquitous motor scooters jamming the pavements as they choked the roads. Squeal, hoot, curse, stop. The four cars in front of the taxi jumped the lights and Ryman's driver muttered to some private god and jerked to a halt, his bent front bumper almost carried away by a swarm of scooters that had started to invade the intersection as soon as the lights changed. Adding to the confusion, two green arrows indicated that on-going traffic in two lanes could make a right turn. This it proceeded to do, taking on the impenetrable stream of buses, lorries, cars and scooters that thundered from the left and challenging them to merge or provoke a multiple pile-up. The screech of horns and brakes was unending. Those

12

denied participation in this particular bout of frenzied movement stacked up against the red lights and revved their engines. The air shimmered with petrol fumes and it seemed that only one glancing collision was needed to spark off the explosion that would reduce the whole mass of metal to the twisted, battered shape of the crumpled motorbike mounted like a trophy on one of the concrete centre sections.

'Stupid bastards.'

This time the target of Ryman's anger was not visible through the window of the taxi. He was thinking of the two men who were the scapegoats for his present black mood. The chief editor and the owner of the paper he worked for. Donald Neville Ryman was a reporter on *The Times of China*, a paper with an imposing title but a circulation that had been dwindling for years. It was a paper remarkable not for its editorial crusades but for the fact that it kept going at all. A bland rehash of ancient international news items and a local section that would have appeared staid and unimaginative even to the most reactionary of British provincial newspaper editors.

Ryman was well aware of his paper's failings and the fact that he ought to have moved on years ago. God knows, he had been told enough times by two wives and a host of other less partial observers. Nevertheless, although the wives had gone, he was still there. For years he had been attending the bedside, puffing up the subs' pillows, placating the printers, even apologising as a last resort when there was no one to take out and get drunk. But now it was over. This time, he told himself, they had gone too far. It was not a question of being passed over for promotion. He would have been insulted to have been offered a job he despised. Nor was it another damn fool change of ownership that nobody had had the courtesy to tell him about. No, it was something that touched him on a deeper level. Something that must be a product of his reaction to his approaching fiftieth year. Something that made him aware that up until now he had always taken the easy way out and that there was not a lot of time left. He was looking down the hill and the view was no prettier than the one outside the window.

On the face of it the issue was not a novel one. A story killed because it might give offence to important people: 'not the kind of thing we specialise in, old boy.' He could still see the chief editor's smug features as he tossed the sheets of paper back across the desk:

'Minister's son owns construction business, gets government contract, building falls down, people die. Nothing unusual there. It happens all the time all over the world. Go and write something heartwarming about the Far Eastern Basketball Championship. We might even carry a photograph.'

Ryman had pressed his point and in time had been rebuffed by the owner, who considered it unnecessary to point out that a policy of co-operation with the government was considered in the best interests of the newspaper. Nevertheless, he did point it out. He had looked long and hard at Ryman with unkind eyes like a host reminding a guest that it is the early hours of the morning and the party is long since over.

Of course, it was difficult to blame them. Ryman had had so many stories like this turned down over the years that he had almost stopped writing them. If his awakened social conscience was suddenly going to arise phoenix-like from the ashes of his apathy then he could not expect the event to be greeted by more than mild incredulity.

Ryman was justifiably suspicious of his own motives. Much as he would have liked to expose Cheng Lung and his voracious brood of relatives he knew that it was a self-destructive gesture. 'Rocking the boat' as the chief editor would have put it. The man could not be blamed for getting cold feet. If he was honest, Ryman knew that his contempt was really a despisal of himself, not the people he went through the motions of working for. Any issue would have done to feed the flames of discontent. A fire was stoking up in his belly and if it did not find a vent it was going to burn him out.

'*Ching ting che.*' The taxi swung into the kerb, triggering off a volley of angry hoots. The driver's face was expressionless as he turned to accept his fare. Ryman gave him a few more New Taiwan Dollars than were shown on the meter and eased himself on to the pavement. He was standing on a street exactly like the one he had left. Only the presence of a nearby food stall brought a new and not unpleasing smell to his nostrils. *Y-t'iao* (fritters of twisted dough) and *pao-tzu* (Chinese steamed buns). A thin column of steam rose from an urn. Ryman plucked at the waistband of his trousers. His belly swelled over the top and pressed against his fingers. He frowned. It was time to lose some weight. 'You're falling apart.' He was surprised to hear himself saying the words

14

out loud. He shook his head and started down the street towards the first drink of the evening.

'Disappointing,' said Mr Chang with a small sniff. He was watching the last of the collapsible chairs being carried from the room at the top of the central tower of the National Palace Museum.

'Yes,' said Henry Burton.

'It appears that the early evening was not a good time for the recital.'

'You were right,' said Burton meekly.

Mr Chang could have been any age between forty and sixty. He had well-ironed, creaseless features and wore wire-rimmed granny spectacles and a grey linen, almost collarless jacket that reminded Burton of the kind of clothes that the Beatles used to wear with their haircuts. He gave assistance slowly and grudgingly.

Now the room was empty save for the dais. Burton walked to one of the long windows and looked down over the terrace and the flight of steps to the distant entrance gateway beyond the lines of cedars. It was dusk and the curved eyelash line of the tiled roof fell delicately as a brush stroke against the dark background. There was nobody to be seen. The National Palace Museum had closed its doors on its quarter of a million treasures, and would not reopen them until nine o'clock the next morning.

Henry Burton was there because the salon at the top of the central tower had been reserved for a violin recital organised by the English-Speaking Union of Taipei. He had been responsible for the event and it had been a spectacular failure. Only five people had attended and the one non-European had been Mr Chang who would have had to be there anyway because he was the museum official delegated to co-ordinate the function. The artist, one of Britain's foremost violinists who had fitted the recital into an already overcrowded Far-Eastern tour, had departed for Chiang Kai-shek Airport barely in control of his temper. Burton felt crushed. This was the second event that he had organised after taking up his post as E.S.U. representative on the island, and it was even more of a disaster than the first; a poetry reading that had failed to touch the sensitive Chinese soul. Trade might follow the flag but culture seemed to lag a long way behind.

Henry Burton was a single-minded, amiable, comparatively unworldly young man of twenty-five. He had passed out in the top

15

thirty at the Royal Military Academy, Sandhurst, yet made little impression on the rest of his intake save for the generally unmemorable quality of being diligent. His father was a professional soldier, and some of his instructors thought that Henry had followed in his footsteps out of duty rather than choice. Now Henry was wishing that he had not resigned his commission. He had begun to enjoy being a soldier, and the reasons for his resignation seemed less pertinent than they had done. At least mess life had provided some camaraderie. Here he felt very much alone. An only child with his mother, and now his father, dead. A job he had never really cared for and only taken because it was offered by an old friend of his father's who had felt sorry for him when he left the army. Worst of all was a feeling of frustration and futility. He was twenty-five and he was making no impression on the world.

The dais was carried from the room and the lights flickered like a discreet hint that it was time to leave. Chang hovered by the door. Burton looked round the room as if it was a battlefield on which he had suffered a major defeat. 'I don't know what to try next,' he said. Chang spoke primly and stood aside to let Burton pass. 'In Taiwan most social contact between the Chinese and other races is done through business. What your government is trying to do is very difficult.'

Burton looked into a gallery of Shang Dynasty bronzes. Heavy witches' cauldrons they might have been, engraved with strange symbols and runic spells. 'I don't know what my government is trying to do,' he said. 'Does anybody know what their government is trying to do?'

'Our government is striving to improve the lot of the people and preserve our heritage,' said Chang seriously.

'Of course,' said Burton, suppressing a sigh. The lift doors opened and he stepped inside.

They descended in silence for three floors. The lift doors opened. Ahead was a Sung Dynasty hanging scroll. Two magpies squawked at a curious hare which twisted its head to look up at them. Ink and paint on silk. Fine in detail but composed in the mind rather than from nature. Burton wondered casually how much it was worth. Impossible to say because it would never reach the open market. It would stay here cooped up with its 249,000-odd friends. There were so many items in the Museum that only one twenty-fifth of them could be shown at the same time. The rest had to be stored in air-

16

conditioned caves hollowed out of the thickly forested hills behind the Museum and connected by a tunnel to the basement of the Museum proper. The exhibits were changed every three months and on this basis it would take ten years to see them all.

Burton started to cross the hall and paused before another painting. A Ch'ing Dynasty landscape. A towering, leaning cliff embroidered with a dragon motif of foliage. A rocky shoreline and a fisherman's boat trailing a line. Distant islands lost in haze. No horizon, no waves, no turbulence. Serenity and great areas of space. The artist's chop a rectangle in the lower left corner.

'Very handsome,' said Burton. He was being polite, but he meant it. Mr Chang nodded as if acknowledging a compliment. 'Wu Li,' he said. 'Seventeenth century.'

Burton was making a calculation. If every object in the museum was worth a thousand pounds — and that must be an enormously conservative estimate — then the whole collection could be valued at, he sighed out loud, two hundred and fifty million pounds. 'Amazing,' he said.

Chang nodded again. Four armed soldiers were waiting at the only door that remained open. They wore thick leather holsters at their waists from which khaki lanyards protruded, fastened to their cartridge belts. The men gazed at Burton faintly disapprovingly, and their expressions did not change when he tried to catch their eyes and smile. Perhaps they resented being kept waiting before they made their evening search of the building. Burton decided he could not blame them. He paused before the door and gripped Chang's hand. 'Thank you again for all you've done. I hope you don't think that it was a complete waste of time.' He waited uneasily, wondering if his confession of failure had prejudiced the future of the third event that he had scheduled to take place at the Museum. Chang retrieved his hand and let it fall to his side. 'We will have to see,' he said. It sounded like the answer to the question Burton had not asked and, feeling faintly disturbed, the young Englishman moved out into the scented dusk.

Harry Crosby glanced at his watch. The express had left Taichung on time and if his calculations were correct they had just passed through Miaoli. That would mean that they would arrive at Taipei shortly after nine o'clock. He yawned and adjusted his seat until it would go back no further. Outside the window, green acres

17

of rice fields stretched away to the invisible sea. In the gathering darkness they seemed even more neat and ordered. Like strips of cloth laid out on a pattern and waiting to be stitched together. Sometimes there were lights, and the dark shapes of buildings huddled together to take up as little space as possible. Where men lived they stole ground that could be used for growing crops. A glint of water and a glow of lanterns revealed anglers still squatting round a communal fishing pond.

The express raced on and the blazing lights of a factory flashed into view like the inside of a glowing bulb. Harry Crosby pressed the foot rest down and stretched out his legs as far as they would go. He folded his hands across his stomach and closed his eyes. Usually he napped well on trains but tonight was different. He felt uneasy. Maybe it was because Feldman had something on his mind. He had worked for the man long enough to know the signs. The taciturnity, the slight tremble of the lips as if he was holding a conversation with himself, the preoccupied expression that avoided the eyes. Crosby wondered what the problem was. Plastics were booming. Labour was still cheap and they had the go-ahead for another factory. There were problems in Korea but there were always problems somewhere in the Far East. China was quiet, that was the main thing. The other China, that was, the one across the Taiwan Strait. The one with 800 million inhabitants as opposed to fifteen million.

Somebody came into the compartment and Crosby opened his eyes, expecting to see Feldman. Feldman had stayed on in the dining-car picking his teeth and staring out into the darkness. But it was not Feldman. It was the tea boy carrying a large kettle which he used to refill the two glasses in the holder beside each brace of seats. It was a skill at which he was adept. A quick tilt and each glass was filled to a half-inch below its brim. The tea was the colour of melted honey. Crosby sipped from his glass and noticed with distaste that there was a smudge of lipstick on its rim. He replaced the glass as Feldman sat down beside him. He glanced up and thought for a moment that the man was ill. His face was tense and drawn and for the first time that day he looked Crosby directly in the eyes. Crosby was suddenly reminded of the man who had told him that he was taking his wife from him.

'Are you all right, Jack?'

Feldman opened one of his clenched fists and held his fingers

18

apart. 'Harry, I've got some bad news for you. I'm sorry, I've been meaning to tell you all day. Couldn't get around to it.'

'What is it, something personal?' Crosby tried to think of all the relations he had that might have died. A sister in Philadelphia, a brother-in-law in New Jersey, if that counted as a relation. He and Lee had never had any children. Maybe it was Lee. He felt a stab of regret that reached across the years. It still hurt.

'Yeah, it's personal. It's about you.'

'Holy shit.' Crosby suddenly knew what it was. The medical he had had recently. Something had shown up on the X-ray. It must be serious or they would have told him direct. Probably they wanted to get somebody close to him to break the news. 'Level with me, Jack. What the hell is it?'

'I'm going to have to let you go, Harry.'

'Let me go?' Crosby repeated the words as if hoping that he had misheard them. There was no correction. 'Why? Did something come up on my medical? Let me tell you, I've never felt better in my life. O.K. I had a little heart trouble way back, but so what? You show me a guy in the company who ...' he broke off as he saw Feldman shaking his head.

'It's nothing to do with your medical, Harry. As far as I know you could swim to China. It's more complicated than that. When Kramer was over here recently he saw a lot of people. He got the idea that things would go better if we recruited some local talent at a senior level in the company. Might open a few more doors. They seemed to like the idea back in the States and, well, that's what's happened. It's a gesture of confidence in our on-going relationship with the people of the Republic of China, I don't have to spell it out for you.'

'That's how you got permission for the new factory?' Feldman looked uncomfortable. 'It smoothed the way.'

'Jesus.' The lights in the compartment suddenly seemed to have gone darker. The figures sprawled around looked like waxwork dummies. Crosby felt alienated from them, from everybody. He was reminded of the after-effects of being knocked out. Everything seemed grey and unreal. 'I don't believe it, Jack. After nearly ten years you're throwing me on the scrap heap.'

Feldman spread his arms. 'It's not my decision. It's company policy, Harry. Believe me, a clean break is in your best interest. I

19

couldn't have you working alongside this guy. I couldn't insult you by inventing some post for you.'

'So you're sacking me.'

'You'll get fixed up.'

'Bullshit! You know how old I am. Fifty-two. Where am I going to get a job now?'

'We'll do everything we can to smooth things out. I know how tough this must be for you. It's pretty lousy for me having to tell you.' Feldman was speaking as if reading from a prompt card. His delivery became more relaxed and confident with every cliché. Crosby started to get up. Feldman looked at him warily. 'Don't take it too hard,' he said.

'Fuck you,' said Crosby.

'Is this the place?' said Burton, but the taxi driver was already reversing down the alley. Burton sighed and looked up towards the sky. Washing hung from every balcony. Air-conditioning units protruded like cages. Burton had flirted with the idea that each one contained a hamster whose labours in a treadmill generated the energy required to make the unit work. 'Hamster power,' he said to no one in particular. He was agreeably drunk for little more than the second time in his life and taking advantage of his condition to do some exploring.

Somebody had mentioned a club called the Gardenia and he was trying to track it down. The name had agreeable echoes of the forties as seen on the cinema screen; Bogart and Bacall outstaring each other across a smoke-filled room. Somebody tinkling away on a piano. Burton looked about him. This might be Bogart territory but an opium den seemed a better bet than a club. Few of the Taipei taxi drivers spoke or understood a word of English. Ambitiously, Burton had started to experiment with some Chinese phrases but results so far had not been encouraging. An old man in a coolie hat cycled past, drawing a coffin-like structure which was constructed round the rear wheel. It rattled dismally over the uneven stones. Some slops spattered down from above, forcing Burton to jump aside. He followed the receding figure of the old man and came to a slender gateway which revealed a small, tiled courtyard with a pool in the middle of it. Beyond the pool was a stone flight of steps leading up to a canopied doorway where spindly neon letters spelt out the words 'Garden Club'. Burton was temporarily disappointed until he took a couple of paces into the courtyard and saw that the last two letters of the first word had not lit up. He had indeed found the Gardenia Club.

There was no noise from the club and the fountain in the pool was not working. Burton felt slightly apprehensive as he mounted the steps and tried the door. It was like entering a private house. Beyond the door was a hallway leading into darkness and on either side of it two low-ceilinged rooms, one of which was a bar, dimly lit by candles. The Chinese barman, wearing a plum-coloured jacket and black bow-tie, slid off his stool and folded a newspaper as Burton came in. He said nothing but waited expectantly. Burton ordered a Singapore Gin Sling and became aware that he was not alone in the room. A large man wearing a rumpled suit was sitting in the corner of the bar against the wall. He was hunched forward with his elbows on either side of his glass and his hands bunched beneath his chin. He twisted his head to look Burton up and down, and nodded. Burton made a noise at the back of his throat that approximated to 'good evening' and perched slightly self-consciously on one of the bar stools. The large man belched noisily and the sound rolled away like distant thunder. 'Squall off the Pescadores,' he observed matter-of-factly. Burton concentrated on his drink. 'Haven't seen you in here before.' The large man was talking again. 'Haven't been here before,' said Burton.

'That explains it then,' said the large man, apparently satisfied by the logic of the exchange. 'How do you find the place? Taiwan I mean.' He drained his drink and stabbed the glass towards the barman with a forefinger like a small turnip. The barman snatched it from the counter as if frightened that it might burn a hole in the wood.

'It's a bit early to say,' said Burton. 'I haven't had time to sort out all my impressions.'

'Very diplomatic,' said the large man good-humouredly. He cleared his throat with a noise like a log jam breaking up, and folded a giant fist round the tumbler of whisky that had been rushed before him so that the liquid still agitated against the glass. 'And how do you pass the time?'

The remorseless questioning was beginning to irritate Burton, and he tried to make this clear by pausing for a few seconds before starting his reply. He explained about the English-Speaking Union and was rewarded by an incredulous shake of the head.

21

'Amazing. I always thought the country was supposed to be bankrupt. How can we find money for this kind of caper?' He lowered his voice so that the barman would not hear. 'I'd have thought the Chinese were about as interested in British culture as they were in making Yorkshire puddings.'

Burton was less than overjoyed to hear his first impressions being played back to him with such fervour. 'Time will tell,' he said defensively. 'You don't have to wait for time. Have the benefit of my incomparable experience of the East.' He held out a large hand. 'Donald Ryman.'

Burton took the hand, which was dry, firm and slightly rough like a well-scuffed baseball glove. 'Henry Burton.'

'Have another drink, Henry.' Ryman jabbed a disparaging finger at Burton's glass. 'Do you really want another one of those disgusting pink things? I hate to be critical but it's the easiest way to be mistaken for a gay tourist.'

Burton was grateful that the darkness concealed his blush. The drink had been chosen for the oriental splendour of its name as seen on a bar card at the Grand Hotel. He could concede that it might have been a mistake. 'I'll have a gin and tonic,' he said. 'Thanks.' He cleared his throat. 'What's your line of business?'

'I'm a male prostitute,' said Ryman agreeably, 'I write for a newspaper.'

'A foreign correspondent?' Burton tried to remember if he had seen the name Donald Ryman on the by-line of any of the articles in the yellowing, airmail editions of *The Times* that sometimes found their way into his possession. The suspicion of a wince passed across Ryman's craggy features, and with this hint of vulnerability Burton felt for the first time that it might be possible to like the man.

'No, I'm on the spot.' Ryman's face split into an unexpected smile as if at a private joke. '*Times of China*. Local rag. They shove it under the door at your hotel. Always gets the television programmes wrong.'

'I've seen it,' said Burton. He tried to think of something relevant and complimentary that did not sound hopelessly contrived. Nothing occurred to him.

'You don't have to say anything,' proffered Ryman. 'Only the advertisers read it to see if their puff is printed the right way up.' He took an impatient gulp at his drink. 'Look, I know it's none of my business but you ought to give Hong Kong a try. Get into one of those big outfits, they've got more pies than fingers. Singapore's all right too, unless you want to grow your hair down to your waist.'

'I've only just arrived here,' said Burton, sipping his drink, in which the barman seemed to have reversed the normal proportions of tonic and gin.

'I can remember saying that,' said Ryman. 'Told myself I ought to give it a fair crack of the rhubarb. Then, in no time at all, the years were clocking up and I'd lost my momentum. I was part of the place, or rather, the place was part of me.'

'But you don't regret it.'

Ryman looked up and his eyes were sharp and hard. 'I'm just beginning to.' His face relaxed into a smile. 'That's probably why I'm giving you this lecture.'

Burton glanced round the empty bar and lowered his voice. 'Ought I to be a member?'

'I don't know,' said Ryman. 'I can't remember when I last paid my subscription. It's a miracle that the place keeps going. You never see an American in here. They can't survive without the iced water and the peanuts.'

'It has atmosphere,' said Burton dutifully.

'Not much else does around here,' said Ryman. 'Culture-wise it's like a Chinese Australia. The odd temple dates before the invention of plastic, but apart from that you have to go to the Palace Museum if you want to see anything.'

'I know,' said Burton. He recounted his stories of the poetry reading and the piano recital.

Ryman nodded his head sagely. 'It's what I told you, old chap. You're wasting your time here. The Chinese are very happy with their own culture. You know how many there are, don't you? A million million. Three times as many as the number of people who speak English in the world.' He lowered his voice again. 'Give them a few years and they'll be swarming all over us like delightful little yellow-arsed flies.'

Burton glanced at the barman to see if he was responding to this speculation on his future movements. The man picked up a glass and began to polish it thoughtfully. 'Mind you,' continued Ryman, 'when you see the stuff in that museum you can't complain. Out of this world. Breathtaking. Just a couple of pieces and you'd be set up for life. You could sell one and look at the other.'

'It would be a difficult decision.'

'Not for me it wouldn't. I can never understand those chaps who live in poverty when they could release a few hundred thou by flogging a family heirloom. And the amount of priceless stuff that museums salt away in their vaults. Nobody ever sees it. Just think what you or I could do with some of those items.'

Burton nodded. Ryman's glass was empty, his own nearly full. It occurred to him that his new acquaintance could become an expensive drinking partner. 'Same again?' he said.

'Good idea,' said Ryman. He glanced at his watch. 'Tell you what. I was thinking of popping up the road to Peitou. Why don't you join me?'

'Peitou?' queried Burton. He could vaguely remember somebody mentioning the name.

'It's a spa,' explained Ryman. 'Sulphur baths, mud baths, hot springs. You can take your pick. A smidgin north of Taipei. Just the place to soothe away the stresses and strains of life in the big city.'

'I was thinking of getting something to eat,' said Burton, deciding it best not to make his eagerness too obvious.

'Absolutely no problem,' assured Ryman with an airy wave of the hand. 'All human whims and desires are catered for.' He rubbed his huge hands together like two grinding stones.

'Well, in that case,' said Burton, 'I'd like to come.'

When the police arrived at the snake shop the crowd was as thick as the flies. The bodies lay inside between the tables, surrounded by an interested group of patrons clutching glasses of snake blood and venom. Only customers had been allowed into the temporary morgue. One of the bodies still wore the ripped, bloody awning like a shroud. The other poured out a seemingly unending stream of blood from the valley in its face.

'This man is living,' said the inspector. He pointed to the slow lift and fall of the exposed stomach. The man with the valley in his face was taken away to hospital, the wailing note of the siren cutting a path through the still growing crowd. The inspector approached the second body and knelt down to pull some of the half-severed strands of material away from the

24

face. Flies rose in the air. The inspector looked and frowned. Nobody was impertinent enough to ask him, but it seemed from his expression that he might know this man. He asked for water to wash his hands and then located a telephone. He made two calls.

'Here we are,' said Ryman. He spoke to the driver who stopped abruptly before a tall pagoda-type building. It was very dark, but the corners of the succeeding curved roofs were lit with coloured lights so that in outline the structure looked like a child's first attempt at a Christmas-tree cut-out. Ryman eased himself out into the open and Burton followed. The air throbbed with the sound of crickets. 'Note the Japanese influence,' said Ryman. 'When Taiwan was Formosa and one of the jewels in the Emperor's crown, the Japanese army had a sort of rest and recuperation centre here.' Burton looked around the square. It was true that the buildings had a more solid, vertical stress than many of their counterparts in Taipei, but he would have been hard-pressed to ascribe it to a Japanese influence. Chinese characters were plastered all over the walls like melting sealing wax, and there was a Christmas bazaar of bright lights and lanterns with their scarlet tassels stirring in the breeze. From somewhere came a peal of girlish laughter.

'Seems a lively place,' said Burton.

'Lively isn't in it, my boy,' said Ryman. He led the way towards a doorway topped by a sign that said 'Eternal Spring of Youth'. Burton followed, and stumbled as he went through the entrance. Some kind of hot bath was probably just what he needed to steam the alcohol out of him. He hoped it was not going to be like the place in Jermyn Street he had once wandered into after a night out from Sandhurst. Some very odd types had loomed out of the steam. Even the chap who handed out the towels had been as gay as a charm of goldfinches. For a moment a horrible suspicion passed across Burton's mind. Could Ryman be queer? Another stentorian belch reassured him. No, no fellow who could belch like that could be queer. 'Heavy weather off Changpin Point,' said Ryman cheerfully. 'Now, I think we need another drink, don't you?'

Burton had been expecting something like the entrance to a swimming bath, but instead found himself in a low-ceilinged room in which there were a number of dimly lit alcoves sheltering behind a fretwork of lacquered gold screens. An elderly woman wearing a long tunic that came down to the ankles of her baggy silk trousers approached Ryman, her hands clasped in front of her. She was obviously glad to see him. A few words of sing-song Chinese were exchanged, and the woman conducted Ryman and Burton to one of the alcoves and went away.

Burton looked around him. On the other side of the room two attractive girls were sitting with what appeared to be a couple of Chinese businessmen. He turned to Ryman. 'Do they allow mixed bathing here?' he asked, slightly surprised. 'All kinds,' said Ryman. He stood up as one of the most beautiful girls that Burton had ever seen appeared around a pillar carrying a tray of drinks. Burton rose to his feet hurriedly and hit his head on a lantern. If the girl found this funny she gave no indication of it. Her red silk *cheongsam* was slit to a point just below her hips and its high neck accentuated the elegance of her long, slim neck. Her hands were graceful and her feet as small and neat as the flower patterns embroidered on her satin shoes. Burton felt a surge of understanding and excitement.

'Henry,' said Ryman. 'I'd like you to meet Ying Pi who is very happy to be addressed as Flower.' He extended a hand towards Burton. 'Henry Burton.'

Burton almost extended a hand and then checked himself. *'Wan An,'* he said.

Flower bowed and placed the tray on the table. 'You speak Chinese?' she said politely.

'Only a few words,' said Burton. ' "Hello", "Good morning", and "Good evening".' He hesitated. 'I intend to learn more.'

Ryman gestured that Flower should sit next to Burton and helped himself to a drink from the tray. 'My father used to say that the only words you needed in a foreign language were "Take off your clothes, my friend will pay." '

Flower met Burton's eyes and saw the laugh die on his lips. He seemed in awe of her, which she found strangely flattering. Normally, the pleasure with which men looked upon her was written in lust across their features. Their eyes stared through her clothing, seeing only what they had bought. This young man with the sensitive features and the slim, graceful hands was almost shy. She warmed to him and instantly warned herself to be wary.

26

Ryman was talking about the Chinese language. 'Did you know that according to how you pronounce it the sound "shih" can mean either history, city, lion, teacher, ten, corpse, stone, room, time, to swear, to recognise, to wait on, and a host of other things? All those jokes about ordering from the menu and ending up with the chef's wife dressed up in a fireman's outfit can take on a grisly reality.'

Burton was looking at Flower. It was hard not to look at her. Her wide almond eyes were dark brown, but they seemed almost black. Black and shining like the sheen on her shoulder-length hair. Her mouth was delicate beneath her small nose and her cheek bones high. Her hair was parted in the middle and she brushed it self-consciously with the tips of her long fingers as if not totally relaxed before Burton's unconcealed admiration. He placed what he assumed was her drink before her and drank from the other. He was grateful for all the alcohol he had consumed. It made the whole thing much easier. He felt relaxed and almost in control of the situation. 'You work here, do you?' he asked. It was not a remark he was especially proud of but a marginal improvement on 'hello' or 'good evening' in bad Chinese.

'Yes.' Flower's reply proclaimed a diffidence that she would have been at pains to analyse. Normally she found it easy to talk to clients. She glanced towards Ryman, but he was looking towards the furthest recesses of the room where a soft rectangle of red light showed the entrance to another part of the building. A figure was moving through the opening. Ryman stood up. 'I'll see you later,' he said. 'I've just recognised somebody I know.' He ducked under the curved lintel and advanced ponderously across the room.

Burton did not watch him go. His attention was totally directed towards Flower. He wanted to touch her skin with the tip of his finger as one might stroke the plumage of a beautiful bird. She turned towards him and smiled, revealing perfect white teeth. 'Do you want to bring your drink?'

She had stood up before he quite realised what was happening. 'Where are we going?'

'To the bath, of course.'

'Of course.' He had forgotten all about the bath. He stood up and then bent down and picked up his drink as instructed. He might need it. It would help if he could be certain who Flower was or what she did. Was she a whore? Half of him wanted her to be.

The other half, the romantic half, hoped that she was something else. But what else could she be? Perhaps in Taiwan the bath girls were just that. Bath girls. Either way, he was soon going to find out.

Flower led the way across the room and past the elderly woman who had greeted them. She inclined her head gracefully. Not for the first time, Burton was struck by how Chinese women seemed to lose none of their suppleness with age. Their movements still flowed. A door loomed up and with it a surge of warmth that one might feel as one approached the grill of a bakery. Flower opened the door and ushered him into a narrow corridor where the heat was almost unbearable and a gurgling, bubbling noise punctuated the silence. Steam clung to the ceiling like smoke and shrouded the already dim lights. Burton was reminded of the stage effects for pantomime hells. After the comfort of the reception area the atmosphere here was one of menacing gloom. The tradesmen's entrance to a house of pleasure. He looked about him for Flower, who appeared carrying two coarse yellow towels. On either side of them were staggered wooden doors placed so that one would not open against the other in the narrow corridor. Flower wiped a wisp of hair from her angelic face and opened one of the doors. Burton's nostrils wrinkled. The smell was that of a malodorous river bank. He looked inside. A stream of thick brown liquid flowed sluggishly past his feet. Steam clung evilly to its surface, which was pocked by sudden convolutions as if an earth tremor was taking place in the vicinity.

'Mud bath,' said Flower.

'I rather thought it was,' said Burton. 'Am I really supposed to get into that?'

'It's very good for you,' said Flower. 'Cures rheumatism and builds strong bones.'

'I don't have rheumatism,' said Burton firmly.

'It is very good for the skin as well.' said Flower. 'Also, it is included in the price.' As if the last argument was incontrovertible she handed over one of the towels. 'Ten minutes, no more.'

Burton looked down at the slowly churning, foul-smelling mud and felt a profound sense of disappointment. 'Is this it?' he said. Flower's fingers dropped to the slit of her *cheongsam* and for a few seconds his spirits rose. Her hand withdrew a key attached to a thin sliver of jade which she dangled before his eyes. She pointed to the

28

Chinese character carved on the jade. 'When you have finished here, come down the corridor to the room with this symbol carved on the door. I will be waiting for you.' She smiled and wrinkled her nose like a rabbit. 'Hot spring.' She dropped the key into the breast pocket of his shirt. 'Ten minutes.' The door closed and she was gone. Burton looked at the glass in his hand. It was covered in steam and the ice had disappeared. He finished it in a gulp and started to take off his trousers.

Crosby flinched as he felt Ryman's hand on his shoulder. 'Evening, Harry.'

'Don, you son of a bitch. You've no business sneaking up on a guy like that.'

Ryman eased himself on to the stool beside Crosby. 'That was my normal butterfly amble,' he said. '"Twinkle-toes Ryman" they used to call me at ballet school.' He glanced at Crosby's glass. 'What are you drinking?'

'I'll get it.' Crosby signalled to the girl behind the bar. 'Scotch?'

'Thanks. I thought you were at Kaohsiung?'

Crosby's face hardened. 'I was.'

Ryman waited, but no further information was forthcoming. Crosby brushed his thinning black hair over his forehead and tightened his grip on his glass. He wasn't drinking from it, just holding it.

'Long way to come for an evening out.'

'Sure is.'

'I believe the train takes about five hours now.'

'Four.'

'Amazing. Still, it must be easier to fly.'

Crosby stared into his glass for several seconds. 'I got sacked today.' There was a long silence. Ryman wondered if the word could mean something else in American. 'You mean fired?'

'Fired, sacked' — he did a bad imitation of an English accent, 'the jolly old order of the boot — fuck the semantics, I'm out on my ear!'

'I'm sorry,' said Ryman. 'I really am. That's terrible news, I always thought you practically ran the place.' He felt a genuine sense of compassion for the small, thick-set American in the shiny Brooks Brothers suit. Like so many Americans he seemed to live for the job. Kicking him out was like expelling a bee from the hive.

'I did run the place,' said Crosby bitterly. 'I practically hung up the paper in the shit-house. Now they've decided to give it all to a tame gook, just so they can keep in with the government, smooth the way for the next land acquisition. I expect he'll be some fucking minister's son.'

'Probably,' said Ryman. He wondered how best to handle the situation. Crosby was reacting as if physically wounded. He looked awful. Grey skin, black crescents under his eyes.

'I sacrificed my marriage to that company. You remember Lee?'

'Of course,' Ryman thought hard and formed a hazy picture of a lard-faced woman with pink hair who had always been beside the Grand Hotel swimming pool when he went to play tennis. She had eventually gone off with a Sino-American travel agent. No great loss, he would have thought, but Crosby had clearly loved her.

'She laid it on the line. Told me that it was either the company or her. I tried to tell her that it had to be both. I was working like a black so we had enough money to retire early and go back to the States. That's why I came out to the Far East in the first place; good money, low taxes. Singapore, Manila, Taiwan. I've served time, and where's it got me?'

'Tough,' said Ryman. He thought of the women in his own life and how he had ridden roughshod over them. Crosby's dedication to one woman seemed to have shown the same return without the fringe benefits.

'I should have listened to her. She said they were a bunch of arseholes. She never liked Feldman, you know, my boss Feldman? Never trusted him.'

Ryman suspected that the erstwhile Mrs Crosby was probably not a specialist when it came to delineating the criteria by which one could trust one's fellow human beings, but it was an impression he kept to himself. 'When did you hear the news?' he asked.

'This afternoon. On the train. You should have seen Feldman. He was shaking. Like Judas.'

Ryman nodded sympathetically. Harry Crosby was hardly the equivalent of Jesus Christ but he must be suffering. 'Any idea what you're going to do?'

'Not beyond coming here and bursting into tears on a whore's tits.'

30

'Hardly practical beyond the short term. What about other firms on the island?'

'Naah!' Crosby shook his head in contempt and drained his glass. 'Once the word gets around, nobody will want to know. You don't take somebody else's rejects out here.'

'It looks like the States.'

'I'm over fifty, Don. That doesn't make it easy, and you know what they think of guys who work in faraway places with strange-sounding names: there must be something wrong with you to be there.' He snapped his fingers to attract the bar girl's attention. 'I'll probably end up pimping for a place like this.'

'Could be the beginning of a fortune.'

'It was for Ignacius Bigg.' Crosby seized his replenished glass greedily. 'You've heard of the guy?'

'Your millionaire buddy from the Korean war?'

'He was never a buddy, and he sure wasn't a millionaire in those days. Just starting out. Boy, he knew how to find girls. He was smuggling them through the minefields from North Korea. Then there was the truck full of morphine and drugs that disappeared. They never pinned it on him but everybody knew he'd set it up. He was uncanny. The rest of us were trying to stay alive and he was going into business. He stayed out there after the war and we thought he was crazy. But he knew what he was doing. The next time I saw him was when he bought his boat.'

'I remember.' Ryman thought back to a story that had been filed about eight years before. Kaohsiung was the island's largest port and world centre of the ship-breaking business. Ships from all over the world arrived there to be broken down so that their parts could be sold for scrap. Ignacius Bigg, a seemingly eccentric millionaire, had arrived to buy an American-built Panamanian gun boat and have it completely fitted to his own specifications. Instead of being scrapped, the vessel had been turned into a miniature floating fortress. That was the impression the article had given, although there were few details. Mr Bigg had not deigned to make himself available to the press. 'What on earth did he want a thing like that for?'

'To house his collection,' said Crosby. 'He was always crazy about works of art. While we were trying to get ourselves laid, he'd be nosing around some Confucian temple.'

'Of course,' said Ryman. He recalled reading that with the

31

opening of the Getty Museum, Bigg now owned the most valuable private collection in the world. A collection that was constantly being expanded. Anonymous bidders at auctions around the world were often subsequently revealed as having operated on behalf of Mr Bigg. Ryman sipped his drink and gazed across the bar to a carved dragon with the pearl of wisdom in its mouth. He had the strangest sensation that an idea was tapping on the side of his mind and trying to get in.

Burton scrambled out of the bath feeling relieved. He did not like swimming in the sea when you could not see anything. This had been worse. The periodic spurts of bubbles felt like wriggling creatures when they met the skin, and the smell did not improve with acquaintance. It was difficult to believe that immersion in this nauseous liquid could provide any physical benefit. Quite the reverse. Those parts of his flesh which were not still covered in mud were pink. Not a pale pink but a colour that one could associate with freshly doused lobsters. He could understand what Flower had meant about the softening of the bones. Fretfully he rubbed himself down, feeling new beads of perspiration immediately replacing old. The atmosphere was stifling. He wrapped the towel round his waist and gathered up his things, nearly dropping a shoe into the mud. The key retrieved, he nudged open the door with his elbow and savoured the minimal reduction in temperature of the corridor. A figure loomed out of the steam and a plump, dripping Chinaman bobbed past, bowing deferentially, his shoulder-blades scoring untidy tramlines in the condensation that clung to the walls.

Burton walked on, looking at the doors. There were no symbols of any kind. He passed though another opening and was relieved to find that there was movement in the air and more salubrious surroundings. A wide hallway with a polished sandalwood floor and panelled doors on each side. Lanterns hung from the ceiling and an entourage of moths agitated in the glow. There was the smell of damp earth and the heavy scent of lilies. The end of the hallway was open to the night, and Burton could see the outlines of trees in an ornamental garden. With returning eagerness he held up the square of jade and looked about him. The door nearest the garden bore the symbol he was looking for. He tucked his clothes under his left arm and inserted the key. His heart was thumping.

For a few moments the key refused to turn, but then there was a reluctant click and the door gave. Burton opened it and peered inside. Before him he saw a couch, a wooden, slatted floor and a sunken pool. What little light there was came from a lantern bonded to the wall. It contained a thick, stubby candle that barely rose above a lunar landscape of melted wax.

At first Burton thought that he was alone and his heart fell. Then he saw the *cheongsam* hanging from a peg in the corner,the satin slippers neatly positioned beneath it. His eyes returned to the sunken bath. Like a naiad, Flower rose from its furthest corner. She was naked and he wondered at the slimness of her body and the black triangle of her pudenda. Her hair was pulled back from her face and the aureoles of her nipples seemed almost too large for her small breasts. She held out a hand towards him.

'Lock the door. This is the part you are going to like.'

'Refresh my memory,' said Ryman. 'He keeps the collection on the boat, does he?'

'That's the whole idea,' said Crosby. 'That's why it's like Fort Knox with a propeller. There are still pirates around here, you know. Malays, Filipinos, Indonesians. The captain of a British merchant vessel was shot dead recently.'

'I know that,' said Ryman. 'I'm a reporter, remember.'

'Then I shouldn't need to be telling you all this,' said Crosby irritably. He waved at the bar girl and nearly knocked over his glass. 'He was here recently. Bet you didn't know that.' Ryman shook his head. 'Yes sir, the *Midas* came in for a refit two months ago. That's when I last saw Ignacius — Jesus, that's some name, isn't it?'

'I could put up with it,' said Ryman, 'if the money was right. You went aboard?'

'No, he rang me up from a bar. He doesn't encourage visitors.' Crosby lowered his voice. 'There's rumours floating around that some of his collection didn't come via Sothebys, you know what I mean?'

'Continue to enlighten me,' said Ryman.

'Well, I met a guy once who said he'd seen a painting twice. Once in the Louvre and once on Bigg's boat.'

'It could have been a reproduction.'

'No, this baby disappeared just after the war when the Louvre

33

was getting started again. Do you remember the Renoir heist?' His tone became sarcastic. 'No, you wouldn't. You're a reporter, aren't you?'

'I don't know everything,' said Ryman. 'Nearly everything, but not everything.' Secretly he was happy to hear Crosby sounding more like his old abrasive self. 'So you think Bigg helped himself to some paintings from the Louvre?'

'I don't know. Let's put it this way; he'd always be in the market for a good piece.'

'No questions asked?'

'No questions asked.'

'Why did he ring you up?'

'Jesus Christ, do you want to write an article about the guy?'

Ryman sipped his drink thoughtfully. 'That's not a bad idea.'

'We sank a few shots, talked about the old times. He'd changed of course, even from when I last saw him. Who said "The rich are different from you and I"?'

'Scott Fitzgerald.'

'Yeah, well, he was right. Iggy had grown a sort of patina. I couldn't break through to him. His name was a case in point. We used to call him Iggy, but this time when I said it he sort of flinched, didn't say anything, just flinched. I didn't call him anything after that.'

'What did you talk about?'

'Shit, I can't remember. He didn't want to talk about what he was doing and he sure as hell wasn't interested in what I was doing. It was a funny evening. You know what I really think he wanted?' Ryman shook him head. 'I think he wanted me to find him some boys.'

'What made you think that?'

'When you've been in business as long as I have you get to know what guys are like. You watch the way their eyes rove about when they're in a bar. If they're important clients you want to make them happy. If they like girls that's usually no problem. Bigg didn't like girls. I took him to this place. Wall-to-wall pussy, you could go out of your mind there. He shrank, physically shrank. He was gripping the side of his chair like he expected somebody to pump twenty thousand volts through it. I got him out in a hurry and we bumped into this kid in the street, he can't have been more than fourteen, his arse hanging out of his shorts. I didn't take any

34

notice. Then I saw Bigg. He was like a parched flower that's been stuck in a vase of water. He'd come alive.

'So what did you do?'

'I didn't do anything. Shit, that's not my scene. Rough trade, kids. I drove him back to his boat.'

'Interesting.' Ryman finished his drink and tapped the side of his glass to indicate to the bar girl that he would like another one. 'I'd certainly like to meet this man. Maybe he could find you a job.'

Crosby pondered. 'That's not a bad idea. I'd do anything at the moment. Why do you want to meet him?'

'Because I've suddenly decided that I want to make a great deal of money.'

'How do you figure on doing that?'

'Something very dishonest, of course.' He nodded towards Burton and Flower who were approaching from the shadows. 'I think this young fellow may be able to help us.'

'Us?' said Crosby.

Burton guided Flower to a bar stool as if she was his bride and approached Ryman. 'What a fantastic girl,' he murmured. 'I'll always be grateful to you.'

'Don't mention it,' said Ryman.

Burton turned from Flower to Ryman as if eager to bestow the fruits of an overwhelming experience. 'Quite unbelievable. I expect you've . . .' he broke off, baulked by his lack of worldliness, uncertain how to continue.

'Yes, I have actually,' said Ryman. 'You see, we're sort of unofficially engaged.'

35

CHAPTER TWO

'Nice of him to send a car,' said Crosby.

'Yes,' said Ryman. They were not driving towards the town, but out on the road that led towards the Api-Api River and the Serangoon Harbour. He tried to think of when he had last come to Singapore. It must have been with Julia. Raffles Hotel before they put up all the buildings in front of it. He felt a pang of sadness. The car was air-conditioned and the unreal atmosphere put a distance between him and his surroundings that seemed to reach back into the past. It made him feel cut off even from his memories.

'We're going to pay for this when we get out.' Crosby was still mopping the last vestiges of sweat from his brow.

Ryman smiled. Even the provision of an air-conditioned Cadillac was not enough to cure Crosby's inveterate pessimism. By the roadside a huge angsana tree released an airborne invasion of tiny yellow blossoms. They piled up in drifts like confetti after a wedding.

Crosby raked his fingers through his hair. 'Shit, I'm worried. I mean, what you're talking about is crazy, absolutely crazy.'

'It depends on what reaction we get from Bigg,' said Ryman. 'If he doesn't want to know, I agree with you. It is crazy.'

'We'll play it by ear. Cheer up, Harry. The trip can't be a complete write-off. You might get offered a job. Maybe I'll squeeze an article out of it. We aren't committed to anything.'

'Feldman got me into all this,' said Crosby ruefully.

'Feldman and the Taiwan Government,' said Ryman. 'You don't owe either of them any favours.'

'And supposing Burton doesn't want to come in?'

'Then we'll think of something else.'

'You're so British sometimes,' said Crosby. 'It makes me sick.'

Outside the window, dusk was falling and the shattered remnants of the sun painted the trunks of the rubber trees with colours of

36

blood. Above, a wagon train of purple clouds trailed across the darkening plain of the sky, edges fleeced with white. A white parakeet soared and then plunged into the jungle.

'You have to watch the girls in this place,' confided Crosby. 'Most of them are men. Look at their hands, that's the giveaway. Hairy fingers, dirty, bitten nails.'

'How did you find that out?'

'None of your business.' Crosby winked.

Ryman nodded. He always took Crosby's references to sexual adventures with a pinch of salt. He might have fixed up his clients with girls but he had probably been boringly faithful himself. It made the departure of the errant Lee that much sadder.

Crosby chuckled. 'I'll never forget the expression on that guy Burton's face when you told him that you were going steady with Flower.'

'You remember what Steinbeck said about marrying a whore: "You can never surprise them and you can never disappoint them"?'

'I think there's a lot of truth in that. It cuts both ways as well.'

He saw an expression of pain flit across Crosby's face and wondered if he had been tactless. He dropped the subject and turned away to look out of the window again. Singapore to him had been a chaste town. A place of love and discovery. On an impulse he wound down the window a couple of inches and immediately responded to the overwhelming scent of a roadside shrub whose name he did not know. Julia had known the names of all the plants on the island. Maybe he should have tried harder with her.

'Are you really going to marry her?' said Crosby.

'Who?' Ryman snapped out of his reverie.

'Flower, of course.'

'Possibly. A man could do a lot worse.'

'I can see their faces at the Club.'

Ryman smiled. 'I can't. Maybe that's why I need to do it.'

The Cadillac swung to the left with a crunch of tyres on gravel and passed beneath the tiled arch of an ornate gateway. Ryman glimpsed the open-work carving of the support pillars and the brilliant colours. Also the Tamil in the baggy trousers standing back against the hedge of pong-pong trees. Inconspicuous but there if anybody needed him for anything. Ahead, the long drive curved through well-manicured lawns and a pool almost choked with lotuses, their large pink flowers swaying forward like inquisitive antennae.

'Impressive,' said Ryman.

'What were you expecting?' said Crosby. 'The YMCA?'

Trellises of vines covered paved paths, and there was a sundial and a mock temple before the house came into view, flanked by palms and fig trees looking green and succulent against the white of the façade. The building was huge and surrounded by a raised verandah. A flight of stone steps closed in on an imposing front door. Ryman looked up and saw a Chinese girl watching their arrival from an upstairs window. Another girl came to her side. Both of them were brushing their hair.

Ryman looked at his watch. 'We're early.'

Crosby reached for the door handle. 'It doesn't matter. It'll be over that much quicker.'

Outside, the clammy heat made the act of breathing seem like an inhalation taken with a blanket over the head. Ryman looked at the white-blossomed frangipani beside the house. How cool it seemed. He ran his finger over one of the blossoms, feeling the sensation of a woman's skin. Memories.

There was a noise from the verandah and a Malay appeared in the kind of old-fashioned dinner jacket that Ryman remembered his father wearing. The bow tie was slightly crooked and looked as if it had been tied in a hurry. At least it had been tied and not clipped on. Ryman knew that his standards might have lapsed in some departments, but there were limits.

'Mr Crosby? Mr Ryman? Please follow me.'

Baskets of orchids hung from wires along the verandah, their too-intricate flowers looking like bloated predatory insects. The roots were dripping on to the rattan furniture. At the end of the verandah an ancient amah disappeared round the corner carrying a watering can.

The Malay gestured towards two high-backed chairs. 'Mr Bigg will be available shortly.' He bowed in a manner that managed to convey disdain rather than respect, and disappeared into the dark interior of the house.

Crosby waited until he was out of earshot before he spoke. 'What do you make of this place?'

Ryman looked down the verandah. There were a lot of chairs

38

and tables, stone seats in the garden. Bottles glinted on the shelves of a bar behind them. It could have been a club.

'I'd say it was a brothel,' he said. 'Superior *boochakong* house. I saw some girls upstairs.'

There was the slap, slap, slap, of sandals on polished wood and an attractive Chinese girl appeared carrying two cold towels on a lacquered tray. She handed them out with a pair of tongs and smiled pleasantly at Ryman.

'You would like a drink, Tuan?'

'A little whisky and water would be very pleasant. No ice please.'

'Why do they always ask you first?' said Crosby.

'Because they see me as a reassuring father figure,' said Ryman. 'The look in your venereous little eyes is enough to scare them into a nunnery.'

If the girl understood what Ryman said she gave no sign of it. She took Crosby's order and her sandals slapped away towards the bar. Crosby's eyes followed her regretfully.

'She wasn't a man,' he said.

'You can't be lucky all the time,' said Ryman.

Neither man laughed at the joke. It was part of a ritual exchange between males. An acupuncture of throwaway lines aimed at deflating a mounting tension. Useful when preparing to go into action. Ryman continued to ponder. What was he going to say when he came face to face with Bigg? He could hardly blurt out the real reason for their visit the moment he crossed the threshold, yet no purpose would be served by pussy-footing round the subject for too long.

Crosby was looking about him. 'Do you think it's just that?' he asked. 'I mean, a cat house?'

'No,' said Ryman. 'Maybe we'll get the chance to look around later.'

'I wouldn't mind if it was a cat house,' said Crosby, almost sadly. 'I was far too faithful to Lee.'

'That's a mistake many men make,' said Ryman. 'Confusing love with fidelity.' He smiled. 'Women too.'

The drinks arrived and a second cold towel. Ryman sniffed his whisky and added a little of the Malvern water that came with it. It was a malt, Glenfiddick at a guess. As he raised the glass to his lips there was a shrill, piercing scream from above their heads. It

39

was a sound difficult to analyse in a split second. Pain was there certainly, but also a faltering note of release. The cry might have come from a woman. Ryman and Crosby looked at each other. There was no further sound. A fan-tailed dove took off from the end of the verandah with an anticlimactic flutter of wings.

Crosby glanced at his watch uneasily. 'Maybe we were too early.'

Ryman didn't say anything. The noise had been unsettling, perhaps because there had only been one sound. A series of screams might have been stepping-stones to an explanation. One scream, once it had died away, was no more than an ugly trigger to the imagination. He found himself listening intently for any sound. Beside him, Crosby sat with his glass poised halfway to his mouth. Finally he drank and the tension was broken. He swallowed and raised his glass.

'Here's to us.'

The words were trite but Ryman knew what Crosby meant: something about this place tells me we're going to need all the luck we can get. He saluted Crosby with his glass and made a deep hole in the scotch.

Minutes passed, and a feeling of unease was replaced with one of irritation. Ryman did not like being kept waiting when he felt that it was merely a gesture intended to remind him that he was an inferior. It was something the Chinese were fond of doing. He had stared at a lot of waiting-room walls in the last few years. Suddenly there was a whiff of pomade and the Malay butler stood beside them demonstrating the gift for silent materialisation that was the copyright of his profession throughout the world.

'Mr Bigg is ready for you now. Follow me please.'

Ryman drained his drink and followed Crosby through the high louvred doors. In the background he heard a car coming down the drive. A Malay girl with large breasts appeared from the shadows and teetered towards the front door.

The room was long, with a high ceiling from which hung an ornate temple lantern. There were glazed tiles on the walls and the polished wood floor was the colour of dried blood. Beyond the bar was a hall and an imposing, carpeted staircase Crosby glanced through some drapes and glimpsed a large room with two roulette tables. So that was it. One of Mr Bigg's interests was a gambling casino. The girls were no more than an

40

extra, like free drinks — although he doubted they were free.

Another Malay girl passed them on the stairs, pushing her thick black hair into place behind a slide. She looked at them curiously, presumably wondering what they were doing there. It was a little early for business. There was a tilted mirror at the top of the staircase and Crosby watched the girl's high-slung bottom ticking away behind him. How his tastes had changed with age. In his youth she would have seemed the ideal bedmate. Now that he lived on Taiwan she seemed almost grotesque, the large breasts and bottom an affront. He preferred the Chinese whisp, something that could nestle in the palm of his hand like a bird. Why? Maybe it was something to do with growing old. The aggressive voluptuousness represented a challenge he was now wary of accepting. It was not a consoling thought.

The Malay turned left at the top of the stairs into a corridor as wide as any that might have been found in an hotel. There was the discreet murmur of high-class air-conditioning. Crosby stopped mopping and put his handkerchief away. Ryman noticed that this part of the house smelt different. The scent of women had been banished. In its place was a pinched, ascetic odour that he associated with the smoking joss-sticks in Buddhist temples. It was dark too. The shade at the end of the corridor was down.

A door opened and a figure came towards them. It was difficult to discern the sex, not because of the light but because the body, though small, was pear-shaped in a way that could have been either male or female. The long jacket and the baggy trousers presented no clues, neither did the walk, a hobbled shuffle punctuated by one thin arm suddenly thrusting out against the wall for support. The black hair was cut close to the head and the cheeks were plump, the lips full. Ryman looked into the face as he went past and met frightened eyes that held the memory of recent pain. The pathway of one large tear bisected a cheek. The features were Mongolian but the sex was still a mystery.

The Malay tapped on a door beyond that from which the figure had emerged and they waited in silence. Behind them, a sudden glow showed that lights had been turned on at the bottom of the stairs. There was a muffled voice from behind the door and the Malay opened it and stepped inside. The smell of his pomade invaded Ryman's nostrils as he went past.

'Ah, Harry Crosby, I see you could make it.'

41

Perhaps because of the name, Ryman had been expecting a big man but the speaker was a good foot shorter than himself and smaller even than Crosby. His features were neat, with a trace of the oriental about the eyes. His hair was cut severely to reveal flesh above his ears, and bore a pepper dash of silver at the temples. The small mouth was guarded by two thin lips barely different in colour to the flesh that surrounded them. It was not a remarkable face but it had an indefinable ability to command respect. Its very anonymity lent it strength. It was also a cruel face. The mouth said that, and the snake eyes that always seemed to be looking for the most vulnerable place to strike.

Ignacius Bigg was standing before a gilt mirror, stuffing a silk handkerchief into the breast pocket of his classically cut, double-breasted dinner jacket. There was a slight flush on the side of his cheeks that suggested he might have changed in a hurry. Double doors connected with the room from which the figure had emerged. A valet, a peon? Ryman wondered.

'Just flew in,' said Crosby. 'Nice place you've got here.' He sounded ill at ease. It occurred to Ryman that after their wait, a few words of apology might have been offered. The reverse was true. 'I see you could make it' suggested that it was they who had been late. Ryman decided that it was going to require an effort to like Mr Bigg.

'I'd like you to meet my friend Don Ryman. Don. Ignacius Bigg.' Ryman stepped forward and offered his hand, which Bigg took after a slight but telling hesitation.

'Delighted to meet you,' said Ryman. 'Harry's told me a lot about you. About the old days.'

Bigg pulled down his cuffs and turned away from the mirror.

'I don't give interviews to newspapers,' he said, addressing his words to Crosby. 'Certainly not to newspapers like *The Times of China*.'

Ryman flinched. Bang, bang. The left barrel after the right. Crosby hurried forward to pick up the pieces. 'We didn't come here to interview you. We had some business in Singapore. This is a social call.'

Bigg moved behind a large teak desk supported by carved elephants.

'Your letter suggested otherwise.' He waved them towards seats.

'I mentioned Don was a newspaper man, that's all.'

42

Ryman was looking round the room. The furniture was good, traditional Indian and Malay most of it, but there was no sign of anything truly outstanding. Nothing that could be a part of the Bigg Collection. He turned to find Bigg's piercing eyes on him.

'You have some nice pieces here,' he said.

'You are referring to the furniture?' There was nothing in Bigg's tone to suggest that he was making a joke but Crosby laughed deferentially.

'It's a hobby of mine.'

'You won't find much here,' said Bigg. 'It's not the setting I'd choose.' He waved a hand dismissively. 'This is business. I own a number of establishments like this in the East. I set a certain style and it is maintained. Like a chain of hotels.'

'I wouldn't mind staying here,' said Crosby.

Bigg looked at him coldly: 'You might find the check a little high.'

'Check.' It was the first Americanism Ryman could remember him using. The accent owed nothing to its Stateside origins. It was more English than anything, overlayed with a heavy Levantine smoothness. It might have been all those years in the East or it might have been cultivated. Ryman tended to think the latter.

'I guess you're right,' said Crosby. 'It's a far cry from the old days, huh?'

Bigg nodded, as if that was the only reply the question merited. 'You're out of a job —'

Crosby hesitated and then nodded. 'That's about the size of it. I was wondering if — er, if there was an outside chance of us teaming up again.'

'Last time I wasn't picking the team,' said Bigg cruelly. He turned towards Ryman. 'Are you out of a job too?'

Ryman had to swallow his dislike of the man before he could speak. 'I'm placed at the moment but I might be interested if the right option came up.' He was surprised at the evenness of his voice.

'I don't know if your credentials are really very interesting,' said Bigg. He looked from one to the other and then to his watch.

Ryman decided that he had had enough.

'I don't know much about your credentials either,' he said. 'But it doesn't stop me from thinking we might be able to do business. Supposing we were selling and not buying?'

43

Bigg's eyes narrowed to slits. 'What?'

'You could name it,' said Ryman.

He looked across to Crosby. Crosby gulped and sat forward in his chair. 'I told him about the boat and your Collection. I believe you've got some pretty fantastic stuff there.' Bigg said nothing. His expressionless face turned towards Crosby like a phase of the moon. 'I know you're always in the market for a good piece.'

Bigg brushed his jacket over his lap and stood up. 'So you have something to sell. What is it?'

'You can make your choice from the National Palace Museum at Taipei,' said Ryman.

There was a silence broken only by a bubble of laughter that floated up from the verandah below. As if stimulated to emulation, Bigg smiled a thin smile. 'If I understand you rightly, you have nothing to sell. Merely the possibility that you might be able to steal something.'

Ryman stood up so that he towered over the little man in the dinner jacket. 'We'd like confirmation that if we came up with something there'd be a market for it.'

'Would I be expected to finance this venture?' asked Bigg. The smile had not completely died from his lips.

Crosby's eyes lit up. 'You wouldn't have to be involved. We're looking for an outlet. You tell us what you want and we'll do the rest.'

Bigg walked slowly across the room and stood with his back to them, apparently staring out of the window. He looked like a figure in a painting, dwarfed by a too-large frame. Crosby looked towards Ryman and made a quick thumbs-up sign. Bigg spun round. 'Gentlemen,' he said, 'I find myself at a loss for words.'

Ryman continued to meet Bigg's eyes. 'I think it would be best if we selected the items together. That way there'll be less risk of any mistakes.' Bigg's hand moved beneath his desk. His face was a waxwork. 'You misunderstand me. I want nothing to do with your impractical scheme.'

'But Ignacius ...'

Bigg held up a silencing hand and an expression akin to a wince passed across his features. It was as if the sound of Crosby addressing him by his Christian name caused physical pain. 'Any further discussion is superfluous.'

Ryman felt as if he had been punched in the pit of the stomach.

What a waste of time and money — and, above all, hope. The door opened and the Malay butler waited respectfully. Bigg spoke without a trace of emotion in his voice and returned to adjusting his handkerchief. 'These gentlemen are leaving.'

The Malay bowed and stood to one side. Crosby walked out without looking to left or right. Ryman nodded and followed him. He had the feeling that Bigg's eyes were boring holes in his back. One of Crosby's fists was clenched as they walked down the corridor.

'Jesus,' he said. 'Jesus, what a bastard.'

'I think you're flattering him,' said Ryman. 'Bastards have mothers, don't they?'

Crosby patted Ryman's arm. 'Gee, I'm sorry, I really am.'

'It doesn't matter,' said Ryman. 'We'll try someone else.'

But who? He was still asking himself the question as they reached the top of the stairs. Multi-millionaire art fanciers with shady backgrounds were not a common commodity in Taiwan or anywhere else that he knew. Bigg was the man they needed. Without his interest the proposition was a non-starter. There was no future in trying to sell treasures from the National Palace Museum on the open market.

'I need a drink,' said Crosby.

'So do I,' said Ryman.

They were standing in the hallway. Outside, lights had been switched on along the drive and a drove of moths were cartwheeling round the lantern that hung from the porch. A car drove away round the side of the house and there was a click and whirr and a murmur of subdued conversation from the gaming room. The girls wore their evening faces, smiling, eager to please; already the aroma of expensive cigars hung in the air. The business of the night had begun. Ryman was moving towards the bar when the Malay touched his sleeve and jabbed a finger towards the front door.

'You go.' Ryman looked at his sleeve as if he expected to find a dirty mark on it. 'We're having a drink, Rochester.'

The Malay's angry features ruckled like perished rubber. He wavered and then jerked his head towards the bar. 'One drink — then you go!' The words came out as if coated in venom. He turned on his heel and walked away.

'Slightly lacking in charm,' said Ryman. 'Also, he bites his

45

fingernails. I don't think I'd care for him polishing the family silver.'

'Jumped-up little arsehole,' said Crosby.

They sat down at the bar next to a prosperous-looking China-man wearing a mohair suit and smoking a cigarette in a long bamboo holder. He sported brown and white co-respondents' shoes and Ryman put him down as an inveterate blackjack player and habitual loser.

The girl behind the bar was a Tamil. Lustrous jet-black hair fell to below her shoulders and she wore a kind of sari with a length of gold-edged transparent cotton thrown over one shoulder and across her breasts. Her midriff was bare and her skin dark as the lacquered surface of the bar. Her eyes were huge and brown, her mouth wide and generous. Ryman could see Crosby beginning to feel better the moment he set eyes on her.

They ordered drinks and drank in silence. It was a small gesture of defiance. There was nothing to be discussed here. Another car arrived and two middle-aged Englishmen appeared, conforming to type by looking both self-conscious and disapproving. They stood in the doorway fingering their regimental ties and peering round the room as if they suspected that a cockroach might drop from one of the drapes. Then they went away, presumably to gamble.

Ryman took his drink and walked out on to the verandah. There was an electric whirr of insects, and somewhere in the darkness a night bird screeched. Away from the air-conditioning the heat was like a hot flannel pressed against the face. Ryman sipped his scotch and looked about him. What he found puzzling was the lack of obvious security. Mr Bigg was a powerful man but what he was doing was illegal. He might have friends in high places but they could not protect him against all the Chinese Secret Societies that existed in Singapore. The Angry Dragons, the Toh Hoh, the Friends. They must have tried to put the squeeze on him. Protection money was a common currency throughout the East. A way of survival. If you refused to pay you took your life in your hands. Mr Bigg was either so powerful that he had nothing to fear, or was paying out a fortune to avoid trouble. Neither alternative seemed entirely plausible.

Ryman stepped out on to the lawn and looked up towards the house. A light was on in Bigg's room but the shades had been pulled. Further along, a buttress structure protruded from the corner of the building like the turret of a mediaeval castle. In its side were two faint bars of light in the shape of a Swiss cross which revealed where an opening had been made in the brickwork. Beneath the cross was the outline of a searchlight, the cylindrical glass glinting like a huge monocle.

With increasing interest, Ryman walked across the lawn towards the end of the house, the turf springy beneath his feet. Suddenly he paused. Something told him that he was not alone. Heart thumping, he turned quickly and peered into the darkness. He could see nothing except the shadowy outline of a clump of bamboo. He started to move towards it and then stopped. Another voice was telling him that he was in great danger, that the next step he took could be his last. Sweat prickled his armpits. The silence seemed to be ticking like a bomb. He knew that if he did not move before the count of ten, something would happen. With an attempt at nonchalance he cleared his throat and turned back towards the house. He had the same sensation as when leaving Bigg's room. A lance was following him, probing for his back. At any moment it would make contact and sink into his flesh. He lengthened his stride.

The pool of light thrown from the verandah greeted him like the frontier post of a friendly country. Crosby was still at the bar making conversation with the Tamil girl. He winked as Ryman came in. 'I thought you'd found yourself a date.'

Ryman did not smile. 'It's time we went.'

'Really?' Crosby looked as if he was going to argue and then read Ryman's expression. O.K.

He slid off the stool and then stopped. A man had come into the room. He was Chinese, but not the milk-fed, affluent variety with two-tone shoes. He was as thin as a reed and the knobs of his cheek bones stood out like knuckles. He wore dark glasses and a tight, short-sleeved black silk shirt, slacks and woven shoes that might have been plastic. Ryman knew the type. A twenty-four carat Chinese frightener raised on bean curd and raw gristle who would cut his own grandmother's throat at the drop of a joss-stick.

The Chinese looked round the bar. There were now half a dozen people dotted about it. Everybody stopped talking. The Tamil girl had been shaking a cocktail and the ice went on clinking as she hurriedly put the shaker back on the counter. It was an eerie sound that punctuated the man's approach to the bar. He extended a skinny arm and pointed to a bottle. 'Blandy.'

It sounded funny but it wasn't. The girl hesitated and then shook her head. 'I cannot serve you. You have to be member.'

'Comere.' The Chinese beckoned with a finger chosen from his left hand and reached down as if he was going to show her something. Frightened but obedient the girl leaned across the bar. Ryman started to move but he was too late. There was a flash of silver and for a second the girl's cheek hung open before his eyes. Then the blood hit the bar-top and she screamed as her hands rushed to hold her face together.

The Chinese was stepping back as Ryman hit him with the bar stool, jerking it up just below the seat and smashing it through the man's raised arm and into his face with all the force that he could muster. There was a rustle from the terrace and a second Chinese appeared carrying a sub-machine gun. The barrel swung up and Ryman plunged sideways as a trail of bullets shattered a row of bottles and sent a shower of glass skittering across the polished floor. The noise hammered at his eardrums and he felt a sharp pain in his right leg. Women screamed and there was a stench of cordite that came back to him from over the years as if someone had wrenched the stopper from a bottle. He scrabbled across the floor and dived against the wall by the door. Beside him the well-dressed Chinese stared up at the ceiling, his cigarette holder still clamped at a jaunty angle between his teeth. He was quite dead. There was a fresh rattle of machine-gun fire but this time from somewhere above his head. A blaze of light flooded the lawn. Ryman put it together in his mind. The buttress he had seen at the corner of the house had contained a strongpoint. The searchlight had just been turned on. The invaders of Ignacius Bigg's privacy would soon be put to flight. He looked around for Crosby.

BOOM!! Ryman's body lifted into the air and his eardrums felt as if they were exploding. The whole building shook and a fresh wave of glass shattered against the floor. The air was full of dust and plaster. Ryman started to pull himself to his feet, his head singing. The garden was in darkness again and the firing from the house had stopped. He glanced sideways into the shattered remains of the bar and saw that a door had been burst open by the blast. Beyond it was a steel, spiral staircase obscured by smoke and the muffled glimmer of flames. With a sickening feeling of fear he realised what must have happened. One of the invaders had knocked out the strongpoint with an anti-tank gun. The stairway must lead to it. A fresh burst of bullets thundered perilously close.

Ryman saw a figure looking through the murk and threw his shoulder against the door of the bar. Sixteen stone shattered the bolt from its mooring and he plunged beside the girl hunched up on the floor with her hands still pressed to her face. A pool of blood spread stubbornly through the welter of broken glass. Ryman stumbled through the door to the stairs, knowing that at any second two skinny hands could be reaching over the bar to pump bullets into his guts. He grabbed the metal stair rail and felt the heat singeing his eyelashes. Above, two hands dangled down, dripping blood on to the machine carbine they had discarded. Ryman snatched it up and swung round. A figure appeared in the doorway and he pressed the trigger. Nothing happened. Fighting panic, he searched for the safety catch and jerked it forward. He squeezed again and bolts of scarlet streaked into the mist. There was a scream and the puppet figure was snatched from view. Ryman ran forward and nearly collided with Crosby. His upper arm was awash with blood. The American looked about him, wide-eyed and desperate. 'Let's get the fuck out of here!'

Ryman said nothing but stepped over the Tamil girl who was still whimpering. The room was thick with dust and smoke and a heavy curtain had collapsed like a sail to block the exit to the terraces. There were bursts of automatic fire and isolated shots, suggesting that the battle was still raging between Bigg's men and the invaders. From the direction of the gaming-rooms came Anglo-Saxon shouts of pain and panic.

Ryman pulled Crosby to him and moved towards the curtain. Through it he could see out on to the lawn and a sight that guillotined hopes of a easy escape. Five Chinese were approaching the house. Two held sub-machine guns, two pistols, and one had a rocket launcher slung over his shoulder like an elephant gun. The men were twenty feet away and scanning the side of the house. Ryman heard the flames crackling behind him and knew that they were doomed if they stayed where they were. The man with the rocket launcher started to unsling his weapon.

V-R-O-O-O-O-M!! An engine roared to life and the men on the lawn spun round. The noise came from the back of the house and a saloon car suddenly hurtled into view, making a run for it across the lawn. There was a squeal of brakes and it slewed round, hurling turf against a clump of palms. The man with the rocket launcher chewed off a guttural gabble of words and, swiftly raising his weapon, rested it on the stooped shoulder of one of the men armed with a pistol. Ryman saw the muzzle swinging round, and then there was a blinding column of light and a flash that forced him to close his eyes. When he opened them, the car was a blazing mass of wreckage, and patches of grass were burning twenty yards away. The noise of the explosion seemed to be wedged in his ears, dying away in waves like the ripples of a gong.

No human being could have survived the blast, but the Chinese closed in with the relish of children approaching a bonfire. Something moved amongst the flames, and a sub-machine opened up at pointblank range, making the sparks dance even higher.

Ryman pulled Crosby with him and brushed past the curtain. The Chinese had their backs to them, and roaring flames on two sides drowned any sound of movement. Over the verandah and on to the lawn. A cloud of smuts stung Ryman's eyes. He glimpsed Crosby on his right and started to raise his carbine, praying that it would not jam. The Chinese were now silhouetted against the flames like thin, black witches at a coven. One of them started to turn.

Crosby fired first, cutting down the two men on the left of the group. A man with a sub-machine gun coolly dropped to one knee and raised his weapon. Ryman shot him through the head before he could fire and the other two turned to flee. One of them was carrying the unloaded rocket launcher. He hurled it at Ryman, who was closing the distance between them like a runaway truck. The weapon hit him a glancing blow on the shoulder and he raised his foot and drove it forward with the full weight of his sixteen stone behind it. The flat of his shoe took the man in the small of his back and catapulted him forward into the burning wreckage. There was a metallic crack as his head met the buckled bodywork, and a greedy hiss and roar from the flames. The outline of the man disappeared as if he had sunk into a crucible of molten metal. The fifth man was running across the lawn towards the entrance gates. Crosby fired a long burst and missed. With his wounded arm he could hardly hold the sub-machine gun. He fired again, and the weapon twitched from his fingers as if it was alive and eager to escape. Crosby clutched his shoulder and dropped to one knee cursing.

Ryman kicked aside one of the wounded Chinese and set off across the lawn. Against all expectation the man he was chasing suddenly turned and fired a pistol. One, two, three. The bullets whistled past Ryman's head, each one closer than the other. He felt death pass an inch from his face and fired a short burst from the hip without slowing up. The man shuddered but continued running. Ryman knew that he was hit, could tell by the twisted, lolling gait that the lights were being turned off all over his body. The lotus lake loomed up and the dying man blundered into it as if it was a shadow in his path. He slapped against the broad leaves and then sprawled full length, the dark water welling up to surge over his head, the closed flowers swaying over his body like striking snakes.

Ryman turned away to find Crosby, feeling a legacy of tiredness sweep over him. The house was burning at both ends with a vicious, greedy crackle that sent regiments of sparks soaring into the air to join battle a hundred feet above the eaves. The blaze gave off an eerie, luminous light and by it he could see a column of people emerging from the front door like ants from a threatened nest. The shooting had stopped and he heard English voices shouting to each other. A car engine started up and the Malay butler appeared walking along the roof of the verandah, still wearing his dinner jacket and carrying a sub-machine gun. It was a surrealist scene and Ryman fought a desire to laugh. Had this all really happened or had it been a dream? A car appeared round the side of the house with headlights blazing and people rushed towards it as if it was the last ambulance from a battlefield. The horn blared and the car took off down the drive and disappeared through the gates. There were angry shouts and a stampede towards the back of the house. Somewhere a woman was having hysterics.

Ryman had taken four steps when he froze. Four Chinese with guns were moving out on to the verandah. He swung up his carbine and then relaxed. Surrounded by the men was the stubby, unmistakable figure of Ignacius Bigg, the white of his dress shirt gleaming like the breast of a penguin. Bigg closed the distance between them with short, bustling strides and glanced approvingly at the corpse in the lily pond. 'Excellent, Mr Ryman. Quite excellent.' He waited as if expecting a reply but Ryman could only stare into his eyes unlovingly. 'I underestimated you.' He paused again before continuing. 'I only do business with professionals and you have pursuaded me that you are one.'

The ghost of a smile hovered around Ryman's lips. 'Thank you,' he said. Ignacius Bigg nodded emphatically. 'I will be in touch.'

CHAPTER THREE

'You don't look German,' said Burton.

'He was my great-grandfather,' said Flower.

Burton drew back along the pillow so that he could study her profile whilst one hand still rested proprietorially on the flat of her belly. They had just finished making love, or — if he was going to be totally honest with himself — she had just finished making love to him. It was something that was beginning to infuriate him in a pleasurable sort of way. On each occasion he would start off with the firm resolve of taking the initiative and then find that he was lying back and enjoying the things she did to him. He resolved to try harder next time.

'When did he marry your great-grandmother?' asked Burton.

'They were not married,' said Flower.

Burton cursed himself for being a clumsy fool. 'I'm sorry,' he said.

'He was hung.'

Burton felt even worse. 'That's terrible.'

Flower turned towards him and smiled. 'My great-grandmother was very pleased. You see, he had raped her. He came here on a ship that was trading for coral. The captain hung him and everybody was satisfied. Of course, my great-grandmother had to marry a poor man but he was kind to her, even when she had my grandmother.'

'Incredible,' said Burton.

Flower smiled ruefully, 'I learned most about my family from children at school.'

Burton nodded sympathetically. 'I can imagine.' It reminded him of things that had happened in his own life. Resting his head against the pillow, he raised his hand from her belly and ran a finger along the soft flesh of her lips. Now that he knew her better he could see that she must be more than thirty. A delicate tracery of lines spread out from the corners of her eyes and there were two marks like silken cords around her neck.

'Thirty-two.'

Burton flushed despite himself. 'What do you mean?'

'You were wondering how old I was.'

'I was thinking how beautiful you were.'

Flower raised herself to kiss him on the corner of the mouth. 'I thank you for the compliment but you must believe that I know enough about men to understand what they are thinking sometimes.'

Burton sighed and lay back against the pillow with his arm across his forehead. 'Why do you do this, Flower?'

Flower turned towards him and drew herself up on one elbow. 'Isn't the right question "What is a nice girl like you doing in a place like this?" I have never found a man who enjoyed my answer but you can hear it if you wish. Most Chinese families would not welcome me as a bride for the reason that I have described. As for sex, I find it easy to separate passion from necessity. Perhaps it is wicked, but I can enjoy the power that comes with bestowing pleasure. Also, I see all the men who come here before I am introduced to them. It is agreed with Mother Ling that I will not go with a man whom I find repulsive. The hours are not long, the work is not arduous and the conditions are clean, very clean. That is perhaps one of the most important reasons.'

'You make it sound very cold-blooded,' said Burton sadly.

Flower was relieved. If Burton had known more about women he would have been aware that she had been waiting apprehensively for a reaction to her calmly spoken words. She was frightened of the growing depth of her feeling towards the young man and she wanted to wean him away from her as painlessly as possible. When she made love to Burton she was not faking her pleasure and that alarmed her. It lessened her control. And without complete control over what she was doing she could not treat it as a job and divorce it from life outside the small rooms and the steamy corridors.

There was a long drawn-out groan of pleasure from the room next door and Burton winced. 'I wish we didn't have to do it here.'

'You don't like the mud bath?'

'Don't make fun of me. You know what I mean. I can't bear the thought of everybody doing it at the same time. I'd like us to be different, special. Why can't you come to my apartment?'

Flower shook her head. 'That would not be fair to Donald.'

'That's ridiculous. As far as he's concerned, what's the difference between making love here and at my apartment?'

'It is as far as I am concerned. Here, what I do is business. At my flat it is private. If I made love to you at your apartment I would feel that I was being unfaithful to Donald.'

'That's a very fine distinction.'

'My life can only work for me if I make very fine distinctions.'

'And I'm hardly flattered to be considered as business.'

Flower moved to embrace him and then checked herself. 'I like you very much,' she said simply.

Burton rubbed his hand across his face. 'I don't understand you. Are you serious about Ryman? He's old enough to be your father.'

'Fathers are very important to the Chinese. Much respected. Great-grandfathers — that depends.'

Burton's face revealed youthful anger. 'You always duck my questions. It gets on my nerves. Do you believe Ryman is going to marry you?'

Flower shrugged. 'One day, maybe. Anyway, we have an understanding. That is important.'

'Very important,' said Burton sarcastically.

Flower turned sharply to face him. 'Do you want to marry me?'

Burton hesitated and felt himself blushing. He tried to take shelter in the hollow of her neck but she held his face between her two hands and forced him to look at her. 'Do you?'

'I don't know,' he said lamely.

Flower took her hands away. 'I think you are a liar. You do not want to marry a whore.'

Burton grimaced. 'Don't use that word.'

'Why not? It is an honest word.'

Burton said nothing but turned away to lie with his back to her. Tenderly, Flower looked down on him, sad in her triumph.

'Jesus Christ, you look awful,' said Crosby.

Ryman dropped to his knees. 'I feel awful.' Sweat lathered his face and chest and fell in large drops on to the sand. His bare feet burned and he felt that his heart might spill out of his mouth with his next breath. Below him the sixty-foot-high dune was scored deep with the irregular pattern of his footprints. He had run up and down it five times non-stop. In the background fishing sampans made picture postcards against the perfect blue of the East China Sea and beachcombers in shorts and coolie hats wandered along the narrow shore.

55

'You'll kill yourself,' said Crosby.

Ryman dusted sand from his body. The singing in his ears was disappearing into the sound of the waves. He took a few more breaths before replying. 'An Australian runner called Herb Elliot used to practise by doing this.'

'Used to,' said Crosby.

'He held the world record for the five thousand metres.' Ryman pulled a towel round his shoulders and winced as it touched the sunburnt flesh. 'How's the arm?'

Crosby was holding a smooth white rock and raising and lowering it at right angles to his waist. The bullet hole in his upper arm now showed only as a recessed white scar. 'It's shaping up.' He gave a short, bitter laugh. 'Sometimes I think we're training for the geriatrics' olympics.'

'It'll pay off,' said Ryman. 'We're going to need to be in top shape.' He patted his waist. 'I've lost two stone since Singapore.'

'You don't have to tell me. I've seen you in a suit. Jesus, Don. You look like a half-struck tent. What do they say at the paper?'

'They think I'm wasting away with an incurable disease. It's an impression I foster with a few discreet sighs from time to time. They treat me as if I'm my own next of kin and a desire to sack me has been replaced by a feeling that if they wait a little longer they'll save themselves the redundancy payments.'

'You still ought to get yourself a new suit,' chided Crosby. 'You'd be less conspicuous like that.'

'And more imposing too. I suppose there's that to be thought of with Bigg's visit looming up. God, do you know what this whole thing reminds me of? It's like being called up in the army.'

'And we're at boot camp,' said Crosby.

'If that's basic training, yes, we are. With our first inspection just round the corner.'

'And a big op on the horizon.' Crosby tossed his stone aside and flexed his arm. 'You're really enjoying this, aren't you?'

Ryman started to pull on his shirt. 'I like the idea of a mental and physical challenge. I'd been stagnating too long. Surely it's been the same for you, Harry?'

'I wouldn't say I'd been stagnating. I was running with my blinkers on. I could only see what lay ahead of me: my job, Lee, early retirement. Now that's all gone and I'm up for grabs.'

Ryman stuffed a billowing mainsail of shirt tail into the sack-

56

like mouth of his trousers. '"There is a tide in the affairs of men, which taken at the flood leads on to fortune."' He turned briskly to his companion. 'What progress on the boat front?'

'I've got one staked out. Pretty sturdy fishing vessel, inconspicuous.'

'And the engine works?'

'As far as I could make out. The guy said he'd just had it overhauled. I opened her right up when I had the chance. He didn't start bawling. There's only one little problem. Feldman knows about it.'

Ryman frowned. 'How come?'

'The guy rang when I was out. Feldman's secretary took the message and gave it to me when I was in his office.'

'Damn! Why the hell did you have to give your office number?'

'How else was he going to contact me during the day? Anyway, it doesn't matter. I told Feldman I was thinking of sailing home. You know, taking a couple of years about it. I spun him a big story about Bali and the coconut palms bending forward to kiss the limpid waters of the lagoon. You know what he ended up saying? He wished he was coming with me. Jesus Christ, that guy would last just as long as it took us to get out of sight of the shore.'

'The sooner you move in with me the better,' said Ryman. 'How much longer are you supposed to be at Kaohsiung?'

'It's up to me, I guess. I've more or less handed over and the apartment is on the market. As far as they're concerned I'm working out my time while I look around.'

'So buy the boat and sail away. Tell them you're getting a refit at Keelung. Can you handle her by yourself?'

'If I can't I'll make sure I don't have too many problems. I'll sail along the shore the whole way.' He smiled wryly. 'It'll bring back memories. Lee and I took a cabin cruiser round Lake Superior one summer. It was one of our last holidays.' His voice faltered as it sometimes did when he talked about his ex-wife. Ryman imagined the strain that a boating holiday on the choppy waters of Lake Superior might inflict on a threatened marriage, and decided not to pursue the subject.

'Don't say anything about me or your future plans. Leave everything vague.'

'And the money for the boat?'

'We'll split it down the middle.'

57

'What about Burton?'

Ryman scratched his head. 'I don't know. I haven't really had it out with him yet. I don't think he's got any cash anyway.'

'All the same, if he comes he ought to make a contribution. It's the principle of the thing.'

Ryman thought and nodded. 'You're right.'

There was silence before Crosby spoke again. 'You've got to talk to him soon.'

'Yes,' said Ryman. 'I know.'

Thwack! The ball shot off the back wall and wide of Ryman's despairing lunge. 'Game!' he said gratefully.

Burton seemed to be breathing as easily as when he strode out on to the court. 'Is it?' he said. 'What a shame. I was just beginning to get warmed up. I don't suppose we could have another ...?'

Ryman wrenched open the door of the court. ''Fraid not. Out of the question. The boss of the American Institute has got the court after us. Very punctual gentleman.' He stepped into the corridor mopping his face on a towel.

'I can see you've played a bit in your time,' said Burton graciously. 'Very effective drop shot.'

'Needs a lot of work. I'm pretty rusty at the moment.'

'I thought you were looking rather fit. Much ...' Burton broke off as diplomacy overtook honesty.

'I've lost a bit of weight,' said Ryman helpfully. He slumped down on a bench and accepted a cold towel from a whey-faced attendant in a high-collared blue tunic. 'Thanks, Ho.'

'I haven't played for a long time.' said Burton. 'Not since Sandhurst.'

'Can't have been all that long ago.'

'No, it wasn't.'

Ryman noticed how Burton's face had suddenly set hard. 'What made you chuck it in?'

Burton hesitated. 'I didn't really feel I was cut out for the army.'

'I was a regular soldier,' said Ryman easily. 'Got out at the wrong time. Became a rubber planter in Malaya. That didn't work out either. Got stuck behind a desk in Hong Kong, that was even worse. Should have come home, I suppose, but when you've been away for a long time everything seems different. You need one hell of a lot of money to survive in the old country these days.'

Burton did not answer and Ryman's eyebrows knitted in concentration. 'Burton,' he mused. 'Did you have a relation who was a colonel?'

'My father.'

Ryman grimaced. Colonel Nigel Burton had been court-martialled and cashiered after three young recruits under his command had died of exposure on a survival exercise in the Cairngorms. The case had aroused considerable controversy and there had been several letters in *The Times* paying tribute to Colonel Burton's brilliant military career. They were printed after he had shot himself. 'I'm sorry,' said Ryman.

Burton's expression showed that he had heard those words before. 'People thought I had resigned my commission out of sympathy with my father but it wasn't totally that. I didn't have enough guts to press on. I knew there would always be somebody around who would make the connection between us. It seemed too much of a handicap.'

Ryman nodded sympathetically. Now that he remembered the affair he could recall the body of opinion that had blamed the death of the soldiers on their own zeal and foolhardiness rather than on any fault of the Colonel. His fault had been to inspire his men with too much enthusiasm. It was something Ryman could understand. His own promising career in Malaya had ended when he took on a band of terrorists who were slashing rubber trees on the plantation he managed. One of them had been a fourteen-year-old boy and in an exchange of fire, Ryman had killed him. There had been a communist-inspired outcry and Ryman had been moved out fast — the first of many steps round the Far East until he had come to rest in the sluggish backwater of Taipei. He leaned forward and patted Burton on the shoulder. 'Come on, I'll let you buy me a drink.'

They showered and changed in silence, and Ryman steered Burton to a deserted corner of the terrace. The red starburst flowers of a poinsettia peeped over the balustrade, and behind them in unappetising contrast lay the untidy grey sprawl of downtown Taipei. The sound of frustrated drivers pummelling their horns drifted up the hill. Ryman waited until the waiter had disappeared into the club before leaning forward confidentially. 'Henry, I've got something on my mind.'

Burton stiffened. He had been expecting this. There had to be a showdown sooner or later. He had felt embarrassed in the shower. Standing naked next to the man and knowing that he had — that they both had — it made it all too close and easy to imagine. Obscene almost. On the squash court it had been different. He had been in control there. Now Ryman looked a figure of authority; his old housemaster about to haul him across the coals for having dated one of the girls from the local Woolworth's. Only it had become rather more complicated than that now. Ryman gazed into space and seemed to have difficulty in choosing his words.

'I wish I could think of a subtler way of approaching the matter. Still, perhaps it's better to come straight out with it.'

Burton nodded. What was the fellow going to say? We'll share her? I'll shoot you? I'll shoot myself? 'Flower,' he said resolutely.

Ryman looked down at the front of his suit as if expecting to find traces of white powder and brushed it absent-mindedly.

'Thank you,' he said. 'Now, Henry, how would you like to make a lot of money?'

Burton was nonplussed for a moment. 'How?' he said eventually.

'By helping Harry Crosby and me ...' he hesitated. 'By helping us remove a few objects from the National Palace Museum.'

Burton's mouth dropped open. 'Stealing?'

Ryman nodded resignedly. 'I suppose that is a more realistic word for it.'

Burton sat back in his chair and shook his head. 'Are you serious?'

'Very.'

There was a pause while Burton tried to come to terms with what he had just heard.

'Why me?'

'I don't want to go into details at this stage,' said Ryman. 'Suffice it to say that you could provide something vital to the success of the project.'

'Robbery,' corrected Burton.

'You do choose such emotive words,' complained Ryman. 'When you think about it, it's not the same as holding up a bank. You're not taking money from somebody.'

'You're taking their artistic heritage,' said Burton.

'Yes, but where did they get it from? It's all been looted from the mainland. Some of the stuff hasn't been outside a box for more

60

than forty years. Since the beginnings of the Sino-Japanese war. Only a scattering of those quarter of a million items ever go on display at the same time. You could say that we'd be liberating it.' Burton continued to look dubious. Ryman took another breath. 'Look, I could understand you being against the idea if we were going to take gold and silver plate and melt it down for the value of the metal. That would be reprehensible, I agree. But that's not the name of the game. We have a private collector who's going to protect these items as if they were his own life. They're probably going to be safer with him than they are in the Museum. Supposing China tried to take this place back. How much would be left by the time they'd finished?'

'And what's going to happen if this man dies?'

'The stuff will probably go back to a museum. It usually does. Our scheme will just take it out of turgid circulation for a few years. We're borrowing it if you like.'

Burton stared towards the distant hills. 'If they caught us they'd put us away for life.'

'With your help we won't be caught,' said Ryman.

Burton pondered and shook his head uncomfortably. 'I don't know if I want to get involved.'

Ryman sighed. 'I hear there were only seven at the tea-tasting. Now I'd have thought that would have been a raging success. I mean if there's something that the Chinese and the rest of the world have in common, it's tea.'

'You weren't there,' said Burton accusingly. 'Neither was Crosby.'

'That would only have made nine,' said Ryman. 'It wasn't anything personal. We just happened to be in Singapore at the time.'

'Flower didn't come either,' said Burton sadly.

'She's a coffee drinker. Didn't you know that?'

Burton sighed. 'I don't think I know anything.'

Ryman leaned forward conspiratorily. 'I'm talking about half a million dollars.'

Burton's eyes widened. 'Taiwan dollars?'

'American.'

'Each—'

'Of course. It could be more. I've still got some negotiating to do.'

Burton didn't say anything. He shook his head and sighed. Ryman drained his glass and glanced at his watch. 'No need to make up your mind right this minute but don't leave it too long. We'll be going ahead whether you come in or not. Frankly, I don't think Crosby will be too upset if you decide it's not your cup of tea. He's got his eye on seven hundred and fifty thou.' Ryman stood up and patted Burton on the shoulder. 'Thanks for the game.' He started to walk away.

'This isn't a practical joke, is it?' said Burton. There was a note of worried pleading in his voice.

Ryman turned and faced him. 'No,' he said. 'It's deadly serious.'

Ryman got out of the car and walked along the track towards the fishing pool. Three men were hunched up round its edge like garden gnomes. All these years of watching, he thought to himself, and I've never seen anyone catch a fish. Yet the ponds must be stocked or the men wouldn't keep coming back. Or would they? It was peaceful here amongst the ricefields. No nagging wives, no screaming children. Just the line trailing away into the brown water. Perhaps they lived in hope that one day they would catch enough fish to be able to sell some back to the owners of the fish pond and make a profit. Ryman permitted himself an ironic smile. Around such slender hopes do men's lives revolve.

The ricefields were a succulent shiny green, stretching away shoulder to shoulder in ordered squares. Only where the ground began to rise did they follow its contours, stepping upwards in graceful, terraced curves. The brilliant white of an egret stood out against the green like a character in a Chinese painting. Nature imitating art. Ryman shaded his eyes against the sun and looked in the direction of the sea. To his relief he saw a small figure silhouetted against the horizon. He walked back to the car and fanned himself.

When Crosby arrived he was sweating profusely, and there was a rime of dried mud and salt on his trousers that reached up to his thighs. His peaked army cap with neck flap was soaked to the brim. He was carrying a small package. Ryman prised the lid off a thermos box and handed over an iced beer. 'You were cutting it a bit fine.' Crosby said nothing but tore the tag off the beer and drank greedily. When the can was empty he

62

tossed it over his shoulder and slumped in the car beside Ryman.

'Those marshes out there are the arsehole of the world. There's a kind of weed that clings to you. It stinks and it's full of little crawling bugs.' He wrinkled his nostrils in disgust. 'I didn't think I was going to get out. I'm not kidding. There's places where you go right down in the mud and you don't think you're going to stop.' He cursed and scratched his thigh savagely. 'I've still got the little bastards.'

'But you hid her all right?'

'I'll be lucky if I can find her myself.' He read the alarm in Ryman's eyes and patted his arm reassuringly. 'Just kidding. Give me another beer, will you.'

'And no problems with the engine?'

'I'd have said, wouldn't I?' Crosby's tone was irritable. He jabbed his finger towards the thermos box. 'Gimme, gimme!'

Ryman slowly prised off the lid. 'How about the radio?'

'I nearly lost it in one of those shitty creeks, but I got it fixed up. Jesus, I'm bushed.'

Ryman handed over another beer. 'The tide's not going to be a problem?'

'Not where I put her. There's only one thing.' Crosby wiped his mouth with the back of his hand. 'When I was checking out the radio I picked up a typhoon warning.' Ryman's jaw tightened. 'West of the Philippines and moving north.'

'Damn,' said Ryman. 'I knew this weather was too bloody good.'

'Probably won't come to anything,' said Crosby. 'Most of them don't.'

'Some of them do,' said Ryman. He knew that a seasonal typhoon could send a tidal wave three miles inland. Past where they were sitting. Where would their boat be then? 'We'll have to watch it.' He looked at the package in Crosby's lap. 'What's that?'

Crosby shook his head. 'I didn't tell you about this, did I?' He pulled open the wrappings and revealed a polished brass bell mounted in a brass frame. 'Feldman's parting shot. It's a ship's bell for my voyage round the world. Touching, huh? You can imagine how I felt when he gave it to me. If it had been a little heavier I might have beaten him to death with it.' Crosby held the bell contemptuously by its clapper and leant out of the window to toss it into the irrigation ditch that bordered the

63

ricefield. There was a complaining tinkle, a splash and silence.

Ryman handed over the folded newspaper he had been fanning himself with. 'This might interest you.'

Crosby spread the paper on his lap. It was a three weeks' old copy of the *Singapore Straits Times*. The story ringed in biro was headed: 'Terrorist Assault On Home of India Merchant'. It described how a band of Communist terrorists had attacked the home of a Mr Ram Nadu and burnt it to the ground. There was speculation on the likelihood of further attacks on the homes of prominent citizens and stern statements from the police and a government spokesman, but no mention of Ignacius Bigg. It might have been a different house had not the location in Tampine been pinpointed.

'It figures,' said Crosby. 'I guess all his stuff is held in the names of nominees.'

'It's impressive the way he's got it all sewn up,' said Ryman. He glanced at his watch.

'What time is he coming?'

'He's late already,' said Ryman. He sniffed uneasily and slapped his leg. 'Why don't you get out of those trousers? I put some clean clothes in the boot.'

'Thanks.' Crosby got out of the car and Ryman dusted the mud from where he had been sitting. He was still thinking about the typhoon west of the Philippines. That would probably melt away into the atmosphere but sooner or later there would be another *tai-fung*: the big wind that destroyed everything in its path. He began to think about a change of plan.

Half an hour later a large but unimpressive black Chevrolet drove past without slowing down. It continued for two hundred metres and turned round in a plume of dust. This time it came towards them slowly and stopped with its nose three feet from their bonnet. The windscreen was tinted and it was impossible to see clearly what lay beyond it. Crosby looked towards Ryman and wiped the back of his neck with a handkerchief. The dust settled and as if in response to a signal, a door on either side of the Chevrolet swung open. The Malay butler got out of the passenger's seat and a Chinaman Ryman did not recognise emerged from behind the wheel. Both wore dark glasses and inconspicuous white shirts and black trousers. They approached Ryman's car slowly and peered inside like policemen about to deliver a speeding ticket. Ryman glanced down and recognised the squat handle of a Browning automatic nestling inside the Malay's waistband. Satisfied that the right contact had been made, the Malay beckoned that Crosby and Ryman should follow him. There was no word of greeting. The Chinese repeated the gesture and Ryman noticed secret-society symbols tattooed across his knuckles. Closed off behind their dark glasses the men were both mysterious and menacing.

Ryman opened the door and got out. He was wearing his new suit and it felt uncomfortably tight in the hot sun. He walked towards the Chevrolet and saw two figures swimming into view through the opaque glass. The back door opened and a familiar but unexpected figure got out. It was the person they had seen in the corridor outside Bigg's room in Singapore. Ryman felt no more qualified to say whether it was a man or a woman. The silk tunic was still designed to conceal any shape the body might have. The hair was modishly short but swept over and behind the ears in a way that might form a hairstyle for either sex. The eye shadow and the dust of powder on the cheeks could have been sported by a fashion-conscious but effeminate young man. It was perhaps the plumpness that was most confusing. The swollen, translucent skin had no direct kinship with either male or female.

Ryman nodded, but the figure jerked its eyes away as if loath to make even the most superficial of contacts. It brushed past Crosby and moved towards the car they had just left, the Chinese in attendance. The eyes were still glistening as if they were a permanent repository of tears. Ryman could not remember having seen a sadder face or one with so much latent terror in it.

Ignacious Bigg sat alone in the back seat of the Chevrolet. 'Get in,' he said brusquely. 'I find this heat insupportable.' His eyes ranged over Ryman, taking in the physical change. There was no affection in the gaze but a slight, grudging respect. Ryman got into the back seat beside Bigg. Crosby sat in the front. 'Wait outside, Quat.' The Malay bowed respectfully and the door was closed. Inside, the air-conditioning hummed dismally and a trapped fly buzzed irritably against the windscreen. Mr Bigg transferred his cold, penetrating eyes to it and the buzzing stopped.

'How long have you been in town?' asked Crosby.

'Long enough,' said Bigg. He felt in the inside pocket of a jacket hanging by one of the windows and produced a sheaf of

65

photographs that he tossed down beside Ryman. 'Those are the items that interest me.'

Puzzled, Ryman picked up the photographs and leafed through them before handing them on to Crosby. They were good quality black and white prints taken as if looking through the glass of a showcase. Porcelain bowls, paintings on silk, bronze wine jars, jade carvings. On the back of each photograph was written the floor and the number of the gallery where it had been taken.

'How did you get hold of these?'

'I took them.'

Crosby frowned. 'That was risky, wasn't it? I didn't think you were allowed to use a camera in the Museum. Weren't we going to make a selection together?'

'That would have been too dangerous. The less contact we have the better. I am not a welcome visitor at the Museum.' He smiled. 'I already have a considerable number of Chinese items in my collection. It is something that is resented in Taiwan. If we were seen walking around together it would arouse suspicion.'

'I'll go along with that,' said Ryman. 'But surely, taking photographs...'

Bigg raised a restraining hand and picked up a pair of dark glasses. He put them on and looked at Ryman, raising his hand to the rim as if to adjust the angle at which they rested on his nose. His hand returned to his lap and his small white teeth showed in a tight smile. 'I have just taken your photograph,' he said.

He removed the glasses and handed them to Ryman. The plastic sides were thick and set in the top of one of them was a tiny plunger. Ryman turned the glasses so that he was looking into them. Next to the hinge was a minute lens no larger than a rhinestone stud and less noticeable. He handed the glasses to Crosby. 'Ingenious.'

Crosby looked and whistled through his teeth. 'Who makes these?'

'I do,' said Bigg. 'I had them designed for my visit.'

Ryman was impressed but took pains to conceal the fact. He thumbed through the photographs again. 'Some of these items are impracticable. This Shang wine vase. It's too heavy. We'd never be able to move it.'

Bigg took the photographs and, for the first time that Ryman could remember, an expression almost of tenderness settled on his small, neat features. It was as if he was looking at a picture of a

66

favourite child. 'I would give a great deal for that piece,' he said, almost to himself. 'It would be the oldest item in my collection.'

'When was the Shang Dynasty?' asked Crosby.

'It started in 1766,' said Ryman.

Crosby frowned. 'It doesn't seem all that old.'

'B.C.' said Bigg. He looked at Crosby with the same cold distaste that he had bestowed on the fly on the windscreen. 'Over thirty-seven centuries ago.'

'I'm sorry, but it's out of the question,' said Ryman. 'I'm not happy about the Chou food bowl either. We'll have to look at it.' It occurred to him that it sounded as if he was quoting for a furniture removal.

'Perhaps you had better tell me what you think you can manage.' Bigg's tone was overtly sarcastic.

'Certainly.' Ryman thumbed through the photographs and selected six of them. 'These are manageable items.'

Bigg looked at his choice. 'Only six?'

'Better six delivered than twenty that don't even get out of the Museum.'

'And how much would I be expected to pay?'

'Three million U.S. dollars.'

There was a silence in which Crosby glanced at his partner nervously. Bigg's face showed no flicker of emotion. Eventually he spoke. 'That is too much.'

'I'm not here to haggle,' said Ryman. 'This is a take-it-or-leave-it offer. The risks involved demand that we make it worth our while. We're not criminals. We have no police records. This isn't just another robbery, it's a one-off job. After this we retire. So the pension fund must be right.' He picked up one of the photographs. 'This Fan Yuan painting alone is worth the price. As you must know it's reputed to be the most valuable work in the Museum.' He selected another photograph of some delicate cups shaped like open flowers. 'With these you'd have over half the Ju porcelain that exists in the world.' He tossed the photographs back on the pile. 'The sum we're asking is realistic and you can afford it.'

Bigg continued to look dubious. 'For this money I could deal with a professional organisation.'

'And then you'd be involved,' said Ryman. 'You'd be doing the recruiting. With us it's different. We only approach you when we have something to sell.'

'And your professionals would want something up front,' added Crosby. 'With us you don't pay anything until you get the merchandise. If something goes wrong you haven't lost a cent.'

'When would I get the merchandise?' asked Bigg.

'If all goes well, sometime in the next few weeks. We'd make contact with you to arrange delivery.'

'How would the exchange be made?'

'At sea. That seems the best solution. You have your ship, we'll have a boat. You hand over the cash and we deliver the goods.'

Bigg reflected and picked up the six photographs again. He thumbed through them as if they were playing cards and brushed the tip of his nose with his little finger. 'Two million.'

Ryman shook his head. 'There's only one price. It's all or nothing.'

'Two and a half.'

Ryman reached for the door handle. Regretfully, Crosby followed his lead. 'All right. Three.' Crosby closed his eyes and resisted his impulse to leap in the air. 'When you have the pieces you will contact me and say that the insurance premiums have been paid. That will be the signal for us to move to the rendezvous point.'

'Where will you be, Singapore?'

'Hong Kong. I am currently negotiating for the purchase of Jardine Matheson. I will contact you later with the details.'

'And the rendezvous point? We only have a small boat.'

Bigg thought again. 'We need somewhere sheltered but isolated. You know the Pescadores Islands?'

'I've visited Mekung,' said Crosby. 'The place was crawling with soldiers. The Chinese communists are only a hundred miles away.'

'There are sixty-four islands,' said Bigg. 'Many of them are little more than coral reefs with a few palm trees. Only a handful of them are inhabited. Below the Tropic of Cancer there's an island with a natural harbour inside a reef. It's easily navigable and I have no recollection of seeing even a fisherman there. I will provide a chart reference and wait for you.'

Ryman hesitated a moment whilst he thought. He then extended a hand. 'Very well, we have a deal.'

Bigg took the hand and Ryman flinched. The flesh was as cold as that of a corpse. Neither was there any returning pressure in the handshake. It was a gesture of literally chilling formality. The ritual was repeated with Crosby, and Bigg rapped on the window. Quat turned from surveying the ricefields and opened the door. For once, Ryman was grateful for the embracing warmth. 'I'll be in touch,' he said.

'I hope so,' said Bigg curtly, glancing at his watch. He was beginning to fade away like the Cheshire Cat but without any indication of leaving a smile behind.

Ryman took the photographs, and he and Crosby got out of the car. Bigg's travelling companion returned with the Chinese. Ryman looked into the bland face and suddenly realised why its sex had been so difficult to analyse. There was no sex. The creature was a eunuch. Ryman remembered the scream and the tear-stained face and wondered how Bigg took his pleasure. There was something infinitely distasteful in the thought of this neutered creature being used for sexual gratification. It measured up to his conception of Bigg as a man who only took and never gave.

The doors closed and the Chevrolet sped away in a cloud of dust. Crosby clutched Ryman's arm. 'Jesus Christ, we did it! I nearly had kittens when you turned your back on that two and a half million.'

Ryman nodded and watched the disappearing car. His elation was more subdued than Crosby's. He felt as if he had just returned a deadly snake to its box. At some time in the future he would have to get it out again.

They got into the car and drove off down the bumpy track past the fishing pond. 'Look,' said Crosby. 'Some guy's just caught something.' Ryman turned his head and saw a silvery bream jigging on the end of a line. He smiled ruefully. 'Let's hope it's a good omen.'

CHAPTER FOUR

Ryman heard himself cry out and woke up with a start. He had just seen the axe go into the man's face; the crease and then the breaking flesh, the juggled features twisting into each other. Then the blood welling up as if from a broken pipe.

Flower's head leaped from his chest. 'What is it?'

Ryman wiped his forehead. He was covered in sweat. 'I had a dream.' He might have said 'I had *the* dream.' He had seen that image several times now. It seemed to arrive with a hideous inevitability every time he fell asleep. Not that sleep was easy to come by these nights.

Flower pulled at a sheet and started to dab his temples with it. 'You were talking in your sleep.'

Ryman felt alarm. 'What did I say?'

'Nothing I could understand. Why do you have bad dreams?'

'I don't know. It doesn't matter. They'll go away.'

Flower nestled her head against his chest. 'It is because your body does not fit any more. You were foolish to lose all that weight.' She moved her hand down and started to massage his stomach. 'I liked you better when you were fat. You were more comfortable. Like a nice old cushion.'

'People sit on nice old cushions.' Ryman stroked her hair tenderly. 'I've had enough of that.'

'You always used to say that you cannot knock in a big nail with a little hammer.'

'Did I?' said Ryman. 'I thought it was Shakespeare.'

Flower reflected. 'I don't know him. Does he work for the Trade Committee?'

Ryman laughed and hugged her slim body to him. 'No, he doesn't.' His voice became serious. 'Flower, if I went away, would you come with me?'

'Where are you going?'

'I might go to England.'

'England? But England is cold and it rains all the time.'

'I know, but my heart belongs there.' He kissed the top of her head. 'Some of my heart belongs to you as well. That's why I want to have both of you.'

Flower stopped massaging his stomach while she considered. 'It is the cold I do not like. I am used to rain.'

'It's only cold in the winter,' said Ryman. 'November to February. And even then you get sun. Real sun. Dry. Not the watery fried egg you get here.'

'And what would I do in England?'

'You wouldn't have to do anything. I'd have enough money to support you, to look after you.'

Flower looked at Ryman suspiciously. 'I do not understand. Why would you have money in England when you have no money here?'

Ryman tapped her gently on the nose with his clenched fist. 'Very good question. Go to the top of the class.'

'That is not an answer.'

'I think I have found a way of making some money. Enough for both of us.'

Flower shook her head. 'You sound like your friend Henry Burton.'

Ryman's expression changed. 'Why?'

'Because he was telling me that he was going to be a rich man. He asked me if I would like to go to Paris with him. Paris, France.'

'As opposed to Paris, Idaho.' said Ryman. It was difficult to keep a feeling of complacency out of his voice. So Burton had taken the bait — or at least started to nibble at it. 'What did you tell him?'

Flower avoided his eyes. 'I told him I would like to go.'

Ryman's face clouded over. 'You're not serious. What about our understanding?'

Flower maintained her innocent expression. 'That is just a joke.'

'He said that, didn't he?' said Ryman angrily. 'Cheeky young whippersnapper. I'll skin his hide.'

'He has said nothing against you,' said Flower, delighted with the response she was getting. 'Anyway, I cannot understand why you are behaving like this. You introduced him to me.'

Ryman looked uncomfortable. 'I felt sorry for him, I thought he needed cheering up.' He hesitated. 'You're not serious about him, are you?'

Flower lowered her head to his chest and this time when she

71

spoke there was no dissimulation in her words. 'I am not certain. I rather think that I do care for him.'

Ryman sighed and drew her up so that he could look into her eyes. 'Flower, I have something to tell you. It's very important. It's about why I haven't been sleeping well lately.'

Crosby stood under the entrance gate and looked up at the long, pink façade of the National Palace Museum. Although only thirty-five years old, it was built in the classical Peking style with glazed green and Imperial-yellow roof tiles and vermilion moon-gates. Five squat towers rose like observation posts to oversee the terraces and the ornamental gardens to the front and the densely wooded hills behind. Viewed from where Crosby was standing, the mass of green appeared like a giant wave about to break over the Museum. Just above the wide, curved roof of the central tower, sitting like an over-large sun hat on a square head, fluttered the national flag of the Republic of China: white sun in blue sky over crimson ground. Blue for equality, white for fraternity and crimson for liberty: Min Chuan, Min Sheng and Min Tsu.

The building appeared solid, brooding and watchful. More a barracks, or even a prison, than a museum; although Crosby would have been prepared to admit that it was his own guilty conscience that saw it in these terms. Or maybe it was the two soldiers standing guard on giant boxes outside the gates. Their uniforms were immaculate: blue tunics, white breeches and high gaiters, gleaming belts, a parade belt with intertwining eagles and a laundered white scarf filling the gap at the back. Their heads were encased in shiny helmets, the silver of which matched the murderous gleam of their stubby bayonets. They stood at ease with their rifles thrust defiantly forward, one fist clenched against the small of the back. To Crosby it was ironic to see these men dressed in what were almost exact replicas of U.S. army uniforms. He remembered the Chinese in Korea. The night attacks with the screaming and the dying men throwing themselves across the barbed wire so that their comrades could scramble over their bodies and continue with the assault. Their contempt for death had terrified him.

Crosby became aware that a pair of wary eyes were watching him from beneath a helmet and turned away.

'Crosby, good morning.'

With a start, Crosby turned towards the road. A nondescript

black Ford was parked at the kerbside and a man with a crewcut was addressing him out of the driver's window. Crosby vaguely remembered him as being called Henderson and working for the American Institute. Quite what he did was a mystery, although he seemed to know most of the American businessmen on the Island and showed up at Trade Conventions.

'Hi,' said Crosby. He turned on his hail-fellow, well-met smile. 'How are you doing?'

It occurred to him that Henderson probably knew about his being sacked, and the thought encouraged another pang of uneasiness. 'Fine.'

'Great.' Henderson nodded as if that was all he wanted to hear. 'Well, take care now.' He drove off, making sure that there was no car within fifty yards of him before he pulled away from the kerb.

Crosby hesitated and went through the gateway towards the Museum. He felt troubled, and when the man who took photographs of tourists and printed them on souvenir plates capered towards him, he told him to go to hell.

Ryman paid his fifteen Taiwan dollars at the kiosk and collected his ticket. Less than fifty cents American. The ticket alone was worth that; large and glossy and expensive-looking. With it he could stay inside the Museum until five o'clock. He walked across the road and through the glass doors. Two commissionaires looked him up and down to see if he was carrying anything that should be checked in at the cloakroom and examined his ticket. There was no turnstile either in or out of the museum. It was difficult to believe that an accurate count could be kept of everybody entering and leaving the building. Already a long double file of school children was wending its way through the doors from the coach park. The girls had cropped, well-brushed hair held back from their foreheads with slides and wore crisp, white short-sleeved shirts and black knee-length skirts with white socks and well-polished black shoes. The boys were dressed identically save for their black shorts. They were very orderly children with serious faces and only occasionally did a couple of the smaller girls hold hands. In their uniforms they reminded him of English schoolchildren from some private school in Kensington. He watched them filing away towards the porcelain section like two lines of industrious ants setting out to gather culture.

73

Crosby was waiting in the main exhibition hall before the bronze statue of Dr Sun Yat-sen, founding father of the Chinese Republic. He started to walk towards an isolated showcase containing a large bronze urn. Ryman fell in beside him.

'Everything's here,' said Crosby, speaking quietly. 'But it's spread out. You were quite right about the wine vase, we'd never be able to shift it.'

'I'll take a walk round myself,' said Ryman. 'No sign of any connecting doors that might be closed at night?'

A man in a brown suit who looked like a museum official walked past and Crosby waited until he was out of sight before replying.

'No, everything's in the main building. But it's under glass.'

Ryman nodded. 'Right. I'll see you later.' He turned on his heel and walked away across the patterned parquet listening to the echo of his footsteps. The bronze features of Dr Sun Yat-sen stared across the room at the wall opposite, full of lofty purpose.

Like Crosby, Ryman had memorised the numbers of the floors and galleries that contained the objects Bigg wanted. He walked round, taking his time and pinpointing the exact location of each item. Then worked out what he reckoned would be the shortest route between the six objects. He tried it and made an adjustment before repeating his tour. It took him fifteen minutes. A fair amount of time when there was no provision for the removal and packing of the objects. The 800-year-old Ju ware of the Sung Dynasty had the translucent bloom of flower petals and would need to be handled with even greater care.

What initially surprised Ryman was the apparent scarcity of security guards. There seemed to be only one official on duty for every two or three galleries. Then he saw what appeared to be an ordinary visitor turn away from an exhibit and approach a door in the wall that had no handle. The man looked around quickly and then produced a key and inserted it in the lock. The door opened and he disappeared through it. The sight made Ryman uneasy. It looked as if the museum had the equivalent of store detectives mingling with the visitors. He made a note to warn Crosby and wondered if his own movements had already been observed and given rise to suspicion. It was fortunate perhaps that he had been a frequent visitor in the past. At the time of his marriage to Julia it had been one of her favourite places. His superficial knowledge of Chinese art and history he owed to her. He began to feel mournful and told himself to snap out of it — the past was the past; the future began here. Now.

A Greyline Tour party was gathered round a glass case of ivory carvings and Ryman mingled with them as if eager to pick up any free information that was going. A middle-aged American woman wearing too-tight pink jeans looked him up and down unlovingly and tried to exclude him with her shoulder. Ryman returned the pressure and studied the front of the show case to see how it opened. One of the objects inside was on Bigg's list — a rhinoceros horn carved into an intricate pyramidal structure that contained three spheres, one inside the other, and all capable of revolving independently. The intricacy of the carving was such that the detail could only be seen with the aid of a magnifying glass. The guide was saying that the whole piece had been carved from a single horn and was the work of three generations of the same family. Ryman looked at it in awe and wondered how many of the craftsmen had gone blind grappling with the interminable intricacies of the design. One slip and the labour of three lifetimes could have been destroyed.

'Gee,' said the American woman, so overcome by admiration that she forgot to push Ryman. 'I sure am glad I saw that.'

Ryman smiled to himself. Perhaps she would soon be able to consider herself even luckier. He looked round the frame of the showcase and saw a keyhole set in the lower right-hand corner. It did not look impossible to force, but there could be an alarm attached to it. Ryman waited until the tour party had moved off and pressed his face to the glass, his hand shading his eyes as if against the glow from the fluorescent lighting in the roof of the showcase. There was a wire tucked under the frame, but that seemed to belong only to the light. Nevertheless, there was no way of being sure just by looking at it. It was something they would have to check out. Ryman twisted his head to make a closer inspection and saw that he was being scrutinised by one of the grey-uniformed security men who was standing in the doorway with his arms folded across his chest. Ryman straightened up and pretended to be absorbed in a Ming carved boxwood, writing-brush holder. In his mind he was making a list of things that needed to be done: the development of a shock-proof, easy to carry packing unit for each item; the drawing-up of an itinerary which would facilitate the quickest possible collection of the goods; and a method of discovering whether the showcases were wired to a central alarm system. That would do for starters. He turned away, feeling a satisfying sense of purpose that dispelled some of his earlier gloom. How they would get in and out of the museum was of course an entirely different problem.

Burton mopped his brow and took a quick look up at the side of the building. Around him, schoolchildren were munching rice cakes out of paper bags and jockeying for positions in the shade. 'Hi,' said one of them in what was meant to be an American greeting. 'Hi,' said Burton, and then as an afterthought, 'Have a nice day.' If they thought he was an American he might as well give full value for money.

Burton had finally decided to throw in his lot with Ryman and Crosby. His mother was dead, his father was dead. There was no family left to be dishonoured. His father had been hounded to his death unjustly. That he, Henry Burton, should take his revenge by doing something wrong and profiting from it seemed ironic justice. There was also Flower. He wanted her, and if he had to buy her he was prepared to do it.

The lowest window of the museum was forty feet from the ground, and only a fly could have clung to the smooth face of the wall beneath it. Burton knew that Ryman had the gist of an idea how they might get into the Museum, but he had hoped to be able to put forward his own brilliant solution. Now this pleasing prospect seemed to be fading. He moved forward to a high concrete wall that appeared to be holding the whole of the hillside at bay and attempted to peer round to the back of the building. There was a path winding up amongst the browning, creeper-hung palms, but a red-framed sign in Chinese at the bottom hardly needed translation — visitors were not welcome. No doubt it was like the other side of the Museum where the bungalows of the museum staff straggled up the hillside guarded by noisy dogs. In neither case did it seem a route worth taking if one wanted to break into the Museum. Nevertheless, perhaps he ought to press on a little further. If he climbed the hillside he should be able to see down to the back of the building.

Waiting until the children had been summoned back to the museum, he stepped quickly on to the pathway and started to climb. Within half a dozen paces the asphalt of the slip road had disappeared below him and he might have been in the middle of the jungle. The sun beat down through the leaves and the noise of insects was deafening. From a nearby clump of bamboo a tribe of seven-year grasshoppers was screeching for mates. A butterfly drifted past like a miniature stained-glass window. Burton sweated and peered through the screen of trees. The two rear towers of the Museum were visible and between them stretched a windowless wall of red brick. He turned back and found himself face to face with Mr Chang. Both men were surprised but only Burton felt that he was blushing guiltily.

'What are you doing here?' said Mr Chang disapprovingly. It seemed to Burton that it was an age before he replied. 'I saw the most fantastic butterfly I've ever seen. I just had to take a closer look at it.'

'You should not be here,' said Chang. 'Only the museum staff may use this path. There is a notice.'

'So that's what it said,' exclaimed Burton jovially. 'I thought it was something to do with parking.'

Chang looked uncomfortable, as if this suggestion was too ridiculous to be taken seriously. 'No,' he said simply.

Burton indicated the direction from which the museum official had come. 'Very handy living so close to the job.'

'I am not living here,' said Chang. 'I was visiting one of our staff who is sick.' He made an annoyed clucking noise. 'It is most regrettable. We have much difficulty in finding men to watch over the Museum at night. They are frightened of ghosts. They think the emperors will come back for their possessions.'

'It must be quite spooky in there,' said Burton, 'all by yourself.'

'They are not by themselves,' said Chang. 'There are always two of them.' He made another exaggerated sound. 'Now with old Ch'ien sick I will have to rearrange the rotas.'

'That's hard luck,' said Burton, congratulating himself on his detective work.

Chang nodded absent-mindedly. 'I am glad that we met. There is something that I wish to talk with you. You will follow me please.' He started hurrying down the path like the White Rabbit late for an appointment. Burton went after him with a returning sense of uneasiness.

Chang's office was on the lower ground floor next to the souvenir shop which sold catalogues, books, sets of postcards and coloured transparencies. There were two exits here with external flights of steps up to the main entrance level and car parks, and it confirmed Ryman's contention that no accurate check was made of the number of people coming into and leaving the Museum. Those who entered by the main entrance and were not seen again could only be assumed to have left via the lower ground floor.

Chang crossed the marble hall and looked round to see that Burton was following. He then felt in the inside pocket of his jacket and produced a key with which he unlocked the door of the office. Burton noted that he then placed the key on the inside of the lock. It was possible that he liked to lock himself in when he was handling rare exhibits, or perhaps it was merely the gesture of a tidy, organised man.

The interior of the office was unremarkable. There was no outside window and the lighting was harsh and fluorescent. Filing cabinets lined one of the walls and there was a desk and table on which were arranged neat piles of papers and a Chinese writing set: brushes in a crystal *pi-t'ung*, a Tuan inkstone, a *mo-ch'uang* or ink holder, paper, paperweights, a water dropper to be used when grinding ink and a *pi-ko* or arm rest which prevented the wrist from touching the paper.

Burton had seen these items before. What caught his eye were the rows of labelled keys on the wall behind Chang's desk. He wondered what they could be for.

Chang waved Burton to a chair and waited politely until he was seated before sitting down himself. Burton sensed that it would be a good idea to take the initiative.

'I've been thinking about our next event,' he began. The moment he had spoken he started to fear the worst. Chang's face darkened and he looked solemn.

'That is why I wished to speak with you,' he said. 'The directors of the Museum do not wish that there should be any more events.'

'No more events!' Ryman's jaw set firm. This was the worst news he could have received. Worse even than the typhoons which, with every day that passed, were becoming a more regular feature of the weather bulletins.

'I suppose this means you won't need me any more?' said Burton.

78

Ryman ignored the question. 'We've got to make them change their minds. How definite did they seem?'

'I only talked to Chang. He gave me the impression that it was a *fait accompli*.'

'What reasons did he give?'

'Nothing very specific. I think they feel that the Museum should be kept as a museum, as a repository of the Chinese culture and its values. They may be suspicious that I'm trying to introduce an alien culture.'

'Which of course you are. Even if you don't have much success.'

'He mentioned attendances as well.'

'They have been rather less than epic, haven't they?' said Ryman. He mused and then snapped his fingers. Burton looked up expectantly. 'Who are the most frequent non-Chinese visitors to the Museum?'

'Must be the Americans,' said Burton.

'You should have put on something that appealed to them. I mean, they speak English. That's what the English-Speaking Union is all about, isn't it?' Burton had no alternative but to nod. 'They're always lapping up culture at the Museum and they're a very influential section of the community. Every time I go past a private room at the Grand there's some thrash going on in aid of the Sino-American Chamber of Commerce.'

'I don't see what you're getting at,' said Burton.

Ryman wondered, 'What do Americans like doing?'

'I don't know. Going to baseball matches, watching TV, barbecuing sirloin steaks....'

Ryman snapped his fingers. 'Eating. That's a good idea, Henry. An American Food Fair: Californian wines, waffles, hominy grits....'

'But it's too late,' said Burton. 'They've shown me the door.'

'But have they opened it?' said Ryman. 'In China you're only out when you're lying in the gutter and you can hear the key turning in the lock behind you.'

'The Chinese aren't going to be very interested in American foods, are they?'

'No, but the Americans are. I'm trying to indulge in what is known as lateral thinking, Henry. If we can persuade them that a Food Fair would be a good idea, then they in turn will bring pressure to bear on the museum authorities and you'll be in again.'

Burton looked sceptical. 'Who do you know who carries any weight in the American community?'

'I'm not on intimate terms with anybody,' said Ryman, 'but I know somebody who's very close to the President of the Trade Committee.'

'Of course,' said Burton. 'Harry.'

'Flower,' said Ryman.

An expression of disappointment arrived on Burton's face. 'She won't be able to do anything, will she?' He thought some more and nodded. 'Yes, she probably will.'

Ryman patted him on the shoulder. 'You go right back to Chang and tell him what you want to do. I'll start things working from this end.'

'So everything goes ahead?' said Burton slowly.

'We carry on until we hit a brick wall,' said Ryman assertively. 'This is just a little bamboo fence.'

Ryman nodded to the security guard and passed into the gallery that contained the Sung and Yuan paintings. He now moved around the Museum with a greater sense of freedom. The guards were beginning to accept him as a regular visitor and the fact that they saw his face frequently would eventually be useful. He paused before a painting of the Empress of the Emperor Ying-tsung and made some notes on his sketchboard. He had enquired if he might bring this with him on a previous visit and there had been no objection. Despite her enormous golden bonnet, her richly embroidered cloak and her bejewelled slippers, the Empress looked unhappy. Perhaps it was the weight of her headdress which looked like a beehive with wings, or perhaps the Emperor spent too much time with his courtesans. He had died in 1066, which was probably not a date that meant much to the Chinese schoolchildren filing past the end of the gallery.

Ryman lowered his sketchboard and moved forward. There were so many crocodiles of immaculately turned-out children filing round the Museum that sometimes he wondered if the head of one did not join up with the tail of another to make an unbroken chain. They were all so well-behaved, too. English children would have been pushing, scuffling, pinching, doing anything but stare obediently into the glass cases of ceremonial jades.

Ryman slipped something from a corner of his sketchboard, and hopefully scanned the crocodile for signs of unruly elements. The object that Ryman held between his fingers was a small but heavy L-shaped lead hook, identical to those that were used to hang items in the showcases. He had noted that when an exhibit was changed, the hooks were often left in the back of the showcase or piled in a corner ready for future use. No museum official would be surprised to find one there.

At last Ryman saw what he was looking for. A small girl with pigtails was being tormented by the boy behind her. Every few paces the boy would reach forward and tweak one of her braids. The girl turned round angrily and threatened to kick him. The boy pretended he did not know what she was making a fuss about.

Ryman reversed his sketchboard and placed the base against his chest. Across the top were three strands of thick elastic. He slipped the hook over the elastic and pulled back hard, feeling the slug of metal cut into his fingers. His heart was thumping. Back in his apartment, a dartboard and the wall around it were pitted with his efforts to perfect his aim. This was the real thing. And he only had one shot.

The children were twelve feet away and nearly level with him. Ryman looked across to the showcase as if framing a drawing in his mind. The boy tweaked the little girl's hair for the umpteenth time. She spun round and raised her arm.

TWANG! To Ryman the noise sounded as loud as a pistol shot, but it was immediately drowned by the tinkle of glass. Children screamed and a teacher materialised from nowhere, followed by a security man with his hand reaching inside his jacket. The little girl stood immobile, with her hand still raised. Behind her the boy who had been tweaking her hair started to whimper. The teacher shook both of them and there was an angry gabble of question, accusation and denial.

Ryman was hardly aware of the commotion. His mind was absorbed by one incontrovertible fact: when the glass had broken, no alarm system had been triggered off.

'Was that a light?' said Burton.

Crosby rubbed his eyes and squinted towards the darkening outline of the Museum. He had been on the point of dropping off when Burton spoke. 'I can't see anything.'

'It must have been a cloud of fireflies or something.'

81

'Yeah.' Crosby changed his position and rubbed his cramped legs. The earth did not get any softer as you got older. It was three hours since a faint light had appeared at one of the Museum windows. If the nightwatchmen followed the pattern of the last two nights, they should be making another tour of the galleries within the next half hour. At the front gates the sequence of events was much more ordered. The military guard changed every three hours. It was they who made a search of the Museum after the doors were closed at five o'clock and before the nightwatchmen came on duty. The watchmen were two old men who appeared from the direction of the hillside housing development carrying bamboo food containers. They stayed at the Museum until the Museum staff started arriving at around half-past eight. The military only approached the building for the evening search, which was usually done by four men and took twenty minutes. To be over in that time it had to be a cursory affair involving checking the washrooms and the few other obvious places where someone might try and hide. The military waited at the Museum until all the staff had left the building. The nightwatchmen were then locked in until the following morning.

Burton slaughtered another mosquito and looked at his watch. Half-past two. He was not thinking of the reappearance of the nightwatchmen, but of Flower. It had occurred to him that while he was marooned out here on the far side of the road from the Museum, she might be with Ryman; that Ryman had expressly organised the two-man vigil with this in mind. She might even be with the President of the Trade Committee, an assignment also organised by Ryman. The thought rankled. Burton could have kept silent, but he was young and had not yet learned how to conceal pain by feigning indifference to it.

'It's difficult to know quite what the relationship between Ryman and Flower is,' he said.

'Very close,' said Crosby. This was not a subject with which he wished to become involved. He was aware of the growing tension that Flower caused between Ryman and Burton and he saw it as a source of potential danger to the mission. At a more personal level, Burton's preoccupation also mocked his own increasing tendency to think about Lee. He had half made up his mind to try and get in touch with her when he got back to the States. He had the feeling that she probably was not very happy wherever she was. There

82

could be no future for her with the travel agent, that was for sure. Running away with him was probably a decision she bitterly regretted. When he, Harry Crosby, reappeared behind the wheel of a Cadillac she would be glad to see him. Crosby frowned. Maybe not a Caddy. That was a bit old hat. One of those Italian cars or even a Jap model. The Japs made some pretty nifty cars these days. Of course, he would have to explain where the money came from, but it shouldn't prove too difficult. He had always told her they were going to be rich. He would say he'd made a killing on the futures market and bought Chinese gold. Lee would pull the mink around her shoulders and believe that. Then there was the question of where to live. People said that California was a geriatrics playground, but shit! Who wanted to spend another winter waiting for the snow plough to show up? New York might be vital, but you lived longer with some sun on your back.

'What are you going to do with the money?' said Burton.

'I'll think about it when I've got it,' said Crosby. 'Right now I'm just concentrating on watching out for that little old light to start drifting past the windows. Why don't you get your head down for a couple of hours?'

'All right,' said Burton. 'Thanks. You wake me when you've had enough.'

'Sure.'

Burton turned on his side, rested his head on his hands and drew his knees up. He looked like a big kid. Harry Crosby turned back to the Museum. He would be glad when the preparation was over and they went into action. Ryman seemed to be moving so slowly, checking on everything before the plan was finalised. Crosby stared into the darkness and frowned. He had bumped into Henderson again at the Central Bank. Of course it was just a coincidence and it didn't mean anything, but for some reason it made him feel uneasy.

Wu Chang sat at his desk and tapped one of his writing brushes against the base of the inkstand. He should have been finalising plans for the Museum's exhibition of porcelain from the Sung and Yuan Dynasties but, most unusually for him, his mind was elsewhere. A number of events had occurred recently that had disturbed him. It was a known fact that throughout the Western World parents were failing in their duty to instil a sense of discipline and respect in their children, but he had not realised until now that the malaise had spread to Taiwan. The incident of the broken showcase was profoundly shocking. Nothing had been damaged, but if brawling children were going to become a feature of life in the Museum, who knew where it might end? They might have to introduce barriers round the exhibits; perhaps even deny entrance to parties of schoolchildren.

Then there had been the business of the English-Speaking Union using the Museum for its functions. First of all, the policy committee had decided that this should cease. Now they seemed to have changed their minds. Not only that, but they appeared willing to allow American foodstuffs to be disseminated. Could this be considered a cultural activity? Hardly. The American cuisine was not renowned for its finesse. If it had been a question of French food, that might have been different. No, this was another example of the insidious and all-pervasive American influence that reached into every aspect of the Island's affairs. And that from a country that had now recognised the Chinese Communist government and diplomatically deserted its former ally. Chang seethed. Burton was an Englishman and everybody knew that the English were tools of the Americans. Perhaps the committee's attitude was conditioned by the fact that there was another bequest in the air. From time to time, prominent Chinese who had made their homes in the United States left valuable works to the Museum. With the approval of the American government these could be allowed out of the country and exported to Taiwan. Some kind of reciprocal gesture was to be expected. Chang sniffed disapprovingly. He would make it quite clear that his heart was not in the venture. Burton could undertake all the arrangements for the Food Fair himself. The Museum staff had better things to do.

Feeling discontented with the world, Chang replaced his brush in its holder and moved to the door of his office. His tea was late. It was another sign of falling standards. Chang swung open the door and found himself face to face with an attractive girl he had never seen before. She stretched out a hand towards him as if seeking help and then began to buckle at the knees. Before Chang could fully appreciate what was happening, she had collapsed at his feet. Confused and uncertain what to do, Chang looked about him desperately and dropped to his knees. Almost immediately, another figure appeared at his side. A tall, powerfully built man.

An Ang Moh, or Westerner, whom Chang recognised as a regular visitor to the Museum.

The newcomer was quick to size up the situation and swooped down to take the girl in his strong arms. Before Chang could say anything he had carried her into his office and settled her on a chair. The girl groaned and held her hand to her forehead.

'I'll go and look for a doctor,' said the man. He strode out of the room and past the few interested bystanders. Chang was left feeling helpless.

The girl opened her eyes and her lips trembled. Her gaze fell on Chang and her plea came in a low voice that was almost a gasp. 'Water!'

Chang looked round the room desperately. There was only his *yen-ti*, a small receptacle in the shape of a frog which he used for dropping water on the inkstone when grinding ink. That would not be suitable.

The girl leaned forward in her seat and her mouth popped open. For one terrible moment Chang thought that she was going to be sick.

'Water, I beg you!'

Chang left the room almost at a run. People were still pressing forward to see what was happening and he closed the door behind him. It was all most embarrassing for a senior official of the National Palace Museum. The women behind the counter at the souvenir shop were gawping and he scolded them with a glance. They were the ones who should be occupying themselves with this unfortunate girl. He hoped there were going to be no misunderstandings. What presumption the Ang Moh had had to place the girl in his office. Still, one must be charitable in this life. Buddha would not wish otherwise.

Chang entered the men's washroom and found to his fury that all the paper cups had been used. Somebody was taking them, he was sure of that. Probably the schoolchildren. They were given so much and yet they resorted to breaking showcases and stealing paper cups. It was perhaps as well that General Chiang Kai-shek had not lived to see such days.

Chang hurried from the washroom and hesitated before the entrance to the women's room. Even in an emergency was he prepared to go this far? The answer came to him in the shape of an American matron emerging through the door and fixing him with a distrustful glare. No. He turned swiftly and crossed to the souvenir shop. One of the saleswomen was instructed to fetch some water and he returned to his office. To his surprise and relief the girl was on her feet and standing by the door. He started to explain about the water, but she cut him short and said that she thought it was fresh air that she needed. Thanking him profusely, she bowed and withdrew from his presence. Chang felt relieved, and when the water arrived he drank it himself. It was only ten minutes later, when he had returned to organising the galleries for the porcelain exhibition, that he remembered that the Ang Moh had not returned with the doctor.

'Excellent,' said Ryman. He tipped the key from its wax impression and tossed it in the air. 'This will save us a lot of trouble.'

'Oh, how my hands were shaking when he went out of the door,' said Flower. 'For a moment I just looked at the key. I could not do anything. Then, when I got out the wax, I dropped the key on the floor.' She laughed deliciously.

'Well, you did it,' said Burton enthusiastically. The affection in his eyes was obvious.

Crosby looked across at Ryman. 'What else are we waiting for?'

Ryman, Crosby, Burton and Flower were meeting in the apartment that Ryman now shared with Crosby. It was situated in the Hang Chou Road near the cable and telegraph offices. Flower had just produced a large dish of dumplings with leek and pork stuffing and the men had eaten hungrily. To get near the stove she had had to move twenty-eight dead beer cans and two empty whisky bottles. She had wondered to herself if Ryman and Crosby ever did anything else but drink.

'Now that Henry's got the go-ahead for his Food Fair, we're in good shape,' said Ryman. He turned to Flower. 'Another vote of thanks, madam.' Flower inclined her head gracefully. Burton looked at the floor uncomfortably. Ryman turned his attention to Crosby. 'American food must be your speciality, Harry. I think it might be a good idea if you gave Henry a hand getting it together. I'd like to be involved at the packaging stage.' He took a swig of beer and belched noisily. 'Sorry about that. Spot of turbulence off Penghu. Now, Harry, talking of packaging, let the others see what you've come up with for the stuff.'

86

Crosby crossed the room and dragged a tin cabin trunk from beneath a rattan table. 'I've gone for plastic,' he said. 'It's light and if, God help us, the worst comes to the worst, it floats.' He opened the trunk and produced a length of grey drainpipe with a permanent cap welded to one end and a screw top on the other. 'Mr Fan Kuan's masterpiece will be rolled up and slipped into this. I've checked out all the sizes from personal observation. Now for the Ju ware.' He delved into the trunk and produced a string of plastic tea cups, each with a clip-on lid attached to it. They were lined with kapok and contained nests of cotton wool. 'Each one will take a cup packed tight like a nut in an avocado.'

Ryman noticed that Flower's face had clouded over. 'What's the matter?'

'I think you are foolish if you try and take the Ju ware.'

'Why? Because it's so delicate?'

'Because it brings bad luck to anybody who touches it.' She watched Ryman's mouth set into a hard, uncompromising line. 'The Emperor Hui Sing was an old man when his wife eventually became pregnant. He was overjoyed, and he ordered the royal kiln to produce a special service for a banquet to celebrate the birth. "Like the sky after it rains," that is the colour he asked for. But the baby was born dead and the Emperor was heartbroken. He ordered that all the dishes should be destroyed because they represented bad luck.'

'Someone clearly disobeyed the order,' said Ryman.

'Yes, and died soon after,' said Flower.

Ryman looked round the three faces before him and took a deep breath. 'I'm sorry, Flower. But I don't think our client is a very superstitious man. We'll get the bad luck if we *don't* turn up with these cups.'

'You could invent a reason why it was impossible to take them.'

'No.' Ryman shook his head. 'I made a deal. For three million dollars, Bigg gets what he wants.'

Flower rose to her feet. 'Then I am not certain that I want to help you any more. I am Chinese, I understand. You are taking a terrible risk.'

'Maybe...' began Burton.

'No,' said Ryman. 'There's no going back. I've made a decision. If you don't like it, that's too bad.'

Burton thought about continuing and then remained silent.

When the steel snapped into Ryman's voice he became a different man from the amiable, easy-going Englishman he allowed the world to see most of the time.

Flower did not hesitate, but threw her silk scarf around her shoulders and moved towards the door. She was gone before Burton had time to open it.

Ryman broke the silence. 'Right, Harry; get on with it.'

Burton rounded on him angrily. 'Is that all you can say? You were pretty hard with her, weren't you?'

'I know her better than you,' said Ryman shortly. 'Now can we get on? There's a lot of other things to discuss.'

'What makes you think you know her better than me?' said Burton.

Crosby stepped in front of him. 'Will you knock it off? We've got enough to worry about.'

Burton looked towards the door and for a moment it seemed he might follow Flower. Then he threw himself into an armchair and folded his arms angrily.

'Right, we've seen the receptacles for the Ju ware,' said Ryman. 'What else have we got?'

Crosby ran through a range of plastic containers and demonstrated how in most cases they could be carried beneath a loose-fitting jacket. The painting was going to be the most cumbersome article to transport, and a Ming bowl also presented difficulties. At the other end of the scale a Ch'ing Dynasty carved Jadeite cabbage, which brilliantly utilised the colours of the stone to achieve its effect, could be carried in a pocket.

Crosby replaced the items in the trunk and Ryman turned to Burton. 'Have you any comments to make, Henry?'

Burton still looked angry but his voice was even. 'What about the question of replacement items?'

'I've talked about that with Harry, and we've decided against it except in the case of the painting — a large empty space against the wall is going to be noticed, so we're taking in a substitute that we've doctored up. We'll never succeed in finding or making duplicates of the other pieces and if we did, purchasing them would raise recognition problems. Since the pieces are all in cases with other items, we'll rearrange the exhibits to fill up the space and hope that it's as long as possible before somebody notices that something's missing. The average visitor will probably never be aware that an item's gone, or will think it's been removed for cleaning or another exhibition.'

Burton shrugged. 'Sounds reasonable. So you and Harry are going to do the job?'

Ryman shook his head. 'No, Henry. I'm changing the plans. I'm desperately worried about these typhoons. When we've got the stuff we need to get away fast. If we have a problem with the boat we're in big trouble. Two days ago, the Babuyan Islands north of the Philippines were devastated by a typhoon. That's less than three hundred miles from the coast of Taiwan. Sooner or later we're going to be hit.' He crossed to the window. 'Look.' The moon was poised above the low hills like a circle of beaten silver. Around its edge glowed a shimmering halo.

'It's been like that for days,' said Burton. 'There's been a halo round the sun as well.'

'They're both signs,' said Crosby. 'Have you noticed how sultry it's been?'

'I want Harry to go up and stay with the boat,' said Ryman. 'If a typhoon blows up he'll take whatever measures he thinks necessary. The rendezvous will be in the marshes. If he's been forced to move away we'll wait for him.'

'So when's he going?'

'As soon as possible.'

Burton's brow furrowed. 'So you're going to lift the stuff by yourself?'

Ryman shook his head. 'I believe we need another pair of hands. Chinese hands. These keys in Chang's office. I'm pretty certain they must be for the display cabinets and showcases. But I can't read the Chinese hieroglyphics on the tags. I could spend all night trying to find out which key went with which cabinet and still end up forcing them. A Chinese would sort it all out in no time. And a fluent Chinese speaker would help afterwards. If we want to use the wireless and not risk rousing suspicions by our accents.'

'And you've ruled out Flower?'

'You heard her. She just ruled herself out. Anyhow, even if she does change her mind, I don't want to get her involved in the actual operation.' Ryman frowned. 'If anything goes wrong the locals will be thirsting for blood.'

'So our cut would go down?'

'Yes, it would be a five-way split. Six hundred thou instead of

89

seven-fifty. Still enough for a trip to Paris.' Burton flushed and Ryman held up a restraining hand. 'The important thing is that we all agree to recruiting someone else.'

Burton sighed. 'Where are we going to find somebody?'

'Crosby's already got somebody lined up,' said Ryman. 'He's called Lee Fong Yu.'

CHAPTER FIVE

The sun, without halo, blazed down from a clear blue sky slightly lighter than the aquamarine of the ocean. The road was a pathetic notch traced unevenly against the corrugated sides of precipitous mountains cut off brutally from the sea as if by a blow from a giant axe. Cliffs rose almost vertically for three thousand feet, their sandpaper faces pitted by the force of torrential monsoon rains and the lop-sided scars of frequent landslides.

To travel on this road was to become immediately acquainted with fear. Beyond its crumbling edges lay a drop of four thousand feet on to surf-battered rocks. In some places it seemed that only a lattice-work of famished vegetation held the mountainside in place. Always there were boulders poised precariously, waiting for the next earth tremor to come crashing down. No man who worked on this road wore a coolie hat unless he was a fool or had lost interest in life. He wore a tin helmet and had ears that were tuned to the sound of a lizard skittling across dried earth, feet that could sense the passage of a worm two metres beneath the ground. By such reflexes did he hope to stay alive. The road had been built fifty years before at a cost of many lives. It had been taking its toll ever since.

'"Far from the madding crowd's ignoble strife",' said Ryman cheerfully. He was leaning back from the wheel of a hired Toyota which bore the battle scars of many skirmishes with Taipei traffic.

Beside him, Crosby jerked his head back from a stomach-churning view of what lay below. 'What the hell are you talking about?'

'Good to be away from the city, don't you think?'

'Keep your eyes on the road!' screeched Crosby. 'Holy shit! I can't take much more of this. Look at that!' He pointed to a pile of rocks half obscuring the road and being shovelled over the precipice by a group of sweating Chinese. 'That was an earthquake.'

'They don't have earthquakes in the typhoon season,' said Ryman calmly.

'You slay me,' said Crosby. He twisted his head and peered up the side of the mountain. High above their heads one fleecy white cloud was lodged between the peaks, as if trapped.

'How did you meet this fellow?' said Ryman.

'He contracted for the marble work when we were extending the factory,' said Crosby. 'He didn't waste any time telling me that I'd earn myself a king-size kick-back if I gave him the job. He also said that he could handle labour problems. I got the idea that he was talking about discouraging any smart ass who wanted to start a union. He'd have rubbed the guy out.'

'Digging up marble seems a strange job for a fellow like that.'

'Don't you believe it. Marble's big business in Taiwan. It used to be just tourist junk but now they're exporting architectural slabs. It's high-grade stuff and they can undercut the Italians by fifty per cent. Australia can't get enough. Iran used to be a competitor, but the Khomeini has put them out of the running. Now it's just the Philippines.'

'I suppose the way the world's going it must be a boom time for gravestones,' mused Ryman.

Crosby darted a worried hand towards the wheel. 'For God's sake, mind how you take those corners or somebody'll be ordering two more.'

'Don't worry,' soothed Ryman. 'It's one-way traffic.'

Crosby looked no happier. 'In this country I always wonder whether the guy coming the other way is saying that.'

'Grim thought,' agreed Ryman. 'So you're saying that our prospective partner Lee Fong Yu is what one might call an entrepreneur?'

Crosby nodded. 'There's a number of small operators up in the hills. All you need is a couple of bulldozers, some of those wild mountain men, and a good head for heights. They blast out the marble, bulldoze it down the mountain and truck it to the processing plants. That's where the sale is made.'

'Sounds as if he's on to a good thing,' said Ryman. 'What makes you think he's going to be interested in our proposition?'

'He's got big ideas and he needs cash to expand. It's going to take him a long time, the way he's going, unless he can build a factory and start processing for himself. With the money we're talking about he could buy a couple of Japanese diamond saws and a stake in some more quarries. The diamond saw is the clincher.

92

With a conventional one it takes a week working nonstop to cut through one boulder.'

'He could get a loan from a bank.'

Crosby allowed himself a small smile. 'I don't think this guy is a banker's dream client. In fact, I don't think this guy is number one on anybody's hit parade. I got a lot of funny looks when I was asking where I could find him. He never left me an address at Kaohsiung.'

Ryman frowned. 'What are you getting at—?'

'I got the impression that one or two people would have liked to have caught up with him themselves. You know what the Chinese are like. They play it so close to the chest that their hands are practically behind their ribs, but you get a feeling. They were interested and they were wondering what I had to do with the guy.'

Ryman frowned. 'What are you getting at — ?'

'Look,' said Crosby. 'We're in a tough spot. We're trying to find a trustworthy hood. That's not easy. They don't move in circles where everybody wears their collar back to front.'

Ryman said nothing. The road had widened to afford a narrow lay-by beneath an overhanging cliff. The Toyota pulled into it and stopped, engine running. 'Good idea,' said Crosby. 'I could do with a leak.' He got out of the car and moved towards the cliff face. Ryman made as if to follow him and studied the beige Yue Looney saloon that was passing. It contained four Chinese wearing a familiar uniform of dark glasses and short-sleeved shirts. None of them glanced towards the roadside as they went past.

Crosby returned mopping his brow. 'Jesus Christ, it's hot. I was pissing steam out there.'

Ryman said nothing. Any sense of release that a trip to the country had brought was speedily disappearing. He listened to Crosby cursing the hot seats and pulled out behind a truck that was belching diesel fumes. Crosby cursed some more.

The beige saloon was waiting round the second bend where the road opened up a bit. Two of the Chinese were urinating into the void. Ryman stood on the accelerator and the Toyota shuddered and shot past the lorry in a shale of loose stones. To Crosby it looked as if they were hanging in space. 'Jesus Christ! What the hell are you doing?'

Ryman flashed a glance at the rear mirror. The two Chinese

were jerking themselves back into their trousers and sprinting for the Yue Looney. Ryman smiled grimly. 'How did you make contact with Lee Fong Yu?'

Bewilderment mingled with alarm on Crosby's face. 'Flower made a few enquiries and I talked to one of his girl friends.'

'I hope she wasn't giving away any confidences.'

'What do you mean?'

Ryman jerked his head over his shoulder. 'We're being followed. Maybe somebody thinks we can lead them to Lee Fong Yu.'

Crosby whipped round, half expecting to see Henderson's black Ford. There was a furious blast on the horn and the nose of the Yue Looney swung out to overtake the lorry. Crosby was jerked back in his seat as Ryman stamped on the accelerator again. Ahead, the road narrowed before disappearing round a bend. Crosby had the impression that they were roaring up a ramp prior to take-off. He tried to concentrate on the brown blurr of the cliff face, but his eyes were remorselessly drawn back to the dizzy void. There was no vestige of a safety wall between them and certain death hundreds of feet below. Ryman was hunched over the wheel, his face grim and determined, sweat dripping to the floor. He revealed no trace of fear. The huge hands moved with the tension in the wheel, exploring what the car could deliver.

A solitary concrete block marked the right angle of the bend. Just as it seemed that they were going to carry it into space with them, Ryman changed down and swung the wheel over. There was a terrifying wall-of-death sensation of imminent destruction, and Crosby could feel the earth breaking away beneath the tortured wheels. Sky and sea smeared together into one vast dimension of space and the seat seemed to be fused to his body. Crosby closed his eyes against the nausea and waited for the impact. When he opened them again they were thundering down a long straight, murderously runnelled by the monsoon rains. A cloud of dust soared into the air behind them.

'If it's any comfort, I had a drive at Le Mans once,' said Ryman, sounding almost cheerful.

'That's in France, isn't it?' said Crosby. He didn't really care. He just needed the reassurance that he still possessed the power of speech.

'Like Indianapolis without the hot dogs.'

The cliff loomed up like a wall and the tyres squealed. Crosby

94

saw rocks cartwheel into space. The Toyota went into a long skid, and her back end slewed to come within a paint-width of a pile of rubble. Then the wheels bit and she shook like a dog emerging from water before roaring up the slope. Behind, the Yue Looney was charging down the straight.

'You'll never shake them off,' shouted Crosby.

'Have a damn good try.' Ryman gunned the motor for the next corner and Crosby's head hit the roof as they plummeted into a pot-hole. He braced himself for the next corner. The Toyota flew round it as if on a piece of string. Crosby relaxed marginally. Ryman did know how to handle a car.

Ahead, the road plunged down towards the sea and there was a welcome glimpse of beach and a steep, boulder-strewn hillside. A ramshackle café stood beside some petrol pumps on a tarmac forecourt. Crosby realised that the vehicles he could see were not parked but waiting at a barrier, a white pole stretched across the road. This is where they must wait for the one-way traffic that was coming towards them. Beside him he heard Ryman unleash an oath. 'Stupid bastards! What the hell are they doing? This stretch should be open now.'

The Toyota swung into a long left-hander and Crosby waited for Ryman to take his foot off the accelerator. Behind, the beige saloon was closing the distance between them.

'Hey!' The seat slapped against Crosby's back and for a moment he thought that they were going to ram the last lorry in the waiting convoy. Then the wheel was flipped over and he saw the white pole looming up fast. A man in a forage cap waved his arms and then dived out of the way. There was a snapping sound like a toothpick being broken and a white object flew over the top of the windscreen. Crosby glimpsed a man desperately waving a red flag and then that image was snatched away as they squealed round a bend and entered a tunnel.

'Are you crazy?' screamed Crosby. The sudden darkness was like a premonition of death. 'We're going to meet something head on!' Ryman's eyes were on the rear mirror. His mouth tightened as two spears of yellow light stabbed the darkness behind them. 'I'll turn off the first chance we get.'

'Jesus Christ,' said Crosby. He was gripping both sides of his seat and waiting for his fingers to meet through the plastic. Desperately he peered into the darkness, waiting for the vehicle that was going

95

to smash them into little pieces. With terrifying speed they shot from darkness into dazzling light. The sea sparkled far below and they were clinging to a ledge that seemed no more than a smudge on the rock face. A pile of fallen stones drove them towards the precipice and Crosby felt his stomach well up into the back of his throat. The Toyota lurched over the stones and slid towards the abyss. The wheels spun aimlessly and Ryman's hands jiggled desperately. For a period that had no place in time they hung between life and death. Then the road was again four square beneath them and they were decelerating into the next bend.

Crosby was unable to speak. Sounds jumped from his throat but they were not words. He twisted round and saw that the beige saloon was still behind them. He turned back and froze in horror. A truck was filling the road in front of them. It took them a second to realise that it was stationary and parked against a cliff. Ryman squeezed past, horn blaring, and glimpsed the astonished face of the driver who was standing beside it. The road widened and a bulldozer hove into view, lumbering over a surface that looked like a dried-up stream bed. Men were working with picks and shovels. There had been a major landslide. That was why the road had been closed. The Toyota ploughed into the scattered stones and Crosby's face was jerked inches from the windscreen. A buttress of rock lunged into the road and on either side of it there were great dark hollows scooped from the mountainside where the boulders had come crashing down. Half the road had been carried away like the broken lip of a plate. Two crossed red flags closed the way ahead and Crosby held his breath as Ryman drove towards them. The men who were labouring looked on, first in amazement and then in alarm. One of them ran forward, waving his arms across his body in a gesture that clearly meant 'stop!' He was snatched from view as they skirted the buttress and came to the second section of the rubble. There was an explosion that rattled the windows of the car, and an ominous rumble.

Ryman ducked to squint up the hillside and realised what the red flags had meant. They were dynamiting the rock face to bring down the rest of the slide. As he looked, he could see the plume of dust and the rocks beginning to move. They were directly above the car. He put his foot down and the Toyota jolted against a small boulder and stalled. Now the sound of the falling rocks was an angry roar like a flood-swollen river in full spate. A spatter of small stones rained down on the roof of the car. Ryman pressed the starter and the engine limped into life. He revved it until it screamed for mercy, reversed and then threw the wheel over. The boulder was nudged aside and they rocketed forward. The earth was shuddering, and ahead another section of the road suddenly dropped from sight. The noise broke down their eardrums and rushed inside their heads, driving out everything but panic. Now the sound was like amplified thunder. A boulder skipped across the ground in front of them and, behind, the earth seemed to be jumping in a mist of inky darkness. Like a surfer cutting beneath the break of a huge wave they were running from the full impact of the fall. A rock cracked one of the rear windows and a spate of stones surged against the side of the car like the first spadeful of earth on a coffin. Then they were wriggling free and hearing the last echoes of the rumble die away behind them.

Ryman slowed and looked behind him into the cloud of dust. Across the smoking rubble of stones could be seen the brooding outline of the Yue Looney. An indistinct figure threw open a door and surveyed the barrier before it.

'Should hold them up for a bit,' said Ryman, hard-pushed to keep the satisfaction out of his voice. He slammed the car into first and roared off up the narrow incline.

Crosby drew out a handkerchief and began to wipe his stinging eyes. 'Oh my God,' he said.

Ryman drove carefully with his finger on the horn. It seemed likely that the road had been closed in both directions but one did not repay good fortune by taking chances. They met nothing and four miles down the descending road came to another barrier and another line of waiting vehicles. The mountains were now falling back from the coastline and ahead was a prospect of green, fertile plains.

Ryman slowed down and was relieved to see the barrier rising. There was a crowd of people waiting and he searched the assembly for signs of the shiny police helmets. Crosby's face was drawn. 'What are you going to do?'

Ryman kept the vehicle moving forward slowly. 'No autographs.'

A Chinese in a khaki jacket and a peaked cap stepped forward with his arm raised. Ryman leaned out of the window and spoke authoritatively. 'A car's been smashed up in a landslide. I'm going to fetch a doctor.' He did not wait to see if his message was understood but accelerated away smoothly.

Crosby read the expression of uncertainty in the official's eyes. There was still some legacy of respect for the words of the Ang Moh even if they were barely understood. He held his breath until they were through the crowd.

Ryman looked about him at the fertile fields of rice, maize and pineapples and felt the sense of unreality that always accompanied a close brush with death. It was so peaceful on this straight, flat sunlit road lined with peach and apricot trees. Almost impossible to believe that their mangled bodies might have been lying under tons of rock a few miles back up the road.

The road jinked right to run beside the Liwu Chi River and then crossed it at the small town of Tailuku. To the south was the seaport of Hualien, but Ryman turned inland towards the mountains that covered seventy per cent of the Island. Men and women wearing coolie hats were working thigh deep in the rice fields, and they passed a team of oxen browsing by the road. There was a banana plantation, and wizened old men fishing with nets in the brown waters of the river.

Crosby only had one eye for the sights. The other was glued to the rear-view mirror. He too found it difficult to come to terms with what had happened. Half of him was still numb as if anaesthetised by the experience. They passed a cement works and then began to climb, the road swinging left and right across the face of the hills. Crosby looked down at the patchwork quilt of fields and then stiffened. A vehicle was moving at speed from the direction of Tailuku. It was too far away to pick out the colour, but there was something ominous about its rapid progress across the flat countryside. Behind it a plume of dust drifted over the fields.

Crosby felt the Toyota jerk forward. Ryman had also been looking down into the valley. 'They must have got that bulldozer working,' he said grimly.

'You think it's them?'

'It could be the half-day cross-island tour.'

Crosby did not smile. The Toyota screeched round a bend and a sign appeared saying 'Taroko Gorge' in Chinese and English. After the next bend was an ornamental entrance arch; curved golden-tiled roofs and scarlet pillars. Ami Aboriginal girls stepped

98

forward hopefully to sell postcards and have their photographs taken with a new batch of tourists. The car sped past them. Crosby glimpsed red jackets and half-melon head-dresses decorated with fur and hanging tassels. The girls looked more like Red Indian squaws than descendants of the oldest inhabitants of the Island.

A creeper lashed the side of the car and they were in the gorge, rattling over a long suspension bridge, the river sparkling far below. On each side precipitous cliffs reared up towards a strip of blue sky. A bus swung round the corner towards them, lights blazing, horn blaring. Ryman threw the wheel over and they entered a long gallery throwing out shimmering images of a thick green beard of vegetation on the cliff wall opposite. Swallows filled the air, shrieking, swooping, darting. Another bridge, dazzling silver in the sunlight, and then they plunged into darkness again, the damp walls magnifying the anguished honking of an approaching vehicle. Out into twilight and then the long ponytail of water dropping into a frothing pool, a concrete bridge and a shrine built on a narrow promontory. Far, far above, a pagoda poked like a missile from the greenery.

Crosby watched the images flash by and scanned the limestone cliffs for signs of the gorge opening up. He felt like an ant trapped in a fold of the ground; at any second the walls might close in and crush the life out of them.

Ryman swung out to overtake a motor cyclist and was grateful that the approaching lorry was proceeding at a snail's pace. It was covered in dust and weighed down by a huge boulder.

'Granite,' said Ryman with some relief in his voice. 'How many bridges have you counted?'

'Fourteen.'

'Me too. Another twenty-six to go.'

Jagged concrete blocks lined a series of openings in a long gallery like rotten teeth in crumbling mouths. Sunshine and shadow mottled the cliffs opposite. Below, the river ran fast through a graveyard of huge stones. Crosby wondered how far behind the pursuers were. The petrol gauge was running dangerously low. As he looked, a red light started to flash below the empty mark. Ryman saw it and said nothing. A petrol tanker filled the twisting road before them. Crosby cursed. The Toyota slowed to a crawl. Seconds passed. Ryman started to pull out and was driven back by an ear-splitting blast on the horn. A second granite lorry squeezed past, wheezing dust. Crosby looked behind him, his heart thumping. At any moment the beige saloon would roar up behind him. They crossed a bridge and entered another gallery. Ryman released a grunt of irritation and pulled out, horn blaring. The road was narrow and they were on a bend. When they were level with the cab of the tanker there was the sound of a vehicle hooting as it came towards them. The Toyota scraped the rock face and the cab of a bus shut out the view before them. Ryman jerked the wheel and they clipped the tanker's mudguard as they pulled in front of it. The bus roared past in a continuous blast of horn, its vibration making the Toyota shudder. Crosby looked at his knuckles. They were white.

'Twenty-five,' growled Ryman. He put his foot down and the anguished bleeping of the petrol tanker died away behind them.

The turning that led to Lee Fong Yu was situated just after the fortieth bridge from the entry to the gorge. The Toyota sped on and the gorge opened out into a steep-sided valley heavy with a matted jungle of vegetation. Only in places had the hillsides been cleared, and here earth and boulders were turned over as if crudely ploughed. Caterpillar tracks traced precarious jerky paths up the side of the mountains. This was where limestone gave way to marble.

Crosby's gaze alternated between the rear-view mirror and the petrol gauge as the miles and bridges ticked by. With every second, he waited for the choked gurgle and the sound of the vehicle jerking to a halt.

At last they came to a long box bridge with a small shrine at its end and the road swung left to follow the line of the river. Almost immediately a steep track rose through a clump of twisted cedars. Ryman braked hard and the Toyota skidded on to the loose earth and started to climb. Crosby watched behind and felt a surge of relief as the thick vegetation shut out the road. Temporarily, they were safe.

The path they were on was heavily pitted by the tracks of vehicles and there were patches of scarred earth and crushed vegetation which showed where marble had been worked. As they climbed higher, signs of this quarrying became more frequent and there were clearings where large segments had been gouged from the hillside and young trees bulldozed into tangled heaps. The ruts became deeper and progress more difficult. Wheels spun in the

100

dust and stones scraped the underside of the car. The heat was suffocating. Ryman's shirt clung to his back like a wet rag. He looked at Crosby. At the front of both their minds was the fear that they had taken the wrong track.

'We're not going to get much further,' said Ryman.

He was right. A man stepped out in front of the Toyota, holding a rifle. The barrel was levelled at the windscreen. Ryman cut the engine. The man was tall for a Chinese and had long hair held back from his face by a band round the forehead. He was naked from the waist up and wore jeans so grimed with brown earth that they shone.

The man held the rifle in the crook of his arm and beckoned for them to get out of the car. His eyes were hard as tungsten chips and his gaze unwavering. Ryman glanced in the rear-view mirror and saw that a second man was coming down from the rocks. He got out of the car slowly, making sure not to perform any jerky movements. Somewhere high in the trees a bird screeched and his heart jumped. A butterfly meandered across the path.

'Lee Fong Yu,' said Ryman.

There was no sign that the name was a password to immediate acceptance. The man with the rifle merely jerked the barrel towards the rocks. '*Dzou.*' Ryman shrugged and did as he was told. Crosby fell in behind him. The other Chinese was standing ten yards away with an automatic pistol resting on his forearm. He wore a green tennis shade which lent him a strange air of unreality. As he scrambled upwards, Ryman could see that the whole hillside was a mass of compressed marble slabs resting on top of each other, like slates on a roof. Trees and shrubs had forced their way into the cracks and their roots were now spread far and wide like arthritic fingers. They served as foot and handholds on the tortuous route towards the summit.

Fifty yards from where they had left the car a wide area of forest had been cleared, and here boulders were strewn across the scored earth like freshly dug potatoes left to dry in the sun. A ramp of earth and stones had been built against one huge stone and on it was perched a bulldozer thrusting a hunk of marble towards a waiting truck. Silhouetted against the steep mountainside, the bulldozer looked like a giant insect toying with its prey.

Another outcrop of rock served as foundation and one wall of a crude corrugated iron structure set back into the hillside. There was a doorway and an opening too shapeless to be called a window. The whole ramshackle building looked as if it had slid down the mountain after a landslide.

Ryman paused to take in the scene. There were five Chinese working around the bulldozer, three of them Aborigines, tough mountain men, ancient warriors and headhunters who had never been subjugated by the Japanese in fifty years of rule.

'*Yu juls dzou!*'

Ryman continued to walk towards the shelter. The man who was driving the bulldozer climbed down and came towards them. He was little more than five feet tall and revealed more bones than an under-nourished whippet. His eyes sped over Ryman and Crosby as if weighing them up like a commodity.

'Mr Ryman, Mr Crosby? I have been expecting you.' He turned to the two guards and addressed them in Cantonese. The men retired the way they had come.

'Mr Lee Fong Yu, I presume,' said Ryman. Yu inclined his head.

Crosby nodded towards the guards. 'You don't take any chances.'

'I have enemies,' said Lee Fong Yu simply. 'It is the price of success. Come, I believe you have a proposition to discuss.' He waved an arm towards the ramshackle hut. There was no attempt at pleasantries or apologies for the humble abode. Ryman respected this. The man looked like a professional.

'Can you think of any reason why we should have been followed here?' he asked.

Yu's eyes snapped towards him. 'What?'

'Four men in a beige Yue Looney. They weren't far behind us coming through the gorge.'

Lee Fong Yu said nothing but ran towards the loading party and unleashed a stream of a dialect that Ryman could not understand. Three of the men started running after the departing guards. Another man with a rifle jumped out of the cab of the truck. Yu turned back, his face serious. 'We will be left alone now.' Ryman nodded and they continued towards the hut. Ryman was uneasy. He was being nagged by an increasing fear that Lee Fong Yu might turn out to be more trouble than he was worth.

They went through the opening in the corrugated iron and Ryman was temporarily blinded by the darkness after the bright

102

light outside. When he recovered his sight he saw a cave going back into the hillside and a line of bedrolls against one wall. There were cooking utensils and a stench of diesel that married with the oil stain on the floor to suggest that the bulldozer bedded down with the men. Crosby imagined what the monsoon rains could do to the terrain outside and could understand why.

A youngish woman appeared from the recesses of the cave and Lee Fong Yu ordered her to bring rice wine. She bowed to Ryman and Crosby and indicated a table and two rough benches by one of the walls. She was a handsome creature with long, black silky hair and Ryman speculated on the other capacities in which she might serve as well as that of cook.

'Is the marble business going well?' asked Crosby.

'All businesses have problems,' said Yu, reaching over to take the bottle. 'What are you offering?'

'Six hundred thousand American dollars,' said Ryman.

The drawing of the cork was the exclamation mark.

Lee Fong Yu poured wine to the rims of three thimble-like glasses.

'How many people do I have to kill?'

'No killing,' said Ryman.

'It's a robbery,' said Crosby.

'A bank?'

'No,' said Ryman sipping his wine. 'You'd be part of a team. Crosby and I would be two of the others.'

'But you do not tell me what we rob?'

'We want to know if you're interested,' said Crosby.

Lee Fong Yu had not touched his wine. He looked about him at the cave which smelt of damp and stale cooking impregnated with the stench of oil. This was where he had been hiding since his escape from the *nanchi*; scraping a secret living from his own little kingdom. Not venturing far from the safety of the mountains and always waiting for the knife in the night, the cry that would tell him that the avengers were coming. Six hundred thousand dollars would buy him a new life. Hong Kong, New York, London. 'I am interested,' he said.

'Excellent,' said Ryman. 'Let me explain what it's all about.'

A rattle of sub-machine fire crashed out from down the hillside. Ryman and Crosby threw themselves against the wall and Lee Fong Yu darted towards the back of the cave. Within seconds he had returned carrying a Belgian FN rifle. There was another burst of firing that seemed to be even nearer. Yu plunged full length and, cradling his gun across his forearms, began to crawl towards the hut opening. Ryman joined him. The rusty corrugated iron would have been hard-pressed to resist attack from a blunt pencil. Ryman edged towards Yu's shoulder and peered down the mountainside. At first he could see nothing. Then a hand appeared over the mounds of earth. The Aboriginal with the headband was climbing laboriously towards them. It was obvious that he had been hit. A patch of red was clearly visible across his stomach and he had difficulty in putting one foot before the other. There was no sign of the other men. Ryman did some counting. Four of Lee Fong Yu's men were either dead or pinned down in the forest. The pursuers must have been waiting for them. Lee Fong Yu growled and slid his rifle forward. The man with the headband, once so aloof and menacing, was now a pitiful sight. He was trying to hold his stomach and Ryman saw his teeth flash in a permanent grimace of pain. The soft earth was like a quicksand to him and each faltering step triggered off a small landslide. He flopped against the side of the hill and tried to dig the stock of his rifle into the ground to stop himself sliding backwards.

There was a sharp crack and Ryman ducked instinctively. When he looked up, the man with the headband had dropped his rifle and was clinging to a protruding root. His hand started to slide, and when there was another crack he jerked sideways and dropped from sight. The shots which had killed him had not come from below, but from further across the slope. Ryman realised that they were being outflanked. Lee Fong Yu fired twice but Ryman could see no target. The sound of the screaming bullets reverberated across the hillside. Ryman looked back into the recesses of the cave. How far did it stretch? There was no escape through the door. As if in confirmation, a murderous hail of bullets ripped through the corrugated iron above their head. A strip crashed down amidst a cloud of rust and choking dust. The burst had come from down the hillside and Ryman saw a man dart behind a mound of earth. 'If we stay here we're dead,' he said.

'Amen,' said Crosby's voice behind him.

Lee Fong Yu's pocket-sized body wriggled backwards. 'Come.' It was an invitation difficult to refuse. Crosby and Ryman rose to a half-stooped position and followed the little man as he ran for the

104

back of the cave. Another burst raked the flimsy façade behind them.

A kerosene lamp hung from the low ceiling and by it the woman waited anxiously. Lee Fong Yu ripped aside a strip of material and more weapons were revealed in an alcove. Ryman recognised a Lee-Enfield rifle that now seemed almost a museum piece. He checked the magazine. It was full. Crosby took a double-barrelled shotgun and a bandolier of cartridges. The best weapons had already gone. Ryman wondered what kind of operation Lee Fong Yu was running. You did not keep a small armoury because you were afraid of burglars.

Lee Fong Yu took the lamp and led the way up a narrow passageway which soon became no more than a fissure in the rock. For him and the woman it presented few problems but Ryman's broad shoulders had to be turned sideways. Roots dangled down about their faces and there was a stomach-turning smell of vegetable decay. Behind was the muffled rattle of firearms.

The passageway narrowed away to nothing and Lee Fong Yu stopped and raised his lamp. Above their heads were earth-caked notches cut in the rock, which showed where other men had climbed. Yu handed the lamp to the woman, slung his rifle over his shoulder and started to climb. Just visible in the poor light was what seemed like a ceiling of rock. Wedged in a seam of the earth, Ryman fought claustrophobia and saw his fear mirrored on Crosby's shining, sweaty face. Dirt and stones spattered down from above. It seemed that at any moment a full-scale fall could bury them. The woman nudged Ryman and gestured that he should start to climb. He slung the Lee-Enfield and then found that it caught on the rock behind him and impeded his progress. He had to sling it over one arm where it was almost as difficult a manoeuvre. With back and elbows scraped raw he arrived at Yu's heels, sweat stinging his eyes, the rifle clattering against the rock. Thin roots dangled down like the tentacles of some nauseous creature, and Ryman smelt damp earth. It was not rock above them.

Lee Fong Yu pressed upwards with his shoulders and there was a cracking noise and a further fall of earth and stones. A beam of light slanted down and Ryman smelt fresh air. So this was the escape route from the lair. They must be about to emerge at a point further up the mountainside. Lee Fong Yu pushed again and the hole grew larger. Carefully he moved aside batons of wood that covered the opening and drew himself up between them. Ryman followed.

A ridge of rock formed a natural protection and Ryman lay behind it and breathed deeply. His arms were aching painfully. Thank God he had got himself into shape again. A few months before he might have been wedged in the cleft like a cork in a bottle.

Crosby emerged, half-blinded by dirt, and then the woman, who had a knotted headscarf pulled low over her eyes. There was fear in her expression but she was calm. This was clearly not the first time she had known danger.

Ryman looked about him. The mountain still rose steeply and behind there were outcrops of rock and patches of scree pinned down by clumps of fir and cedar. The quarrying had not reached this point. There was not a lot of cover for the first fifty yards, but after that came the trees where it should be possible to make an escape. Ryman looked towards Lee Fong Yu, wondering what he was going to do.

Two rifle shots and an answering burst of automatic fire jerked his attention back down the slope. He crawled forward and peered through a natural crenelle in the rock. Below them was the ramp with the bulldozer on it and a man with a rifle knelt behind one of the tracks. It was he who had leapt from the cab of the truck. A fresh burst of firing came from below his position and bullets ricocheted off the vertical blade and screamed across the hillside. Ryman tried to pick out the spot where the firing was coming from. The attackers were working systematically, like a well-trained unit. Ryman felt grudging admiration. He searched the hillside beneath the hut and then turned his attention to the area beyond the bulldozer. It was likely that the attackers would try and outflank their adversary: keep him pinned down whilst a man moved round behind him. Sure enough, a figure scrambled nimbly across the stretch of open hillside and ducked down behind a boulder. Automatically, Ryman slid back his safety catch and checked his sight. Within seconds he had taken up position with his legs spread and had his weapon trained on a spot slightly uphill from the boulder. When the man next moved he would be ready for him.

Crosby crawled close. 'Why don't we get the hell out of here?

This isn't our battle.' He spoke in a low hiss. Ryman said nothing: he was concentrating on his potential target, his finger already taking the pressure of the trigger. The man's head and shoulders appeared and moved into the firing line. Ryman squeezed, his whole hand contracting round the rifle to prevent the shot being jerked. The butt thumped into his shoulder and the man bounced back like a jack rabbit. He clutched his thigh and rolled down the slope after his weapon. Ryman frowned. 'She's firing low.'

'Shit,' said Crosby. 'Now we're in it.'

Lee Fong Yu opened up and there was an answering burst that set the scree dancing to their left. Below them, the truck driver leaned round the side of the steel blade and fired twice. There was a single returning shot and he pitched forward, his rifle falling from the ramp.

Ryman swore softly and rolled over on his back to address Crosby. 'Give me your shotgun.'

'Why?'

'I'm going down there. You can cover me better with this.' He slapped the breech of the Lee-Enfield and passed it over.

'What are you going to do?' asked Lee Fong Yu.

'Try and get that bulldozer working.' Ryman took the shotgun and watched the others move into position.

Crosby's face was glum. 'You're crazy,' he said. 'You're going to get us all killed.'

'Shoot straight,' said Ryman. He glimpsed the uncomprehending face of the Chinese woman and rolled sideways away from the shelter of the rocks. The mountain sloped sharply and he half fell until his feet touched its side and skidded downwards in a shale of stones. Brambles tore at his legs, and he dropped ten feet to land on a dirt ledge where the bulldozer had started its devastation of the hillside. His knees buckled and a firecracker of bullets kicked up dust to his left. There was an answering 'crack', 'crack' from above. Ryman plunged forward and left the ledge as if diving off a board. A boulder loomed up and he crashed against it, smashing his knuckles against the rock. He dropped to his haunches and slid down the slope on his backside, feeling the pain burn through him as if he was sitting on a hot iron. More bullets whistled past, their angry insect hum sounding like the call sign of death. Battered and bruised he fell to his knees on another ledge and saw a man taking aim at him from behind a fallen tree. He unleashed a barrel of the shotgun and leapt again, landing on two feet in soft earth as if in a long-jump pit.

Now he could see the cab of the bulldozer below. Stirred by the sight, he took off again and crashed down the hillside in a gathering avalanche of dust and stones. The bulldozer loomed up and he slammed down beside it sobbing and gasping for breath. Above, the landslide he had unleashed continued to roll down the side of the mountain. A bullet whistled perilously close and he urged himself forward and began to scramble for the driver's seat. Instinct, like a hand on his shoulder, made him turn. Twenty yards away, the man he had shot was hobbling towards the ramp trying to get into position to use his rifle. His thigh was a slippery wash of scarlet. Ryman swung round and brought up his shotgun. He fired and the man was jerked away like chaff before a gust of wind. Ryman threw the weapon aside and hauled himself into the seat. A bullet whistled off one of the stanchions that held the flimsy cab in place, and others beat a tattoo on the clearing blade. He could see where the men were now — grouped behind an uprooted tree that lay obliquely across the fall line of the slope. Bullets from Crosby and Lee Fong Yu kicked up dirt around their position.

Ryman found the ignition and fumbled with the gear lever. There was a resentful judder and the engine slowly sprang to life. His hand closed about the mighty hand brake and he squeezed and released. The bulldozer jerked forward towards the edge of the ramp and then steadied as Ryman found neutral and pushed the lever into reverse. Perched in the cab like a mahout on an elephant he felt terrifyingly exposed and vulnerable. The bulldozer shuddered and retreated down the ramp, sending stones flying. It was only then that Ryman realised how precarious its hold on the hillside was. The angle of descent was steep and the path no more than an impression. At any second the bulldozer might tilt and topple over and over until it eventually came to rest amongst the trees below. Ryman braked and engaged first gear. There was an angry roaring from the engine and then it jerked forward and skirted the ramp. The lorry was to the right with the door still open and as he came abreast of it a fresh volley of fire thundered from the position below. Ryman braced himself and hunched forward over the controls.

With a skill remembered from his Malay days he engaged the blade mechanism and the heavy curve of steel sank towards the

108

level of the uneven ground. Like a plough shear it picked up a lip of earth and began to push it forward, picking up stones and the shredded roots of trees that lay in its path. The blade dug deeper and the edge of the dirt wave began to spill down the hill. A lump of marble was dislodged, and then a boulder that bounced away to gather speed and crash through the trees. A noise of snapping branches went on long after it had disappeared. Ryman changed course and the bulldozer lurched towards the edge of the path. For what seemed like seconds he had the sensation of falling into space, and then the machine tilted forward and he felt the controls thumping the wind out of his chest. He was poised at the angle of a roller-coaster going down an incline, the blade of the bulldozer serving as a crude brake and his body sprawled forward barely making contact with the seat.

Below him at an angle of forty-five degrees lay the uprooted tree with the three men behind it. A wave of earth and debris was now breaking over them, propelled by the descending bulldozer. One man, alerted to the danger, threw himself forward across the trunk to take careful aim. Ryman could see the glint of the barrel and sensed an invisible line tracing a path to his heart. At any split second the trigger would be pulled and he would be dead. Then the man's head dropped and he lay still as if he had fallen asleep whilst praying. He had been shot dead from above.

Now a full-scale landslide had been started. A section of the mountain was breaking away and it was no longer certain whether the bulldozer was instigator or part of the descending mass. Two slabs of marble cleared the fallen tree and a third smashed against its side, ripping away a section of bark to reveal white wood. The tree jolted back with the impact and there was a scream that cut through even the deafening roar of the slide. Another man turned and ran. He had taken three plunging steps when a rock caught him between the shoulder blades with a sickening force that made even Ryman wince. The man disappeared into the dust. Crunch! The blade was underneath the tree and lifting it in the air. The force of the impact jarred every bone in Ryman's body. He clung on desperately and glimpsed a puppet figure jerking back into space. The caterpillar tracks chewed up anything that lay beneath them and the fallen tree was carried like a battering ram smashing down a clump of young saplings and scourging the earth of rocks and boulders. As the bow wave of moving matter built up to spill over the blade, Ryman dug it in even deeper. Ahead he could see the tops of fir trees. The mountainside sloped sharply to become almost a cliff face. It was here that he had climbed with Crosby. The bulldozer shuddered, slid and finally came to a halt on the very brink of the drop. The dust began to clear and a fast-diminishing trickle of earth and stones pitter-pattered away down the slope.

Ryman slumped over the controls, drained and barely able to believe that he was still alive. Sweat began to prick through the mask of dust that clogged his eyes and he rubbed his face and clambered down from the cab. Behind him the ground smoked and showed the uneven descent of the caterpillar tracks. There was no sign of a human being. Ryman breathed deeply and walked round to the mound of driven earth and the tree. Like an offering, the barrel of a machine carbine protruded from the debris. Ryman pulled and felt a slight resistance before he held the weapon in his hands. He checked the mechanism and found it was still working. The bullet that might have killed him was still in the breech. Warily, he began to descend the hillside. No birds were singing; there was an eerie silence. It was on the bluff above the car that he came upon the first man. He had been shot in the chest and back and fallen whilst trying to escape into the trees. Three more Aborigines were lying dead beside the car. Their killers must have waited behind the vehicle and opened up at pointblank range. There was a contented hum of insects.

Ryman's face screwed up into an expression of disgust. There was a sound behind him and he spun round swinging up the rifle. It was Crosby. He looked down at the bodies and winced. 'Jesus Christ! What have we got ourselves into.'

Ryman didn't answer immediately. His eyes were searching the trees behind Crosby. 'Where's Lee Fong Yu?'

'He's O.K. He's back there somewhere.'

But when they returned up the hillside there was no sign of either Lee Fong Yu or the woman.

CHAPTER SIX

Burton lay in the half-darkness and listened to the subdued roar of the air-conditioning. Lights flickered against the blind as if the building opposite his apartment was on fire, but it was only the neon sign outside the Szechuan Restaurant. He closed his eyes and could smell the fried eels in sauce, hot-sour soup, steamed pomfret and the crispy duck skin that was served in a hot bun. In this membrane-walled flat you lived other people's lives as much as your own. The sound of mah-jong tiles slapping together and the rattle of an abacus on one side; the man who woke up shouting in the middle of the night; the woman upstairs who talked to her flowers. You knew when and what they were eating, when they took a shower, when they made love.

'I must go,' said Flower.

Burton burrowed closer to her. 'Stay until morning.'

He felt her shaking her head. 'No.'

The vehemence that the gesture lent to her refusal annoyed him. 'Why not? You're not still feeling guilty, are you—?' It was the first time he had persuaded her to make love at his apartment.

'No.' This time there was no shake of the head.

Burton was not prepared to let the matter rest. 'You don't still love him, do you?'

Flower closed her eyes. There were questions she did not want to answer even to herself. Sometimes she wished that both men would go away and leave her alone; they only added to the confusion. Where did she belong? She had once taken a perverse satisfaction in her German blood, using it to explain her lack of harmony with the Chinese world. Now, her reaction to the planned theft of the Ju ware was forcing her to realise how deeply engrained her heritage was within her.

'Why don't you answer?' asked Burton.

'Because I do not know what the answer is.' A great feeling of despair welled up inside her. 'Why don't you just use me like a whore? It is so much simpler.'

Her head started to move down his body until he seized it angrily and pulled her towards him. 'Listen to me! You don't

111

know what you're saying. Flower, I love you.' His arms moved round her and she started to cry softly. 'Don't worry about some stupid old superstition. That was a thousand years ago. You and I, we're now.' He spoke more urgently. 'Don't you understand? You're the reason why I'm doing this.'

'Is that supposed to make me happy?' Flower's voice was bitter. Burton did not understand what she was saying. 'If you don't want to come with us, I'll tell Ryman that I'm not going ahead.'

Flower thought of Ryman and of all the planning, and of the risks he had taken. She remembered other places and other times. Could Burton really understand the nature of the blackmail he was exerting? Burton listened in the darkness and heard the creaking of the shutters that gave on to the balcony of the apartment above. Old Ching would soon be talking to her geraniums. 'Well?' he said.

Crosby came up on deck and tore open another can of lukewarm beer. He could never remember a night like it. The air seemed to have been replaced by hot cotton wool. It was impossible to sleep. Especially in the narrow berth with the high wooden surrounds. When he got in it he felt as if he was lying in a coffin. And the mosquitoes — they were as big as daddy-long-legs. His neck and shoulders were swollen with bites. You slapped your skin and three died. The moon hung lonely in the sky except for a bank of clouds on the horizon. It still wore its halo and with it seemed as saintly and insubstantial as some faded icon. The silver path it traced across the water had more reality. And what a sea — its surface was a slab of marble. There was no wave, no ripple. The tide rose and fell like a rich man's bath being filled and emptied: discreetly. The lack of movement and the heaviness of the air would have been disturbing even if their significance was unknown.

To Crosby it was frightening; even more frightening than — there was a rustle from the reeds and he spun round. In this terrible silence any unexpected sound made the flesh creep. He hated the marshes and the stinking mud and the labyrinth of creeks. Sometimes there was the noise of something dropping in the water and he saw dark shapes swimming. What were they? Water rats? Otters? He wondered if they would start coming on to the boat, if he would go into the galley and see a pair of yellow eyes looking at him from the table. Such fantasies became more and more frequent as the time passed. It didn't take long for loneliness to start playing tricks on the mind.

He stared into the dark banks of reeds, his ears tuned for any sound. Somewhere, deep inside their quagmire recesses, a creature was moving. He drank some beer and, on an impulse, hurled the half-full can into the reeds. The noise it made was almost pitiful in its brevity. He walked aft and struck out blindly at some mosquitoes. He was powerless here, even against the marshes. And somewhere below the horizon the barometer was dropping like a hot coal through butter and the first muttering winds would be building themselves to cyclic fury. And in Taipei, a man called Henderson would be thinking of his meeting with Crosby and the things that had been said and the things that must be done.

Ryman woke from a bad dream. He had the impression that there had been a noise but it must have been in his dream. All he could hear now was the hum of traffic and the occasional bark of a horn. He hated sleeping with the air-conditioning on. He glanced at his watch. A quarter to four. The hour to imagine that your children have been killed in a car crash, that your wife is about to leave you, that your life is wasted. But Ryman had never had any children and his wives had left him; and his life?

He reached out for the bedside light and knocked over a tumbler of neat whisky. The gesture reminded him that he was drunk. Professionally drunk, so that there were none of the symptoms of headaches and gummed eyes felt by amateurs. You had to work it out for yourself when you discovered your body lying stretched out on the floor beside a bed instead of in it.

It was not going well, he knew that. Lee Fong Yu had disappeared into thin air, presumably for ever, leaving a number of scores to be settled, with Ryman's name at the head of the list of creditors. The typhoon danger was worsening hourly rather than daily. Flower had not been near him, and Burton's Food Fair was imminent. Crosby was on the boat and he, Ryman, had to make all the decisions. Could he pull it off by himself? It would be difficult but possible. It was either that or scrubbing the operation; or perhaps persuading Flower to come into the Museum. No, as soon as the thought occurred to him he rejected it. He had left scar tissue on two women's lives and that was without sending them to prison, or worse.

He looked beside him to the place on the bed where Flower would have been lying. He could see her hands drawn up against her face in sleep. He took a drink of whisky. Steinbeck had been right: you could never disappoint them, you could never surprise them. She was a whore, he had whored away his life. If not made for each other they had settled into each other like two adjacent buildings weathered by age. Perhaps one day he would regret her more than anyone else.

Something creaked and he froze, senses ticking. Sooner or later they would come looking for him. Three bodies bulldozed into the hillside, ten men dead. A reckoning would be made. There was silence and then a light tap at the door. Ryman hesitated and then felt a glorious sense of relief. He knew who it must be. He swung his legs from the bed and pulled on a dressing gown. Running his fingers through his tousled hair, he crossed the room in two strides and threw open the door. Before him stood a slight Chinese figure. Ryman's face clouded over. He was not looking at Flower but Lee Fong Yu.

CHAPTER SEVEN

'This is real nice,' said Mrs Budkiss.

'I'm glad you're enjoying it,' said Burton. He glanced quickly round the room. It was going well. He had never seen so many people he did not know and most of those that he did know he had met at other people's events. The food was disappearing fast. For a moment he felt a pang of regret. At last he had achieved a success and he was never going to get the chance to repeat it. This might have been the turning point.

'Where did you get the meat?' asked Mrs Budkiss.

'Wei Yang,' said Burton. 'You know, Min Sheng Road. East, I think.' Mrs Budkiss bit another large hunk out of her hamburger and drew closer to lay a hand on his sleeve. 'You know, I never understand how they eat dogs.'

'I'd have thought it was very easy to understand,' said Burton. 'I mean, Americans love hot dogs, don't they?'

Mrs Budkiss gurgled delightedly and squeezed his arm. 'Oh, you are terrible. I'll never eat another one again.' She continued to enjoy the joke and called over one of her friends so that she could repeat it. Burton looked around for somebody else to talk to and saw Ryman disappear behind one of the screens that concealed the food and cutlery boxes. Nobody appeared to notice him go. The wine had been circulating for an hour and the warm throb of conversation suggested that the guests had profited from it. Burton flinched as another hand fell on his sleeve.

'You never dropped by, did you?'

Burton turned and recognised an engineer's wife who had once extended an open invitation to her pool. He wondered what she did to her hair to get it looking as if it had frozen at the prow of an arctic trawler. 'I've always been meaning to,' he said. 'Just never got around to it, that's all.'

'You must come. I'm having such a good time I'd like to repay the hospitality.' She winked and lowered her voice huskily. 'Wednesdays are good. That's when I'm a golf widow.' Burton had heard of American hospitality, but this invitation seemed to be hinting at an intimacy greater than that achieved by helping the lady add chlorine to the filtration system. Again he experienced a twinge of resentment. It was all happening too late. Of course it would have changed nothing as far as Flower was concerned, but it might have been amusing to have made more contact with the locals.

Ryman strode behind the screen and pulled it close. There was a tight feeling in the region of his heart. He set down his empty glass and quickly pulled two of the tin boxes together end to end. They were empty save for an inch of cushioning on the floor. He dropped to his knees and removed the steel pins that held one of the end panels of each box in place. There was a pin at each corner and they pulled out between finger and thumb. Within seconds the panels had been removed and hooks swung out to fit into beds and hold the two boxes together. Now there was one long space inside them. Ryman swiftly climbed inside and pulled a lid down over his legs. A catch had been made which penetrated the side of the box and could be locked from the interior. He heard a warning cry from outside and quickly lay back and lowered the lid of the second box. There was a click and he lay alone in the suffocating darkness.

'Very nice to talk to you,' said Lee Fong Yu. 'I will phone you about the marble.' He pocketed the business card and turned away. The American had been interested in obtaining marble for the side of his swimming pool. He would have to wait a long time. Lee Fong Yu looked round the room cautiously. It was as well that there were few Chinese present. He had recognised only one; a judge. The man had looked at him as if sifting through a card-index system in his mind, but the faces of sentenced criminals were clearly not filed; or perhaps there was no anticipation that they might be met on social occasions. The moment had passed without danger. Lee Fong Yu sipped orange juice and pretended to be studying the view of the Museum Gardens. He could have stood with Burton, but the man was talking to the wife of the Ang Moh he had just left. He had no wish to get involved with these people, but there was no alternative. He must get away from Taiwan. Here his days were numbered to a figure any child could count on its fingers. They had already smashed every stick of furniture in his flat and thrown acid in the face of his woman. There was nowhere

116

on the Island he could go. This was where he would have to buy his ticket to a new life.

Lee Fong Yu skirted the room and approached the row of screens. He cleared his throat loudly and paused a few seconds before passing beyond them. Before him a few slim metal boxes and canteens of cutlery were strewn about. He moved a tray of glasses on to two boxes that were lying together and approached a small, portable chest of drawers. He pulled one of the knobs and the whole front of the piece came forward to reveal that the drawers were false and the area inside an empty space. Swiftly, he squatted inside and drew his knees up before his chest. He pushed his arms between them and made contact with a rail. He pulled it towards him and the 'chest' was one again.

Mr Chang glanced at his watch. It was time for the event to be over. He looked about him carefully and dropped his barely eaten hamburger on to an abandoned plate. To his relief it seemed that nobody had noticed. How anybody could serve almost raw pieces of ground-up meat in a bun was beyond him. And the difficulties involved in eating it. The tomato fluid and the mustard that leaked over one's clothing at every bite; the unpalatable slices of raw onion. There was something so clumsy and vulgar about the whole concoction. That it should be produced here in this shrine dedicated to the protection of the wisdom and ability of the past and the creation of an even loftier civilisation was painfully incongruous. He proceeded towards Burton and was nudged aside by a large red-faced American with a glass of wine in his hand. The man hardly seemed to notice that contact had been made. That was another thing. The two waiters had not stayed behind the bar but made incessant sorties with bottles of red, white and pink wine which they had poured into the guests's glasses whether they asked for it or not. This had been done specifically at the Englishman's instigation. Chang had been subjecting him to close scrutiny and he knew. Well, if the man was trying to curry favour amongst his guests with this gesture, he would very soon learn that he was taking the wrong route. This was certainly not the way that he, Wu Chang, expected to be entertained on a social occasion. He would make it a point of duty to ensure that this lamentable affair was the last function held at the Museum.

'Going rather well, don't you think?' said Burton.

117

Chang looked down his nostrils. 'There is smoke on the ceiling,' he said.

'Not very much,' said Burton. 'There must be a draught coming from somewhere. Those grills are usually very reliable.'

'They are better outside,' said Chang pointedly.

Burton showed no signs of being ruffled. 'If the worst comes to the worst, we'll get the mark off with a mop on the end of a pole. A drop more wine?'

Chang shook his head firmly. 'I regret to remind you that the Reception should have ended half an hour ago. That was what you agreed.'

Burton glanced at his watch and simulated the degree of alarm and penitence that he thought would please. 'Good heavens! I'd no idea it was so late. I am sorry. You're sure you won't have one for the road?'

Chang made no attempt to hide his exasperation. 'Everybody must leave! The soldiers are waiting to make their inspection. The Museum is officially closed.'

Burton controlled his desire to smile. 'Damn! I was going to say a few words. I don't suppose ... '

'No!' said Chang, firmly.

'Right,' said Burton briskly. 'Well, we'll be back tomorrow to get everything tidied up.'

'Early,' said Chang, almost ferociously. 'You will be here when the Museum opens.'

'On the dot.' Burton paused as another malicious inspiration occurred to him. 'By the way, I've an idea I'd like to discuss with you. Pets. Do you know how many people in this room have a cat?'

'No!' shrilled Mr Chang.

'About three-quarters of them. We could ... '

'It is out of the question! You will have to find somewhere else. I am going to talk to the Directors about it.'

Burton looked downcast. 'Well, then. There's nothing for it. We'll just have to steal away quietly.'

Ryman lay in the darkness and wondered what the time was. He had heard nothing since the last guest had been wheeled away and the military had made their evening check. That had been a heart-stabbing moment. He had listened to one of the soldiers opening the tin box that rested on the two he was in. Seconds had passed whilst he held his breath, and then the lid had slammed down again.

Ryman screwed up his eyes and tried to peer through the holes that had been bored in the roof of the box above his head. His eyes were so drowned in sweat that he could see nothing. His flesh seemed to be cooking. His clothing stuck to his body and his body stuck to the padding beneath it. He could feel the sweat trickling down the side of his chest. Where were the nightwatchmen? The vigils made by Crosby and Burton had suggested that they usually made their first tour of the building an hour after the military. It must be past that time now and there was no sound from them. Why had they changed their routine tonight?

Ryman's hand moved to the catch on the box that concealed the upper half of his body. He had meant to lie hidden until after the first tour, but the conditions inside the box were insupportable. There was a pain in his ears and in his chest and he was losing consciousness. His fingers made contact with the catch, then froze. He had heard something. The sing-song rhythmic cadence of a Chinese voice. It must be the nightwatchmen patrolling together. This fitted in with what Chang had told Burton about their fears of spending the night in the Museum. They would not wish to make a tour alone. Ryman twisted his head so that his ear was nearer the breathing holes. Seconds passed and he heard the scrape of a screen being moved back. The men must be very near. His heart was beating so loudly that he wondered that neither of them could hear it. There was a pause and then one of the men said something and the other laughed in agreement. There was a chink of bottle against glass and a hearty '*jye jye ni*'.

Ryman realised what was happening and fought a desire to groan out loud. The men were helping themselves to a drink from the remains of the buffet. How long would they be? He couldn't stay cooped up here much longer. There was more conversation and then, to his horror, he heard the sound of wraps being moved on the table. The remaining food was being uncovered. The men were going to have their own private banquet. Ryman twisted his head upwards and pressed his nostrils against the perforations. He was becoming dizzy. If the men didn't leave soon — something grated against the roofs of the boxes and he jumped. What the hell was happening now! Were they getting a knife from the cutlery box? Without warning, the light above his eyes was blotted out and the box quivered. One of the men had sat down on it.

Panic stampeded through Ryman's swirling brain. He was going to be suffocated. The man was going to sit there and eat and drink, and while he did so, Ryman would be dying. Unless he shouted and kicked and beat with his fists. Ryman closed his eyes tight. He must not do that, not yet. The box could not be completely airtight save for the perforations. He breathed as slowly as he could and felt his skin burning. The pains in his head and chest were worse. How long would it take to use up the air that remained in the box — if there was any? He gripped and un-gripped his hands and then told himself to stop. Even this pathetic, futile gesture must use up oxygen. The pain in front of his eyes was now throbbing like a neon sign. He could see it in the darkness; yellow, yellow, yellow. The inside of his mouth was dry, his throat ached. His tongue seemed to be swelling so that at any moment it might explode through the side of his head. He wasn't prepared to die, not like this. He knotted his fist and drew it back across his chest.

The box quivered and the muzzy circles of light reappeared. The man had stood up. There was a guttural clearing of the throat, ending in a spitting noise. '*Wo bu che jei ge!*' The man was saying that the food was uneatable. '*Bu hau!*' agreed his companion emphatically.

There was the sound of food covers being put back into place and then the voices faded away. Ryman waited until he thought his head was going to shatter into splinters and then pressed the catch that released the lid. Nothing happened. Frantically, he pressed again and the lid jumped open an inch. The air seemed to rush in like cool water and he lay back, not moving, drinking it in. Slowly, his head began to clear, and he warily pushed the lid up a couple of inches more and peered out. The moon had come up, and shafts of ghostly light broke through the windows. There were no sounds. Ryman pushed the lid back and gritted his teeth as he hauled himself into a sitting position. The cramp in his limbs was agonising. He released the second lid and drew his knees towards his chest. Every muscle ached. He felt exhausted and yet the real work had not begun. He listened again and then clambered out of the boxes and closed both the lids. He was glad to do so. The inside of the boxes stank of the sweat that still lathered his body.

He crossed to the chest that held Lee Fong Yu, and pressed the

120

release catches. The man was hunched up like a newly hatched chick. For a moment he did not move and then his sticky limbs began to separate and he climbed unsteadily to his feet. Ryman said nothing, but poured a glass of red wine and thrust it into his hand. Lee Fong Yu shook his head, replaced the wine glass and pulled the stopper from a bottle of brandy. He gulped from it as if it was lemonade, then wiped his mouth with the back of his hand and nodded emphatically in a gesture that said '*Now* I am ready'. Ryman drank some mineral water and found a dish cloth to wipe himself down with. Ablutions over, he approached one of the food containers and lifted up its false floor. Revealed were the packaging materials made by Crosby and several sets of overalls and cord-soled shoes. Swiftly, the men changed and placed their discarded clothes in Ryman's tin boxes. The packaging materials were divided as had been previously agreed and rehearsed. Lee Fong Yu professed not to share Flower's qualms concerning the Ju ware but was still happier that Ryman should carry it. With containers slung round their necks and over their shoulders, the two men replaced everything as it had been before they emerged, and moved silently to the short flight of stairs that led from the tower room. Outside, it was light enough to see to the main gate where the soldiers would be on guard. Ryman looked up at the less-than-saintly moon and cursed its halo.

They went past the lift and started to descend the stairs, listening at each bend. One piece of information that Ryman did not have was the exact whereabouts of the nightwatchmen when they were not making their rounds. From the observations made by Crosby and Burton it would seem that the light always appeared from the area of the staff offices. This would be a sensible location for a rest room but it would mean that the two men were not far from Chang's office, and that was where they were going first.

Ryman looked across to a row of Western Chou wine vases shaped like ornamental fonts. In the moonlight it was easy to see the squat shapes as skulking hobgoblins, creatures from another time taking shape before his eyes. The brooding intensity of the thirty-seven centuries of Chinese history crowding in about them played havoc with the imagination.

They approached the lower ground floor and Lee Fong Yu restrained Ryman by the sleeve and tapped his nose. Ryman sniffed. There was the odour of stewing bean shoots. The nightwatchmen must be preparing a meal. So much the better. It would keep them occupied.

The staircase came to an end and Ryman peered across the marble hall. The shutters had been lowered over the souvenir stall and only the faintest glimmer of moonlight penetrated to the bottom of the steps, making the glass doors gleam black like the lenses of reflecting sunglasses. A grass blade of light fell across the marble and this came from a door on the far side of the hall that was slightly ajar. There was the murmur of distant voices as if the men talking were in a room beyond that from which the light was shining.

Ryman touched his eyes and pointed towards the door opposite. Lee Fong Yu nodded. Ryman removed the key to Chang's office and stepped into the open. He crossed swiftly to the door and inserted the key. He twisted and his heart gave a little jump. Nothing happened. He tried again and then pulled the key towards him. Damn the lock! He was about to turn again when there was the sound of a Chinese voice, muffled but strident. He turned and saw Lee Fong Yu gesturing him back furiously. He attempted to withdraw the key and found that it was stuck. Fighting panic, he abandoned it and flattened himself behind the nearest pillar. He heard a door opening and the sound of approaching footsteps. An old man with grey hair walked past, almost brushing his shoulder, and headed for the washroom. Ryman willed him not to turn round, not to see the key sticking out of Chang's door. The washroom door creaked and the man disappeared. Ryman looked towards the staircase. A hand beckoned. Running on tiptoe he reached the stairs and moved with Lee Fong Yu to the first bend. Both men crouched shoulder to shoulder, trying to control their breathing, and listening.

Eventually, the washroom door creaked again and elderly feet slip-slopped back across the hall. There was a pause and then the sound of a door closing.

Ryman let out a sigh of relief and retraced his footsteps to the hall. All was in darkness and there was no sound. He waited a few seconds and then returned to Chang's door. This time he agitated the key back and forth until he felt it bite against the mechanism and something turn. There was a subdued click and the door opened. Lee Fong Yu moved to his side and together they entered

122

the room and closed the door. Ryman produced a shaded torch and closed in on the keys behind Chang's desk. He held the torch whilst Lee Fong Yu screwed up his eyes and studied the tags. Ryman watched him anxiously. The man's face revealed no hint of understanding as he moved from one hieroglyphic to the other. Eventually, he beckoned that Ryman should bring the torch and crossed to the wall map of the layout of the museum, making several trips before he selected six keys which he laid on the table while Ryman made a note of the positions they had hung in on the wall. Everything must be put back in its original place to minimise the risk of the alarm being given immediately the Museum opened.

Ryman gathered up the keys and crossed to the door. After a moment's reflection he left the key to Chang's office on the inside of the door. One of them might want to slip inside in a hurry. There seemed no possibility of the nightwatchmen trying the door. He indicated what he had done to Lee Fong Yu, extinguished the torch and gently turned the handle. The door opened half an inch to reveal the hall, still silent and in darkness, and Ryman ushed Lee Fong Yu out, closed the door softly and followed his partner to the stairs. Working as they were now with the keys, it had been decided that they should stay together and not collect three items each. One man could stand guard whilst the other worked and they would be able to help each other with the delicate items.

They ascended the stairs and Ryman glanced at his watch. It was only nine o'clock but it seemed like the early hours of the morning. The nervous tension and the living death of the tin boxes had taken their toll. He glanced quickly at Lee Fong Yu. The man's face was shiny but there was no intimation of fear or fatigue.

They entered the Porcelain Gallery and moved silently towards their prey. Ryman had drawn so many plans of the Museum that he could have found his way around it blindfolded. He approached the section devoted to the Sung Dynasty and walked slowly past the crowded showcase listening for any sound.

Ting, Chun, Kuan, Lung-ch'uan, Ko, Ti. The names of the different wares struck the ear like musical notes. Even the dim lights could not totally conceal their beauty. They seemed to glow like precious stones in the darkness. He paused and gazed down at the perfect shape of the Ju cups. Why did Bigg covet them more than any others? Did their sad history touch some chord in that stony heart? It seemed unlikely, but there must be some aesthetic feeling there capable of nurturing a hint of warmth.

Ryman sunk a hand into the commodious pocket of his overalls and produced Chang's keys. Lee Fong Yu flicked them over with small skeletal fingers and selected one. Ryman gestured to the showcase and returned the remaining keys to his pocket. He withdrew the torch and pointed it at the lock. Somewhere in the darkness a piece of furniture fidgeted and both men froze. Seconds passed and there was no other sound. Ryman switched on the torch and Lee Fong Yu inserted the key. Ryman waited for it to turn and held his breath. Supposing *some* of the showcases were connected to an alarm system? His experiment with the catapult would not have revealed that. The key turned and the door jumped open with a tiny squeak. Ryman told himself that it was his imagination that made the noise sound almost human — some tortured spirit fleeing into the dark recesses of the Museum, desperate to escape the pillage.

The glass door opened and Ryman found himself a foot away from the first prize. The plastic cups were slung like a garland around his neck and with shaking fingers he pulled open one of the closures. He was reminded of the feeling that he had had when robbing a bird's nest as a child. A sensation of guilt that nearly overcame the desire to possess; nearly but not quite. He stretched out a hand and gently lifted the first cup between finger and thumb. It seemed no thicker than an egg shell and just as fragile. Lee Fong Yu steadied the plastic cup and Ryman gently released his booty into its new nest. It fitted perfectly and he pushed in some more padding and pressed down the lid. No unseen devils lunged for his throat. His heart continued to beat normally. He looked at Lee Fong Yu and smiled. For the first time he began to believe that they might just get away with it.

The swell had started to run at ten o'clock. Crosby had heard it tapping against the hull as he lay on his bunk and tried to sleep. At first he thought it was a passing fisherman's boat, but there had been no engine noises and no light when he went up on deck. Just the thud, thud, thud of water starting to come alive. And then there was the wind. It worked its way into the reeds, which hissed and rustled as if passing on rumours of what was to come. The wind was nothing at first, but then there were sudden gusts and the water cut up as if rubbed by a rasp. What was most sinister was the horizon. It seemed to be rising as if a great wave was casting a shadow across the sea and rushing towards the shore, silently and inexorably, bent on overwhelming people in their beds. But the rising horizon was not a wave. It was the bar of the storm that would surely come; the black nimbo-stratus clouds, the plumed outriders of the typhoon.

The noises in the reeds had stopped. A frightening calm prevailed. It was as if the creatures of the marshes had read the signs and known that this was a bad place to be. They had already retired to seek what shelter there was. He was left alone.

Crosby stood on deck and listened. The swell was stronger. The boat was stirring at its mooring. The swell came first before the winds. The typhoon could be as much as a thousand miles away, driving the sea before it. Crosby ignored the mosquitoes which browsed unhindered on his flesh and crossed to the barometer. It was sinking slowly as if it had sprung a small leak. That might be interpreted as a good sign — maybe the typhoon was heading for another part of the coast. If it was coming towards him the barometer would be sinking fast. Most likely it was a question of time. If the descent speeded up he would know that the destructive winds were on their way.

Crosby went below and switched on the wireless. Slap, slap, slap, the noise of the sea against the hull was almost angry now. He turned the knobs and picked his way through the static, his ears cocked for the familiar Chinese word *'tai-fung'*. Ryman and Lee Fong Yu would be inside the Museum now if all had gone well. He envied them each other's company — here there was nobody to share a decision with. He was on his own.

He thought he heard the word *'tai-fung'* and fiddled desperately with the dials. A blare of static obliterated the message. He fought the conditions for five minutes and then gave up. Why was reception so bad tonight? Was it because of the electricity in the air? The nearness of the approaching storm?

Crosby stood up and moved, stooped, to the tiny engine-room. A pool of bilge twitched ominously between the joists. Should he start her up and make a run for it, or stay where he was in the hope that the typhoon would strike elsewhere? The longer it took him to make up his mind, the less available became the options. His hand strayed out towards the engine rail and then dropped back again.

125

Always there were decisions and always, at the back of his mind, there was Henderson.

Plop. Carefully rolled, Fan Kuan's *Travellers Amongst Mountains and Streams* slid to the bottom of the length of plastic piping. Ryman pressed the cap on the painting and sealed it with a length of insulating tape. Five down, one to go. It was merely a question of hanging the substitute painting and they could go in search of the last item, the ivory carving with the concentric balls. Ryman was still keyed up, but feeling an increasing sense of satisfaction. Three trips had been made back to the tower room, and merchandise carefully packed in the tin boxes. All the display cases so far had opened with the keys and without problems. He might have accused himself of being over-confident, but there were times in life when it was excusable to think of hardship as an insurance taken out on future success. After what they had been through, cooped up in the tin boxes, they were due for some good fortune.

Ryman carefully moved the tubing to one side and packed up the replacement painting that had been inside it. This bore little resemblance to the work of the gifted Northern Sung artist, but he was hoping that it would be some time before a specialist looked at it and noticed the substitution. In his experience, the guards spent all their time watching the visitors and scarcely glanced at the contents of the display cases.

Ryman unrolled the painting and then rolled it the other way to correct its tendency to curl. Grasping it by the top corners, he stepped towards the case. There was a sharp hiss from his left. Ryman turned and saw a torch beam stab three times from the darkness. It was Lee Fong Yu signalling that someone was coming up the stairs. Ryman hesitated. Should he try and hang the substitute painting and risk discovery, or gamble that the night-watchmen would go on to another floor? The space on the wall was the danger. If they did go past they must notice it. Ryman stepped forward and released one edge of the painting so that he could spring one of the two hanging clips. His fingers were fumbling and the scroll folded awkwardly against the chest. He pressed the paper home and felt for the second clip. Now he could hear the sound of voices. The clip refused to open and he struggled desperately, bending one of his nails back. The men were coming

126

closer. He forced the parchment between the metal jaws and retreated, leaving the painting swinging. Pressing the door closed, he started to run for the nearest archway. Then he realised that he had left the tubing lying at the foot of the display case. He turned back and snatched it up just as a light appeared at the end of the gallery. Expecting to hear a cry of alarm at any second, he darted back to the archway and pressed himself into the shadow beside a showcase. Through a gap in the open-work moulding he could see across to the case he had just plundered. As light flooded down the gallery and announced the approach of the two nightwatchmen, the substitute painting separated from one of the clips and dangled lop-sidedly across the case.

Ryman watched, not so much hypnotised as stunned. The nightwatchmen must see the painting. At the very least they would report its condition in the morning and the deception would be discovered immediately. What the hell could he do? Suddenly, there was a rattling noise from the direction of the stairs and the advancing light stopped. There was a quick flurry of Chinese and the sound of footsteps withdrawing fast. The nightwatchmen must be going to investigate. Ryman moved forward, his senses jangling. He heard another exchange and then the light faded away like a descending plume. The men were going downstairs. Ryman moved swiftly to the display case, opened the door and stepped inside. In his hand he held one of Chang's keys. He prised open the stubborn clip and secured the painting. No sooner had he done so than he heard the noise of returning footsteps. The nightwatchmen had found nothing and were continuing their round. Ryman thrust the door closed and darted back to the archway and the protection of the display case. He sank down into the shadow as the torch beams probed down the gallery throwing a mirror image on the paintings against the glass. The nightwatchmen went past, one of them glancing over his shoulder as if still seeking an explanation for the noise.

Ryman moved his hand to the left side of his chest and rubbed it up and down. It was a gesture he was perfecting to reassure his heart that it was still working. He waited until the lights and the sounds of footsteps had disappeared and then emerged silently into the gallery. There was no sign of Lee Fong Yu. He crept back towards the head of the stairs and hissed through clenched teeth. There was an answering hiss from the shadows and the small

Chinese glided to his side. He shook his head in a gesture of self-reproach. 'Sorry. I drop my torch.'

Burton stepped back from the curtain and let it fall into place. There was no sign of the men now; they must have been waiting for somebody to come out of the Szechuan Restaurant. He must not allow his imagination to start playing tricks. There had been no car following him when he picked up Lee Fong Yu and drove him to the Museum. The men waiting outside after the party were members of the staff who lived nearby. There was a logical explanation for everything. Logical, if not always convincing.

He opened the fridge and found to his disgust that he had forgotten to fill the ice trays. Too much on his mind. But that was no excuse — Ryman and Crosby were the ones bearing the pressure at the moment. He could sleep if he wanted to; if he was capable of it. He poured some fruit juice into a glass and carried it to the window. Tension started to build. It was like some kind of stupid children's game: pull back the curtains; will the bogeymen be there? He paused and pulled back the curtains. The bogeymen were there.

Ryman emerged from the gallery and approached the octagonal showcase isolated in the middle of the hall. Stepping into the open, he felt as if he was going up to receive an award. The cases full of exhibits ranged round the four walls were the spectators; the centre case was the presentation dais. In it was his prize, the Ch'ing Dynasty carved ivory balls.

He approached the display case and looked through the glass. He swallowed hard and his eyes darted to every corner. He moved to the next case, and the next, tracing a circle round the five sides in a state of mounting alarm. He stopped where he had started, the palms of his hands damp. The ivory carving was not there.

Flower turned off the wireless and cupped her coffee between her hands with her upper arms close to her body. It was a posture she often adopted when she was worried. The announcer had said that a typhoon was expected to strike the north-west coast over an eighty kilometre area between Hsin-chu and Tan-shui. If the forecast was correct, it would mean that the edge of the storm would sweep over the spot where the boat was moored. The typhoon was moving at a speed of twenty-five kilometres per hour and was expected to make contact with the coast in four hours' time. Coastal dwellers were advised to move to high ground and take their livestock and possessions with them. Taipei would bear some of the brunt of the storm, and Flower knew what was at its source; the removal of the Ju ware had awakened the wrath of the ancient gods. It was no accident that the typhoon had chosen this night to strike. She sipped her coffee ruminatively and looked at the bundle of her things prepared for the morning. She knew that something terrible was going to happen.

Ryman stared at the case trying to tell himself that his eyes were playing tricks. The carving must be there. Suddenly it would jump into view and he would feel a great surge of relief and curse himself for his stupidity. Then he noticed that the whole display had been changed. For a second he wondered if by some incredible aberration he had come to the wrong floor. Then he thought of something else and a feeling of doom closed in about his heart.

The day before yesterday had been a public holiday in honour of the birthday of Confucius and the Museum had been closed. He knew that because it had originally been the day they had arbitrarily chosen for the Food Fair. Since the Museum was open on Saturdays and Sundays it could only be on public holidays that the exhibits were rotated with some of the enormous stock in the underground warehouse. This was clearly what had happened whilst the rest of Taipei were attending ceremonies at the Confucian temples. Ryman smothered a groan and told himself what a fool he had been not to think of this and make one final check of all the items to be removed. Wearily he retraced his steps to Lee Fong Yu, who was watching the stairs.

He explained what had happened and Lee Fong Yu cursed softly in Chinese. 'Can you take another item?'

'No. He specified exactly what he wanted.'

'He will have to take what we can give him and adjust his price.'

Ryman said nothing and tried to think. He knew that Bigg was not going to be happy unless he got everything. There was also a strange kind of personal pride involved. Ryman lost a lot of little battles but not the big ones. He wasn't prepared to be beaten here.

'We've got plenty of time,' he said. 'We'll try and get into the warehouse and see if we can find it.'

129

He was expecting Lee Fong Yu to argue, but the man merely reflected for a few seconds and then shrugged his shoulders without expression.

'Very well.'

Not for the first time, Ryman wondered what kind of partner he had recruited.

The two men moved towards the staircase as the first flash of lightning scissored across the sky.

The rain was coming through the deck-house as if it did not exist. Crosby pressed his chest to the wheel and braced his feet against the support timbers. Only in this way could he hold himself upright and exercise some meagre control over the course of the vessel. The swell was mountainous, and the bow and propeller never in the water at the same time. The sky was black and the moon had disappeared as if blown away by the wind. The only light came from flashes of lightning and the white crests of angry waves. Each horizontal gust carried a spray of spume and torrential rain that rattled against the side of the boat like rifle fire. Crosby groaned and hawked, nausea riving his empty stomach. Ahead, a gutted candle in this terrible darkness, gleamed a jagged patch of grey. Crosby was running south towards Hsin-chu and what he prayed was the edge of the typhoon.

Ryman listened to the squalls of rain battering against the windows and thought of Crosby. What would conditions be like on the coast? A mood of black depression descended upon him. The operation seemed to be cursed. Maybe Flower had been right. He thought of her hopefully tucked up snug in bed and wondered why fate persisted in making things so difficult for them.

None of the public lifts or stairways descended to the level that led to the warehouses under the hills. This meant that they must go down from the offices on the lower ground floor. And it was in these offices that the nightwatchmen had their rest room. Ryman looked at his watch. If the pattern of events observed by Crosby and Burton was to be repeated, the men would soon be making their penultimate tour. When they left it might be possible to enter the offices, descend to the warehouses, locate the ivory carving, wait until the nightwatchmen went out on their last tour and then leave the offices, returning all the keys

130

to Chang's office *en route*. It was complicated but it was feasible.

Ryman explained the scheme to Lee Fong Yu and again met with neither query nor criticism. He was grateful but, at the same time, he wondered what exactly was going on behind the watchful grey eyes.

Moving carefully and trying to listen for any sound not drowned by the noise of the storm outside, the two men descended to the ground floor and took up shelter behind the counter of the cloakroom. Lightning forked the sky outside and raindrops formed a million tiny eyes against the glass doors. Ryman sat back and smothered a yawn. Minutes passed and then a half hour. Just as he was about to close his eyes there was a distant sound of a door opening and the murmur of Chinese voices. Ryman jerked himself fully awake and leaned forward. After several minutes, during which the men had presumably visited the washroom, there was the noise of footsteps and the two nightwatchmen came fleetingly into view as they rose from the lower ground floor and started to walk across the hall. One of them yawned loudly and was chided by the other. Ryman waited until the noise and light came from the storm and then moved forward to the stairs. The tour of the Museum took approximately twenty minutes. That should provide more than enough time to get down to the warehouses.

Ryman arrived at the lower ground floor and crossed swiftly to the door from which he knew the men had emerged. He took the handle and listened with his ear pressed to the wood. A man's voice from within made him freeze. Then he relaxed as he heard the sound of music. He was listening to a wireless. He opened the door and peered inside. There was an ante-room with a desk and a row of hooks for hanging coats. He beckoned to Lee Fong Yu and closed the door behind the two of them. Before them was another door with a light shining underneath it. It was here that the music came from. Ryman opened the door and found himself in a sparsely furnished room with a small stove and extractor fan; a sink, a couple of chairs and a bamboo table on which rested a transistor and some dirty dishes and chopsticks. Ryman did not give the room a second glance but passed through the door at the far side of it. This gave on to a narrow corridor with other doors at intervals down its length. The corridor was in semi-darkness.

131

Ryman switched on his torch and moved forward. Half a dozen paces brought him face to face with what he was looking for; the door of a lift. He quickly thought of the position of the other lifts in the building and then pushed the button. There could be no possibility that this shaft continued up into the rest of the Museum. To do so it would have to protrude through the floor of the scroll room where Dr Sun Yat-sen's impressive bronze statue now stood. At the back of his mind was the fear that the nightwatchmen on their round would suddenly see an empty lift descending.

There was a low hum and the lift jogged to a halt. Ryman opened the door and followed Lee Fong Yu into the scuffed interior. The lift seemed to have brought some of the cold of the caves with it, and the morgue-like atmosphere bestowed no favours on nerves already strained to breaking point. Standing in darkness, they descended into darkness, and Ryman felt as if he was going down in a bathysphere to plumb the depths of some uncharted ocean. Every metre extended the slender lifeline that connected him to safety.

The lift trembled to a halt and there was a hiss of an opening door and a rush of cold air. Ryman hesitated, confused, and then realised that the door had slid open behind them.

They emerged into an open space from which led a brick-lined tunnel wide enough and high enough to receive a truck. There was no illumination, but a row of lights could be made out stretching down the roof of the tunnel. There was also the hum of a ventilation system. Ryman remembered having read that the caves were air-conditioned. That was one of the reasons why they seemed so cold. Around the entrance to the lift were half a dozen trolleys with rubber wheels and long handles. Their use was obvious. It was in them that exhibits would be ferried to and fro between the warehouses and the Museum.

Ryman saw a row of what must clearly be light switches, but ignored them. Better to work in darkness than risk discovery should the nightwatchmen choose to descend below ground. He turned to Lee Fong Yu.

'There must be some order in which the stuff is laid out. We'll go through and take a look round. Tell me if you see any signs relating to ivory or carving.'

Lee Fong Yu nodded. 'Maybe it will be done by dynasties. We want Ch'ing, yes?'

'Yes,' said Ryman. You had to hand it to the little man. Nothing seemed to ruffle him.

Ryman led the way and they walked into the tunnel. It was straight and level and the only sound, apart from the rhythmic slapping of their cord-soled shoes, came from the water that dripped in places from the roof. Ryman thought again of the night outside and the fate of Crosby and the boat. If that was wrecked then the dice were loaded even more heavily against them. Stored in Ryman's mind was the chart reference for the rendezvous with Bigg which had arrived in a telegram from Hong Kong. He craved the chance to use it.

The tunnel was a hundred metres long and debouched into a high-vaulted cave which had been laid out in rows of racks — larger versions of those that might have been found in a wine cellar. The number of levels depended on the height of the cave but each rack was packed tight with dusty boxes bearing a graffiti of Chinese calligraphy.

Ryman flashed his torch but could decipher nothing. He turned to Lee Fong Yu. 'Can you read what it says?'

Yu twisted his head to follow the lettering. 'This row is bronzes from the period of the warring states.'

Ryman grunted. He had never thought that their task was going to be easy, but looking around him proved that what the Museum visitor saw was only the iceberg tip of the collection. This was where ninety-six per cent of it resided. He walked down one of the rows and the torch beam picked out a fork-lift truck. Some of the packing cases were stacked six high. The ceiling lowered and they came to the entrance to another cave, the opening fortified by brickwork. Again, rows of shelves stretched away in orderly lines.

'Well?' said Ryman.

Lee Fong Yu stepped forward. 'More bronzes. Shang Dynasty.'

'We'd better press on,' said Ryman. There were ten dynasties of bronzes represented in the Palace Museum and this was but one category of exhibit amongst thirteen. Unless they moved fast they could still be down here at daybreak.

They walked on past rows of dusty, cobweb-strewn boxes that looked as if they had not been opened for years. The air was cold and damp and Ryman shivered. His sweat-soaked shirt was clammy against his skin. Tiredness was catching up with him and the cold sapped his resistance. He stumbled and paused to swing

133

his arms and drive the blood round his body. They stood at the cross point of two aisles and, on impulse, Ryman made a right-angled turn and continued until he came to the edge of the cave. Here a brick wall had been built up to the limestone ceiling and the torch picked out several heavy metal doors that resembled those found on refrigeration units. Ryman approached one and pressed down the lever. There was a hiss and the door opened as if it had been sealed.

Ryman shone his torch inside. The small room was cold as a morgue and from its ceiling a row of scroll paintings hung down like pennants. Ryman pondered for a moment and then realised why they had been placed there. The paintings were a thousand years old and it was feared that exposure to light and air would destroy their already faded pigments. The paintings would stay here, sealed away from the masses, with only the occasional art historian to disturb their slumbers. Ryman put his shoulder to the heavy door and it closed with a soft sibilant sigh like the warning hiss of a snake. He pressed the lever down and turned to Lee Fong Yu who was at his shoulder. 'Nothing there for us.' He considered the advantages of the two of them splitting up, but there was also the danger of them getting lost, coupled with his own limited ability to decipher Chinese. Best to stay together. He glanced at his watch. The nightwatchmen would now be back from their round.

Ryman led the way along the wall past several more heavy metal doors. The roof descended and they came to another cave. This time the containers were more fragile and had many different shapes, a tall, slim cylinder being the most frequent. They were scattered over and beneath a wilderness of tables that stretched beyond the furthest range of the torch beams. 'Porcelain,' said Lee Fong Yu.

Ryman felt cheered. There were signs that work had been going on in the area; sawdust and straw packing surrounded a table on which were laid out half a dozen Ming bowls covered with a cloth. Ryman gazed down at one of them, admiring the perfect colours of the glazed enamel decoration: mandarin ducks resting amongst lotus flowers. These six items alone must be worth a king's ransom.

Lee Fong Yu was diligently examining containers on another table. He closed a box and moved on like an eager browser in an antique supermarket.

'Hei!' The excitement in the exclamation made Ryman spin round. Lee Fong Yu was waving his arms. 'This area here is for sculptures.'

Ryman hurried to his side. A dozen tables stretched away to the brick wall. 'It should be here.' Ryman shone his torch around trying to find any container that looked as if it had been opened recently.

'I will start by the wall.' Lee Fong Yu moved away.

Ryman dropped to his knees and flashed his torch beneath the table. Only certain boxes were the right size to hold the carving. He isolated one and reached forward into the darkness. A cobweb brushed against his skin and in the next instant something ran up his arm. It was a furry spider three inches across. He dashed it from his shoulder with an exclamation of disgust and brushed the remains of the cobweb from his fingers. His heart was pounding. Breathing deeply, he withdrew the container and prised off its lid. A thick wad of paper served as packaging and then there was the gleam of intricately carved ivory. With fumbling fingers, Ryman withdrew his prize. Excitement died. He was looking at a beautifully carved drinking vessel sculptured in the shape of a ship from either an elephant tusk or rhinoceros horn. Sadly he replaced it in its silk-lined leather case. It was exquisite and worth a small fortune, but to him, valueless.

He had returned the container and was reaching for another when he found Lee Fong Yu by his side. 'I think I have found it.'

Ryman's spirits leapt. His eyes sped to Lee Fong Yu's empty hands. 'Where?'

The little man said nothing but turned on his heel and moved towards the far tables. Ryman saw that one of the doors in the wall was open. Surely it could not be in there? But yes, Lee Fong Yu was gesturing with his torch and standing to one side. Eagerly, Ryman pressed forward and stared into the room. Illuminated by a beam of light, the carving stood on a table against the far wall like a religious relic on an altar. The shadow of its tracery projected like a rood screen on to the bricks. Ryman advanced towards it and then stopped. Like a flash of lightning from the storm outside came the realisation that he had stepped into a trap. The carving would never be stored here. Before he could turn, the heavy jade seal that Lee Fong Yu had dropped at the top of the staircase crashed down on the back of his head and the room filled with light. A bomb went off inside his brain and an unbearable pain seared through him as if a white hot poker had been thrust into one of his eye sockets. Something hard and cold smashed against his face and he realised that it was the concrete floor. That was all.

Flower could not understand why the telephone in Burton's flat did not answer. He must be there. Maybe the storm had caused a fault on the line. She pulled her cape around her shoulders and peered out into the rain-washed street. Already the water had overflowed the pavement and was nearly up to the box. Cars were going past behind a bow wave, their frenzied wipers barely making an impression on the downpour. She listened to the ringing tone for another weary minute and then hung up. He must be asleep. Perhaps he had taken a pill. No, that didn't make sense. If he was sleeping tonight he would be sleeping like a cat. She couldn't sleep. That was why she had tried to call him. Now she was worried; more worried. The box was steaming up and she rubbed her hand against the glass. An empty taxi was waiting at the lights. Flower pulled her cape over her head and ran out into the pouring rain.

Ryman moved his head and screamed. Something was sticking to the back of his scalp. Primed by the pain, his memory slowly filtered back through the throbbing waves. He was lying on his face on a cold floor and every time he moved, it hurt. It hurt a lot. But at least he could move; that was something positive. He slid his hand round towards the back of his head and realised he was lying underneath something; something that covered his body like a shroud. His fingers reached the base of his skull and nausea ploughed a path through his belly. The covering that had been thrown over him had stuck to his congealing blood. There was a swelling on his head like a growth.

Slowly, Ryman began to find out if his body was still working. He moved his toes, flexed his legs, twisted his shoulders, pressed the palms of his hands against the concrete and pushed; all the pain that arrived came from his head. Lee Fong Yu had only struck one blow. He could afford to conserve his strength. Trapped in this airtight chamber, Ryman knew that he would not survive until daybreak. The material thrown over his body was presumably intended to conceal it. Lee Fong Yu need not have bothered. Who was going to come near this empty, disused chamber? Perhaps the smell of decomposing flesh would eventually be distinguished from the overall pinched scent of decay that permeated the caves, but most likely his bones would be scoured white before anybody found them.

Ryman clenched his teeth and seized a fold of the material that covered his wound. Bracing himself, he pulled and wrenched his head sideways. Again a wave of pain and nausea swept through him, but his head was free. Moaning to himself against the throbbing agony, he struggled to his knees and crawled to the nearest wall. A milky way of stars burst before his eyes but he twisted and slumped with his head against the bricks. What in God's name was he going to do? He tilted his head back and then jerked forward as the swollen scalp made contact with the wall. His foot nudged something and he slowly edged a hand forward to meet his torch. Lee Fong Yu had obviously forgotten this in his eagerness to be on his way. Ryman hooded his eyes and switched on the torch. At first the bright light threatened to bring on an attack of vomiting, but he controlled himself and slowly moved his head to look about the room. The ivory carving had disappeared, which was no surprise, and apart from the worm-eaten table the room was empty.

He flashed the torch about and saw that all four walls were made of brick. The one in front of his head had a dark patch near its top and this, coupled with the musty smell, made him surmise that the brickwork must be damp. Bracing himself, he pushed his heels against the concrete and slowly forced himself into an upright position. The throbbing ache in his head was intense and he wondered if the blow had fractured his skull. Whether it had or not, there was no advantage in staying where he was. Slowly, and painfully, he felt his way along the wall to the door. There were no surprises here either. There was no handle on the inside of the heavy steel and it did not flinch when he put his shoulder to it. Gritting his teeth, he threw his weight forward, but only his head suffered. He had to stand still for almost a minute before it cleared.

Already the air in the room seemed stuffy and he wondered how much longer it would last. Was there any grain of comfort in the fact that water had permeated through some of the bricks? He felt his way round the wall again and raised his arms above his head.

His fingers made contact with a thin, slippery mould. This was the wall that had been built against the side of the cave; but presumably not flush against it. The sides of the other caves that he had seen had tailed away at an angle. If this was true then there must be a gap on the other side of the wall and also some kind of opening, however small, through which the water descended.

Ryman rubbed the mould from his fingers against a patch of dry wall. The presence of damp could well be a reason why the room was not being used to store materials. It had a weak point. Now that he had something to occupy his mind, Ryman found the pain easier to bear. He thumped the side of his fist against the wall which abutted on the limestone and then moved to the other walls to see if there was any difference in sound when he struck them. If there was, he had to confess that it probably only existed in his imagination. They all seemed intimidatingly thick. He felt in his pocket and searched for the keys. They had gone. Bloody fool! He had never really trusted Lee Fong Yu but he had never expected that the danger would come here. It was after they had left the Museum that he had resolved to keep his eyes skinned. The fury he felt against himself almost outweighed his desire for revenge.

Ryman thought again and felt inside his loose-fitting overalls. In case of problems with the display cabinets he had brought with him a steel screwdriver which would serve as a jemmy. He withdrew it from its stitched recess and approached the damp patch. Raising himself on tiptoe, he probed the space between two bricks. With a surge of excitement he felt the steel sink into the soft mortar. Eagerly, he dug deeper but was forced to stop by the wave of nausea that swept over him. He waited for his head to clear and slowly dragged the table across from the end wall. He tested that it would bear his weight and then climbed on to it with his torch wedged in the pocket of his overalls. He was only a couple of feet from the floor, but in his half-concussed condition it seemed as if he was looking down from a mountain top. He swayed and leaned stooped against the wall whilst another spasm passed. Steeling himself, with legs apart, he took the screwdriver and began to chip out the mortar around one of the bricks. The first one was going to be the most difficult. If he could prise that out, then it would be easier to attack the others. A blister appeared on the palm of his hand and was rubbed away; his fingers ached. Wedged as he was with his head nearly against the limestone it was becoming

138

difficult to breathe. Certainly the throbbing pain was as persistent as ever. He flicked out another section of mortar and inserted the screwdriver halfway up the brick to the depth of an inch. He pressed as hard as he could until he felt the blade about to snap. Nothing budged. He pressed again and a piece of the brick broke away. His heart plummeted. Was he going to have to chip out the brick bit by bit? He would be dead before he got it out.

Working slowly and painstakingly, he probed and scraped at the mortar until he could draw the blade round the brick to its full depth. Holding his breath, he moved the screwdriver to the opposite end and started to lever. For several seconds nothing happened, and then there was a click and the brick slid sideways to become firmly wedged against its neighbour. Forgetting pain, Ryman stuffed his fingers into the widened crack and tried to prise the brick out. It refused to move. Ryman took the screwdriver and inserted the blade where the brick was flush against its neighbour. Easing and teasing he edged it slightly forward and away from the surface of the wall and then returned to the other side to repeat the movement. Slowly the brick began to protrude from the wall until he was able to close his chafed fingertips about it and throw it triumphantly to the floor.

The success gave him strength and in the next half hour he had removed seven more bricks and was ready to start on the second layer. He drove himself because he knew that he dare not stop to rest. Not only the fear of suffocation dogged him but the realisation that every time he stopped it became more difficult to start again. His fingers were so raw and numb that they could hardly hold the screwdriver; his arms dropped automatically to his sides when they were not wedged in the opening. In this condition the blinding pain in his head was almost an advantage. It jarred him into a state of permanent wakefulness like a goad jabbing beneath his flesh. He might fall unconscious but he could never fall asleep.

Another twenty minutes and the first brick of the second layer was out. Ryman prayed that the wall might be only two bricks thick, but it was not to be. He reached into the cavity and tapped with the haft of the screwdriver. There was a hollow ring. That must be the last layer. He moved the torch onto the ledge he had formed and struggled on. Below him the table creaked and swayed. The constant motion had begun to loosen its ancient joints. Ryman smiled grimly to himself. His own ancient joints were hardly in any better condition. He jabbed, probed, scraped, prised and another half hour passed. The smell of damp was now strong in his nostrils and the bricks were cold and slimy. At last, one in the third row was revealed in its entirety. He set to work and the mortar came away easily, pattering down to the floor at his feet. He waited until there was a dark shadow round the brick and then pushed. It stirred. He pushed again and then drove forward with his fist. This time he felt it recoil. Forgetting pain, he smashed his barked knuckles against the brick. His arm carried on into space and his cheek stopped an inch from the wall. Like a stone dropped into a well, he heard the hollow thud of the brick hitting earth on the far side. A wave of cold, damp, stale air met his nostrils. It smelt like perfume.

CHAPTER EIGHT

Flower got out of the taxi into a small river. The rain had eased but the blustery wind was still kicking up flurries of water. The driver had said that one of the power lines was down on the north side of the city. Maybe this was why Burton's telephone was not being answered. Flower hobbled past the parked cars and rows of scooters. The street was in virtual darkness; only a few shop signs were illuminated. She reached the doorway of Burton's apartment block and shook the water from her cape and stamped her feet. The temperature had dropped twenty degrees and it now felt quite cold. Usually there was an old man, an ex-soldier, who had served with General Chiang Kai-shek on the mainland, who sat outside and acted as watchman, but the storm must have driven him away. Flower pressed against the door and stepped over the high threshold that was supposed to keep evil spirits from entering.

It was dark in the hall and she opened the door again to try and see the light switch. A shadowy figure skipped past through the rain, making her jump. She found the switch and flicked it down. Nothing happened. With a sigh of exasperation she felt her way along the wall to the staircase and started to climb. She felt uneasy and the darkness did not help. A flash of lightning cleaved the sky and illuminated the next bend in the stairs and a patriotic portrait of General Chiang We-kuo. Flower gritted her teeth and tightened her grip on the handrail. She reached the first landing and started to climb again. Apart from the sound of the rain and the wind gusting against the windows there was no sound. She envied everybody who was tucked up comfortably in their bed. This was no night to be out alone with an uneasy conscience. The second landing loomed up in another flash of lightning and she saw the fire doors which shut off the corridor in which Burton had his apartment. Eagerly she stepped forward and pushed open the door. A hand closed over her mouth and pulled her head back into the darkness.

Ryman writhed and wriggled and felt the jagged edges of bricks scoring his body. His head and shoulders were through the hole and he was ready to plunge into the unknown. Already the torch had shown a sloping wall of slippery limestone that pressed down just above his head. Whether he could find his way along it and back to the warehouses was something that might decide his life. He dropped the torch to the ground and pressed firmly against the wall, projecting himself forward. His testicles dragged painfully over the bricks and he plunged down trying to protect the back of his head. His hands and forearms took the first impact and he toppled over sideways with the breath driven from his body. The pain inside his head whirled into a million stabbing particles like the snowstorm in a paperweight. Ryman waited until the pain had subsided to a dull ache and picked up the torch. Taking a deep breath he scrambled to his knees and then to his feet.

Ahead of him, the rock sloped down steeply to a limestone floor. It was as if he was pressed against the wall of a tent. He shone the torch in both directions and set off back towards the tunnel. He had hardly covered a dozen paces when his hopes collapsed. The cave wall closed in flush against the brickwork. There was no way through. Wearily, he retraced his steps and set off in the opposite direction. Soon he was forced to drop to his hands and knees to crawl beneath rock that descended almost to ground level. He was entering a series of small caves where the roofs pressed down lower and lower. The effect was claustrophobic and the air impregnated with an odour that made him want to gag. Stretched full length, he wriggled forward and lowered his throbbing head beneath yet another barrier. Twelve feet ahead, the torch's dim light showed the brick wall meeting the limestone with barely space for a hand to squeeze between them. This was the end of the road.

Ryman closed his eyes and rested his cheek on the damp stone. After all he had been through, it looked as if he was going to perish here in this miserable fold in the ground that stank like a fox's earth. He spat the evil taste from his mouth and wondered what the smell was. It was more than damp or vegetable decay. He shone the torch again and saw that there was a dark shadow to the left of the chamber before him. He wriggled forward and the shadow became an opening. The roof made a half-open mouth where it failed to descend to floor level.

Ryman hesitated and then crawled forward again. There was no point in holding back. If he was going to die he might as well die fighting. He held the torch before him and wriggled forward on his elbows. Immediately the smell became more nauseating. There was a scent of animal decomposition and Ryman wondered if some creature had crawled down to the bowels of the earth to die. It was an unhappy omen for his own chances of survival. He approached the opening and paused. Before him he could hear a sound: the rhythmic drip, drip, drip of falling water. It induced a faint hope that there might be some kind of course carrying the water down from above. He wriggled forward and found the rock opening up above his head. It was not so much another cave as a cleft in the limestone made aeons before when the earth was still finding its shape. Ryman shone his torch and sucked in his breath in amazement. At the top of the fissure was a section of square metal piping following the line of the wall. It must be the source of air for the ventilation system. His heart exulted. If it was, then it must surely lead to the side of the hillside. All he had to do was follow it to be free. He stumbled forward and thumped his fist against the metal. There was a satisfying ringing noise that echoed away into the darkness. Feeling a new surge of strength he rested one hand on the piping and began to pursue it along the narrow defile. The metal was wet and the ground beneath his feet slippery. The storm rain must be leaking down through the hillside.

Only one thing was still worrying him. With every step, the stench was getting worse. It became so bad that he had to hold his hand over his mouth and nostrils. It puzzled him and it frightened him. Ahead, the ground began to descend and he had to reach up to continue touching the pipe. Something glinted in the darkness and the smell became unbearable. He shone the torch and saw that the space before him opened up into a chamber filled with water. The water was moving and in it there were objects. He came closer, feeling that he was going to throw up. A welter of human faeces met his eyes and amongst them the body of a dead dog grossly swollen. On its grey, furless back, three rats looked up inquisitively into the torch beam. Ryman jerked his torch away from the living nightmare as there was a splatter of water from the far side of the cave. Over a lip of rock slopped a fresh wave of sewage. Ryman scanned the brown, foam-flecked scum around

143

the walls and realised what had happened. The rain had flooded the storm drains and overflown the natural cesspools that the hollow limestone provided for the dwellings on the hillside. Now the nauseating waste was finding a new level.

Ryman shone the torch to pick out the route of ventilation piping. It followed the wall ten feet above the swill of human detritus and then turned off at an angle to disappear into the roof of the cave. Apart from the narrow opening by which the sewage entered the cave and the passage he had followed from the wall, it was the only way out. Fighting the tide of revulsion that surged up inside him, Ryman sank to a sitting position and lowered his legs into the noisome liquid. When it had reached chest level his feet touched bottom and he began to wade forward slowly, holding his torch above his head.

Flower struggled desperately and turned to see the man who was holding her. He drew her close to him and gestured that she should be silent before releasing his hand.

'Henry!'

'Sh! Don't say anything.' He drew her behind him up the stairs that led to the next landing. 'I think somebody's watching the flat.'

'Who would be doing that?'

'I don't know. What are you doing here?'

'I was frightened. I couldn't sleep. I didn't want to wait until morning.'

'You came to a bad place to sleep.' He brushed a rain-sodden strand of hair away and thought how beautiful she looked.

'What do you mean? Can we not go to your flat?'

'If anybody comes we'll be safer here.'

'But who would be watching the flat?'

'Maybe it's something to do with Lee Fong Yu.'

'You think he is trying a trick?'

'A double-cross? Maybe. He knows we're all meeting up here tomorrow with the stuff. He doesn't know what's happening after that. It would be the right moment to try something.'

'Or maybe the men are looking for him.'

'I thought of that too. I had the feeling that somebody was following us when we drove to the Museum. Either way I thought it better to stay out of my room.'

'You cannot stay here all night.'

'Do you have a better alternative?'

Flower hesitated. 'Come to my flat. We can get out by the fire escape.' She squeezed his arm. 'I have done it myself. The van is in the garage and we can drive past tomorrow to see if the men are still here. If they are, we must try and contact Donald and Lee Fong Yu when they leave the Museum.'

Burton thought over what she had said before pulling her to him and kissing her on the forehead. 'You're a treasure,' he said.

Ryman gagged and shone his torch up the chimney that held the ventilation pipe. The sewage was an inch below his chin and rats were squeaking from the rocks a few feet away. They seemed to have no fear and looked at him merely with curiosity. There were struts running from the piping to the wall and these had presumably been placed by somebody descending the chimney as the sections of the ventilation system were installed. They were not going to be easy to circumvent; especially for somebody of his size. He thrust the torch into the top pocket of his jacket and dragged himself to the rock. He had only one thought: to get away from this hideous place. Seizing an outcrop of rock he started to pull himself upwards. It was not easy. The limestone was as slippery as soap and there were few footholds. He had climbed about three feet when the rock squeezed from between his fingers and he fell backwards. The fetid water closed over his head and he fought his way upright as the rats squeaked in alarm and derision. Even in his disgust and panic he clapped a hand to his chest to make sure his torch was still there. To lose his only source of light in this awful place would be to abandon all expectation of survival. Trying to stay calm and not to let nausea overcome him, he rubbed his hands against a crust of rock and started again.

Pressing with his knees and elbows he managed to lever himself from the stinking flood and spread his weight so that he could edge his way upwards scarcely separated from the rock. At last, timorously, inch by painful inch, he was able to extend a hand and seize the first strut that supported the ventilation piping. He started to draw himself up and soon realised that the bars were not intended to bear a man's weight. He could feel the base stirring in its mooring and the metal sheeting of the piping creaking under

145

the strain that was being placed on it. As quickly as he was able, he found a foothold and braced his shoulders against the beginning of the chimney. He rested for a moment and then forced himself to continue. The minute he stopped moving he felt the cold embalming hands of death pinching his body as if checking for the onset of rigor mortis. At least he knew that somewhere above his head there must be a way out. All he had to do was find the strength to reach it.

An hour later he was still painfully easing himself upwards. Above and below him like the buckled rungs of a metal ladder stretched the irregularly placed struts that held the ventilation piping in place. Sometimes they ascended vertically, sometimes at an angle. Sometimes there was the noise of water pattering away in the darkness that suggested other fissures. Always there was pain and an increasing weariness. The ache in his head now seemed to have spread out through his whole body, but in a disjointed way so that there was no rhythm to it, only an acupuncture of sly thrusts and needle-sharp jabs that came when and where they were least expected. He felt that small pieces of him were dying with each rung of the interminable ladder.

How far did he have to go? That was the question he could never answer. Was he clawing his way towards the side of the hill or towards its top? There was no point in trying to detect whether the air smelt purer. The stench of sewage still clung to him like a film. No draught or hint of wind disturbed the deathly silence of the tunnel. When he stopped, all he could hear was his own laboured breathing and sometimes the sound of water; usually dripping.

He dragged his watch to his eyes and saw that the dawn would soon be coming up. It was good to have a watch to tell you things like that. How did earthworms tell? Perhaps they didn't care. At least they could pop their heads above ground when they felt like finding out. Ryman ground his teeth and stretched out his arms towards the next strut. If worms could do it, so could he. He wasn't going to die down here. If he could just force himself to keep plugging on, sooner or later he must suddenly see a circle of light above his head. If the reward was the rest of his life in Taipei gaol, it was still worth it.

Another half hour and he was on a gradient. He liked gradients. Not only was the going easier but there was always the prospect

146

that when you got to the end you could look up and see sky above your head. When you were hauling your tortured body up a chimney, you could see exactly what lay ahead of you — and it was always more chimney.

Ryman paused. He could hear something. Something other than the trickle of descending water. A squeaking noise. He flinched with fear and disgust — not more rats. The memory of what he had left behind was one of the things that kept him going. The thought of those filthy, quivering bodies passing anywhere near him made him want to scream. He listened again. The noise was higher pitched than the sound the rats had made. He sniffed and shook his head. Was it his imagination or was there a fresh stench apart from that which clung to his body like a second skin; a sharp, acid putrescence which burnt the inside of his nostrils? Prey to new horrors, he continued to edge forward towards the bend in the chimney. The torch revealed what might be an opening ahead. It was from this that the squeaking was coming.

He was four feet from the hole when the torch started to flicker. He turned it off and then turned it on again. The darkness magnified the noise and fear; the smell became more pungent. He was terrified. He must get past the hole and to the bend in the rock. The torch flickered and then the light oozed away to the glow of one tiny filament and went out.

Ryman struck the torch against the rock and the noise echoed away along the chimney. The squeaking became more strident. Still holding the torch, but now as a weapon, he scrambled forward in a panic. The rock closed in on the casing of the ventilation system and he struck the back of his head a blow that sent white-hot coils of pain expanding through his body. He blundered into a strut and felt something wet and slimy squeeze onto his hands.

The squeaking came from beside his head; he could feel a disgusting breath of warm air that came from living creatures. With every tortured second he expected to feel something touch him. Something that would complete the nightmare and drive him mad. His scrabbling hands met solid rock and he clawed desperately. This must be the bend. He twisted and felt upwards. At first he could not believe what he saw: a jagged circle of grey tinged with pink. It was the sky showing the first signs that dawn was approaching. His heart started to lift and then fell. He was

147

looking at the heavens through a grille and as he watched, horrible shapes began to squeeze through the bars and drop down towards him. Bats returning to their lair after a night's hunting. Not one or two, or half a dozen, but a dense mass that had soon blackened out the sky above his head. He glimpsed the terrifying pointed teeth and then saw nothing; only felt them jostling past him, their wings and claws scratching his face, their angry squeaking filling his ears. Their sheer weight nearly brushed him from his perch and carried him with them. He wanted to scream but his mouth was tight-closed and his face pressed against the rock. There seemed to be no end to them as they poured down on him. The smell and the sensation of them wriggling past his body was the most sickening thing he had ever known; the slithering wings, the furry bodies, the clawing feet.

At last the tide slackened and a deafening cacophony of squeaking rose from beneath him. Returning bats still fluttered past but he was able to continue his climb. The walls were streaked with fresh excrement, but his only thought was the grille and whether he could get past it. Spattered with filth, he hauled himself up the last few feet until the top of his head was six inches from the bars. The grille was set in concrete but there was a trap-door in its centre, secured by a rusty padlock. Ryman cast his useless torch away and with fumbling fingers withdrew his screwdriver. He thrust a hand through the bars and inserted the blade between the jaws of the padlock. Another flurry of bats arrived and he saw their hideous long-eared faces in close-up as they squeezed by. Desperately he wrenched at the screwdriver. There was a snapping noise and he fell backwards heavily against the wall. The blade had snapped. He heard the sound of it tinkling away into the darkness. He looked up. The padlock was swinging to and fro, its hasp had sprung open.

Forgetting the pain, Ryman threw himself forward and tore away the padlock. He thrust upwards and the trap-door creaked and lifted a few inches. He pushed his arm out and seized the grille, striking out with his legs so that he could find a foothold and propel himself to safety. His shoulder pressed against the bottom of the trap-door and he forced it up until it clattered backwards sending the sound ringing across the hillside. Calling on his last reserves of energy, he hauled himself out and knelt shaking beside the fine mesh grille of the ventilation in-take.

A pool of water had formed against the concrete projection and Ryman tore off his overalls and bathed his naked body until all the filth had been washed away. Then he took his overalls and soaked and pummelled them; rinsed them out and stretched them over a bush to dry. Where he had emerged, the vegetation was thick and there were no landmarks. Rain was dripping from the sodden trees and there was a wash of grey in the sky. Ryman looked about him and found that his head was spinning. His knees buckled and he took an unsteady step before toppling sideways and sprawling across the wet earth. Before his head had touched the ground, he had fallen into an exhausted sleep.

'Good morning,' said Burton with forced brightness. '*Tsau an,*' perhaps I should say.'

Chang winced. He did not care for Burton's attempts to speak Chinese. 'Good morning,' he said coldly. 'I am glad you are punctual.' They were waiting on the steps, watching one of the Museum officials open the doors. Burton could see the two night-watchmen on the other side of the glass carrying their food containers. He was relieved to see that their faces bore no hint of alarm or consternation. One of them yawned.

'I'll just pop across and buy some tickets,' said Burton. 'No reason why we shouldn't pay our share.'

Chang watched him cross the road to the ticket office and sniffed. If the Englishman thought that he could ingratiate himself by such trifling gestures he was wrong. There were going to be no more events at the Museum. Chang turned away and looked beyond the straggle of waiting visitors to another source of annoyance: the debris of foliage that had been brought down by the typhoon. Burton returned, brandishing three tickets. He followed Chang's gaze. 'Terrible storm last night. I hardly slept a wink. I suppose we're in for quite a few of those.'

'It is the season,' said Chang.

The door was open and he started forward. Burton beckoned to the two youths who helped him manhandle materials whenever there was an event. Another taxi full of tourists arrived, cameras flapping. The window of the ticket booth slid back. Burton stepped over the threshold. Christ! he thought, this is it. There was a nervous pain in his chest that seemed to be hardening into a rock.

149

He glanced back again at the two nightwatchmen who were standing back respectfully. They inclined their heads as Chang went past. No word was spoken. Two security men who had arrived earlier were flexing their arms as if preparing for a long day. They bowed as Chang approached. A sharp crack like a pistol shot made Burton jerk round nervously. One of the cloakroom attendants had dropped a coat hanger.

Chang paused by the stairs. 'I will leave you to remove your things. You will come to my office when you have finished. I would like to see that everything is' — he paused to choose his word — 'correct.' 'Of course,' said Burton. He watched Chang's precise little footsteps measure their path towards the staircase and turned back to the main entrance. The first visitors were coming in now; showing their tickets and fanning out into the Museum or pausing to check-in their cameras. A coach went past. Good, let there be more of them. Somewhere in the building, Ryman and Lee Fong Yu would be hiding, waiting to mingle with the visitors and eventually walk out by the lower ground floor exit.

Burton moved to the lift and pressed the button. The doors hissed open immediately, making him jump. He stepped inside, the two Chinese with him. 'When we've loaded everything in the van I'll drop you off downtown. I'm going to take the stuff back later. There's no need for you to hang around.' The two youths nodded. That suited them.

The lift shuddered to a halt and Burton noticed the long pause before the doors opened. It was the first time he had been so painfully aware of it. He led the way up the steps and entered the tower room. The light was strong, but the outside of the windows was patterned with leaves and undulations of brown mud deposited by the storm. The air stank of dead cigarettes. Some flies were crawling over the paper sheets that covered the uneaten food.

Burton pushed back a screen and gestured to the crates that were reserved for the plates and the dirty glasses. 'These should be big enough for what's out there.' He wrinkled his brows self-accusingly. 'I think I must have over-estimated the numbers.'

The Chinese appeared unconcerned. They put the crates on two trolleys and wheeled them outside. Burton waited until he heard the sound of cutlery being loaded and approached the tin boxes. Now they had been separated and lay a few feet apart. He dropped to his knees, his heart thumping. He listened to make sure that the two Chinese were still at work on the other side of the screen and pushed in the catch. He lifted the lid and peered inside. Like a treasure trove, the box swelled with the bulky outline of familiar packages. He closed the lid firmly and locked it with a small padlock. The stuff was here. They had done it!

Lee Fong Yu heard the washroom door open and swung his feet from the ground. There was a gap beneath the door of the cubicle in which he was sitting and with it the chance, the faintest chance, that somebody would see his legs and wonder what he was doing there at this hour. He listened intently and was rewarded with the sound of a tap being turned on, followed, shortly afterwards, by the screech of a roller towel. He waited a few more moments and the door banged shut.

Lee Fong Yu lowered his legs. He would stay where he was for another few minutes and then go out. He patted the inside pocket of his jacket that contained the Kuei seal and congratulated himself for his quick thinking in having told Ryman that it was the torch that had fallen outside the gallery. In his pockets were three other small but priceless objects that he had filched unbeknownst to Ryman: two jade cicadas and a ram and shepherd carved in flawless black jade. These alone were more than adequate recompense for his night's work. In addition he could look forward to his increased share of the larger items left in the metal boxes. He would catch up with those later at Burton's apartment. Ryman's absence would of course be a complete mystery to him. He would shrug his shoulders and say that perhaps the big man had gone straight to the boat. As time passed and nobody arrived they would have to believe him.

Lee Fong Yu stood up and adjusted his jacket. At a later date he would take further steps to reduce the number of people with an interest in the treasure. He would have preferred to have done it sooner but he was going to need assistance to get out of the country. The door creaked and somebody else came in. Lee Fong Yu flushed the lavatory and left the cubicle. The man standing with his back to him did not turn round.

Outside there was nobody in the gallery and he walked to the lift and looked about him as he waited for it to come. On the wall opposite was the mosaic of a serpent with its forked tongue protruding. Lee Fong Yu's eyes flickered uneasily. The image stirred unpleasant memories. He thought of the Snake Man behind the Lung Shan Temple and his premonition that his time was running out. The doors hissed open behind him and he spun round to be faced by a middle-aged Japanese leading a small child by the hand. He stepped aside and got into the lift, surprised by the sudden feeling of fear that had gripped him. The eye of the snake gleamed red as the doors closed on it.

Lee Fong Yu smoothed his hands down his jacket and watched the amber light that indicated each floor as he descended; third, second, first, ground, lower ground. The doors opened and he could see the exit to his left. He started to walk across the marble. The woman behind the counter of the souvenir stall looked up, but he avoided her eye. There was no sign of a security guard. Five more paces and he would be outside the building. 'Excuse me.' Lee Fong Yu kept walking. 'Excuse me.' A figure hurried from behind a pillar and touched his arm. 'Are you leaving?' The man wore the uniform of a security guard.

'Yes, I have to meet someone.'

The guard did not seem to require any further explanation. He held out his hand. 'I will stamp your ticket.'

Lee Fong Yu felt as if he had been subjected to a powerful electric shock. 'Of course.' He swallowed and started to pat his pockets. He could feel the jade seal bulging against his chest.

The guard stretched out a finger helpfully. 'Is it there?' He felt Lee Fong Yu's jacket and his brow crinkled.

'I think you dropped this.' Burton rose from a stooped position and approached the two men holding out his entrance ticket. He had just descended the stairs to go to Chang's office.

Lee Fong Yu hesitated for the fraction of a second and then almost snatched the ticket. '*Jye jye ni*. Thank you. Thank you very much.'

The guard smiled and stamped the ticket. 'It is foolish to have to pay twice.'

'Very', said Lee Fong Yu. He accepted the ticket and bowed to Burton and the guard before going out.

Outside, the steps rose steeply to the parking area and the watery rays of a hazy sun reached down to greet him. Still clutching the ticket tightly between finger and thumb, he emerged from the shadows. He took a deep breath and savoured the feeling of release that swept over him. A private car went past, and then a battered taxi pulled out from beside a parked coach. He raised a hand to hail it and then dropped it again. There were passengers in the front and back seat. He had hardly turned round when an uneasy thought struck him. How had a taxi managed to pick up a fare here at this hour of the morning? Before he could do anything, the taxi had stopped beside him and a door swung open so that it nearly hit him. He looked down to see a pistol pointing up at him. 'Get in!' For a second, the passage of all life through his body seemed to be suspended. The man holding the pistol had a snake tattooed on the back of his hand.

Ryman shivered. Putting on wet garments was disagreeable. Putting on wet clothes impregnated with foul-smelling ordure was even worse. At least the pain in his head had diminished to a dull ache and the swelling had subsided; his skull had not been fractured. If his physical condition gave some faint cause for optimism, other things did not. It was now past ten o'clock. The drugged sleep into which he had fallen must have been some kind of concussion. If there had been no slip-ups at the Museum, then Lee Fong Yu and the others would be converging at Burton's flat before setting off for the rendezvous with Crosby and the boat. He needed to get there fast. Lee Fong Yu had tried to kill him; it was a matter of conjecture as to how long he intended to let the others live.

Ryman forced his feet into his sodden shoes and pulled himself to his feet. A wave of nausea passed through him, but he shook it off and clawed his fingers through his tangled hair. Where the hell was he and how long was it going to take to get back to Burton's flat? He rubbed his cramped limbs and set off along an overgrown path leading away from the grille. The vegetation was high and he could see no more than a few feet in front of him. It was hot and clammy but there were still clouds in the sky — wispy cirrus clouds, mares' tails that boded ill and meant that another typhoon was lurking. There was a crackling above his head and a small monkey swung away, chattering in alarm and anger. It clutched some berries in its paw and the sight reminded him of how hungry he was. His stomach ached.

The path veered sharply to the right and disappeared into fresh, green grass, high as a man. Ryman cursed and then saw something. Poking over the horizon was the tip of an electric pylon. It must be carrying the power line that ran over the hill behind the Museum. It must also have some access to a road.

Ryman pressed forward into the grass and a mad chirping of grasshoppers. The lower half of his body was soon soaked and covered in a rash of seeds and burrs. It was not a discomfort he noticed; he was trying to keep his eye on the tip of the pylon that rose and dipped like a float in the undulating sea of grass. He brushed clouds of pollen from his cheeks and ploughed on, distracted only by the occasional rustlings in the grass about him and the difficulty of keeping his feet on the slippery rain-soaked slopes.

At last he could see the pylon through the trees, rising in stages like an open-work pagoda on the summit of the hill. He dropped into a low ditch, took evasive action as a toad the size of a door-stop sprouted beneath his feet, and scrambled into another patch of thick grass which he found was sharp enough to cut him to the bone. Leading with his elbows, he pushed forward and suddenly found the pylon rising above the grass immediately in front of him. He had taken two more steps when the earth disappeared below his feet and he emerged from the grass as if thrust through a swing door. A steep bank fell away beneath him and he slithered down it to arrive at the bottom of a narrow path, soggy from the overnight rains.

Five yards away, three Chinese were staring at him in amazement. They wore white tunics and yellow, metal helmets with the insignia of the Electricity Corporation on them. At their belts hung a selection of spanners, pincers and wire cutters. The reason for their presence was obvious. Twenty yards down the pathway an uprooted tree had toppled against the wires. Its topmost branches were burnt black. Ryman realised that his own appearance was going to be more difficult to explain.

He pulled himself to his feet and brushed himself down briskly. 'Good morning.' The words emerged from his mouth with a jauntiness that encouraged him. 'This damn storm's got a lot to answer for, eh?' He watched the reaction of his words closely. The Chinese looked at each other, each one secretly willing the other to reply. If they did speak any English it was clearly not a tongue they were happy with. Good. This gave him an advantage. As he dusted his sleeves, he was looking about him quickly. The pylon blocked the route behind him and there were no footprints in the

154

mud. The men must have come up the path. He moved towards them and gestured in the direction he had come. 'Bad slide down there. Threatening some of the houses. Going to have our work cut out to block it off.' He purposely spoke fast and slurred his words making himself as difficult to understand as possible. One of the Chinese nodded a response and pointed to the tree as if indicating that everybody had their problems. None of them wanted to lose face before each other or the Ang Moh by saying that they did not have the faintest idea what he was talking about or what he was doing there. Ryman started to walk down the track. 'Another *tai-fung* and we're going to be in trouble.' At the mention of the word '*tai-fung*' there was a general nodding of heads, and Ryman waved cheerfully and authoritatively and set off down the track walking easier with every step.

'Where the hell are they?' said Burton.

'Calm yourself,' said Flower. 'They will not want to leave too quickly. It will create suspicions.' They were waiting in Burton's flat, Flower sitting, Burton pacing up and down that part of the floor which was not covered with the containers removed from the tower room at the Museum.

'It's nearly eleven,' complained Burton.

'Maybe they are stuck in a traffic jam — like everybody else in Taipei.' Flower smiled up at him reassuringly. 'You must not always think that the worst is going to happen. Look at this morning; there was nobody here, was there?'

It was true. When they had driven past the flat a few times before Burton had gone to the Museum there had been no sign of anybody watching it. Maybe he had imagined being tailed with Lee Fong Yu and the two men outside the Szechuan Restaurant. If this was so he was grateful. However, he resented Flower's suggestion that he was an alarmist. 'You're a fine one to talk about worrying,' he said. 'What about the fuss you made over the Ju ware?'

Flower flushed angrily. 'That is different.' She tapped her slender breasts. 'It is something I feel in my heart. I am still unhappy. But I do not look for things that do not exist.'

'Yes, but...' Burton threw his arms apart in a gesture of exasperation. 'What's the point of talking to you about it?'

'Because I would not understand?' Her voice was taunting.

Burton said nothing but walked into the kitchenette and wrenched open the door of the refrigerator. The arguing was making him feel hungry. The shelves were almost bare. He had purposely let stocks run down. He flipped open the vegetable tray; one banana more black than yellow.

Flower appeared at his elbow. 'Don't you have any food to offer them when they come? They will be very hungry. You should have thought of that.'

Once again Burton knew that she was right but he was not prepared to admit it. 'There's plenty of food left over from last night. If you were so worried, you could have provided something.'

Flower said nothing but crossed to one of the cutlery boxes and struggled to pull back the catches. Burton followed her into the room. 'Not that one.' He opened one of the food boxes and then straightened up in surprise. Ryman's shoes, jacket, trousers and tie had been crumpled up and shoved into one of the corners. 'That's strange. He hadn't changed back into his clothes.' A terrible thought struck him. 'He can't still be in the museum.'

Flower peered down into the box. 'Perhaps he found another way out. A safer way.'

'Then why isn't he here now?'

Flower didn't answer immediately. She touched the clothes, almost tenderly, as if Ryman might still be inside them. 'Perhaps there is some reason why it is not safe for him to come here!'

'So what are we going to do?' The edge of desperation in Burton's voice had returned. Flower looked at him and saw him for what he was. Little more than a boy. She was going to have to make the decisions. 'I think we should go to the rendez-vous point with the boat and wait there. That was what was agreed.'

Burton crossed to the window and pulled down a section of the blind to peer out. 'I did see something.' His tone was one of unhappy resignation.

'Donald and Lee Fong Yu have probably gone straight to the coast. They will meet us there.' Flower was trying to persuade herself.

'Yes.' Burton crossed to the treasure box and dropped to one knee. He opened it and prised open the container that held the ivory carving. Withdrawing it carefully he savoured the roughness of the intricate openwork tracery against his fingers and probed one of the concentric balls. It glided round carrying the other eighteen miraculous little spheres with it. All this painstakingly carved from one rhinoceros horn. It gave a reality to the enormous stakes they had been playing for. Burton slid the carving back into its case and looked up at Flower. 'At least we have the stuff.' He read the sudden weariness that had flared up in Flower's eyes and hastened to correct any wrong impression. 'I didn't mean...'

Flower's voice cut in firmly. 'I will fetch the van. You bring down the box and some food.'

Burton did not argue.

'I hope your cold is better,' said Chang politely. He moved his arm rest to show that he wished to continue drawing up his plans for the Porcelain Exhibition.

Suo Chih-ming did not move. 'Much better, thank you. I am sorry that I was forced to miss the changing of the exhibits.'

Chang sat back in his chair and pushed aside his brush-holders; the gesture of a man whose work routine has been totally destroyed. 'It does not matter. We managed very well without you.' Chang did not like Suo Chih-ming, whose special interest was the 3,894 jade items held by the Museum. He found him complacent, narrow minded and pedagogic — charges that most of the Museum officials levelled at each other in the privacy of their own thoughts. Furthermore, he suspected that his colleague had not been ill, but had been malingering so that he might don his yellow robe and attend the ceremonies at the Confucian Temple in Talung Street.

After his ambivalent response Chang imagined that Suo Chih-ming would take the hint and retire, but he continued to hold his ground. Chang knew the man well enough to tell that there was something on his mind. The peevish expression and the pinched nostrils suggested that he had fault to find. Chang waited impatiently and the words were not long in coming.

'I thought it had been agreed that the Jadeite cabbage would be on permanent display?'

'It was.'

'Then why has it been removed?'

Chang tapped the base of his brush against the desk. 'It has not been removed.'

Suo Chih-ming tilted his head censoriously. 'When I returned this morning I walked round all my exhibits to ensure that the changes I had asked for had been made. The Jadeite cabbage was not there.'

Chang pushed back his chair. 'Then there has been some kind of mistake. I was here when the exhibits were being exchanged and I gave very explicit instructions which were based on the suggestions made by each Director.' He stood up. 'Come, we will go and look together. I am certain there is a very simple explanation.'

Ryman hurried down the deep furrow of the track, yearning to see some sign of civilization ahead. He must get to a telephone and warn Burton. Every second that passed increased the danger.

Something glinted ahead and he picked out the grey shape of a Toyota Land Cruiser. He drew nearer and recognised the insignia of the Electric Corporation on its side. The vehicle was parked at the edge of a wide waterlogged track running at right angles to the path. There was nobody in the driving seat. Ryman glanced to right and left. The road was empty. Tense with nerves, he broke into a stumbling run and squelched to a halt beside the cab. He brushed mud from the window to glance inside and was rewarded with the sight of two keys dangling from the ignition. Heart pounding, he wrenched open the door and slid across the seat. He turned the key and the engine sprang to life immediately. His foot slipped on the clutch and he let it out too fast and nearly stalled. The vehicle jerked forward and he had started to make a U-turn before he realised that the handbrake was still on. He released it and the Land Cruiser skidded, hurling a spray of mud against the wheel flaps. He swore at himself and eased his foot off the accelerator. Like a sailing vessel righting itself after a squall, the vehicle stopped shuddering and bumped off down the track. The first bend loomed up, and beyond it, down the thickly wooded hillside, could be glimpsed Taipei.

Lee Fong Yu screamed, and the sound seemed to be made not by

158

his vocal chords but by the actual physical disintegration of his body. It was the sound of the strings that gave the marionette life being ripped from their moorings.

'Where have they taken the boxes?'

Through the thin slits between his grotesquely swollen eyelids and cheeks he could squint into a red mist of pain. In the mist swirled a face, and from it one cruel, vengeful eye peered down at him. The other eye and most of the features, save the mouth, were obscured behind a swathe of bandages. It was the man he had taken the axe to at the snake stall. Through everything they did to him he cursed himself with one reproach: 'Why did I not strike harder?'

'Talk!'

The gimlet of pain twisted again and he screamed, his body arching from the table. A contemptuous blow smashed him flat again. The heavy jade seal floated above his head and then disappeared. They had searched his clothes and found everything. Now they were searching inside him, picking over his bones for scraps of truth. If only telling them were a guarantee that he would die quickly... There was a hiss and a roar, and a brilliant blue and white flame stabbed the air before him like the feather of a beautiful bird. Its noise was the noise of fear; the noise of a snake rearing up to strike; but its power to mutilate and inflict pain was more terrible than that of any serpent.

Lee Fong Yu felt his legs being pulled apart. He swallowed blood and began to talk.

'So how many items are missing?' said the inspector. He was a small, precise man who spoke flawless Mandarin with a clipped accent.

Chang looked round his tiny office in bewilderment. 'I cannot be certain yet, but it seems that we have lost our most important exhibit in every category. If one had to select a range of pieces that represented in themselves everything that was finest in our cultural heritage, then these would have been they.'

The inspector nodded. He was well aware of the seriousness of the situation. 'And there is still no indication of how the thieves got into the building?'

'We have found nothing, no.'

159

'And of course there is no indication that any of the cabinets have been forced. You would agree with that?'

'Emphatically,' said Chang.

'How many people hold keys to the cabinets?'

'Each Director will have a set of keys that correspond to the exhibits under his control. The Managing Director holds a complete set of keys as, of course, do I.' Chang gestured to the wall behind him.

'You keep your door locked when you leave the Museum at night?'

'Whenever I leave the room.'

'And how long have the nightwatchmen been with you?'

'None of them less than ten years. They live on the site. They are like part of the Museum family. Surely you do not think...'

The inspector raised a reassuring hand. 'We have to consider every possibility. You must agree that from the evidence we have at the moment some interior collusion seems likely, if not inevitable. Every man has his price.'

The inspector did not search out his eyes when he uttered his last words or give them any special stress, but they awoke in Chang a terrible possibility. Could anybody think that he was involved in this affair? It was almost too terrible to think about. He noticed that one of the policemen was taking notes. The inspector continued to speak calmly and methodically. 'Now, let us return to the subject of when the theft was committed. You say that you yourself saw some of the pieces two days ago?'

'That is correct. On the occasion of the public holiday. These are the only times we have to change the exhibits. I certainly remember seeing the Ju ware because I was thinking about it in connection with a porcelain exhibition we are planning to hold.'

'So there would have been a fair number of people in the Museum at that time?'

'The department heads and their assistants. About twenty-five or thirty people on this occasion. I could give you the exact figure.'

'All of them you know well?'

'The department heads certainly. Most of their assistants as well. The staff here does not change a great deal. People consider it a privilege to work at the National Palace Museum.'

'Very understandably,' said the inspector. 'Well, we will talk to

160

all these men as soon as possible. They may have noticed something unusual. Is there any other exhibition or event that had taken place here recently?'

Chang shook his head. 'No, the last exhibition we had here was of paintings of animals and birds....' He broke off. Sitting in front of him on his desk was an antique *Chen-chih* or paperweight that much to his surprise and embarrassment Burton had given him that very morning. He poked it with his finger before continuing. 'You could hardly call it an exhibition, but last evening the English-Speaking Union held a function in the Tower Room.'

'You know the people responsible for that?'

'Oh yes. A young Englishman called Henry Burton.'

The inspector nodded to one of his subordinates. 'Take his address. We will send somebody to talk to him.'

Ryman parked as close as he could to the flat without being visible from it and flung open the door of the Land Cruiser, nearly knocking a Chinese off his scooter. The man started to remonstrate and then quickly continued on his way. A dishevelled Ryman in grimy, stinking overalls was an intimidating sight as he reared up from the driver's seat.

Ryman was worried. There had been no answer when he had eventually found a telephone and called the flat, and he needed to know why. Had they left for the coast or had something gone wrong at the Museum? In the latter case, he would have expected Flower to be at the flat and to have answered the telephone. Hammering away inside him was the terrible fear that Lee Fong Yu had done away with both Flower and Burton so that he could make off with the loot. Their bodies would be lying in the flat in a pool of blood.

Ryman ran across the road and kept close to the wall, ignoring the chattering of the Chinese who pointed at him as if he was a visitor from another planet. A child who approached him was snatched away by its mother and an old man selling cinnamon sticks looked up from his wares, mouth agape, as he stalked through the scooter-strewn cloisters and the gutters overflowing with storm rubbish. He reached the entrance to the flats and the old soldier with his rice bowl, chop sticks and mouth all converging, glimpsed him only as a shadow as he went past.

Ryman went up the stairs two at a time and dropped his shoulders into the swing doors. Half a dozen strides and he was outside Burton's flat. He seized the door handle and flung his weight forward as it twisted. The door burst open and crashed against something lying on the floor. It was an emptied canteen of cutlery. The room looked as if a bomb had exploded inside it. The contents of half a dozen boxes collected from the Museum were strewn everywhere, plus the interior of every cupboard and drawer in the flat. There was a noise behind him, and Ryman whirled around expecting to see Lee Fong Yu. The hatchet-faced Chinese with the gun was unknown to him. Hardly had he turned, than his feet were kicked from beneath him and he crashed down amongst the debris. Two men had emerged from the kitchen, one of them with his head swathed in bandages and only his mouth and one eye visible.

'Where are the pieces that you stole?' he said.

Ryman tried to unscramble his thoughts. 'I don't know what you're talking about.'

A kick landed on the side of his ear, making his head ring.

'Do not lie, you are part of the conspiracy. The material was here. Where is it now?' The flesh that was not covered by bandages was unhealthily pale; the lips like pale slugs. Ryman was trying to think fast. These men could not be working with Lee Fong Yu. Perhaps they had also been double-crossed. At least it looked as if Flower and Burton had got away with the stuff — and Lee Fong Yu?

Another savage kick reminded him that a reply was expected.

'I can't tell you something I don't know.'

'But you do know. Your name is Ryman. Lee Fong Yu described you to us before he died. He died in great pain, and so will you unless you co-operate.'

Ryman tried to control his features. 'What makes you think that I can tell you anything?'

'You did not tell him where you were going after you left this flat. That was very wise of you. He was a very untrustworthy man. We both have experience of that. If you had told him he would have told us. He would have told us anything by the time we had finished with him.'

Ryman felt a chill current curdling through his veins.

'Let's make a deal,' he said.

162

The man with the bandages shook his head. 'You are not in a position to make a deal.' He nodded to the man who had emerged with him from the kitchen and Ryman steeled himself for another blow. Instead, an agonising burning pain seared through his thigh and a brown smoking hole appeared in the material of his overalls. He cried out and clawed at his stinging flesh. The pain seemed to burn deeper like a white-hot needle. He looked up and saw a small glass phial poised above him. Acid.

'That was only one drop,' said the cold, nasal voice. 'If you do not tell us what we want to know, your face will be next. After that you will wish that we had killed you.'

Ryman clutched his leg and bit his lip. The agony had now translated itself into a deep, throbbing ache. He scraped the inside of his mind to think of something to say.

'Where have the pieces been taken?'

There was a sharp rat-tat-tat on the door, coincident with the bell ringing. A heartbeat, swollen like an over-inflated balloon, exploded in Ryman's chest. Even as he looked towards the door, the muzzle of a pistol was thrust beneath his jaw and he was dragged backwards. He scrambled to his feet and retreated into the kitchen as there was another volley of banging. His head was thrust against a cupboard and the weapon pressed into his flesh so that the muzzle seemed to be inside his mouth. There was the sound of the door opening and exclamations of surprise in Chinese. Almost immediately there was a shout and a shot and a scream. The gun against Ryman's flesh jerked away an inch and the pressure against his cheek relaxed. Ryman took his chance and swung his hand up to grip the pistol and knock it aside. There was an explosion in his ear and powder stung his temple. He drove his knee up and felt it lift the man off the ground. An electric iron was lying on a work surface and he snatched it up and swung it with all his force. There was a sound like somebody stamping on a box of matches, and the man crashed back against the sink unit and slid to the ground.

From next door came the noise of a rifle range; dust and plaster were swirling through the doorway and a volley of bullets shattered glass. The muffled roar of a police automatic sounded from outside in the corridor; bullets were chewing through the door and spewing a chaff of splinters around the room. Ryman ran for the window. The man with the bandaged face was kneeling in the

163

doorway that led to the living-room, but he was concentrating on the main point of attack. Ryman glimpsed a policeman lying face down in the debris, and swung a leg over the window-sill. The man with the bandage turned and fired, but the bullet went wide. Ryman saw the air-conditioning unit attached to the wall and used it as a stepping stone as he launched himself towards the balcony of the next flat. It held his weight for a second and then crashed away as his fingers closed about the balustrade. For a moment he clung in space, and then his scrabbling feet made contact with the wall and he clawed himself up to topple over the rail and flounder amongst a welter of washing. Below him, there were screams and shouts and, behind, another burst of automatic fire; all was noise and confusion. He scrambled across the balcony and glimpsed a woman cowering in the shadow of her flat, clutching a baby. She screamed as he looked towards her. On the far side of the balcony was a fire escape attached to the wall and beyond that a billowing mass of drying sheets like a galleon under full sail.

Ryman flung his foot over the balustrade and leaped for the rusty iron platform. For a second it sank and he thought that the whole structure was coming away from the wall; then there was a splatter of falling rust and mortar and he was able to start climbing towards the roof. A bullet scored the wall beside his head and he saw two policemen tearing aside the folds of laundry so that they could get a clear shot at him. An awning jutted out, cutting him from their view and he saw the watery, haloed sun above his head as it peeped over the edge of the roof. A rusty rung disintegrated beneath his foot and he slipped and nearly fell before hauling himself up the last few feet and flopping over the edge of the parapet.

The roof was flat save for box-like clusters of ventilation units and the raised sentry boxes of stairheads. Panting for breath, Ryman ran to the nearest door and tried to open it. It was locked on the inside. Frantically he ran to the next one. It wore the smooth, blank, unyielding face of its neighbour. On the stair side he could hear the muffled sound of boots clumping up the concrete steps. Desperation gave way to panic. He ran to the back of the roof and looked down. Laid out below him like an ornamental garden was the glittering complex of a many-buildinged Buddhist temple; flying dragons, a phoenix, mystical Ch'i-lins crowding the corners

164

of the curving roofs; the polished glass of the roof tiles gleaming like rows of bamboo. The nearest of its buildings was twelve feet away, across a narrow alley and behind a high, green brick wall topped with spikes. The roof was thirty feet below the point where Ryman stood.

There was an echoing boom and one of the stairhead doors burst open. Ryman did not wait, but launched himself into space. He cleared the alley, and the concave roof rushed up to meet him, dashing the wind from his body. His legs crumpled beneath him on the undulating tiles and he felt a sharp pain in his ankle. He started to scramble upwards, and immediately slipped and fell back; the roof was far steeper than appeared from above and still slippery with typhoon rain. Feverishly he twisted and spread his hands wide to stop his descent. He came to a halt with his head looking down at the spikes.

Expecting a bullet at any second, he pushed himself unsteadily to his feet and set off along the edge of the roof. Ahead of him was a dazzling row of mythical beasts that decorated its rim and rose to the apex of the building. They were the only hand-holds available. He hobbled painfully and threw out an arm to grip the undulating tail of a winged dragon. The structure trembled and he transferred his weight to the parapet and started to haul himself upwards. The roof rose more and more sharply and he was a foot from its apex when there was a shrill cry from above. He lunged forward and for an instant was straddling the cavalcade of mythical beasts that followed the gentle, sagging tightrope curve of the roof. A shot rang out and chips of glass clattered down the runnels between the tiles. Ryman scrambled forward, released his hold and found himself sliding into the unknown. Gathering speed he saw the lip of the roof racing towards him. Instinctively he stuck out a hand to slow himself down and felt burning pain. For a second he was in space, and then he crashed down on a second roof. Feet first, he slithered towards the edge and then crashed down on a table laid out with offertory gifts. It shattered beneath his weight and he sprawled on his back with the wind driven from his body and a piercing pain in one elbow. There were shouts of alarm and surprise and the faithful, standing with their joss-sticks before the candle-strewn altar, opened their eyes and wondered whose prayers this visitation answered.

Ryman drove himself to his feet and ran past the squat incense

165

burner and the granite pillars encrusted with carved snakes, past the ornamental pool where the fat carp browsed listlessly on the surface; into another courtyard and down a flight of stone steps, past gift stalls and the booth where worshippers retrieved the pieces of paper that set out the answers to their secret questions. Ahead lay the noble tri-tiered gate and beyond the painted railings were the teeming streets of the congested Lungshan area. As Matsu, Goddess of the Sea, plump and benign, beamed down at him with supreme indifference, Ryman staggered past the last puzzled faces and through the narrow side gate.

He had taken four steps into the crowd when there was a shout behind him. A policeman with a carbine was emerging from the alley. Ryman started to run again. Ahead, a dense crowd of people waited at the level crossing. Lights flashed and bells rang. A train was approaching. Cars, taxis, scooters, cycles; Ryman weaved through them clumsily, praying that the policeman would not shoot for fear of hitting an innocent passer-by. Two boys had lifted their bikes over the barrier and were crossing the line. They started to run as an express glided round the bend. Engines were revving and there was a corporate howl of anger when the train came to a halt straddling the crossing. This was a frequent happening. Trains often slowed down and stopped before entering Taipei Station. Ryman heard another shout above the cacophany of the horns. On all sides he was hemmed in by a swarm of scooters. There was a burst of firing and the crowd looked about them thinking it was a firecracker. Ryman could see the impersonal faces of the train passengers staring down at the rabble beneath them. He threw himself at the barrier and scrambled over it. There were shouts and jeers; the crowd pressed forward. What was the crazy Ang Moh doing?

Ryman threw himself down and wriggled under the train. He smelt the sickly sweet odour of hot oil and glimpsed the legs of the mass of people pressing against the barrier on the far side of the line. A bullet screamed off one of the bogies and he threw a leg out to crawl to the other side. The train lurched and started to move. Ryman scrabbled sideways desperately as there was a noise like a pair of rusty scissors closing. The wheels bit into the grooves and as he rolled to safety, one flicked the end of his shoes as easily as it might have sheared off his leg. Ryman heard the gasp from the crowd and scrambled to his feet. The train was gathering speed.

He ran beside it, leaped on to the footplate and clung precariously to a vertical rail. The shouting died away.

A quarter of an hour later the train pulled in to Taipei Station and was over-run by police. But, minutes before, Ryman had jumped clear and scrambled across the lines towards the North Gate and the Tanshui River.

CHAPTER NINE

'Have you noticed?' asked Burton. 'We're the only ones travelling towards the coast.'

Flower had noticed but she had said nothing. Every vehicle that came towards them was loaded down with items of furniture. There were even carts being pulled behind bicycles; people rescuing their possessions from the last typhoon or fleeing from the next; on the way to seek shelter with relations in the big city.

Flower looked towards the sky. The sun had almost disappeared behind a lowering mass of grey. It glowed dully as if seen through thick opaque glass. By some strange effect the halo seemed to have more intensity than the sun itself.

'At least we got through to Bigg,' said Burton. 'I only hope we don't get bogged down. Have you seen some of the tracks around here?'

'We told him we might be late.' Flower was thinking about Ryman and Lee Fong Yu. The fact that they had never appeared at the flat was ominous. Had they been caught leaving the Museum? She had listened to the van radio with trembling heart, but there had been no announcement. That proved nothing. There was strict censorship in Taiwan. The authorities might well consider that news of a successful robbery from the Palace Museum was bad for the national morale. More to the point, they might rightly think that it would alert any accomplices still at large. She fiddled with the dials of the radio as Burton continued to try and soothe himself with the sound of his own voice. 'Of course, this could help us. With everything in turmoil it should be easier to slip away.'

Flower held up a restraining hand. 'An important message has just been announced.'

Burton darted glances at her face to see how she was reacting. 'What are they saying?'

'Another typhoon is forecast for this evening. Between Chunan and Taichung.'

'That's where we're sailing, isn't it?'

Flower snapped off the radio. 'How can we sail anywhere if the others do not come?'

'We can't wait indefinitely. As soon as the theft's discovered and they start putting two and two together, the whole island will be looking for us.' Flower continued to stare ahead of her. 'We'll keep their share. You seem to think I want to profit from what's happened.' He turned his gaze back to the road. 'The only profit I want from this business is you.' He waited hopefully for some sort of reply on to which he could build a conversation but Flower remained silent. It was not the first time that she had listened to Burton's protestations of love. Once they had flattered her, now they made her feel guilty. There was a balm in the passion of youth that softened the pangs of growing older, but it had to be reciprocated from the heart and not from vanity. Flower blamed herself for not having been more ruthless in her attempts to prise Burton away. He was a boy and, as the world turned crazy around her, she was beginning to realise that she needed a man. If he wanted her.

'We'll see what Harry has to say,' said Burton.

'I hope they're there,' said Flower.

Ryman knew that time was running out fast. Any second now there would be a general alert out for him which would include both the police and the military; and a six-foot-four-inch Englishman did not fade easily into the background of Taipei's crowded streets. Once they started looking for him there would be no place to hide. Ryman emerged from an alley and crossed the Huanho road that ran beside the river. Below him was the Chungsing Bridge and the road that led to Taoyuan and the south. That was where he wanted to go. On the bridge was a traffic jam of encumbered vehicles coming in from the coast — refugees from the typhoon. Country bumpkins, they did not hoot as frequently or frenetically as their town cousins. The traffic going out of town was running smoothly. He should have been part of it hours before. Below him, the river was the colour of mud and in full spate. Swollen by the torrential rains, it was swirling down towards the sea in a precipitation of whirlpools and angry currents, its surface sprinkled with branches torn from trees and accumulated debris stored against the banks since the last storm waters had started to ebb.

Fifty metres up the road towards the Taipei Bridge, there was a gap in the wall and a crumbling flight of stone steps leading down towards a mooring stage that was already under water. Three decrepit sampans jostled on the end of a painter like fish on a line. Ryman looked at the boats as part of the landscape and then he looked again. Around him, people were hurrying past as if anxious to get home before a storm broke. The blare of the traffic horns had an increased edge of panic to it. The signs were obvious; the sky was darkening and an oppressive, sultry heat hung over the city. It was as if an air-raid warning had been sounded and people were fleeing from the streets.

Ryman started to move towards the gap in the wall and then paused. A traffic policeman was on duty at the nearby inter-section. He stood on a white box in the middle of the road, complete with helmet, whistle and a pistol at his waist. The truncheon in his hand waved and jabbed as if he was practising a fencing movement. Ryman dropped to one knee and pretended to be doing up his shoelace. He waited until the policeman had turned his back to beckon out another line of traffic, and then hurried forward. The gap in the wall was twenty yards away. Near the intersection was a sentry box, its sides painted a brilliant white. A light outside it began to flash. There was a message for the policeman on traffic duty. Ryman looked at the throbbing light and was afraid. A familiar inner voice told him what the message would be.

Walking as fast as he could without breaking into a run, Ryman arrived at the gap in the wall and ducked down the stone steps. No inquisitive head peered after him. He reached the jetty and cold water broke over his ankles. The boat furthest from him had a paddle and he took it and threw it beneath the semi-circular deck housing of the vessel nearest to the steps; its awning covered nearly the whole length of the boat. He clambered aboard swiftly and ducked under the thatch. The sampan stank of fish, and brackish water swished around his feet. The fast-flowing current pummel-led the hull. Ryman fumbled with the knot that bound it to the others, fearing that at any second there would be a shout from above. Eventually it came free, and he shoved off with the oar and shrank back into the obscurity of the deck awning.

As the current bore him away, he heard the familiar see-saw siren of a police truck cutting through the traffic noises.

170

The man's head bounced up and down on the floor as the bandage was pulled from it. He felt no pain because he was dead. The last four bullets of a burst sprayed at random through the shattered door were lodged against his backbone.

The cotton wool came away with the final strip of bandage and the inspector looked down at the exposed face, easily suppressing any emotion that he felt. His lieutenants looked at him expectantly. '*Na lin-yen*?' They nodded emphatically. The inspector pondered. 'New territory for him. The Three Pearls have always been content with extortion up till now.' He nodded across to one of the other bodies in the room. 'Any sign of life?' The police surgeon shook his head. The inspector frowned. The man who had tried to jump from the window had fallen on to a car and been killed by the bus following it. That left nobody to question.

The inspector straightened up and looked at the blood-stained debris. 'These are almost certainly the boxes that were taken into the Museum. Bring Wu Chang here to identify them. Fingerprint everything.'

'The Ang Moh will tell us everything,' said one of the lieutenants confidently.

'When we find him,' said the inspector quietly.

He turned as another policeman came into the room and saluted. 'We have located their car, sir. There is a body of a man in the boot, very badly mutilated.'

The van wheels spun for the fifth time and the engine screeched in protest. Mud spattered on water twenty yards down the inundated track and the wheels dug deeper. Burton withdrew his aching shoulder and staggered towards the cab through the sucking mud.

'Cut it! We're never going to drive out of here. We'll have to walk.'

Flower pulled her foot off the accelerator and switched off the ignition.

'Nobody else has been here, have they?'

'You mean Don? No, it doesn't look like it.'

They had arrived at what had once been the strip of coastal rice fields but was now a swamp with the rice pressed down against the earth like wet hair. A tidal wave had swept three miles inland, breaching the sea wall and carrying away half a fishing village further down the coast. The crop was ruined, the land would be unusable for years. All around was a stench of decay as sea creatures that had been swept inland gave up their lives in evaporating pools and began to rot. The only sound came from the buzzing of flies that had arrived in great black swarms. The air was sullen and brooding, the sky dark on the horizon; the sun a memory. Ahead, the sea beyond the slight lift in the ground seemed like the edge of the world.

As Flower had pointed out, the track in front of them bore neither footprint nor tyre mark to suggest that anyone had passed this way since the passage of the typhoon. There was nothing to inspire hope.

Burton squelched back to the rear of the van and wrenched open the door with muddy hands. Already the sweat was dripping from his brow and mosquitoes circled his head. He pulled the box towards him and began to organise the distribution of the treasures. How incongruous it seemed in this wasteland. Priceless works of art encased in cheap plastic and stowed like a crate of vegetables. He draped the Ju ware round his neck and read Flower's expression as she glanced at it. 'I know,' he said with a trace of bitterness. 'It's all because of this that things have gone wrong.'

Flower said nothing; Burton's drawn expression as much as his words revealed that the strain was beginning to tell. He needed all the support she could give him.

'What do you want me to carry?' she said calmly.

A look almost of shame came over Burton's face. 'I'm sorry,' he murmured. He delved in the back of the van and handed over one of the Ming bowls, the ivory carving and the Jadeite cabbage.

Burton added a haversack of food to the items they were carrying and they set off towards the sea. All manner of stranded creatures littered the way: small squid, star fish, crabs, sea horses — some of them still attached to life, others putrefying. One stretch of the path was a disgusting, glutinous mass of decomposing jellyfish, their transparent bodies piled on top of each other as if they had been tipped from a lorry. The touch of their slippery yielding forms beneath the foot set the teeth on edge. A crow flew over and then another. Soon there was a flock of them cartwheeling over the drowned rice-fields, plunging down to strut and gorge on the unexpected banquet. Their exultant cawing echoed over the desolate waste.

The sea wall, which was no more than a pathetic earth mound

breached in several places, wore a crown of foul-smelling weed in which tiny shrimps still danced their lives away. Beyond it was a lagoon and the beginning of the marshes where Crosby was supposed to be moored. The reed beds had been beaten down and the whole area looked like a rank wheat-field after a violent storm. Only in places did the sedge still straggle up towards the sky. Burton looked at Flower and they both shivered. The place stank of death; it was purgatory with scant promise of heaven at the end of it.

'I can't believe he's there,' said Burton. 'Surely we'd be able to see him.'

'Not if he is hiding as he should be.'

Burton screwed up his eyes. 'God, I wish Ryman were here.'

'So do I!' said Flower.

Burton led the way and they waded into the water, which was soon over their waists. Their feet sank into the ooze and a thick layer of surface weed made progress difficult. Burton thought uneasily of any sharks that might have been washed shorewards and come to rest in this tidal lagoon. There had been a recent report of a net fisherman taken in a few feet of water. Something nudged his leg and veered away and a current of terror passed through him. The water was dark brown and it was impossible to see anything below the surface. Only touch and imagination afforded details of anything that might be lurking. A sharp stinging pain against his stomach made him cry out and he saw the repulsive outline of the jellyfish that had breached the opening in his shirt. He started backwards and saw that the way ahead was dimpled with them, tentacles swaying, bodies pumping in and out. Calling Flower to close up behind him, he took the food bag and used it as a sponge to clear a passage for them both.

A few feet from the first reed bed, the ground beneath him disappeared and he was choking on a mouthful of brackish water. The Ju ware floated from his neck as he went down and he had to swim clumsily to retrieve it. Obviously, some dyke or river had flowed here before the sea came in. He reached the muddy bank and lay coughing until he could breathe naturally. The taste in his mouth was vile.

'I cannot swim,' said Flower.

Burton swore and unburdened himself of the tube that held the painting, the Ju ware and the second Ming bowl. He left them in the reeds and went back to take Flower's packages. One more journey and he was ready to stand before her with his hand cupped underneath her chin. 'Let your feet float up and try and lie on top of me. I'm going to swim backwards. Imagine we're making love.'

Flower said nothing but prepared to follow his instructions. She could sense that with a physical role to play he was beginning to gain in confidence.

Burton sank backwards, kicking out with a back-stroke leg action and drawing Flower with him. Her slim neck was arched from the water and there was fear in her eyes, but she did not panic. His shoulders collided with the bank and he turned on his side and pulled her up beside him. She splashed desperately and clutched at the reeds. 'Excellent,' he said. 'You're going to be very good.'

She smiled bravely and Burton pulled her on to the bank and scrambled to his feet. Inside him there was still the hope that he would see the boat a few yards away, but there was nothing. Only the flattened marsh and the leaden sky; the oppressive heat and the insidious smell of animal and vegetable decay. The horizon was now a thick black line and the sea unnervingly calm, lit by a strange light that made it seem like some vast silver salver. In the far distance the heavens were combed into tresses.

Flower read his face. 'Nothing?' Burton dropped to his knees beside her and shook his head. 'He must be well hidden.'

Burton said nothing. There was no point in spilling out his thoughts; that Crosby and the boat had been lost in the previous typhoon or forced to run far down the coast where they had encountered problems. Flower probably thought the same thing but was trying to wear a brave face. Burton pulled the canisters and packages towards him and ran his eye over them. Nothing seemed to have been damaged or taken in water. He did not want to look any closer. To find that something had been smashed would set the final seal on their disaster. Not only to have failed but to have destroyed a masterpiece for nothing. He could understand any vengeance that might be meted out to them.

Flower was rising to her feet and picking up her share of the packages.

'We must go on.'

'And if we find there's nobody there?'

'Then we wait.'

'How long? There's another typhoon on the way! You know that. Look at that sky!'

'We will wait as long as we can.' Flower started to pick her way through the reeds. 'Where else can we go?'

Burton had no answer to this question. He shouldered the painting and carefully draped the other containers round his neck. His body was smarting as if from hundreds of little bites. Some kind of water parasite must have attacked him in the lagoon. He swatted mosquitoes and stumbled on through sodden reeds that twisted round his ankles like snares. Occasionally the overall smell of decay was punctuated by a localised stench as the reeds offered up the body of a drowned creature — a huge rat that must have been trapped in its burrow, yellow teeth showing in a rictus of death; a goose, its neck twisted over its shoulder, its beak open; a snake glistening with flies. Every step over the greasy, squelching mud threatened an unpleasant surprise.

They came to a narrow dyke where the stinking, sucking mud rose to their thighs, and then to a wide stretch where the reeds had managed to assert themselves again and were making some show of rising from the marsh. It was here that Burton's spirits began to rise; it was just possible to believe that there might be a boat tucked into a secret creek behind the next clump. He called out, but there was no response save from a sea eagle that lifted clumsily into the fetid air a dozen yards away. He watched it flap away, making a wide sweep towards the shore, and told himself that Crosby was asleep or taking no chances. He thought of a cold beer and the chance to wash the filth from his body; above all the protective feel of a deck and bulkheads about him, the smell of polished wood and a well-maintained engine — safety, if only temporary, from this terrible wasteland.

The sedge bowed down again and Burton saw what lay ahead. A deep cut into the reed beds made a perfect natural harbour. It was empty. Beyond, the marsh petered out into the open sea. The bar of black on the horizon was thickening.

Ryman had passed Tanshui to the north, and the gap between the banks was widening. The river still moved at a reckless pace, but there was now a choice of currents and it was easier to avoid the floating branches and the clusters of intertangled foliage that bumbled down the flood like huge discarded bouquets.

175

Ryman still kept beneath the thatched awning and steered with the oar trailing behind the sampan. The last time the river had come close to a road on the south side he had seen soldiers manning a road block. Whether it was anything to do with the robbery or because the authorities wished to prevent people entering the area of typhoon damage he had no way of knowing. In neither case did it give him an incentive to show himself. With aching eyes he peered through the arch to see what lay ahead. Now, neither bank was visible. What lay ahead was the open sea, with China a hundred miles away. The marshes where the rendezvous was to have been made lay round the flooded sand banks to the south.

Ryman leant on the oar and felt his arms creaking in their sockets. The palms of his hands were raw from finger to wrist. They stuck to the oak. The sampan shifted and turned laboriously towards the south bank. It was still difficult to make an impression against the swirling current. If he was carried out to sea he would never get back again before the storm broke. Before him, dark layers of nimbo-stratus cloud fell like the bars of a venetian blind. They promised only one thing. A typhoon. Ryman ground his teeth and leant his shoulders against the oar. The water-logged banks sped by.

Chuang Lien-kwei looked at the square face of the digital watch given to him by his father and wondered when the van would come back. He had been in the ditch trying to unlock one of the flooded field drains when it had gone past down the track, and that was over an hour ago. He had looked up just in time to glimpse the tense face of the Ang Moh at the wheel. What could he be doing down there? Perhaps he was an American adviser helping the government to cope with the aftermath of the typhoon. There were many men like that in the country — engineers and agricultural experts — although usually they drove in vehicles with big wheels that had the insignia of government departments on the sides. This van had not been like that.

Chuang Lien-kwei opened another sluice gate and scrambled up the bank. It was not time for the sun to go down yet but already it was as dark as night. A big *tai-fung* was coming. He would be foolish if he did not hurry back to the road and ride his motor scooter home. He paused on the track and looked down at the deep furrows made by the van's tyres. Rice could have been planted in them. He looked towards the sea. Maybe the van had become bogged down. As a Junior Leader it was his duty to aid those who were helping his country. He should go and see what had happened. Perhaps he would be able to help.

Chuang Lien-kwei left his rake by the side of the track and started to run towards the sea. He was not wearing his sandals and the ground was slippery; but it did not matter because very soon he saw the van. As he came nearer he noted that it was indeed axle-deep in mud. He looked about but there was nobody to be seen. Only two sets of footprints leading towards the marshes. Why would people who had become bogged down walk towards the marshes? They must have known that they were going towards the sea and that there could be no help there. It was strange.

He looked up at the sky and hesitated before going on towards the marshes. It seemed to be getting darker with every minute that passed; as if somebody was turning down the wick of a lamp on the edge of the world. His mother would already be worrying.

But he must take one quick look to see what the Ang Moh and his companion were doing. He arrived at the low sea wall and looked about him with mounting surprise. The marshes stretched away flat and desolate and there was no sign of any living creature. He peered into the gloom until his eyes ached and then started to run back to the van. Now he felt doubly uneasy; not only the storm but two people who had driven to the sea's edge and disappeared. It was like the stories he had been told as a little boy; angry sea gods who came ashore demanding human sacrifices. As the darkness rolled down there were certainly fearful omens in the air.

Chuang Lien-kwei steeled himself and peered into the back of the van. There was nothing there save an empty tin box. He breathed a sigh of relief and set off down the track. It was puzzling, but there was probably a simple explanation. His father would be able to supply it when he came back from work at the police station.

Burton swore and wiped his hand across his forehead. It came away wet with sweat and heavier by the weight of three mosquitoes. Even as he brushed them away so did more settle on the backs of his hands. They were insatiable. Beside him, Flower sat with her knees drawn up against her breasts. Her head was tilted down towards the reeds; she might have been asleep.

177

Burton took a deep breath. 'Flower, we can't stay here much longer, you must see that. With the storm that's brewing, Harry's not going to come back here. He'll lay off till it's over and so will Don and Lee Fong Yu. They'll expect us to do likewise.' He listened to silence for a few seconds. 'I'm not trying to run away; I'm just talking common sense. If we stay here we're committing suicide.'

There was another long pause and then Flower slowly nodded her head as if having arrived at a difficult decision. 'Yes, you are right. We will have to go back.' She shuddered. 'Through that terrible water.'

'I'll help you.' Burton scrambled to his feet. 'If we . . . ' he broke off and listened. Across the dark waters came the rhythmic thump, thump, thump, of a small boat's engine; the noise magnified by the eerie darkness of the sea.

Flower rose to her feet and stood shoulder to shoulder with Burton peering into the inky darkness. Her hand sought his and squeezed with a pressure that grew greater as the noise increased. They stared out to sea and suddenly, beyond the furthest fringe of the marsh, there was a glint of light and a shape even blacker than the darkness that surrounded it. The engine note faded and then picked up again to continue growing louder. The boat was coming towards them. Burton's stomach tightened. A torch shone out and began to play along the banks of reeds. The helmsman must be looking for the creek. A shape detached itself from the Stygian gloom and Burton recognised the flat outline of a high-prowed vessel. The torch light splashed over them and the engine was cut as the boat nosed into the reeds and rocked against the mud. Water washed hissing through the sedge.

A figure leaned towards them from the deck housing.

'Where are the other two?' said Crosby.

Ryman was standing in the stern. Now that he had got the hang of using the paddle, he was making good progress. It had taken a long time to shake off the grip of the river currents. The great mass of brown, flood-swollen water was billowing miles out to sea, carrying everything with it. He had become entangled in a small island of foliage and nearly capsized before he freed himself. The incident had done nothing to improve the seaworthiness of the sampan; it was carrying too much water and the hull was creaking ominously.

Ryman leaned on the oar and peered ahead for sight of the shore. In this sepulchral gloom there was no sound of waves breaking, no noise to hint at the presence of land. He might, terrifying thought, be steering in the wrong direction — into the widening jaws of the typhoon. He twisted the long oar and pulled again. It was an action he had watched a thousand times without ever thinking that he might be called upon to imitate it. God, how tired he was. He would have given anything to be able to drop onto the rotting boards and fall asleep; anything but his self-respect. Even if there was no hope, he had to keep going, to try and find the others. That was the only thing left.

'The tall man is almost certainly called Ryman,' said the lieutenant, pronouncing the name with difficulty. 'He works for *The Times of China* but he did not appear today. We have searched his flat and found a briefcase with his passport and some American dollars in it. Also a bag with clothes. He does not appear to have a car.'

'And the other man?' said the inspector.

'We could find none of his papers at the flat. Chang says that he drives a grey van which he uses for his business. The old man who is the watchman at the flat says that it is usually parked nearby, but we cannot find it.'

'You are checking the number?'

'Of course. And I have alerted all units to be on the lookout for it.'

'Good. I take it that the watchman had seen the big man before?'

'Several times. He was a frequent visitor to the flat in recent weeks.'

'I suppose the watchman did not recognise the man who was in the boot?'

'No, he was too badly burnt. But he did speak of another Ang Moh and a girl who came to the flat. We are getting a detailed description.'

'Good.' The inspector rubbed his hands together thoughtfully. 'It is very possible that one of them is hiding this man Ryman. He will not dare...'

He broke off as a wireless operator came in with a scrap of paper in his hand. The man's face revealed a barely suppressed excitement. 'Excuse me, sir, but we have just received a message

179

that I think may be important. A grey van has been discovered abandoned near the sea between Chuwei and Bali. Apparently it was driven by an Ang Moh and there is an empty tin box in the back.'

The inspector moved with unusual speed, and his finger traced a circle round an area of the wall map which hung nearby. That part of the coast was less than twenty miles from the city. 'Alert the nearest coastguard unit immediately. They must be trying to get away by sea.'

The wireless operator looked solemn. 'Sir, there is a typhoon warning in the area. All vessels have been instructed to leave those waters. The coastguard units will be in the deep water harbour at Keelung.'

'Well, some of them will have to get out!' said the inspector angrily. 'This is a national emergency.' He snatched the piece of paper from the wireless operator. 'Is this the exact location? I will talk to the naval authorities from the car.' He beckoned to his lieutenant, who was already falling in behind him. 'Come, we do not have a moment to lose.'

'I don't know how the hell I'm still alive,' said Crosby. His face was haggard, and even in the ghostly half light of the cabin they could see the bruises wherever his flesh was exposed. He looked as if he had been in a prize fight. 'It didn't let up for four hours. I was bouncing about like a pea in a pod.' He touched a raw bump on his cheek and winced. 'When the water came into the engine room once, it was as if somebody was filling a bath in a hurry. I was swimming in there.'

Burton looked into the hollow eyes and believed him. Crosby seemed to have lost a stone in weight and aged ten years. There was still water slopping in the bunks, and tins from the galley rolled about the floor. A swell was getting up; a great, ominous, switchback, whip-crack of rolling water that lifted the prow on to the mud bank and then jerked it off again. It was a sign that Crosby knew well; the typhoon was coming.

'Thank God you came back,' said Burton.

'I needed the money,' Crosby gave a mirthless laugh. 'Look, we gotta get out of here. Strike north; lie up round the other side of Shihmen if we can. We'll come back for the others when the thing blows over. We've got to pass this way, anyhow. Where's Flower?'

'Still up on deck. She's got this feeling that Ryman's going to appear.'

'Crazy dame. She can't make up her mind, can she?' Crosby retreated towards the engine room. 'I'm going to take this old tub out before she founders in this goddam creek. Cast off, will you?'

Burton went on deck and leaped into the reeds to retrieve the land anchor. A fine rain was now falling, and a terrible blackness closed in from all sides. The sea washed over his feet and it seemed as if the marsh might suddenly sink beneath him, leaving him to struggle in the swirling water. He tore the anchor from the mud and threw himself onto the rolling deck.

'Where are we going?' Flower was beside him as he scrambled to his feet.

'North. Crosby wants to get round the headland before the storm breaks.'

'It is breaking.' Flower spoke without emotion.

She was right. The rain was coming down harder, lashing the water with an angry hiss. Burton took her by the arm. 'Come below.' She shook him aside. 'I feel he is out there.'

Burton turned away. His own feeling was that he was losing a battle he had never really stood a chance of winning.

The boat moved slowly astern and then shuddered as Crosby brought her round to lie broadside to the swell. For a moment, water licked over the scuppers and Burton looked down into a trough that could have been his grave. Then the prow came round and the screw made an impression on the water; the vessel slipped over the top of a wave and was under way.

Burton was turning to go below when Flower shouted. Immediately there was an answering shout and a shape loomed up ahead. A sampan lay across their bow and for a few seconds it seemed that they must cut it in half. Then it was clattering against the side of the hull and a huge figure struggled with an oar in the stern.

'Don!' Flower's scream cut through the sound of the sluicing rain. She threw herself forward and tried to steady the sampan. It ground against the hull and she nearly lost her fingers.

'You'll have to jump!' Burton clung to the rail that ran along the deck-housing and stretched out his arm. The sampan lifted to the height of the deck and then dropped again. 'This time!' Ryman's head and shoulders loomed into view and he threw himself forward. He stumbled as he landed and Burton's arm saved him from pitching full length and falling over the side. The effort nearly wrenched Burton's arm out of its socket. Crosby stuck his head out of the deck-house. 'Where's Lee Fong Yu?'

Ryman accepted Flower against his chest and clamped an arm around Burton's shoulder. 'He won't be joining us.'

There was no room for a vehicle to get round the abandoned van, so the local police pushed it down the bank into the rice field and the inspector's truck churned its way on to the beginning of the marsh. A powerful searchlight mounted on the back of the vehicle swept along the shore in both directions and then out across the lagoon to the desolate track of reeds. Two pairs of footsteps disappeared at the water's edge and there was nothing else to be seen. As the inspector ordered the searchlight to be turned off, the rain beat down harder.

'We have lost them,' said the lieutenant.

'They are lost,' said the inspector, calmly. 'If they go north the patrol boat will pick them up. If they go south they will never survive the typhoon.' He looked at the torrential downpour kicking up mud before the truck's headlights. 'And if we don't get away from here, neither will we.'

'Which way are you going?' said Ryman.

'North,' said Crosby. 'If we get as far as Chinshan we'll be in the lee of the headland.'

The rain was lashing against the cracked glass of the deck-house, reducing visibility to a few feet. Ryman shook his head. 'There's a coastguard boat patrolling up there. The swell was running so high the searchlight passed over me. We won't be that lucky.'

'So we steer into the typhoon?' said Crosby. 'No thanks. I've already brushed the edge of one. I don't want to go through that again.'

'It'll be different with four of us.' Ryman turned to Burton. 'What do you think?'

Burton rubbed the side of his jaw. 'I don't want to spend the rest of my life in gaol. We've come this far, let's go south as we planned.'

'Flower?'

Flower's eyes moved from Ryman to Burton and back again. 'I will stay with you.'

182

'Go for broke,' said Crosby. 'Everything we've done so far has been crazy, but this is the craziest thing of all.' He looked into the face of his own private demon and began sawing at the wheel to bring the boat round.

CHAPTER TEN

When the typhoon started to screech it was like no noise that Burton had ever heard. Sometimes it was like singing, sometimes like a million drowned souls howling for the last time before the water closed over their heads. It was an angry noise, yet at the same time spine-chillingly plaintive. The mad wind snatched away the crests of waves and drove the rain horizontally with the force of buckshot. Aboard the vessel, Ryman wrestled with the wheel whilst Crosby and Burton nurtured the engine and Flower went where she was needed — when she could move without being dashed against a bulkhead. The night was rent not only by the eldritch wail of the wind but by the hideous screaming of the propeller when it shook free of the water and railed at the spray-filled air. The boat felt as if it was coming apart. Each wave that thundered down on it in a maelstrom of white foam made the timbers groan and creak; sent a shudder through the hull. The bilge water that slopped from engine room to fo'c'sle could as easily have burst through the yielding timbers as pour over the sides. The engine hissed and spat like a decrepit steam iron, and the companion way had become a waterfall.

Ryman braced himself against the wheel and screwed up his eyes against the driving rain. The bottom had dropped out of the barometer and he guessed that they had entered the first radius of the anti-clockwise winds; the gusts must be blowing at nearly a hundred miles an hour. The darkness was impenetrable, but sometimes there were terrifying streaks of white that reared up, up, up in their path until they crashed down in the form of another mountainous wave. The boat dived into a trough, wallowed, struggled to right itself, scaled a wall of water and then plunged into another drowning pit. Hardly had the sea started to stream from the decks before the next wave swamped them. Sometimes it seemed to Ryman that they were never going to come up; that the boat must fill with water and lurch towards the bottom. He struggled to keep the vessel's prow pointing into the mountainous waves and wiped the sodden hair from his eyes. There was a sharp crack to his right and one of the side windows of the deck-housing shattered, showering him with broken glass. The whole structure filled with spray and emitted a tortured grinding noise as if about to snap from its mooring and disappear into the night, carrying him with it. He braced himself and the boat pitched into the next trough. He was exhausted, and felt near to death.

Down below, the engine was on the point of breaking apart. Wheezing, coughing, braying, the driving assembly churning jerkily and irregularly, the propeller screaming hysterically when it left the water. Crosby presided over the death rites with a greasy handkerchief tied round his forehead. This had originally served to keep the sweat from his eyes, but when the typhoon had swept down on them the temperature had dropped more than twenty degrees. Now the handkerchief was soaked with sea water and got a new dousing every time a fresh wave cascaded down the companion way.

Crack! One of the engine linking arms burst adrift under the strain and threshed the air like a demented limb. The vessel groaned and yawed into another wave. Water swirled around their feet. Somewhere in the flood was the bolt head that secured the rod to the drive shaft. Terrified, Burton fumbled in the tin of dancing nuts fastened to a joist and found something that he judged to be the right size. He pressed it into the breast pocket of his shirt and tried to line up the frenetic movement of the linking arm. His hand darted out and he screamed in pain as it smashed against his knuckle. For an instant he saw gristle and then the blood welled up. The agony seared past his elbow. He was still pressing his hand to his mouth when Flower lunged past him with the speed of a striking cobra. Her slim hand plunged into the whirling mass of metal and closed tightly round the head of the jointed linking arm. She gritted her teeth and clung on with her arm circling until Crosby and Burton had launched themselves forward to relieve her and force the socket over the bolt of the drive shaft. With numb fingers, Burton screwed on the nut and tightened it with the spanner. Flower had turned away and was valiantly trying to bail water over the raised threshold. Burton looked at her, love and admiration filling his eyes.

Ryman turned as Burton appeared behind him. The wind had dropped a little and there was even a patch of light in the sky.

'Are we coming out of it?'

185

Ryman shook his head grimly, 'Not for long. We're passing into its centre. It'll be calmer for a while but then we have to go through the radius again. The typhoon is a moving circle all around us.'

'We can't stay where we are and weather it out?'

'We'd have to go ashore with it. It's only going to die down when it hits land.' He jerked his head towards the stern. 'How's the engine holding up?'

'God knows.' Both men ducked as a vicious gust of wind drove a swirling wave over the starboard side of the vessel, nearly causing it to broach. For several seconds, only the deck-house was above water. Burton clung for his life to a rail and thought of Flower below.

Ryman leaned towards him and raised his voice above the storm. 'Check out the merchandise.' Burton nodded and waited for the right moment to gain the companion way. In the last couple of hours he had been too occupied trying to save his life to think about the treasure. He plunged for the companion rail and slithered down into the heaving bowels of the ship. What was referred to as 'the merchandise' had been stored away in a natural compartment behind two timbers in the fo'c'sle. Burton struggled towards it, thrown from spar to bulkhead, and found that everything was still intact. Only the running seam of water between the timbers filled him with fear. The caulking was coming out like mortar from an old wall. If Crosby's containers started to leak then the painting would be ruined: if, as seemed more likely with every minute that passed, the timbers started to break away from the joists, then everything would be smashed.

Burton hobbled back to the engine room and the oily, water-specked confusion of pistons, valves and tappets that was somehow driving them through the storm. He found a cooking pot bobbing amongst the welter of floating debris and settled down to help Flower to bail.

Up on deck, a flash of forked lightning cleaved the sky. By its light, Ryman saw a terrifying sight; the seascape that stretched ahead. A range of white-capped mountains reaching away into infinity; giant waves, their over-hanging crests tobogganing down with the building force of an avalanche. The second half of the typhoon.

Ignacius Bigg pushed aside his cup of jasmine tea practically untouched. No one looking at his cold, impassive features would have been aware that he was experiencing a sensation of excitement; but it was unusual for him to reveal any sign of emotion. Excitement, too, was a comparative stranger to his repertoire of feelings and thus had had scant occasion to develop a recognisable personality of its own. The cause of Bigg's elation was a message he had received the previous day. It had come from Taipei and informed him that some insurance premiums had been paid. Wary at first, he had made discreet enquiries and discovered that the National Palace Museum was closed. There was no public holiday in Taiwan and this was therefore a most unusual occurrence. He alone of all who learned the news was best placed to hazard an explanation for it. The coup must have been successful; the promise contained in the message was correct.

Ignacius Bigg looked round the stateroom of the *Midas* and began to allocate his new treasures. The Renoir and the Fragonard would have to be moved; also the Goya obtained from the laxly guarded collection in the Episcopal Palace at Castres — it had been changed during restoration work in the Museum and nobody had yet noticed the substitution, rather to Bigg's annoyance. Perhaps it would be best to move the Gobelin tapestry to the far wall. Bigg pressed a button on his desk and a steel shutter slid up to reveal a display case set into the wall, full of priceless Delft pottery. He was going to need more of these display cases. It was a satisfying thought.

Bigg stood up and moved towards the private lift that would carry him to the deck. The weather outside was exceptionally fine and he always enjoyed leaving the suffocating purlieus of Victoria Harbour and pushing out into Kowloon Bay and the freedom of the South China Sea. Hong Kong was best at night, when it could be viewed as a static firework display rather than an ant hill.

He stepped inside the lift and frowned. The weather, that was the main problem. It would be a tragedy if his prizes were lost in a typhoon. There was also the question of his reception of the men who had procured the items; men who had already, or would soon, be branded as thieves; men who had already slipped out of circulation and to all intents and purposes disappeared.

Ignacius Bigg reflected for a moment and then pressed the button that would conduct him towards the deck. The faintest hint of a smile hung at the corner of his mouth.

The engine died when Ryman judged that they lay east of the Pescadores. There was a brief, hysterical railing from the propeller, a backfire shudder, a noisy confusion amongst the hammering tappets and then a dying fall which ended when the last grasshopper leg of circular movement had stuttered away to nothing.

'Shit!' said Crosby.

His frustration was understandable. They had just emerged from the perimeter of the typhoon. The swell was now a creamy, undulating wash and the wind had died away to an exasperated moan with only a hint of menace to it.

Ryman gave the helm to Crosby with instructions to hold her steady against the swell and prevent her broaching, and went below.

Burton had infiltrated the driving arms and pistons so that he looked as if he had been trapped by a huge insect. Ryman watched warily. 'Can you get her going?'

Burton twisted himself round the propeller shaft so that he could grunt a reply. 'Some of the pins have sheered off and she's seized up. It's not a big job but we need to beach her.'

'You can't patch her up?'

'Not till we get ashore.'

The vessel rolled and a surge of water swept over Burton's body. Flower and Ryman plunged forward to pull him clear of the engine and he emerged, coughing his lungs up. Ryman left him in Flower's care and went in search of the charts. The fo'c'sle was under water to the depth of several feet and he looked anxiously to the position of the merchandise. Water was spluttering through the timbers as if under pressure. A couple more hours and they would founder, if the vessel had not broken up first. A small waterfall was dropping on to the wireless set. Ryman flicked the switch; no light came on. The batteries must be drowned. Now they could receive no information from the outside world, nor make contact with Bigg. Ryman retrieved the chart case and peeled away the thick clinging leaves. There was no question of them choosing somewhere to beach; they would have to take what they could get, if they got anything other than a coral reef tearing the bottom out of the boat.

Ryman squinted into the faint light afforded by the one lamp that was still working and made out three islands to the east of

188

Penghu, the largest island in the Pescadores group. One seemed little more than a long coral reef, the other two had settlements marked on them. Whether there were people permanently living there or not he had no way of knowing. Most probably they were only visited by fishermen or coral merchants.

A shout from above sent him scrambling up the heaving companion way to find Crosby's face pressed against the rain-spotted glass of the deck-housing. 'What do you make of that?' There was terror in his voice. Ryman squinted into the inky darkness. At first he thought he was staring at the white line of a huge tidal wave; then he realised that the wave was not coming towards them. It was suspended against the night like a tightrope.

'It's a reef.'

'Holy shit.' Crosby recoiled from the glass.

'Can we steer past it?'

'Not a chance, Harry. You know we'll broach if we try and bring her round.'

'Fuck that engine!' Crosby's fist smashed against a panel. 'What the hell are we going to do?'

'There's nothing we can do. We'll have to ride out the swell and hope it takes us over the top. Hold her steady and keep your fingers crossed.'

'And on the other side?'

'We'll worry about that when we get there.'

'And the merchandise?' Burton had hauled his way to their sides. Ryman hesitated. If the boat broke up on the reef then they would lose everything, including, most probably, their lives. If they took to the water with the merchandise then it would hamper their efforts to survive, and almost certainly be smashed. There seemed only one alternative. 'It stays where it is. Get Flower up here.'

Burton nodded and disappeared. Crosby's face was once again pressed to the glass. 'Don! Look at this.'

Momentarily, before the vessel tilted into a trough, two lights could be glimpsed as if resting on the long comber of the reef. Crosby wrestled with the wheel and both men's eyes probed the darkness. The boat settled and then slowly climbed up the crest of the swell; white water streamed past the deck-house. The two yellow lights could now be clearly seen beyond the reef.

'What do you make of it?'

'A passage through the reef.'

Crosby cupped his eyes against the glass. 'It all looks the same.'

'We can't tell from here. Anyway, I don't think we've got a lot of choice.'

Ryman took the wheel and braced himself. Above the pounding of the sea and the wind came an even more ominous sound — the hungry roar of the surf, millions of tons of water smashing down on razor-sharp coral. Even after what they had been through it was a noise to freeze the blood.

Flower and Burton crowded into the tiny deck-house and Ryman saw the girl's jaw tighten as she recognised what lay ahead. 'We're going through or over that reef. Whatever happens, stay with the vessel as long as you can. The water must get calmer on the other side.'

Burton put his arm round Flower's shoulder. 'I'll stick with you.' He smiled down at her. 'Just in case you need another swimming lesson.'

Flower returned the pressure of his hand and together they looked towards the reef.

Now they were being carried remorselessly forward by the swell and the sound of the surf was thunder. No sooner had one clap started to die away than another echoed across the broad expanse of angry white before them. Individual pockets of turbulence became recognisable but no sign of the passage promised by the lights; the horizontal line of frenzied water was unbroken. Ryman fought to hold the boat steady as the noise deafened him. If they came broadside on the reef then they would be swamped and broken in seconds.

'Hang on!' The words were meaningless. He shouted them as a war cry to prove that his voice could carry above the fury of the elements and quench his fear. There was a wall of white before them; spray leaping a hundred feet into the air; a glimpse of gleaming, sea-washed coral like teeth exposed in a hungry mouth; a cannon roar of surf; the sea suddenly ran crazy like a river approaching a waterfall, the boat was sucked forward and swept towards the maelstrom of white; there was a terrifying grinding noise and she slewed sideways and seemed to explode in the surf; Ryman felt himself turning through ninety degrees, bodies crashing down on top of him: he could see nothing in the firework burst of spray. The boat shuddered to a halt on the coral and a wave broke over it. Ryman thought that he was going to die, felt water over his head: then whatever lay beneath them seemed to lift into the air and sweep them forward again; the wheel spun and nearly broke his wrist; he could feel the boat careering sideways and water breaking over them.

Something struck his head and he was free as if tipped out of a box beneath water. He lashed out in a last frantic effort to survive and felt only the currents tearing at his body; for terrible seconds it seemed that he was never going to reach the surface and then his head broke clear and he saw grey sky above him. The angry roar of the surf was behind him, and in the distance was the outline of the shore and the two lights that now trembled in the darkness. Ryman spat and looked about him desperately. Where was the boat? Where were the others? There was still movement in the water but it was sluggish compared to what lay outside the reef. Somehow, the force of the tide had carried them across the coral and into the comparative safety of a lagoon. But had they all survived? Ryman shouted and trod water whilst he searched the darkness. There was an answering cry and a black shape suddenly obscured one of the lights. It was the outline of a capsized boat. Ryman struck out and blundered into a flotsam of fuel cans and spars. The boat was on its side, and Burton and Flower were clinging to the hull. Ryman felt his heart lift as he recognised the slim arms spread out against the timbers.

'Where's Harry?'

Before Burton could reply there was a pained, spluttering noise and Crosby struggled out of the darkness, swimming an untidy side stroke. With Ryman in attendance he reached the boat and clung to the rudder, making each breath sound as if it was going to be his last. Ryman rested against the propeller and saw to his relief that it appeared to be undamaged. He turned towards the beach. That they had survived was no thanks to the two bonfires that he could see blazing on the sand. He was prepared to swear that there had been no passage through the reef. Doubtless they had misread the signs, but it could have cost them their lives.

Crosby's breathing was easier and his groans sounded more like prayers for his continuing existence rather than indications that he was injured.

Ryman sculled to Flower. 'Are you all right?'

She nodded slowly. 'Thanks to Henry.'

'Can you make it to the shore?'

'She'll be all right.' There was a proprietorial edge to Burton's voice that Ryman could understand.

'O.K. Let's go.'

Ryman pushed away from the hull and almost immediately was brought to a halt. A thick mass of weed swelled up against his body and robbed it of movement. He stopped swimming and tried to tread water, but it had wrapped itself round his legs and clung tenaciously. Alarm gave way to panic; he called out to warn the others and kicked violently, eventually freeing himself. Like dead men's fingers, the weed brushed against his body and he scudded clumsily across its surface, fearing that if he stopped again it would be for the last time. He took in a mouthful of water and then another, and he was forced to let his feet drop. The weed coiled round his arms and as its slippery mass closed about him greedily, his foot struck sand. He had reached the beach at last. He saw the flickering light of a fire take solid form and he drove himself forward, the weed a barrier against his chest. He rose up from the water and then stopped. A figure was approaching with the light behind it. The silhouette was unmistakable; the pudding basin helmet turning the head into a button mushroom, the gaiters pinching the legs above the boots; the carbine gripped menacingly between two hands. With a sinking heart, Ryman recognised a soldier of the Taiwan army.

CHAPTER ELEVEN

'*Dyou byan chuan!*'

Burton did not understand the order to turn left and was rewarded with a blow from the rifle butt. With Flower, Ryman and Crosby he had been dragged from the water and promptly relieved of his wrist watch and the small amount of Taiwan dollars he had been carrying. He could remember seeing four soldiers — dirty, dishevelled men, one of them wearing four wrist watches like bracelets — but he was so tired as to be hardly able to take in what was happening. Even the crushing disappointment of capture had been pushed quickly into the background. All he wanted was to be left to sleep; the misery could come later.

Ryman looked about him as the party was driven off the narrow, sloping beach and into the rocks. It was cruel luck that this small coral island should be one of the ones fortified against attack from the Chinese mainland. As a stepping stone to Taiwan it did not appear to have a great deal to offer. Perhaps it had some strategic importance in relation to the rest of the Pescadores Group. Whatever its military value he was not impressed with the soldiers who were guarding it. The Taiwanese Army was usually a model of smartness and efficiency. These men were dirty and brutal; their uniforms had not been cleaned nor their bodies washed. Ryman did not trust them. He looked forward to seeing an officer.

'*Ting-yi-ting!*'

Flower plucked at Burton's arm to save him from another blow. They had been ordered to stop where a slab of concrete showed white amongst the rocks. There was a doorway in it and it was towards this that they were driven. Flower was not surprised to find steps going down and an unpleasant musty smell combined with that of human excreta. She knew that there were islands like Quemoy and Matsu near the Chinese mainland that were honeycombed with tunnels against air and sea invasion. Men could spend weeks below ground.

The steps went down to a narrow corridor and the smell got worse. The floor was littered with an accumulation of sand, empty bottles, tins and screwed up pieces of paper. Cobwebs festooned some doorways, and beyond them could be glimpsed small cell-like rooms either empty or containing untidy piles of ammunition boxes. Ryman was becoming more and more puzzled and worried. This grubby mausoleum did not give the impression of being a military base. It appeared to have been abandoned.

Some steps loomed up and there was a welcome breath of fresh air. Crosby gritted his teeth and prepared for the ascent. Like Burton, he was ready to keel over and barely conscious of his surroundings. He felt the muzzle of a rifle thrust into his back and struggled forward in the jerky light of the torch. The rough treatment came as no surprise. He had never entertained any illusions as to what would happen if they were caught.

Flower had listened to every word the soldiers spoke, but she had heard no mention of the National Palace Museum or the fact that they were being hunted. Their captors had talked about recovering the boat in the morning, that was all. Perhaps it was because they were only simple soldiers. Their officers would probably have been alerted by wireless.

Burton saw a door open in front of him and ducked as he was thrust into a small low-ceilinged room with one barred window. Ryman and Crosby appeared beside him and the door slammed shut. Burton turned slowly and saw to his horror that Flower was not with them. Galvanised, he launched himself at the door and kicked and beat with his fists until he was pulled away by the others. Ryman shouted at him angrily, 'Shut up! That's not going to do any good.'

Burton stared at Ryman contemptuously. 'I thought you loved her.'

'I love her enough to save her life,' said Ryman calmly. 'And my own. If one of those clowns decides to empty his carbine through the door we're not going to be in shape to help anybody. I think we're in more danger than you probably realise.' He crossed to the window and pressed his face to the bars. Above the dark outline of the rocks a faint pink flush told that dawn was approaching. The wall was thick and the bars set into it securely. Ryman wrenched but there was no hint of movement.

Crosby sank to the floor. 'Sorry, I'm bushed.'

Ryman dropped down beside him and spoke urgently. 'I don't think our reception committee is part of an army unit. I think they're deserters. They've probably come here from some other island: the defences here have been abandoned, that's obvious. I think those fires on the beach were lit expressly to lure any passing boats onto the reef. Did you see the man with four watches on his wrist? Where do you think they came from?'

'Wreckers,' breathed Burton.

Crosby jerked himself up to a sitting position. 'That weed was thick with wreckage. I didn't think it all came from us.'

'And they took everything we had, didn't they? I thought it was strange: soldiers taking our watches. Christ...!' a thought occurred to Burton and he shook his head in disgust. 'One of them shone his torch in my mouth. He was probably checking if I had any gold teeth.'

'You think they're going to kill us?' Crosby suddenly found himself staring at the dark stains on the walls.

'And they've got Flower,' exclaimed Burton.

'I don't think they're going to kill her,' said Ryman calmly. 'She could last longer than any of us.'

'Bastards!' hissed Burton.

'Why haven't they killed us already?' said Crosby.

'Maybe they need us for something: perhaps they don't have a boat and they want to get ours working so they can move on. They can't stay here for ever.'

'So they don't know anything about the merchandise?'

'I doubt if they've even got a wireless.'

'So what are we going to do?'

'Be ready for anything. Watch me. When we move we're going to have to move like lightning. There may never be another chance.' Ryman looked at the haggard faces about him. 'Right now you might as well try and sleep. Nothing's going to happen till morning.'

Crosby sighed and lay down again. 'Shit! And I thought I was tired. Now I don't want to shut my eyes.'

But he did. Twenty minutes later all three men had fallen into an exhausted sleep. Ryman was the only one to wake when the door cracked open and Flower was thrust in with them. Her lips were swollen, her mouth was bleeding and one of her eyes was closed. She slumped to her knees and Ryman took her in his arms. He didn't need to ask her what had happened. He could feel her beating heart and hear her crying softly. He stroked her hair and gently massaged the back of her neck. Just when he thought she had fallen asleep her fingers slipped inside her torn sleeve and withdrew a bayonet shaped like a dagger; its blade gleamed wickedly in the half light. 'I was able to take this,' she said.

'Good,' said Ryman. 'Very good.' He withdrew the bayonet gently from her fingers and continued to stroke her hair.

When Ryman woke again, there was a patch of lop-sided light on the wall and the sky was steely blue. He carefully laid Flower's still-sleeping body on the floor and moved to the window. The sound of the surf pounding on the reef could be heard quite clearly. A flutter of wings made him turn his head and he saw a large crow alight on the sand a dozen yards away. It cocked its head to one side and then hopped forward to peck at something that protruded from the sand. At first Ryman thought it was a root; then he recognised the fingers. The crow was pecking at the hastily buried remains of a human being. Another crow arrived and Ryman turned his back on the loathsome sight and leaned against the wall. What he had just seen confirmed his worst suspicions. There was probably more than one body buried in the sand and plenty of room for four more.

Seen in the light of day, the inside of the cell was hardly more reassuring. There were smears of blood on the walls and the brick work was pock-marked with bullet holes.

Ryman woke the others and told them to look out of the window. As he listened to their exclamations of disgust, he was looking round the cell to see if it afforded any opportunity to take their captors by surprise. The door opened outwards and the only furniture was a latrine bucket. The ceiling was low and there was no possibility of hiding. Only in the last extremity could they make a stand here. Ryman addressed the others. 'We mustn't let them know we've seen what's outside that window. They might decide to finish us on the spot. Act as weary as you can, give them the impression that there's no fight left in us' — he revealed the bayonet — 'but be ready to move at any instant.'

'Where did you get that?' asked Crosby.

'Flower got it,' said Ryman grimly. The swelling round her eye had gone down slightly but was still puffy. Burton looked at her and there was pain in his eyes. 'What did they do to you?'

'They raped me. I saw the knife on the floor so I struggled. When they threw me down I was able to take it.'

196

'My God!' Burton clenched his fists in fury. 'I'm going to kill those bastards.'

'Not if you lose control of yourself,' said Ryman. 'Remember what I said: act beaten, not angry.' He turned back to Flower. 'What else did you see last night? How many of them were there?'

'Only the four that were on the beach. I do not think that there are any more. They were drinking *kaoliang*.'

'What the hell is that?' asked Burton.

'White lightning,' answered Ryman. 'Distilled sorghum; sixty per cent alcohol by volume. Potent.'

'They were very drunk,' continued Flower. 'That is why they brought me back; they could hardly stand up.'

'So there's going to be some thick heads and mean tempers around this morning,' observed Ryman. 'We have been warned.'

'The one with the watches is the leader.' Flower shuddered and touched her swollen eye. 'He is crazy. The others are frightened of him. The one with the scarf round his head; he is simple and I do not think that he sees very well.'

'They didn't say what they were going to do with us?'

'No, but' — Flower shivered again — 'there are bundles of clothes in one of the rooms; also sandals, all sizes. These are not soldiers' clothes. I think they have stolen from fishermen who come here, and killed them.'

Whilst they talked, Ryman had removed his shirt and made four small cuts in the material beneath his left armpit. He threaded the bayonet through these from the inside and put on the shirt again. The bayonet now rested vertically against the side of his ribs with the two small areas of blade that showed, concealed by his arm. Hardly had he stuffed the shirt back into his trousers than there was the sound of footsteps approaching down the corridor. Ryman gestured to the others to lie down and sank to his haunches with his arm positioned to snatch the bayonet if the right moment arose. His heart was pounding and his mouth dry as the door flew open. Nobody came in, and for a moment he expected a hail of bullets to wipe them out. Then a guttural order was barked, telling them to come out one by one.

Ryman emerged first and was met by a blow from a rifle butt that smashed against his upper arm and propelled him down the corridor towards a second man who was covering him with a sub-machine gun from one of the doorways. There was no chance of

197

retaliation. Ryman nursed his arm and staggered on down the corridor towards the direction they had come from the night before. Behind him, Crosby and Burton suffered their turn. He heard the sickening thud of butt against flesh and prayed that Burton would keep his head. There was a discussion amongst the Chinese as to whether Flower should accompany them, and then a decision that she would be needed as an interpreter. This suggested that there was some task awaiting them, but also left the lingering fear that with the exception of Flower they were going to be disposed of afterwards. She would be kept alive to amuse their captors.

Ryman emerged into dazzling sunlight and shielded his eyes. There was a strong wind blowing but all traces of the typhoon had disappeared. The air carried the smell of rotting seaweed. On all sides the rocks rose up to the height of a house and on the landward side there was a low cliff. A stunted banyan tree was the only vegetation to be seen. It sprawled across the sand on spindly roots that supported the weight of its foliage like makeshift crutches.

Ryman looked carefully at their captors as they emerged from the tunnel. He could see what Flower had meant about the man with the scarf round his head. He appeared to have a wall eye and moved clumsily, clutching his carbine as if it was a stranger in his hands. The other two men were more dangerous. They were wary and their fingers never strayed far from the triggers of their weapons. One of them would always stand back and keep his distance if the other closed with the prisoners. They were not taking any chances, and if the white lightning had had any effect on them it had only been to increase their viciousness.

The fourth man came into view as they left the shelter of the rocks and stepped out on to the hot sand. He was still wearing his helmet as if it were a symbol of authority and stood up in a small boat that he was propelling through the weed with the aid of a long pole. The vessel that had brought them from Taiwan lay on its side on the far edge of the weed bank that acted as a buffer between it and the shore. Beyond it, the reef curved round in a semi-circle, with an opening close to the shore that had been invisible from their position of the night before. The two treacherous fires were still smouldering. Ryman looked around at everything, feeling his senses sharpened by the proximity of death. The weed was strewn with pieces of wreckage and there was the burnt-out hull of a fishing boat further up the beach, the remains of its nets lying across its thwarts.

The man in the boat started to shout in Cantonese and gesticulate towards the capsized vessel. Ryman looked towards Flower for a translation. 'He wants us to bring the boat up on the shore.' Ryman felt a sense of temporary relief. So there was a task for them; they were not going to be cut down on the beach. Not yet.

'*Dzou!*'

The muzzle of a machine carbine jammed into Ryman's kidneys, driving him towards the sea. He felt the steel of the bayonet cold against his flesh, and bit back the desire to whip it out and plunge it into his tormentor's ribs. For the moment he must show no resistance. Pretending to stumble, he shambled to the water's edge and waded into the weed. Soon it was a heavy barrier against his chest and his arms were festooned with it. It was impossible to forge a permanent pathway; with every step taken the weed closed in behind.

Ryman glanced round to see Crosby, Burton and Flower entering the water. The man with the machine carbine waited on the beach; the two other Chinese shouldered their weapons and started to wade after their prisoners — they were presumably going to help. Ryman pushed on through the weed and felt nervous excitement building inside him. The man in the boat had now paused ten metres from the capsized vessel and was retrieving a fuel can which had come to rest in the weed. There was other flotsam in the bottom of his boat; also another machine carbine.

Something moved in the water to his left and Ryman turned to see a large yellow croaker twitching on its belly. The weed was a repository of human and animal waste; under the hot sun its surface was steaming, a scent of death and decay filled the nostrils. Ryman came to the edge of the fishing boat and pushed against its hull. It stirred listlessly. He pushed again and watched what was happening about him. To his dismay, the man in the helmet stood up with the machine carbine in his hands. Now they were under two guns, from the shore and from the boat. In a response to orders and a translation from Flower, Crosby and Burton moved to the stern of the vessel with the Chinese who had been responsible for meting out most of the physical abuse. The man with the head scarf was at the prow with Flower, trying to clear a path through the weed.

'*Ni men dzou!*'

With water up to his chest, Ryman started to push. Beside him, Crosby was nearly treading water and the Chinese was barely in his depth. Ryman looked across to the small boat and the pole that was lying across it. The sand stirred beneath his feet and at ankle level there was no resistance from the weed. It was a floating mass between him and the boat, but there was a way underneath it. He pretended to be pushing with all his strength and whispered out of the corner of his mouth to Crosby, 'I'm going to take our friend in the boat. Don't do anything until they see I've gone. Tell Henry.' He slipped his hand underneath his shirt and quickly withdrew the bayonet and lowered it beneath the water. He nudged Crosby with the hilt and nodded downwards. 'Take it.' Crosby hesitated and then closed his fingers round the weapon. The boat was now advancing slowly and Ryman edged his way round the stern as if looking for a better point from which to push. He was waiting until he was out of sight of the man on the shore and his leader in the rowing boat. He scrambled round the lop-sided keel and bent low as if pushing with all his might. He was now temporarily invisible to the Chinese nearest to him, who was occupied in goading Crosby and Burton to greater efforts.

Ryman took a final glance between the keel and its housing to pinpoint the exact position of the small boat, and then sucked in a deep breath. He ducked beneath the water and folded himself into a ball until his knees touched the bottom. Feeling the sand against his chest, he struck out with all his might and drove off towards the man in the helmet. The weed pressed down on him and the view ahead was a glaucous blur; the light that penetrated was not enough to reveal the whereabouts of the boat. Five strokes and his arms became enmeshed in weed. He struggled on and felt himself being held back as if by tightening bonds. Some of the weed was rooted in the sand and he was blundering into coils of slippery fibres. The strain on his lungs was building up and bright lights flashed behind his eyes; surely the confusion beneath the water must be seen from the boat. He thrust on again and the darkness closed in about him; his chest was going to explode. More clinging tentacles wrapped themselves around him and he drove from the bottom and broke surface. The thick mass of weed smeared against

200

his face and he tore it aside to find himself staring at the pole which lay across the boat. There was a cry of surprise and he seized the pole and drove at the man's legs. There was little force in the blow but the man stumbled and fell backwards. A burst of hot metal screamed past Ryman's head and he threw himself forward and seized the barrel of the carbine before it could be fired again. The man struggled to break free, but Ryman lunged across the gunwale and closed the fingers of one huge hand round the lip of the helmet. He tightened his grip and pulled the man towards him. For a moment he smelt foul breath and then he took both hands to the rim of the helmet and wrenched viciously. There was a sharp crack and the pressure of the strap against the Adam's apple slackened. The man was dead, his neck broken.

There were sounds of commotion from the large vessel and a burst of firing from the shore. Ryman snatched the carbine as bullets kicked up the water around him. He struggled behind the boat and fought to free his arms and shoulders from their mantle of weed. The man on the shore was standing with legs astride, and spraying the small boat. Splinters skipped in the air and there was the unnerving whine of bullets. Ryman felt a searing pain as if his arm had been touched with a white-hot poker and threw the carbine to his shoulder. More bullets spattered about him and he fired a returning burst with his head barely above water. He saw a dust of sand rise in the air and the man turned and started to run up the beach. Ryman took careful aim and fired two short bursts. As his finger eased off the second, the man was falling to his knees. He scrambled a few feet further and then rolled on his side, slowly drawing his legs up towards his chest.

Ryman turned towards the fishing boat. Only the Chinese at the stern was visible. With one hand he was clinging to the rudder; the other was pressed to his body below water level — a tide of scarlet stained the green. Ryman pushed forward and the man lost his grip and slid beneath the weed.

There was a burst of firing from the prow, and Ryman bypassed the stern to see Crosby lowering a rifle taken from the man killed with the bayonet. A flurry of sickening movement and the weed closed over another corpse. A long ripple died away through the green carpet and pressed gently against Ryman's chest. He waded towards the spot where Burton was comforting Flower. Her face bore the marks of blows and there was a vicious-looking swelling at her temple. It was easy to see what had happened: she had tried to stop the Chinese firing at Crosby and Burton, and had suffered accordingly. Without Burton's support she would have sunk below the surface. Ryman reached out and squeezed her hand. It was no more than a gesture but it was all that he had the power to give. He nodded to Burton. 'Look after her.' He turned to Crosby. 'We'll see if we can lay our hands on some food and then organise a burial party. After that we'll get the boat organised.'

There was no reply. Everybody was too exhausted to speak. They started to wade towards the shore.

CHAPTER TWELVE

'Well?' said Ryman.

Burton spoke with quiet satisfaction. 'I think I've done it.' It was the next morning and they had beached the boat on rusty steel rollers found amongst the debris in the tunnels and built a large fire against the rocks. A primitive but effective set of bellows had been constructed with the aid of some rubber tubing and tins fitted inside each other, and Burton had set up business as a blacksmith. The fruits of his labours were now cooling in front of them: three of the pins responsible for the breakdown of the engine, complete with newly welded heads.

'Whether they hold is another matter,' said Burton.

'We'll test them out round the lagoon,' said Ryman. He looked across to where Flower was caulking the timbers with a makeshift oakum of the fibres from the fishing nets. 'If we don't hit any snags we'll get under way tomorrow at sunrise.'

'Good.' Burton's gaze took in the three freshly dug graves beneath the banyan tree. 'It can't be too soon as far as I'm concerned.' Ryman started to move away but Burton stopped him. 'Don.' He tossed aside his coal hammer and nodded to where Flower was industriously using a bayonet to fill one of the gaps between the planks. 'What are we going to do about her?'

Ryman flushed angrily. 'What is there to do?'

'I want her.'

'She can make up her own mind.'

'You never say what you feel about her, do you?'

'Not to you, I don't.'

'I love her.'

'That's your privilege.'

Such exchanges made Ryman feel uncomfortable. Not only because their directness embarrassed him, but because they drew out into the open something that he wanted kept out of the way until their main business was completed. Single-minded co-operation was vital to the success of the mission. This intermittent sparring over Flower created tensions that should not exist. Ryman knew he was capable of feeling jealousy towards Burton and was aware that the younger man had saved Flower's life coming over the reef. It was not something he wanted to be reminded of. Until the deal with Ignacius Bigg had been completed, Burton must remain an ally, not a rival.

'I'll try and get these pins mounted. I'll call you if I need some help.' Burton had rightly construed Ryman's tense replies as an indication that the subject was not one he wished to pursue.

'Right.' Ryman watched Burton walk towards the boat and saw him kiss a smiling Flower on the shoulder as he went past. He turned away.

In the shadow of the rocks, Crosby was working on the radio set. Ryman was relieved to hear a crackle of static as he came near. 'You've got her going, then?'

Crosby quickly switched off the set and removed his earphones. 'Yeah, I think she was just soaking wet. I've dried her out and baked up some batteries. Should be all right if we take it easy.'

'Well done. It looks as if Burton's licked the boat problem, and I've been checking the fuel. We only lost a couple of cans coming over the reef and I've located some drums over by the tunnel opening. The unit that was here must have left them when they pulled out.'

Crosby stood up and dusted his hands. 'That's great. Some frigging luck at last.'

'And we'll take the weapons with us.'

Crosby's face clouded over. 'You think that's a good idea?'

'Why not?'

'Supposing something goes wrong and we get caught? They're going to give us even more trouble if we're carrying arms.'

'We need something up our sleeve. What if we find ourselves in another situation like this one? The sea around here is crawling with pirates. And how far do you think we can trust Bigg once we hand the stuff over?'

Crosby sighed. 'I don't want to get involved in another shooting match.'

'We'll hide the guns; just like we did the treasure. Nobody will know they're there unless they have to.' Ryman shook his clenched fist. 'Come on, Harry! We're in the final straight. Don't turn soft now.' He walked away towards the sea. Crosby flicked at the wireless set with his forefinger and looked after him, thoughtful and worried.

Safe under an overhanging boulder lay three million dollars' worth of art treasures. None of the items had been damaged in the typhoon or its aftermath; each container had been opened and its contents removed and examined by nervous fingers. Each one was intact. Ryman gazed down at the treasure. Every time he looked upon it he was seized by a kind of fear and awe. He expected a great bird to swoop down and carry it away, or a boulder to topple over and smash it to smithereens. Some act of God was always lurking round the corner waiting to snatch away what they had so nearly given their lives for. He turned to find Flower standing behind him. Her face was still beautiful despite its injuries. She looked sad. 'You have not talked to me,' she said.

'I'm trying to think about all the things we must do.'

She nodded towards the merchandise. 'So you can make a lot of money. Henry says that is not important to him.'

'Then he's a damn fool to have put up with what he's been through.' Ryman immediately regretted his vehemence but there was nothing he could do about it. He looked up to see tears forming in Flower's eyes.

'Donald, what is going to happen to us?'

'I don't know. I've talked about us going to England. Maybe you've had a better offer.'

Flower continued to look at him and the sadness deepened. 'Maybe I have.'

'Well, you think about it,' said Ryman brusquely. 'I've got to think about hiding some guns.' He looked at the bayonet in her slim fingers and thought of the price she had paid to obtain it. He wanted to take her into his arms and beg her forgiveness; he knew what she was asking for, but for some reason he could not give it. Not yet. 'Is that hull watertight?'

Flower said nothing, but turned and walked back towards the boat. Ryman looked down at the treasure and cursed under his breath. He hoped he knew what he was doing.

The wind woke Ryman and he looked at his watch. Three o'clock. They were sleeping on the beach because nobody wanted to be near the rocks or the tunnel. Ryman had already dreamed about it; he was lost in a labyrinth in which each turn brought a new horror, fresh intimations of how his mind was haunted by death. He sat up quickly and looked about him. Particles of sand were skipping across the beach with an eerie hissing noise. For a second he had a terrible premonition that the boat would not be there, but when he turned his head it was gently rocking where they had moored it beyond the weed. It looked like a ghost ship in the grey light of a full moon. The surf was booming against the reef and tiny wavelets agitated against the shore.

Ryman glanced towards the depression in the sand where Flower had been lying and saw that she was not there. His heart jumped. He looked around. There was no sign of either Burton or Crosby. Now he was wide awake. He threw aside his blanket and stood up. The fire they had lit was still burning and the wind ruffled the embers sending a shower of sparks dancing down the deserted beach. Ryman felt uneasy. Where had they gone? A sound made him whip round, but it was only a frond of dried palm blowing across the sand. He knelt and picked up the carbine that lay beside where he had been sleeping. At least the weapons were still there. He flicked off the safety catch and set off down the beach away from the tunnels. Ahead lay some broken rocks, and beside the water's edge the moonlight helped him make out two sets of footprints, one more pronounced than the other. Listening for any sound, he watched the shadows and tried not to see human shapes stalking him. A causeway of rock rose up and he clambered on to it, taking care not to strike anything with the rifle.

He started to walk along the natural breakwater and then stopped. A shadow moved beneath him. He froze and saw two bodies that were almost one: Burton and Flower making love, totally impervious to anything except each other. He saw the undulating movement of Burton's body and heard a reciprocating moan. A bitter ache filled his heart and he turned away silently and ran his hand across his eyes as if wishing to brush away the memory of what he had seen. If it had just been jealousy, that might have been an easier emotion to come to terms with, but there was more to it than that; he felt as if a vital organ had been removed — that bitter ache was not filling his heart but the place where it had been. For the first time, he realised that he could lose Flower, and with this realisation came the revelation that he had always taken her for granted; like the other women in his life, Maggie and Julia, who had got tired of waiting and packed their bags and silently stolen away. The same thing was going to happen again — was happening in his very presence. He had thought that he could put Flower into cold storage whilst he sorted out his plans for the days ahead, but it was not going to be as easy as that; she was not going to stay compartmentalised. Through Burton she had come to terms with the fact that Ryman's magnanimity in professing to love a whore was no more than self-interest; he could not accept the responsibilities entailed in having her to himself. Not until now; and now perhaps it was too late.

Ryman retreated as quietly as he had come, but this time was almost oblivious of his surroundings. He was conscious only of his own misery. It was not until he was nearly level with the boat that he became aware of a faint noise borne on the wind. It sounded like Crosby talking to himself. It was a strange noise and it filtered slowly into his troubled thoughts, reintroducing the fears that had started him on his nocturnal wandering. It was only when he heard the crackle of static that he realised that it came from the boat and that it was Crosby testing the wireless set. Quite why he should be doing so in the middle of the night was something that Ryman was too preoccupied to consider.

CHAPTER THIRTEEN

Ryman took them through the reef at sunrise. The water was clear, and the pitted surface of the coral undulated only a foot or two beneath the keel; the swell lifted them and shoals of brightly coloured fish darted away in total synchronisation like clouds of sparks. Soon there was only a sandy bottom and there the water became opaque and the sea choppy. The atoll disappeared and minutes afterwards its attendant island slid beneath the waves. Once again they were alone in the open ocean.

Ryman examined the charts and calculated that it would take them the best part of the day to reach their rendezvous. They were south of Penghu, but he wanted to give all the islands in the group a wide berth and also nurse the engine. With every second that passed, one ear was tuned to its rhythmic thumping as they chugged through the white crests. Below, Burton stood in attendance like a surgeon with a patient in the aftermath of a difficult operation.

If he was preoccupied, then Crosby appeared ill at ease. He said little, complained hardly at all, and wandered round the boat like a confined animal seeming to want to keep away from the others. Ryman wondered if the horrors of the island had made a deep impression on him. He did not seem himself.

Flower made tea and spent most of her time close to Burton. Ryman sensed a rejection and hoped that the pain and longing he felt did not show. There were now a lot of things that he wanted to say but he knew that this was not the time to say them. He must try and concentrate on the events of the next twenty-four hours.

By ten o'clock they had seen two fishing junks and passed through the Tropic of Cancer. The sky was cloudless and the wind had dropped; the sun came through the windows of the deckhouse as through a magnifying glass. Ryman screwed up his eyes against the glare and continued to hold course for Chi Mei to the south-west of the Pescadores Group. He made a routine sweep of the horizon and then looked again. A vessel had appeared on the starboard bow and even at a distance he could see that it was neither a junk nor a fishing boat. The sun was picking at it like a jewel.

Ryman watched uneasily. Penghu, Paisha and Yuweng, the main islands in the group, had been left behind; they were sailing in the open sea with Taiwan fifty miles to their east. The ship that was bearing down on them was coming from the south-east; from the direction of Kaohsiung, the Island's largest port and main naval base. Ryman called to the others and cursed the fact that their only set of binoculars had been carried away in the typhoon. The ship was closing the distance between them fast and he could make out the radar mast and the sleek lines of the triple deck; it looked like a compact destroyer.

Burton appeared, wiping his hands on an oily rag. 'What do you make of that, Henry?'

Burton's face fell. 'Christ.'

'That's what I thought.' He turned to Crosby. 'Any ideas, Harry?'

Crosby's expression was intriguing. He revealed more animation than at any time since they left the Island. He shaded his eyes and peered forward eagerly, almost devouring the vessel with his scrutiny. It was coming at them obliquely and they could see lifeboats hanging athwart the stern. Suddenly he burst into a short jackass laugh. 'It's a ferry boat. There's a daily service from Kaohsiung to Makung.' He laughed again, almost nervously. 'What did you think it was, a ship sent to hunt us down?'

Ryman was feeling too relieved to answer. He moved astern, and the small, brilliantly white liner loomed nearer so they could see the red of the Nationalist flag at the masthead. 'Flower, take the wheel for a bit. The rest of us had better get below. We don't want anybody reporting that they've seen three Ang Moh cruising round the South China Sea.' He led the way down the companion way, continuing to observe Crosby. He was getting worried about the man; there was a morose expression on his face that was almost disappointment. A minute passed, and there was a couple of greeting blasts from the ship's siren. Shortly afterwards the deck beneath their feet pitched and rolled as they cleared the wake.

Ryman looked towards the radio set which was mounted aft. 'Another couple of hours and we'll try and make radio contact.'

Crosby looked uneasy. 'You think that's a good idea? Supposing somebody picks us up?'

209

'We've got a waveband and a frequency. Who's going to be listening? We'll get Flower to do the talking; there's no reason why anybody should be suspicious if they do pick us up.'

'Surely they must believe that we're dead by now,' said Burton.

'That's what worries me,' said Ryman. 'If Bigg believes we're dead and sails off somewhere then we've got problems. We're behind schedule anyway. He'll hang around for a while, but not all that long.'

'Don's right,' said Burton. 'If there is a risk then I think we've got to take it.' He looked at Ryman supportively and then turned away, unable to hold his eye.

Crosby's expression grew more sullen. 'I think we should wait till we get to the lagoon. If Bigg's not there, then we can open up.'

'I don't agree, Harry.' Ryman's tone was relaxed but firm. 'We'll send out a call at midday when we're well south of Wangan. Just one.'

'When was it ever agreed that you made all the decisions?'

Burton put his hand on Crosby's shoulder. 'Harry, you've left it a bit late to start talking like that.'

Crosby shook the hand away and turned his head angrily. 'Why don't you mind your own fucking business? Go and screw your girlfriend.' Burton's fist swung back and Ryman caught it just in time.

'That wasn't necessary, Harry. I think you'd better apologise.'

There was a strained pause and then Crosby nodded in a gesture which pleaded guilty. 'I'm sorry, I guess I'm getting too keyed up.' He pushed past them and paused at the bottom of the companion way. 'O.K. to go on deck now?'

'Fine,' said Ryman.

In the hours that followed, they stopped to make minor repairs to the engine, and cooked and ate a large *tinhsian* fish that had been caught by trailing a line from the stern. At midday and thirteen hundred hours, Flower went on the air to send signals to Mr Bigg, but there was no reply. Ryman began to worry, and the atmosphere was tense between all on board. The sun moved overhead towards the coastal province of Fukien a hundred miles away in the People's Republic, and the timbers creaked. It was too hot to stay on deck outside the wheel-house, and stifling below. They passed four small islands that seemed little more than atolls and on one of them saw signs of human habitation and fishing boats pulled up on the shore. Apart from the occasional junk, they had the ocean to themselves.

'Hello Rainbow, hello Rainbow. Starfish calling. How do you hear me, over?' Flower spoke the words self-consciously in Mandarin as if their symbolism had no meaning to her. The others clustered round the set listening to the dry crackle of the static. In the background a Chinese voice could be faintly heard speaking urgently between what sounded like drum beats; probably a propaganda message being beamed either from the mainland or one of the Nationalist-held islands opposite Amoy and Fuchow.

There was a pause and Flower repeated her message. Again there was only the sound of the tiny disembodied voice ranting in space. Then, totally unexpected, there was a dip in the static that brought their hearts towards their mouths. It was the change of beat that presaged a message coming back across the air waves. 'Rainbow to Starfish. Rainbow to Starfish. You are very weak. Repeat, very weak. Report position, over.'

Ryman waited for Flower's confirmation of the precisely spoken words and joined Burton in a whoop of joy.

'It's them! We've done it.'

Ryman moved towards the companion way. 'Tell them we'll be at the rendezvous point in a couple of hours. I'll get the chart and give them our precise position.'

He climbed the steps, wanting to clench his fists and punch holes in the sky. After all they had been through it looked as if they were actually going to pull it off. He wondered why Crosby showed hardly any emotion. There was definitely something wrong with the man; perhaps he was sickening for a fever. He entered the deck-house and approached the gently rocking wheel. The chart lay beside it, and as he stretched out his hand he glanced around the placid ocean. A ship was bearing down on them out of the haze. Ryman looked again and told himself not to jump to conclusions; the ship was not bearing down on them; it was probably another ferry. But it was coming out of the sun, from the direction of the Chinese coast. There were only a handful of uninhabited atolls between them and the mainland and they had long ago left the shipping route between Makung and Kaohsiung. If it was not a ferry, what could it be? Most probably a warship of the Taiwan Navy on routine patrol; that made sense.

Ryman grabbed the chart and ducked back down the companionway. Before he could say anything, Burton turned with a worried expression on his face. 'We've lost them.'

Crosby had replaced Flower and was fiddling with the tuner.

'I was trying to get a better signal. I think the batteries are kaput.'

'We may have another problem,' said Ryman. 'Come on deck.'

Crosby flicked off the wireless and removed his headset. The expression on his face was difficult to read. Burton glanced at Flower and made for the companionway.

The approaching vessel was now taking on a shape: slim, high-decked, a cannon mounted aft of the bridge, a pennant with a red flag flying. She looked like a coastguard sloop; impossible to outrun and capable of blowing them out of the water. She was also on course to intercept them.

'Keep down,' said Ryman. 'She's probably got a glass on us.'

'Do you think she's looking for us?' said Burton.

'I doubt it. Better get below anyway. Flower, you take the helm. Act like a crazy woman if they hail you. Say your husband is sick and that Matsu will put a curse on them if they don't go away and stop frightening the fish.'

Flower did not reply. She was peering towards the approaching ship as if she could not believe her eyes.

'Did you hear what I said?'

Flower shook her head. 'It is not possible.'

'What is it?' said Burton.

'The flag.'

Ryman strained his eyes across the shimmering water and then understood. The flag he was looking at was not the familiar red, white and blue. It was bright red with a large yellow star in the canton and four smaller yellow stars in the crescent facing it. It was the flag of the People's Republic of China.

'What the hell are they doing here?' said Burton.

'Get below!' Ryman shoved him towards the companionway and turned to Flower. 'Do what I said and act scared.'

Flower smiled grimly. 'I will not have to act.'

Ryman squeezed her hand and followed the others below deck. The Chinese sloop was less that two hundred metres away and closing the distance fast; he had to think of the best thing to do. Burton and Crosby looked at him anxiously. 'You know where the

212

guns are. We'll only use them if we have to; I'm not giving up without a fight. If they board us they won't be able to bring that cannon to bear. We'll wait for them to come down here and then try and take them by surprise. I'll knock out everything I can with the sub-machine gun, you try and get aboard with the carbines. We may be able to catch them cold.' He waited for Crosby to demur, but the American said nothing.

Burton looked bemused. 'I still can't understand what they're doing here. These are Taiwanese waters.' He stationed himself by one of the bunks. Beneath the mattress was a machine carbine. Ryman moved to an oilskin that was hanging from a peg and draped over the sub-machine gun. Crosby picked his way to the fo'c'sle. A second carbine rested on two nails hammered into a joist.

Ryman listened and heard the powerful whine of the sloop's turbines override the lazy sound of water slapping against the hull. There was an ear-splitting shriek of a hooter, and a screech of Chinese spewed out of a loud hailer. The deck rocked beneath his feet and the hull creaked.

Ryman licked his dry lips and heard Flower reciting her piece. There were more orders and then the teeth-grating sound of two hulls grinding together; a shadow fell across the deck at the foot of the companionway. Ryman looked at Burton. Bubbles of sweat traced the line of his upper lip; his eyes were needle points. At the sound of feet dropping on to the deck above their heads, his hands moved towards the mattress.

Ryman raised one hand to the stock of the sub-machine gun and the other to the oilskin. Not only was he frightened, but he had a distaste for what he might be called upon to do. In all his years as a soldier, he had never killed in cold blood.

The sound of more men arriving on the deck coincided with the first footstep on the companionway. Ryman silently removed the oilskin and unhooked the sub-machine gun.

As he drew it down he saw that it had no magazine. Stupefied, he glanced about him, and at that instant two Chinese sailors appeared carrying snub-nosed automatic weapons. Their arms lunged forward and for a second he thought he was going to die; then a guttural order was barked out and he let his weapon drop to the floor. Beside him, Burton did the same, and behind came the sound of Crosby's carbine clattering to the deck.

213

'What the devil do you think you're doing?' exploded Burton. 'Are you pirates?'

'Save your breath, Henry,' said Ryman.

The two sailors stood aside and pointed to the companionway with their weapons. As Ryman ascended, he could hear the sounds of the compartments being pulled apart behind them.

Flower was standing on the deck, and with her a lieutenant in a white peaked cap and two more armed ratings. Another officer surveyed the scene from the bridge of the sloop and beside him stood a helmeted marine clutching a sub-machine gun that he looked as if he would dearly love to use.

'*Dzou!*' The lieutenant pointed towards the sloop. Ryman did not argue but clambered up on to the deck and waited for the others to join him. They were led past the davits and a brace of depth charges to a companionway at the stern. At rifle point they descended a passageway so narrow that it scuffed Ryman's shoulders, and were pushed into a tiny, steel-walled enclosure. The door slammed behind them and they were left in the suffocating heat.

Ryman turned to Crosby and hit him in the face with every ounce of force that he could muster.

CHAPTER FOURTEEN

Crosby's head jolted back and crashed against the bulkhead. His knees buckled and he slid down to arrive in an untidy heap on the floor.

'You bastard!' said Ryman. 'You told them, didn't you? I wondered what the hell you were doing with that wireless last night.' He glanced quickly at the startled Flower and Burton, as if in apology.

Crosby's hand rose slowly to the side of his jaw. On his face there was only an expression of miserable resignation. The hull trembled as the sound of the turbines picked up. They were getting under way.

'And you removed the magazines from the weapons,' continued Ryman. 'You really set us up. Why, Harry? Don't tell me you did a deal with the Chinese. Wasn't six hundred thousand enough for you?'

'Not with the Chinese,' said Crosby slowly. 'With the CIA. A guy called Henderson started haunting me. He's officially a business attaché but his real job is to keep tabs on everybody. He knew that I had been sacked. He started asking me why I was still in Taiwan. I told him I was thinking of starting a little export business in jade curios. I don't think he believed me and he knew I was staying at Ryman's apartment. He called me round to his office one day and suddenly produced some photos of the packaging for the merchandise. He'd had the apartment searched.'

'So you told him everything,' said Flower contemptuously.

'Not right away; I didn't know what to do. But he was clever. He gave the impression that he knew what we were going to do and that he *wanted* us to do it. He talked about the People's Republic's attachment to its cultural heritage. He said that there was an increasing need to maintain close and friendly relations with China. At the same time we had a commitment to Taiwan and should take care not to alienate her by appearing to move too closely towards the People's Republic. After a while I began to see what he was getting at. If we took the stuff and the Chinese were tipped off where they could intercept it, then the US would have done the People's Republic a big favour and nobody on Taiwan would know the difference.'

'So you volunteered to do the tipping off,' said Burton angrily.

'I didn't volunteer. My arm was twisted. First of all I got a lot of patriotic shit about my duty to the United States. When that didn't seem to be having much effect, Henderson started dropping hints. He said that if I didn't play ball he knew enough to have all of us put away for planning a seditious act against the people of Taiwan. He also said that once we were inside we'd never get out again.'

'So you did it for us,' sneered Burton.

'Henderson guaranteed that if the stuff was handed over to the Chinese he'd ensure that we came to no harm and were put across the border into Hong Kong.'

'So why didn't you tell us this was going on?'

Crosby looked uncomfortable. 'There didn't seem to be any point. Henderson kept saying that even if we didn't go ahead he still had enough to put us away. He was twisting my arm.'

'And there was no question of you making any money on the deal?'

Crosby hung his head.

'Well?' said Burton.

'A hundred thousand dollars.'

'You bastard.'

Burton drew back his foot and Crosby cowered. 'Don't you see? It was the only way anybody was going to make money out of the deal. You'd have done the same, there was no choice. I'll share the money if you like: twenty-five thousand bucks. All I want to do is get back to the States; find my wife.' He was almost crying. 'I wish I'd never got involved in this whole rotten business.'

Burton turned away. 'You make me sick.'

Ryman looked down at the pathetic bundle at his feet. Part of him felt sympathy; Crosby had been promoted beyond his means; the scheme had always been too ambitious for him. He had been ready to crack right from the beginning. Nevertheless, he had betrayed them. That could never be excused.

The door burst open without warning and the lieutenant was revealed with two armed ratings. He saw Crosby crumpled up on the floor and quickly gabbled an order. Ryman, Burton and Flower were forced back against the bulkhead with their hands on their heads, and the American was hauled to his feet and led towards the threshold. 'I am sorry,' he said pitifully. 'Jesus Christ, I'm sorry.' Tears were running down his cheeks as the door slammed behind him.

Burton lowered his hands and kicked the door savagely. 'Hell! And they were there, just a couple of hours away. It's not possible.'

'Soon after that we'll be in China,' said Ryman. 'This thing must be capable of forty knots.' He sank to his haunches and cupped his chin in his hands. He felt bitterly self-accusing. If he had not been so preoccupied the night before he might have realised the significance of Crosby's presence at the wireless; or at least been suspicious and pressed the matter.

Ryman looked at Burton and Flower and read the misery in their faces. It was ironic after all their suffering that they had merely succeeded in transferring the treasures from one set of Chinese to another. And with every second that passed they were sailing further away from Ignacius Bigg.

'Still no word?'

The wireless operator removed his headphones deferentially. 'No, sir.'

Bigg pursed his almost non-existent lips and moved away. This silence was strange. It probably signified no more than a technical fault or a fear that a communication might be intercepted, but it was still puzzling. Was it possible that some kind of psychological manoeuvre was being put into motion; an attempt at further whetting the appetite and introducing the fear that something had gone wrong? The whole intended to make the purchaser part almost gratefully with his money when the merchandise did eventually arrive?

Ignacius Bigg laid his hand on the polished brass rail that would conduct him to the scoured deck. Such reasoning was probably far too sophisticated. Ryman and Crosby were blunt men of action; effective at their craft, as they had proved, but not followers of Machiavelli. They would arrive with the merchandise and he would be waiting with their reward.

He stepped out on deck and pulled his yachting cap lower over his eyes. The sun was strong and the glare intense. His eyes spent most of their time in rooms. Such picture-book sights as were now afforded them arrived but rarely; a deep, natural harbour inside a

217

coral reef, palm trees admiring their reflections in the water, a narrow fringe of steeply sloping beach. Bigg shaded his eyes and looked across the calm waters of the lagoon to the opening in the reef and beyond. The sea shimmered away to the horizon unmarked by the imprint of any vessel. He swallowed a slight disappointment and leaned over the rail. The water was deep and the bottom invisible. A shoal of small fish scored the surface with their dorsal fins and nuzzled the side of the hull. Bigg watched them for a few moments and then let his eye wander to the recessed hatch two feet below the gunwale. It was this that concealed one of the four two-inch guns aboard; capable of firing through a hundred degrees and ripping into sheet metal as if it was toffee. He looked down and saw the fresh rust where the hatch runners had scored the paintwork of the hull during the last training session. It was only a detail, but it offended his punctilious eye for neatness and cleanliness. He would have it painted as soon as possible. He frowned; that would have to be after he had received his visitors.

'How many men did you see?' asked Ryman.

Burton wiped his arm across his forehead and reflected. 'Two, four, the lieutenant, the captain, the fellow on the bridge, there was a man near the companionway, maybe two — about a dozen all told, I suppose.'

'Plus the engine room. I'd say the whole crew would be between fifteen and twenty.'

Flower raised a weary head from her knees. 'What difference does it make?'

'I want to get some idea what our chances are if it comes to a fight. We're never going to get out any other way.'

'What about the safe conduct to Hong Kong?' said Burton.

Ryman shook his head scornfully. 'Do you really think they're going to let us go? Henderson would prefer us dead; we know too much. He's probably passed that on to his Chinese friends. They've got their treasures, we're criminals. They won't give a damn what happens to us.'

'Don is right,' said Flower, earnestly. 'They will probably kill Crosby too.'

'And save Henderson a hundred thousand dollars.' Ryman nailed Burton with his eye. 'It's the tidy way out.'

218

Burton shook his head. 'You talk about "our chances". What chance have we got against fifteen men, maybe twenty?'

'If we can get to the bridge and take over, that will knock the fight out of the rest of them. The ratings are raw recruits, probably fisher boys plucked off the waterfront at Chang-Chou. That's why they've got that marine with the sub-machine gun on the bridge. He's the professional. It's a long shot, but we can do it.' He watched Burton's face for signs of a reaction. 'The alternative is to stay here. You know what I think — if it gets any hotter they won't need to shoot us.'

It was true. The bulkheads were hot to the touch and glistened with their sweat. There was no movement of air. Burton shrugged his shoulders in a gesture of resignation. 'All right. I go along with what you say. How are we going to do it?'

As Burton looked at Ryman, Flower spoke. 'I will lie out on the floor and pretend to have fainted. You two will kneel beside me. You will appear to be very agitated. You will lift me to my feet and I will act as if I need both of you to support me. You will say that I need air and start to lead me towards the door. The guards will step forward and you will seize them.'

Ryman reflected. 'That seems as good as anything. I don't think the lieutenant is armed. Try not to fire a shot if you can avoid it. Club them down with their weapons and high tail it to the bridge. If we can put the squeeze on the captain then we've got a chance.'

Burton shook his head. 'It still sounds like suicide.'

'So is staying here, waiting to be killed.'

There was a silence, broken by Flower taking the initiative and lying with her back against the floor. Burton filled his lungs with the hot, clammy air and joined Ryman in kneeling beside her.

Flower took one of their hands in each of hers and smiled up at them. Ryman felt a range of conflicting emotions; it was like a deathbed scene. There was the incongruity of kneeling beside the woman he now knew he loved, but with his rival only a foot away; having so many things to say but being denied time and opportunity to say them; the words welling up but being swallowed down again as his ears strained for some sound to say that their gaolers were approaching. He squeezed the slim hand and felt the pressure returned. Perhaps that mutual gesture said everything.

There was a sharp crack and the door opened. Ryman leaned forward solicitously and out of the corner of his eye saw Burton

219

doing the same. Flower groaned and looked towards the open door through half-closed eyes. The pretence vanished from her face and her eyes opened wide in horror. Ryman braced himself and turned his head.

Crosby stood behind them with a knife protruding from the side of his neck and a rivulet of blook soaking his shirt. A self-loading rifle clattered from his fingers and he crashed to the floor.

CHAPTER FIFTEEN

For a second nobody moved. Ryman saw a look of horror on Burton's face that must match his own. Flower recoiled as Crosby's blood spread across the floor towards her. His hand moved and jerked clumsily towards the door. He was urging them to escape. 'Sorr-sorr-sorr —' At first the ghastly, guttural noise meant nothing: it seemed to come from a machine rather than a man. Then Ryman realised that Crosby was trying to say 'sorry'. In trying to make amends he had given his life.

Ryman scrambled to his feet and snatched the self-loading rifle. He crossed to the door and peered out. Near the companionway a pair of feet protruded into the corridor. The ship was vibrating, humming with its movement through the water; the dim lights flickered. Ryman beckoned the others into the corridor and closed the door. Crosby's hand had risen to the knife in his neck and stopped moving.

Half a dozen steps brought them to the foot of the companionway. A Chinese sailor was lying half out of a cabin with his bonnet askew. There was a large bump on his temple and he was moaning softly. The knife sheath at his waist was empty. Ryman heard voices on deck and dragged the man back into the cabin. A plate of chop suey lay across the floor beside a bunk. It looked as if Crosby had received his fatal wound in a battle with the man who had brought his food.

Burton and Flower piled into the cabin and the door was closed. Ryman started to speak and then broke off as he heard the clatter of footsteps coming down the companionway. Hardly had he time to move towards the door than it burst open and a sailor with a rifle peered in. Ryman shoved the muzzle of the self-loader underneath the man's chin and his opening mouth closed fast without uttering a sound. Burton stretched out a hand and hauled the man over the threshold to propel him the length of the cabin against a bulkhead. Ryman brought down the stock of his weapon and the Chinese sprawled unconscious beside his comrade. Flower closed the door silently and the sound of heavy breathing filled the confined space.

'The bridge,' said Ryman. He waited whilst Burton snatched up the fallen rifle, and pressed his ear to the door. The turbines whined and there was the sensation that they were losing speed. Ryman swung open the door and waited in the corridor for the others, before closing it and sliding home the bolt. Above their heads, a rectangle of blue sky showed at the top of the companionway. Ryman took the steps three at a time and burst on to the deck. Two men were on their hands and knees beside one of the depth charges. They spun round as Ryman appeared and there was an instantaneous screech of alarm. Ryman clubbed down one man and the other fled down the deck towards the bridge, screaming at the top of his voice. Ryman raised his weapon but could not fire. He chased after the man and heard Burton's footsteps behind him.

The ship was still travelling fast and he glimpsed white water surging past the two-tier wire rail. He veered towards the superstructure to preserve his balance and the change of direction saved his life. A rating with an automatic opened up from above and bullets furrowed the deck where he had been running. There was a shot from behind and the automatic stopped firing. Ryman kept running. An unarmed sailor cowered near one of the davits and, ahead, the man he had been following dashed into a companionway howling like a stuck pig. Ryman saw the corner of the bridge protruding round the radar stack and raced for the steps. As he did so, the menacing snout of an automatic lunged round the rail and he glimpsed the helmeted marine who had been on the bridge when they arrived. Ryman changed his plans fast and dived behind a ventilation hatch as a spray of bullets chewed splinters out of the deck around him.

The situation was desperate. Their only hope had been to take control of the bridge fast and now he was pinned down on the open deck. He looked back towards the stern. A man lay sprawled across the deck with one arm stretched out towards the automatic that lay just beyond his reach. Beyond him, Burton was sitting with his back against the superstructure, clutching his thigh. Ryman could see blood pumping through his fingers. As he watched, Flower darted from the meagre shelter of a stack and swept up the fallen automatic. As her fingers closed about it, there was a burst of firing from the bridge. Ryman jerked round and saw the marine poised at the top of the companionway. His weapon was trained towards the stern and the flash eliminator glowed with the length of the burst. Ryman threw the self-loader to his shoulder and depressed the trigger. Bullets screamed off stanchions and the man trembled as if leaning into a gale, and then fell backwards with one foot protruding into space.

Ryman started to run forward and then sprawled full length as the vessel changed course violently. He started to slide towards the sea and felt a cloud of spray burst over him. One foot collided with a rail, and he braced himself and scrabbled to avoid pitching into the sea. Water sluiced through the scuppers and soaked him up to the waist. Another tilt and he was rolling backwards towards the superstructure. Something struck his arm a heavy blow and he clung to it through the dizziness to find that it was the bottom rail of the companionway to the bridge. He started to haul himself upwards and was struck by the corpse of the dead marine, hurled towards the deck by the force of the latest turn. The shock knocked the weapon from his hands and he looked up to see the Captain braced in the opening at the top of the companionway. He held a pistol in his hands and it was pointed at Ryman's heart. A shot rang out and Ryman flinched. Then the barrel of the pistol wavered and the outstretched arms dropped; the head tilted forward and the man pitched down the steps to smash with sickening force against the body of the gunner.

His place at the top of the stair was taken by Flower holding an automatic in her hands. Hardly had Ryman launched himself towards the woman who had saved his life than there was a teeth-grating, grinding noise and he was forced to cling on as the vessel lifted in the air and careered through forty-five degrees. A wall of spray burst over him and when he looked up, Flower had disappeared. He struggled upwards and suddenly became aware that the seascape around them had changed. Waves were breaking as if on invisible beaches; there were white plumes of surf and an exposed strand of coral stretching away like the surface of a pitted tombstone. Their course had taken them past a small atoll and they were in danger of tearing themselves apart on it.

Ryman burst through the doorway on to the bridge and found Flower struggling with the wheel. A sailor lay against a bulkhead, holding his wounded arm. Ryman launched himself at the wheel and clung on desperately as the ship veered to starboard. 'Tell them to cut the engines!' He jerked his head towards the speaker and braced himself as he saw an area of angry white water looming ahead. He swung the wheel and the sloop jinked like a whippet,

223

nearly forcing him to release his hold. White gave way to grey and he saw the ridges of turbulence ahead like jumps in a steeplechase. Any one of them could indicate a strip of coral capable of ripping the hull open. Another patch of wild water loomed up and Ryman took evasive action that sent the wounded Chinese sliding across the deck. At least it was going to be practically impossible for the crew to marshall their forces. A figure appeared in the corner of his eye and he spun round to see an ashen-faced Burton clinging to the rail. His right thigh was spurting blood in two places. Three hundred metres ahead, a strip of coral blocked their path like a harbour wall. The sea lapped over its edge and ran riot in streaming pools of boiling foam. On all sides they were enclosed by razor edges of reef. There was no passage to steer through.

In desperation, Ryman turned to Flower and at that moment the engine note began its dying whine. Two hundred metres from the reef and they were losing speed; one hundred metres and they were coasting. The lethal shelf reared into view like the lower half of a devouring jaw and Ryman spun the helm to bury it in a wash of white water. The stern swung round and the sloop was riding in deep water less than a dozen metres from the murderous coral.

Ryman left the wheel twitching and seized a loud hailer that was swinging from a hook. He tossed it to Flower as he headed for the main deck. 'Tell them I want everybody to assemble in front of the bridge. Anybody disobeying will be shot. Henry, can you move?'

The loud hailer shrieked into life and Burton cursed the pain and staggered after Ryman. The wounded Chinese hobbled down the companionway before him without demur.

Ryman moved to the stern warily. The muzzle of a weapon protruded from the aft companionway, and Burton cried out a warning. As Ryman threw up his self-loader a rifle clattered harmlessly on to the deck and its owner followed with his hands in the air. Flower's message was beaming out with ear-splitting distortion. Three more ratings emerged and hurried towards the bridge encouraged by a short burst that Ryman fired over their heads. He heard Flower's voice falter and decided not to repeat the manoeuvre. A glance at Burton showed that the pain of his wounds was becoming difficult to bear. Ryman gestured towards the prow. 'Keep an eye on them. I'll send up any more I can find.'

He watched Burton hobble away and continued towards the

stern. The towline to the fishing boat had snapped during their erratic passage through the coral and their old vessel was drifting a quarter of a mile away. Two figures were visible on the deck. Ryman began to make some quick calculations. He could account for nine men on the sloop, eight of them dead or disabled. With two on the fishing boat, that left an estimated four to nine men, some of whom must be in the engine room. He approached the stern companionway and two tousle-haired men appeared in shorts, looking as if they had been woken from sleep. Their hands shot up when they saw Ryman and they filed obediently towards the bridge. Warily, Ryman checked the starboard side of the superstructure. The man who had been sprawling on the deck had disappeared, presumably swept overboard. The door to the radar cabin and wireless room slid open, and a man appeared still wearing his headphones. Ryman gestured towards the deck with his weapon and the man moved with such alacrity that the headphones were pulled from his head as he descended. No doubt he had been in constant communication with the Chinese mainland, but it was highly unlikely that the People's Republic had another vessel in the area or would risk an international incident by sending reinforcements. Ryman saw the man on his way to the prow and hurried to the stern companionway. There was no sound from below and he descended to the corridor and passed the cabin where Crosby had been imprisoned. The bolt was still slid home. There were cabins on either side of the corridor and he braced himself and threw open the doors, waiting for the burst of fire from any zealot who preferred death to surrender. Each time the cabin was empty.

At the end of the corridor, beyond the cabin in which they had been imprisoned, another companionway led down to what Ryman surmised must be the engine room. There was no sound beyond the eerie, subdued whine of the idling turbines. Ryman turned his body sideways and slowly felt his way down the narrow metal treads. Before him was a heavy door bristling with rivets and secured by a wheel closure. The heat was almost unbearable and the confining steel walls glistened; there was a stench of engine oil and human sweat. Ryman banged on the door with the stock of his weapon and the sound reverberated in the enclosed space. There was no reply and the door did not open. Ryman braced himself for action and spun the wheel in a clockwise direction. He felt the watertight closure relax and pushed forward hard, at the same instant stepping swiftly to one side. Nothing. He waited, feeling the tension build inside him, and stepped into the doorway. Three men stood before him wearing only shorts, slippers and sweat bands round their heads. Their hands and bodies were covered with oil, and this combined with the glistening sweat to give them the appearance of savages from some primordial jungle. They stood beside the wire-mesh grilles that surrounded the turbines as if in attendance upon primitive gods. There was fear, not malice, in their eyes, and as Ryman looked round the chamber, one of them approached him with a scrap of paper that had clearly been folded many times. It showed a photograph of the late General Chiang Kai-shek and Ryman recognised it as one of the safe-conduct passes that were flown over to the mainland by hot-air balloon together with other inducements to defect.

'*Hau*,' he said, meaning 'that's fine', and waved towards the companionway with his weapon. The man carefully refolded his pass and beckoned to his shipmates with a gesture that was almost jaunty. They scuttled past Ryman, bowing deferentially, and he wondered if they had any knowledge of the mission they had been on or who he was. They probably thought that he was an American and some kind of adviser to the Taiwan Forces who had taken over the ship.

The two dazed men nursing their heads in the cabin by the stern companionway were released, and joined their three comrades from the engine room in the climb to the deck. Ryman did not relax. There was no sign of the lieutenant who had come aboard the fishing boat. Perhaps he was one of the men still aboard her.

When they arrived before the bridge, Flower was quick to approach him. 'More than half the crew say they wish to go to Taiwan. They have had enough of the People's Republic.'

Ryman's face broke into a broad smile. 'Excellent! From Communism to Capitalism in one bound. I'm all in favour, but I think it may be in our interest to impose a few conditions.' He turned to a grimacing Burton. 'How's the leg?'

'Wishing that our friends had changed their minds a little earlier. It's stiff as a board.'

'We'll have a look in a moment. Do you think you're going to be able to make the pick-up?'

Burton snorted. 'Try and stop me.'

Ryman turned back to Flower. 'Are all hands accounted for? I haven't seen the lieutenant.'

'He's on the fishing boat with two other men.'

'Good.' Ryman swept an eye over the silent, wary group of Chinese standing disconsolately before him. 'I'm going to make these gentlemen a proposition and then we'll go and pick him up.'

CHAPTER SIXTEEN

About time. Ignacius Bigg thought the words with such intensity that he almost believed that he had spoken them out loud. The fishing boat was lost to sight behind the reef but would soon be coming through the opening. For what seemed like an age he had watched its slow progress across the dappled ocean. The wireless message had come through just before dawn and since then he had suffered with increasing impatience. Was this going to be another false alarm? Would the treasure ever materialise? Ignacius Bigg did not enjoy being placed on racks of this kind and it was with a vengeful spirit that he raised the binoculars to his eyes and trained them on the opening in the coral. The big Englishman was clearly trying to achieve some kind of psychological ascendency which put him on an equal footing with his superior. This could not be tolerated.

There was a discreet cough behind him and Bigg turned to see Quat waiting respectfully by the table that contained the breakfast things: the jar of Cooper's Olde English marmalade, the remains of the toast wrapped in its thick linen napkin, the silver entrée dish that had held the devilled kidneys and the thin rashers of bacon cooked to a crispness that turned to dust at the touch of a fork. The butler knew that his master was in a bad humour because the empty shells in the twin cup had been turned upside down and battered into fragments with a spoon. Some people lost their appetites when they were preoccupied; Bigg merely let his mood show in the way that he ate. Ignacius Bigg nodded his head and the arms of the table were folded down, its wheels released and the whole propelled towards the lift that would carry the victim of his appetite to the galley, presided over in air-conditioned comfort by an over-paid and under-employed former head chef of L'Archestrate in Paris.

Bigg returned his attention to the reef. Hardly were his glasses focussed than the high prow of the fishing boat breasted the gap and entered the lagoon. Bigg looked upon it and found it difficult to control the grudging admiration he had felt when exposed to Ryman's capacity for survival in Singapore. That this puny, battered craft could have ridden out the full force of a typhoon was really something exceptional. These men almost deserved their delivery fee of three million dollars. The thought was uncharacteristic and Bigg punished himself with a flicker of an eyelid. Such largesse was akin to altruism and the word had no place in his vocabulary. Bigg was interested in honey, not bees.

He lowered his binoculars and frowned. The fishing boat was not coming directly towards him but hugging the inner lip of the reef like a threatened adversary warily circling the ropes. No sooner had he started to examine reasons and meanings than there was a buzz from the intercom system. He flicked open the nearest box and took the receiver in his hand. It was the wireless operator stating that Ryman wished to speak to him. Bigg swallowed his irritation at being summoned in such peremptory fashion and ordered that he be connected. There was a splutter of static and he raised his glasses again to study the fishing boat. It had hove to about three hundred metres away against the reef. Only one member of the crew was visible, a Chinese isolated in the deckhouse.

'Mr Bigg, can you hear me, over?'

'Bigg speaking. I can hear you. Why are you standing off?' Bigg's voice was calm and assured. It gave no hint of the anger that he felt.

'We have the merchandise. Please send over the money so that we can confirm that everything is in order and make the exchange.'

Bigg ground his teeth together. 'Your attitude suggests that you lack confidence in my honesty.'

'I prefer to think of it as professional prudence.'

Bigg allowed himself a long pause in order to give the impression that he was racked by doubt. 'Very well. Twenty minutes.' He replaced the receiver and moved to the landward side of the deck. A flock of parrots took off from the palms but they hardly engaged his attention. Below him, out of sight of the sailing boat, a pinnace was moored at the foot of a gangway. Visible only from directly above it were six pump-action Remington shotguns equipped with special heavy-duty cartridges filled with tear smoke. Fired from close range the cartridges would turn the hull of the fishing vessel into a colander and asphyxiate anybody inside it. Conventional Heckler and Koch 5.46mm self-loading rifles were available to finish off anybody who reached the deck. There was the danger that a cartridge might strike a work of art, but this unfortunate contingency had to be allowed for in the overall scheme of things. Ignacius Bigg congratulated himself on his acumen in having legislated for the kind of problem that now faced him. Always, one had to remain one jump ahead.

Ryman stood by the wireless and listened to the hum of the sloop's turbines as she churned through the water. It was five minutes since he had last spoken and they would soon be in sight from the lagoon. The important thing was that Bigg had believed him to be speaking from the fishing boat which in fact was being propelled by two Chinese crewmen from the sloop. Now he waited for the signal that would tell him that Bigg's men were on their way to the boat. The more of them making the trip, the better. With Bigg's forces divided they were in a better position to take counter measures should there be an attempt at treachery. Nerves stretched tight, Ryman stared at the wireless and willed it to come to life. There was a dip in the static as if somebody was about to come on the air, and then the scratchy crackle returned. The gambit was repeated three times. The signal had been given. A boat had been put out from the *Midas* and was closing with their old vessel. The big moment had come.

Ignacius Bigg replaced the receiver on its hook and snatched up his binoculars. For once his face betrayed emotion; not one emotion but several. Dismay, anger and even a flicker of uncertainty passed across his bland, puppet features. That a vessel from the Chinese People's Republic should sweep out of nowhere at a moment like this was a cruel stroke of fate. What business could they have with him that they wished to put alongside? They were outside their territorial waters even if this lonely atoll was the nearest to the mainland.

Bigg watched the prow of the sloop cutting through the reef and thought again of blasting it out of the water. But the 25mm cannon on its foredeck was a formidable weapon and it was far from certain that even if he crippled the vessel with his first shot he would avoid suffering retaliatory fire. There was also the question of his relations with the People's Republic. If news got back that it was he who had accounted for one of their coastguard sloops, then his valuable heroin trade would be irrevocably prejudiced. An additional factor that weighed heavily was the temporary loss of his most effective fighting arm. Eight men and their sophisticated weaponry were to all intents and purposes marooned in the middle of the lagoon equidistant between the *Midas* and the fishing vessel. The Chinese could not have arrived at a worse moment.

Bigg tapped the tips of his fingers together lightly and reached for the telephone of the intercom. The answering voice had replied almost before it reached his ear. 'Yes, sir?'

'Gun crews to fire on red alarm. Armourer prepare to issue weapons. Crew on general alert.'

'Yes sir.'

Bigg moved to the rail, wishing that he was in radio contact with the pinnace. A loud hailer could reach them, but it was hardly the most discreet form of communication. The presence of the Chinese vessel would also mean that their mission would have to be temporarily suspended. Grim-faced, Bigg looked out to the fishing boat and wondered what the big Englishman was making of it all.

'Astern of the anchor opening.' Ryman handed the binoculars to Burton, who propped his elbows on the ventilation hatch behind which they were sheltering and peered towards the vessel that was taking shape before them. Just behind where the anchor trailed down into the sea was an indented rectangle like the sliding door of a cupboard. As Burton watched, it seemed to tremble, and a black bar of shadow appeared. Heart beating faster, he continued along the hull until he came to another recessed panel near the hull. This was still closed. He returned to the anchor opening. The band of black had not widened.

'Looks as if they've got us in their sights.'

'I bet their trigger fingers are itching.' Ryman saw Burton grimace and looked towards his thigh. The blood had started to seep through the bandage. 'How's the leg holding up?'

'Better. That morphine worked wonders.' Ryman looked round at the nearest Chinese crew members. 'Keep our new friends on their toes but try not to move about too much.'

Burton smiled grimly. 'It's amazing how quickly the profit motive can be re-instilled. Chairman Mao must be turning in his grave.'

'At least some of the faithful remained loyal.' Ryman was

231

referring to the lieutenant and five other crew members who had opted for one of the lifeboats and enough provisions to get them back to Fukien. They must be approaching the coast now. Ryman thought of the reception that they would get and winced.

Fifty metres to the left the fishing boat rose and fell on the slight swell and Ryman wondered if he would ever set foot on it again. He was trying to stay calm and appear relaxed, but with every split second that passed he was watching for the stab of flame that would herald the sound of screaming death; the shell of the *Midas* that would rip them apart in a mass of twisted, flaming metal. Now they were passing the pinnace and its crew of sullen, hard-faced men who looked like mercenaries. A blond Aryan, two blacks, a man with his head shaved down to stubble. One of them spat contemptuously as the slim cutter rode out the sloop's waves. There was no sign of any container that might hold three million dollars. Ryman looked at the satchel of hand grenades by Burton's side and thought how one of these lobbed into the pinnace might ease their problems. Still, there was no concrete evidence that Bigg intended treachery. Ryman forced himself to remember that the man might simply pay for the merchandise with a good grace and let them sail away. He looked ahead to the gaunt, menacing outline of the *Midas* and frowned. Somehow, it did not seem very likely.

Ignacius Bigg watched the cutter sweep round in its approach and noticed that there were two men manning the 25mm cannon. They were raking it through one hundred and eighty degrees, testing a field of fire that stretched from the pinnace to the ship they were bearing down on. The flag of the People's Republic fluttered proudly at mast and stern. A strange feature of the vessel was that there were hardly any crew members visible on deck. Were they expecting trouble or did they intend to make it? Bigg began to question his decision not to open fire. Now it was almost too late. The sloop had cut its engines and the bow wave was thudding against the hull of the *Midas*. Men advanced with heavy-duty fenders and Bigg saw that one of them had a bandage round his head. Though he was far from squeamish, for some reason the sight disturbed him. The bandage was so white, so recent. It added to Bigg's growing feeling that things had been happening that he knew nothing about. He heard the grating sound of the fenders scraping against the ship's side and saw men making fast with ropes. The main deck of the sloop rode beneath that of the *Midas* and she was poised between the two lethal guns positioned at stern and aft. With grim satisfaction Bigg noted that they could be brought to bear and inflict crippling damage from point-blank range. Something plummeted into the sea beside one of the fenders, but Bigg's attention was only half engaged. He had caught sight of the man emerging onto the deck from one of the companionways. It was the tall Englishman and with him was a slim Chinese girl who was helping to carry half a dozen oddly shaped packages.

Ryman paused and raised an arm in salute towards the top deck of the *Midas*. 'Permission to come aboard, Mr Bigg?'

CHAPTER SEVENTEEN

Burton watched Ryman and Flower disappear up the companion-way and let his hand drop to his throbbing thigh. The effects of the morphine were wearing off and the pain was coming back. He stared into the wary faces looking down at him from the decks of the *Midas* and then glanced sideways. A length of wire ran along the deck and dipped into the water beside one of the fenders. Beyond it, the gun hatch by the stern of the *Midas* remained closed like the eyelid of a light sleeper.

Burton swallowed and walked along the deck away from the wire. Half a dozen paces took him across another length of flex which also fed into the water between the two hulls. He glanced round, trying to appear casual and saw that half a dozen pairs of eyes were on him. As far as he could make out nobody appeared to be taking any notice of the wires. So much the better. Fearful but determined, he retraced his steps and turned into one of the companionways. The wires crossed the threshold at his feet.

'I don't understand,' said Mr Bigg. 'I thought you were on the fishing boat.'

'I was, but I thought better of it,' said Ryman. 'You must forgive me, but my experience in Singapore has made me very wary.'

Bigg's eyes narrowed. 'And Harry Crosby?'

'Dead. He was indirectly responsible for the transportation that brings me here. However, it's a long story and one that has no direct bearing on the purpose of my visit.'

'Nevertheless, I'm fascinated,' said Bigg. 'Surely you haven't replaced Harry as a partner with the Chinese People's Republic?'

'Only on a very temporary basis.' Ryman turned to Flower. 'This is Ying Pi. She is what you might call my principal partner.'

Bigg nodded formally. 'I am delighted to see both of you. And, of course, what you appear to be bringing me.' He gestured towards the lift. 'Let us go below. It is becoming rather warm up here.'

Ryman noticed that Bigg's eyes shot a wary glance towards the sloop and the pinnace that was standing off the fishing boat in the background. His own took in the immediate surroundings of the top deck. Through moist, wary eyes, Bigg's eunuch surveyed them from a position by one of the companionways. A glance from its master and the creature turned and disappeared from view. Another corner of the deck was commanded by Quat wearing a white mess jacket and black trousers. His hands dangled almost too casually at his sides and there was an unwieldy bulge in the area of his left armpit. In the lookout point on the main mast another man had the deck under surveillance. A rifle was fitted into the rack by his side.

The lift doors opened silently and Ignacius Bigg ushered his visitors inside and produced a small key attached to an antique gold chain. There were three floors marked, each with a button beside it. Bigg inserted the key in a lock below the buttons and turned it. Immediately, the doors slid shut and the lift glided downwards. Lights flashed in sequence but the lift by-passed all floors and continued to descend. Ryman felt Flower press against him and tried to smile reassuringly. It was not easy. With every foot that they descended the bright sunshine became more of a memory, the route between them and safety more difficult to follow.

The lift rippled to a halt and the doors slid open. There was a click and Ryman was momentarily dazzled by a battery of lights that could have illuminated the sound stage of a motion picture studio. They were arranged round the walls and ceiling of a long, rectangular room, playing on paintings and display cabinets, some of which were set into the walls with their own lighting system. So this was it. Bigg's private gallery where he could gloat over his collection and know that every ounce of pleasure that it provided need never be shared.

Ryman stepped from the lift and looked about him, finding it difficult to select one item to focus on. There was so much to seduce the eye. A Toulouse-Lautrec that he recalled having seen reproduced in the national papers when it disappeared from the collection at Albi; a set of icons finished in gold leaf and encrusted with precious stones, no doubt removed from some remote monastery in Crete. On all sides stretched a treasure trove of items that had once made headlines but were now probably only remembered by a handful of bereft museum custodians, private collectors, and, with special sadness, insurance brokers.

235

Ryman took in the beauty but noticed one disturbing feature of the room. There seemed to be no other entrance save the one they had come in by. The lift.

Bigg crossed to a large desk covered in plum-red hand-tooled leather and swept some papers impatiently to one side. 'Show me,' he said. The words had almost a lover's compulsive urgency. His eyes were gleaming.

Ryman raised a hand to the garland of Ju ware about his neck and then paused. 'I take it there is no problem about the three million dollars?'

Bigg threw his arms apart. 'It is on the way to the fishing boat. That is what you requested, isn't it?'

Ryman rubbed his chin. 'Perhaps it could be delivered to the sloop. I would be happier to know that it had arrived safely before I finally hand over the goods.'

'You're playing a very complicated game, Mr Ryman.' There was a hard, unloving edge to Bigg's voice. 'Do not become obsessed with that money. I can pay you from the funds I hold here. Let us examine the merchandise.'

Ryman said nothing but removed the necklace of cups and placed them in a circle before Bigg. Flower looked in the man's eyes and was reminded of how some of her clients gazed upon her when the moment to make love had come. The face that seemed so cold suddenly began to come alive. As Ryman prised the lid off one of the covering plastic cups, stored-up desire flowed to the surface; the head tilted forward in anticipation, the eyes moistened, the tongue darted snake-like along the thin lips. To Flower it was repellent. As Bigg stretched out a possessive hand she could almost feel cold, damp fingers beginning to pull open her clothing.

With a surgeon's delicacy, Bigg pulled out the packing between finger and thumb and gently drew forth the wafer-thin cup. He held it in the air so that the light passed through it as if it was fabricated from transparent glass and then let it down on the plum-coloured leather. His small nostrils moved as he breathed in deeply; his concentration was totally absorbed by the small, exquisite object before him. He swallowed, and then his mouth came open and his eyes narrowed and momentarily closed. Ryman felt uncomfortable; he was watching a man enact a private sexual experience. This, to Ignacius Bigg, was making love.

Moments passed and then Bigg's eyes began to count the rest of

236

the cups. He picked up the one before him as if it was a petal and returned it to its container like a child replacing a favourite toy in its box.

'The others are intact?'

'Everything was in perfect condition when we arrived.'

Bigg's eyes darted over the other items and lighted on the container that held the painting. 'I would like to see *Travellers Amongst Mountains and Streams*.'

Ryman moved to open the canister and then paused. 'I would like to see three million dollars.'

Bigg shook his head in irritation as if he had been woken peremptorily from a pleasant dream. 'There is little pleasure in doing business with a man who is always talking about money.'

'I didn't enter into this transaction for pleasure,' said Ryman. 'And in the last few days I've known precious little of it. My pleasure will come when I sail out of this lagoon with the money you owe us.' His grip on the canister did not slacken.

Bigg's eyes hardened into agate chips and his lips disappeared into the pallor of his skin. 'Very well.' He stood up and moved precisely to an alcove beside the lift. It contained a handsome Florentine urn on a carved stone table. Bigg stretched out a hand to administer a light tap and the whole structure slid effortlessly to one side to reveal a four-foot-high wall safe mounted at chest level. Bigg's agile fingers toyed with the dials and Ryman glanced uneasily at Flower. There was a final click and the door flinched. Bigg's fingers closed about the handle and then relaxed. He turned to Ryman at his shoulder with a glance that was openly contemptuous. 'Perhaps you would feel more assured if you opened it?'

He did not wait for a reply but stepped to one side. Ryman hesitated. He felt singularly un-reassured. What lay on the other side of the door? A weapon rigged to put a bullet through his heart? He stretched out a hand, feeling the sharp prick of danger. To delay longer or to refuse would be to invite humiliation. Ryman had long since decided that he hated Ignacius Bigg; he would as readily accept death as lose face before him.

With a firm hand, Ryman reached out and pulled open the heavy door. What he saw robbed him of speech as effectively as any bullet. All round the walls were shelves stacked high with thick piles of bank notes: American dollars, Swiss francs, Deutschmarks, yen, rials, krona, cruzeiro, yuans and even roubles. The capacity of the safe was much greater than that indicated by the area of its door. From floor level rose a neatly stacked pile of interlacing gold ingots that reached the level of the bottom shelf. In the background could be seen neat rows of drawers such as might be found in a bank-deposit vault; their contents defied imagination. Ryman's eyes travelled to the floor of the safe. Neatly stacked was a pile of large, self-inflating buoyancy bags that could be used to house the fortune in case of emergency. Ryman looked and wondered.

A rustle of movement to the left side made him jerk his head sideways. Bigg's hand was withdrawing from the mouth of the Florentine vase. It held a 9mm Browning self-loading pistol.

'Ready for any contingency.' Bigg's gaze did not embrace the safe as well as the prisoners but his meaning was obvious, his satisfaction evident. No change of tone or facial expression was needed to emphasize the message.

'Don't be in a hurry to press that trigger.' Ryman's tone gave no hint of fear. He spoke quickly. 'If we don't walk off this boat in the next ten minutes with three million dollars, then you and your Collection are going to be lying at the bottom of the ocean.'

Bigg said nothing for a moment but jerked the cruel barrel of the Browning back towards his desk. 'What do you mean?'

'When we came alongside, we dropped two depth charges to rest against your hull. If we don't reappear in the next...' Ryman broke off to glance at his watch '... eight minutes and fifty-five seconds, then they'll be detonated. You'll go down like a stone.'

'Taking you with me.'

'We've sacrificed nearly everything except our lives to get this far. If you renege on the deal then we're prepared to go the whole way.'

Ignacius Bigg moved round behind his desk and sat down. The expression of doubt and irritation on his face gave way to one of understanding. 'You leave me no alternative, do you?' His hand moved surreptitiously and pressed the red alarm button.

CHAPTER EIGHTEEN

Burton looked at his watch and tried to regularise his breathing. The sweat was dripping off him and yet the inside of his mouth was dry. The minutes were going by so fast; they had not left enough time; Bigg would want to inspect the merchandise before he made any move to hand over the money.

There was movement on the top-deck of the *Midas* and Burton craned forward hoping to see Ryman and Flower. A man in a white mess jacket was peering down at him suspiciously. All along the decks of both vessels men were waiting warily like characters in the final stages of a Western shoot-out.

Burton glanced at his watch again and found that another minute had rippled by. It was impossible to stay where he was; he had to move. He dragged his leg over the battery and the knotted wires and emerged from the companionway. The sun was breaking through the rigging of the *Midas* and turning into an explosion of light. Burton looked towards the stern of the huge yacht and stopped dead in his tracks. The gun hatch was sliding open; something glinted from the darkness. Burton turned towards the prow; there he could see the dark shadow expanding and the murderous circle of metal lunging out towards them like a deadly snail emerging from its shell. He staggered into the mouth of the companionway and fell painfully to his knees. He heard a cry of alarm that had heralded his sudden movement and snatched up the wires. Below him was the battery. All he had to do was make contact and the depth charges would explode. He looked down and watched the drop of sweat that had stained the dust. His hands had frozen; he could not bring himself to do it in cold blood.

VROOM!!

The explosion seemed to have taken place inside his head and torn it apart. A terrible pain in his ears made him scream. He saw a flash of yellow light and felt his body lifted into the air. Above his head there was a roar of flames and a wave of heat singed his hair.

As the sloop buckled and his body smashed against sheet metal, he pressed the wires against the battery contacts.

239

Hardly had the sound of the first explosion thudded in their ears than Ryman found himself hurled against the desk as if he had been struck a violent blow in the back. Bigg disappeared and the floor came up to meet him like a heavy weapon. The wind was driven from his body and he had the sensation that blood was coming from his ears. Suddenly he could hear nothing, although glass was breaking all around him. The room lurched sideways and a chair slid past him, gathering speed. He was dazed and in pain yet aware that he was still alive and not seriously wounded. The ringing in his ears was agony. He tried to scramble to his feet and then slid sideways as the floor tilted again. After the twin explosion of the depth charges, the vessel had reared into the air and was now toppling into its own watery grave.

Ryman sprawled against a cabinet and saw the top half of Bigg's body poised above him. Blood was streaming from a cut above one eye and he looked about him desperately trying to pinpoint his adversaries. Ryman ducked and saw Flower lying a dozen yards away. The stricken ship lurched again and Flower rolled over on her back, one arm flopping out beside her. Bigg raised his arm and Ryman saw that it still clutched the Browning. He raised another hand to hold the pistol steady while he took aim at Flower. The deck rolled and he staggered sideways, fighting to regain his balance. Ryman half scrambled to his feet and dived as the shot rang out. His shoulder drove into Bigg's chest and two hundred pounds swept the little man backwards to smash through a display cabinet as if it was made of matchwood. Bigg's body hit the tilting floor with Ryman still on top of it and skidded backwards. Fuelled by gut hatred, Ryman continued to press down with all his weight. There was a sharp pain against his shoulder and he wrestled for Bigg's hand only to find that it hung limp. A glistening point of steel protruded from Bigg's chest. Ryman twisted sideways and saw two bifurcating blades lunging from his adversary's back like the arms of a pair of dividers. Ryman recognised the weapon; it was a Burmese three-bladed throwing knife, its jewelled heart sunk into Bigg's flesh like a baneful eye. The first blade had entered his back as he crashed into the display cabinet. As Ryman watched in horror, Bigg's eyes opened wide and a gulp of blood spilled from his mouth. His lips trembled convulsively and then were still.

His head ringing, Ryman scrambled to his feet. His ears popped and his hearing came back. Around him there were strange

240

groaning noises as the hull twisted in torment; the lights flickered and he had the sensation that he was sliding downwards. Striving to clear his head he scrambled across the floor to where Flower lay. She sprawled on her back and a thin trickle of blood descended from one temple. Her eyes were closed. She looked as if she was dead.

Burton saw the square of blue above his head and continued to drag himself upwards. The companionway was still rocking and a surge of water broke over him as if a dam had burst. Terrified of being swept down into the bowels of the ship, he clung to the metal rungs with all his strength. The flood abated and he forced himself on until he could look over the threshold on to the deck. Before him, the *Midas* was listing and the ropes that secured her to the sloop were strained tight. There was a smell of burning paint and a crackle of flames. Water was breaking over the deck and it seemed that the sloop was doomed to go down with the *Midas*. Men were hacking at the mooring ropes and as Burton watched, one of the cables parted with a noise like a whip crack.

He looked up at the superstructure and saw that the bridge and wireless room had disappeared; there were only cruel talons of blackened metal and a cloud of dense black smoke laced with flames; a body dangled obscenely from the buckled girders and leaked its baked juices on to the deck. Burton dragged himself forward to help a man who was trying to dislodge one of the mooring ropes. Water was bubbling up from the gap between the two ships and swilling round his ankles; bullets whined off the hardened steel; from somewhere in the smoke and flames men were still firing at each other. Burton clawed at the rope and glanced towards the stern of the *Midas*. To his horror he saw the barrel of a two-inch gun protruding from the hatch and ranging towards him. The gun crew were trying to compensate for the list of the vessel so that they could finish off the stricken sloop. Desperately he scrambled back towards the companionway and the satchel of hand grenades.

Ryman called Flower's name and searched her face for signs of life. Seconds passed and she did not move. 'Flower!' An eyelid fluttered and her eyes opened. Relief surged through him. Trembling, he drew her tenderly against his chest. 'Are you all right?'

She nodded slowly. 'Where is Bigg?'

'Dead.' Ryman rose to his feet unsteadily and pulled Flower with him. The floor beneath them was still a slope. Broken glass and priceless treasures littered the Bakhtiari carpet. 'Pray to God that the lift is still working.' He led the way as they heard the terrifying noise of water swirling powerfully against the neighbouring bulkheads. The metal groaned under stress and more objects started to slide.

Before them, beside the lift, the door of the safe still yawned open revealing the treasure trove inside; the gold bars, the stacks of currency, all the money they were owed and more. Ryman saw Flower's eyes following his own. Then she turned to him and spoke one word. 'Yes.'

Ryman moved forward and snatched up one of the buoyancy bags.

Burton plunged into the companionway, cursing the pain that flooded through his leg. For a second he could not see the satchel of grenades and feared that it had been swept down into the hold. The heat about him was now unbearable and the metal too hot to touch. He spluttered against the smoke and felt another surge of water swirl beneath his feet. The satchel lifted into sight behind the battery and he snatched it up and staggered on to the deck. A bullet whined past his head and he drove himself towards the stern. Three steps and the last mooring rope parted, setting the sloop free of the *Midas*. The shock threw Burton sideways and he fell heavily against the superstructure. The satchel of grenades jerked from his hands and skidded across the deck.

Ryman dragged the now bulky bag after him and into the lift and momentarily thought of Bigg's body whose space it now occupied; the reality replaced by its symbol. He plucked Flower to his chest and pressed the top button, his heart thumping. There was a pause and the doors slid shut. He waited and the lift began to rise.

Burton threw himself on the satchel and tore it open. His fingers closed round a grenade and he limped on, feeling the water round his ankles suddenly turn boiling hot. One of the boilers on the *Midas* must have burst. He screamed in pain and saw the yacht's

242

stern tilting before him. The gun port was almost directly ahead. He could see the murderous muzzle and the flesh of the men glistening in the shadow. He drew the pin and hurled the grenade through the opening, throwing himself to one side. There was an explosion and, almost coincident with it, a louder blast that sent a column of yellow flame soaring over his head, singeing his water-soaked body with its heat. The grenade had detonated the ammunition in the gun emplacement. There was a terrible hissing noise and steam filled the air. As Burton turned his head the water was beginning to pour through the side of the *Midas* and she was sinking fast.

The lift stopped. The light went out. Ryman sweated and waited. No doors opened. All around him he could hear the ship groaning in its death agonies. Most terrifying of all was the sensation of slow, remorseless descent. His fingers jabbed at the lifeless buttons. He pressed and then pressed again harder as if somewhere, an infinite fraction of an inch away, there was a contact that could be made if he could only find the strength to make it. They clung together in their black coffin listening to disembodied sounds. Ryman fought the waves of panic and despair that swept over him. They must try and remain calm. The ship was foundering and the generators had broken down. It was only a question of time before the water got to them or they ran out of air. Even as he tried to think, he heard the sound of water splashing down on the roof above their heads. The *Midas* must be totally submerged and the sea sweeping in through the lift-housing on the deck. Desperately he felt above his head. There must be some kind of hatch. Terrified, he felt water dripping on to his face. His fingers traced the outline of a recessed square and he fumbled for a catch. The water was now dripping faster and the sound of it pouring on to the roof had disappeared. The lift shaft was filling up. Ryman found a small lever of metal and pulled it with all his force. It gave slightly. The water was now around his ankles and entering the lift so fast that it was difficult to breathe. He felt Flower clinging to him and returned to the lever. He tore at it with the strength of desperation. There was a grating sound and it slid through ninety degrees. Ryman changed his stance and with head bowed to avoid the water that was now leaking down in a constant stream, he thrust upwards until it felt as if the sinews in his shoulders must snap. The hatch

243

did not move; the weight of the water pressing down on it was too great.

Ryman let his arms drop to his sides; the water had now risen above his knees. He knew that there was only one thing that he could do: wait until the water had risen to the roof and the pressure inside and outside the lift was equal; then, with the water above their heads, he would hope to push open the hatch and swim up to the head of the shaft. What happened there would depend on the strength of the grille that enclosed the lifting mechanism.

Burton watched the *Midas* slide beneath the waves with a feeling of dread and terror. A great swirl of oil and water bubbled to the surface and the sea was suddenly full of men and debris. The main mast stood above the water but nothing else remained. A submarine explosion went off like another depth charge and a roman candle of turbulence pushed the sloop away like the thrust from a great hand. Burton gazed down into the maelstrom, desperate for sight of Ryman and Flower. He saw three men who were still alive and clinging to a half-submerged lifeboat, but no sign of his comrades. Tears filled his eyes. The sloop was holed, but the fire on the bridge had been got under control and she was holding steady in the water. The bulkheads had been secured and the immediate danger of sinking had been averted. But the *Midas* was threatening to suck her down into the same grave. As the white turbulence creamed and eddied, the hull twitched like a huge cork bobbing on the lip of a whirlpool. Burton staggered and fell to his hands and knees with water breaking against his chest. A wave washed him sideways and he was forced to look out to the reef.

The fishing boat was still moored near the mouth of the lagoon, but the pinnace was drawing closer to the sloop. As he clung to a radiator cowling a chunk of metal was torn from it and sent screaming into space. A fusillade of fire was being brought to bear and it came from the approaching pinnace. Burton felt the ship bucking and rearing beneath his body and tried to scramble to his feet. Why had the 25mm gun not opened up? He had seen it intact after the first broadside from the *Midas*. A sense of bitter rage swept over him and with it came a burning desire for revenge. Dragging his wounded leg behind him, he hobbled towards the prow. Men were trying to pull themselves on to the half-submerged deck and gusts of dense black smoke blew in his face. It was oil not water that

244

now seemed to be swirling round his feet. He scrambled past the twisted metal of the bridge and saw the gun with one of its projection plates bent back at right angles to the other. The body of one of its crew was wedged against the scuppers, the other had been washed overboard. Burton launched himself forward. Bullets screamed past him and another chunk of metal was chipped away like a layer of flint. He reached the pedestal and desperately spun the handles to depress the barrel.

Now he could see the faces of the men in the pinnace, crouching low beneath the gunwale, pressing in against their weapons; the man at the rudder hunched up with his knees before his face. Another bullet ricocheted from the sheet of metal beside his head and he pressed the trigger as the deck rolled. A screeching hornets' swarm of bullets hissed into the sea and the pinnace kept coming; he had missed by ten feet as the sloop wallowed. For a moment the barrel of the 25mm clawed at the sky and then it plunged again. Burton tried to line up the open sight and fired haphazardly as the circle of metal swung across the bow of his target. The heavy gun shuddered and yammered as if crazy to break free from its mooring and its banshee wail splintered against his eardrums. The heavy cannon shells tore into the pinnace and shattered it to sawdust; the water boiled and columns of spray rose twenty feet in the air. The sea was full of struggling streaming men. Burton fired until the gun was too hot to handle and the pinnace no more than a flotsam of floating spars. As the survivors clung to anything that would keep them above water, the widening circle of oil spread out to meet them.

In the lift, the water was above Ryman's chin and continuing to rise. He supported Flower before him, terrifyingly aware that she could not swim. He could feel her neck straining back as she pressed her nose towards the last few inches of air. The ship had just ridden out a violent spasm that had convinced him that it was about to turn turtle. They had both been thrown against the side of the lift with the water momentarily closing over their heads. Through all this, Flower had remained calm. Now she stood against him, hands resting on his shoulders. Waiting.

Ryman thrust his arms above his head and prepared to push. The water was up to his nose and still showering through the hatch closure. He took a last gulp of air and held on, saving his energy until he was certain that there was only the sea above him. Pray God that the hatch lock had been properly released. He braced his legs and thrust. There was no resistance and the hatch swung upwards. He felt Flower starting to struggle and pushed her through the opening. Her feet struck his face and his lungs began to ache; every movement seemed to take an eternity. At last, Flower was free and he scrabbled for the bag of money bobbing at his feet. He swung it up and thrust it into the aperture, where it jammed like a cork in the mouth of a bottle. Now came the terrifying realisation that death was upon him. His head and lungs seemed about to explode. He struck out blindly and the bag slowly squeezed through the opening.

As it swayed free he drove his arm after it and found one of the lift cables. His shoulders scraped the edge of the hatch aperture and he hauled himself upwards and clawed the water in search of Flower. Far above his head a square of luminous green showed in the darkness. In desperation he released the bag and started to fight his way towards the surface. He had taken half a dozen strokes when something struck him in the face; it was one of Flower's legs. He pulled her with him and struggled on, feeling that with every propulsion of his legs his tortured heart and lungs might explode out of his body. Suddenly, like the underbelly of a giant insect, the lift machinery loomed up above his head. There was now unmistakable light shining through the water and he could feel the surge of a current. The sight gave him strength and his fingers glided from the smooth metal sides of the lift to the rough wire of the grille surround. He kicked his legs up and drove them out with the force of desperation; he felt the mesh give and another kick tore it open. Flower was struggling beside him and he bundled her through the opening and wriggled after her, feeling the severed wires lacerate his flesh. Something bobbed against his leg and he reached back to touch the money bag. He pulled it after him and struck out for the surface.

No sooner had Burton seen that the oil was on fire than Flower's head broke the surface. For a moment he was mesmerised, powerless to take action. He had given up hope; this seemed like an apparition. Then Ryman appeared, his face furrowed with exhaustion, his eyes almost invisible. He sucked in mouthfuls of air and cast about until he saw the floundering Flower; she was

246

half-drowned, choking and hawking. Ryman struck out with clumsy, ill-coordinated strokes and grabbed her by the hair. Burton looked about him for a rope or spar and shouted at the fishing boat that was chugging towards them. His voice was carried away in the crackle of flames and the screams of men dying in the thick black smoke. The slick had caught where the survivors of the pinnace were clinging to the remains of their boat and only a strong offshore wind was slowing its progress towards the sloop, which was completely surrounded by oil.

Burton shouted and waved his arms and the fishing boat changed course. The remaining members of the sloop's crew thronged the edge of the listing deck and Burton pushed through them to reach Ryman and Flower as they struggled towards survival. He dropped to his knees, almost oblivious of the pain in his thigh and stretched out a hand to haul Flower on to the deck. She lay on her stomach and he watched her retch as if her whole body was coming apart; a mixture of mucus and oil spattered his thighs. Drifts of black smoke swept across the deck and he turned to see that the wind had changed and that the fire was now speeding towards them; outriders of flame leading the thick black cloud that obscured the edge of the reef and the palm-fringed beach.

The fishing boat ground against the hull and Burton looked for Ryman. For a second he thought that he had slid below the water and then he saw him striking out ponderously towards the flames; trails of smoke drifting above his head. Burton shouted after him, certain that he had taken leave of his senses. At his feet, Flower had now stopped coughing. He hesitated, still stunned by Ryman's disappearance. The flames crackled a warning and he picked up the slim body and carried it to the fishing boat. Men were scrambling over the side and he joined them and laid Flower before the deck-house. When he looked towards Ryman, he could not see him.

Ryman swam clumsily, blundering into the assorted debris from two ships. Every time he touched something he prayed it would be the money bag. His strength was almost finished. He saw something breaking the water ahead of him and struck out desperately; this would have to be the last chance; he counted the strokes, one, two, three. His fingers made contact with something bulky yet

247

yielding, floating almost entirely below the surface. He pulled at it and it slid towards him through the oily water. In horror he gazed into the face of Bigg's drowned eunuch.

The crackle of flames roared in his ears and a column of fire ran along the surface of the water. Ryman released his hold of his grisly prize and twisted away. At any second he was going to be engulfed. He struck out desperately and could feel the heat behind him. Spirals of smoke raced past him like the vanguard of an all-conquering army. He started to cough and suddenly realised that there was no more air. All around him was black; the fire was consuming everything. He blundered on and heard a shout. Before he could reply the bow of the fishing boat loomed up before him. He fought to clear his throat and rasped out a cry. He saw terrified faces staring down into the water and recognised Burton. A hand stretched out and he seized it gratefully. As he was drawn towards the boat, his body struck something. He clung to it and did not let go until he was lying half blinded in the bottom of the boat. He rubbed the oil from his eyes and blinked at what lay before him. It was the money bag.

Burton shouted to the man at the helm but there was no need for words. Black water was already churning from the stern as the vessel pulled back from the holocaust and her prow swung round towards the open sea. As the flames raced to the edge of the oil slick she was already clear of it and heading for the gap in the reef.

CHAPTER NINETEEN

It was after the SS *Fairmead* left Kuching with her cargo of rubber, sago and pepper that Burton recalled that he had not seen Flower and Ryman for several hours.

The *Fairmead* had come to their rescue in the Luzon Strait where, after they had handsomely paid off the remaining members of the crew of the sloop and transferred them to a junk bound for Hong Kong, the engine of the fishing boat had finally and irreparably broken down. They had drifted for several hours before being picked up by a battered tramp steamer plying a trade between Japan and the China and Java Seas. The captain of the *Fairmead* was a mildly eccentric Scot who had seemed quite happy to believe a story of a thwarted voyage from Hong Kong to Laoag in the Philippines and had only asked that his new passengers made no demands on his prescribed itinerary. This they had been content not to do.

The presence of two bullets in Burton's thigh had been ascribed to a brush with a pirate junk north off Cape Bojeador, and again this had been considered thoroughly plausible by the good captain who said that a colleague of his had been shot dead by pirates only three months before.

Burton watched the jungle of Sarawak steaming away to his left and hobbled along the deck towards Flower's cabin. The heat was clammy and oppressive and she was probably sleeping, as he had been whilst the loading and unloading was in progress. He reached the door and tapped lightly. There was no reply, and he tapped more loudly and then opened the door. There was no sign of Flower, nor that her bunk had been slept in. Suddenly worried, he hurried on towards Ryman's cabin. He raised his hand to bang on the door and then paused. Supposing they were making love? A wave of despair and jealousy swept over him. As their three minds and bodies healed he had been waiting for some kind of showdown. Their relationships had been almost artificially calm since their escape from the atoll, but undermining everything had been a tension that he knew sooner or later must be resolved. He banged on the door and then banged louder as there was no reply. A

249

passing lascar seaman looked at him curiously. He waited and then threw open the door.

Ryman's cabin was empty. Now Burton's worry had turned to a sick pain in the pit of his stomach. They had left the boat at Kuching and gone off together. Perhaps he had always expected this but it made it no easier to support. Feeling miserable he returned towards his own cabin. Half a dozen steps and another thought struck him — the money! It was unbelievable but it was just possible. Hobbling as fast as he could, he reached his cabin and unlocked the door. The pillow lay on top of the cupboard and he tore it down, immediately feeling relief as the notes ruckled beneath his fingers; over a million dollars. He peered into the neck of the pillow and then saw something on the floor. It was a letter that must have been pushed through the window grille whilst he was sleeping. He had got up without noticing it.

Burton bent and snatched up the envelope, recognising Ryman's handwriting. At least they had left him a few words. He pulled out two sheets of paper and started to read: 'Dear Henry, before I say anything, I think you had better cast an eye over the enclosed.' Puzzled, Burton turned to the second sheet and immediately recognised the thin spidery handwriting that seemed almost a variation of Chinese calligraphy.

'Very dear Don and Henry, by the time you read this I will have left. I have decided that it is time to make my own life before it is too late. I could not do this if I stayed with you — either of you. Thank you for everything — not least the money. Always loving, Flower.'

Burton paused and read what Ryman had scrawled beneath the letter: 'You'll never believe this, but I feel worse than you do. All the same, she may be right. We need to break up and go our own ways. We've been through too much together. I'm away too. Good luck and hope to see you some day. Don.'

Burton read both pieces of paper again and then crumpled them into a ball. Still holding the bulging pillow, he left the cabin and walked to the ship's rail. He felt sad, but the pain of loss and rejection was somehow not so acute when shared. It also seemed immoral to be miserable when you held a million dollars in your arms. He tossed the ball of paper into the sea and started to make plans for Jakarta.

POSTSCRIPT

It was a month after the disappearance of the treasures from the National Palace Museum, Taipei, that *The Times of China* received the one and only scoop of its existence: an anonymous letter with a London postmark stating the exact chart reference of the lagoon where the missing items could be recovered in the hold of a sunken yacht. Not only they, but other valuable works of art pillaged from private and public Collections around the world. The letter concluded by saying that none of the awards offered by insurance companies would be claimed, as a reasonable sum had already been deducted from the estate of the individual responsible for the thefts.

The Times of China pondered long and hard over the desirability of publishing any details of their scoop and, in the end, referred the matter to the Taiwan Government. They, in turn, decreed that any reference to the affair would be against the national interest and promptly sent a salvage boat to the chart reference specified. All the items taken from the Museum were recovered safely with the exception of one of the Ju cups which suffered a slight chip to one of its rounded crenellations. This can still be seen amongst the items on display in the National Palace Museum. Ninety per cent of the other items in Bigg's Collection were recovered intact or in a reparable state and are believed to be still housed in the caves behind the Museum awaiting a decision on their future. This is a delicate matter as the Taiwan Government is loath to release any details that would reveal that a successful theft of items from their showpiece Museum had ever taken place. It may be that the most important repository of Chinese art in the world has enlarged its collection to an extent that may never be seen by the public.

The inhabitants of a small and virtually inaccessible privately owned Cotswold hamlet near the Slaughters were understandably distressed when they heard that as a result of taxation, death duties and inflation and other twentieth-century bugaboos, their village had been sold lock, stock and every barrel in the village pub. For a while, wild rumours circulated that the purchaser was an Arab oil

251

sheik and much was the rejoicing when the new Squire turned out to be an amiable gentleman of means returned from the Colonies. He moved easily amongst his tenants and spent a great deal of money in restoring the village to something approaching its former glory. Houses were re-thatched, sanitary arrangements adjusted to the standards of the twentieth century, and even the meanest cottage completely re-wired and brightened by a coat of paint.

If the villagers had one regret, it was that their Squire was not married with a son to ensure the continuation of the good work. He did receive occasional visits from a handsome Chinese lady, but of course only the most devious minds imputed that there was any romance involved in the relationship. She was merely considered to be a good friend from his past.

One extraordinary rumour that flourished briefly — and was believed to stem from a travelling friend of the doctor's who should have known better — was that the lady owned the finest brothel in Hong Kong, where the girls wore Paris fashions and were gifted, amongst other things, in painting and the playing of musical instruments. This fanciful suggestion was considered for no longer than it took to find it ridiculous. Nobody could imagine the Squire ever setting foot in such an establishment.

If the Squire and the Chinese lady shared an interest, it was perhaps in sitting before a roaring log fire in the panelled drawing-room of the Manor and planning a visit to a mutual friend who lived in Australia. From the infrequent letters that this young man wrote, they had learned that he owned a large cattle station on the borders of Queensland and New South Wales where he also raised thoroughbred horses. After a promising start he had suffered cruelly from a prolonged drought and lost many head of cattle. However, sooner or later the rains would come, the grass would grow and he would rebuild. Like his friends, he had overcome adversity in the past and they were certain that he would do so again.